M000199148

"Williams populates her historical fiction with people nearly broken by their experiences."

— *Foreword Reviews INDIES Finalist (Soul of a Crow)*

* Gold Medalist - 2015

— *Independent Publishers Awards (Heart of a Dove)*

"Set just after the U.S. Civil War, this passionate opening volume of a projected series successfully melds historical narrative, women's issues, and breathless romance with horsewomanship, trailside deer-gutting, and alluring smidgeons of Celtic ESP."

— *Publishers Weekly (Heart of a Dove)*

"There is a lot I liked about this book. It didn't pull punches, it feels period, it was filled with memorable characters and at times lovely descriptions and language. Even though there is a sequel coming, this book feels complete."

— *Dear Author (Heart of a Dove)*

"With a sweet romance, good natured camaraderie, and a very real element of danger, this book is hard to put down."

— *San Francisco Book Review (Heart of a Dove)*

Also By Abbie Williams

The Shore Leave Cafe Series

Summer at the Shore Leave Cafe

Second Chances

A Notion of Love

Winter at the White Oaks Lodge

Wild Flower

The First Law of Love

Until Tomorrow

The Way Back

Return to Yesterday

Forbidden

 The Dove Series

Heart of a Dove

Soul of a Crow

Grace of a Hawk

The First
Law of Love

a
SHORE LEAVE CAFE
novel

Abbie Williams

central
avenue
publishing

2017

Published by Central Avenue Publishing, an imprint of Central Avenue Marketing Ltd.
www.centralavenuepublishing.com

THE FIRST LAW OF LOVE

978-1-77168-110-0 (pbk)
978-1-77168-022-6 (epub)
978-1-77168-023-3 (mobi)

Published in Canada

Printed in United States of America

1. FICTION / Romance   2. FICTION / Family Life

BECAUSE WHEN YOU KNOW, YOU JUST KNOW...

Chapter One

RAIN SPATTERED THE GLASS A FEW INCHES FROM MY NOSE as I sat in the gloom of my apartment. I blew a long stream of smoke toward the five inches of screen near the bottom of the window, cranked open in my attempt to ensure that no one would complain about the scent of the cigarette. I was stressed. I needed nicotine right now, not a lecture.

The city was dismal under a weeping sky, an hour from sunset. The streetlight a block away went through its paces in a repeating array of blurry color, starbursts of red, green, yellow and then back to red; I watched like one mesmerized. The orange neon *L* on Papa Leone's Pizza sign needed replacing, zizzing in and out, flickering like the tail end of a firefly. I closed my eyes, conjuring up an image of fireflies at dusk. In the background I could see Flickertail Lake gleaming blue promises and my heart clenched on a hard note of longing.

Landon.

Shore Leave.

Home.

I hadn't been back to Minnesota, where my mother's side of the family had run the Shore Leave Cafe for generations, in over a year. This seemed inconceivable, but what did I expect as a student in the JD program at Northwestern College? Free time? A boyfriend? The ability to see my family now and then?

I expected none of these things, as my father warned me over three years ago, after I'd been accepted to his alma mater, Northwestern Law. As I'd been staying in Chicago with them the warm, windy afternoon

I'd received my letter of acceptance, Dad and his wife Lanny took me out for dinner at Spiaggia and I felt as though the universe was presenting me with an incredible gift—a chance to make something of myself.

Euphoric could not begin to describe me that evening, buzzed as I'd been on my own glory, real and imagined. The *juris doctor* program. Chicago and all its glittery bustle. Dad's beaming smile. Visions of myself standing triumphant before judges, winning case after important case through the decades of my career, stormed my mind as I sipped wine, too revved up for food. That was also the evening I first met Ronald Turnbull, a business associate of my father's, a brief introduction as he'd paused at our table to chat with Dad and Lanny.

"Ron, this is my daughter, Patricia," Dad had said, and I'd delicately placed the wine glass on the table to offer my hand.

Ron, silver-haired and intimidating, confident of his place in the world, produced a smile as our hands met. "Ms. Gordon. I understand congratulations are in order. Your father speaks highly of your academic abilities."

"Thank you," I responded. "I plan to prove myself and then some."

He chuckled, seeming amused, and I felt my shoulders square in immediate defense, but then Ron surprised me by saying, "I've got my eye on you, Ms. Gordon. I'll see you in appellate court. And perhaps we can chat next May, when you're on the hunt for summer work."

I was stunned by this offer but I'd kept all of that from my expression, maintaining a professional mien. "I appreciate that very much. Again, thank you."

Dad couldn't keep from grinning as Ron was led to another table. He leaned toward me and murmured, "I would love to see you ground floor, Turnbull and Hinckley. That's promising, Tish, promising indeed."

"He sits on the appellate court?" I peered discreetly after Ron. The appellate court was comprised of alumni and faculty; as a first-year student I would present mock cases before them, arguing against fellow students. Nervous anticipation prickled along my spine.

"Alumni," Dad confirmed. "And Ron is an old friend. I've talked about you for years, honey, but you'll prove yourself."

That he thought so sent the warmth of pride through my heart. Dad was an expert schmoozer; a sincere compliment from him was a rarity and so I let myself bask in the one he'd just bestowed.

"Favors," Lanny said, caressing her wine glass. She had not yet touched the appetizers, but for reasons other than my own; she didn't remain a size two for nothing. My stepmother wasn't exactly the evil witch I'd once believed; though her personality was as shallow as a wading pool she was my father's wife, and I was mature enough to be civil to her. She elaborated, "Favors are what get you ahead. You scratch Ron's back now, he'll return the gesture." Her full, candy-tinted lips plumped into a speculative pout as she regarded me. I studied her flawless eyebrows, her professionally-applied false eyelashes as she added, "It doesn't hurt that you're young and beautiful, either."

I wasn't sure if I should thank her or consider this a smoothly-delivered insult. Implication: that's how a woman gets ahead in the corporate world. Certainly she had used her own considerable talents in that department to hook a successful lawyer like my father. Dad noticed my rising temper and grinned. "Ron *does* have a very eligible young nephew."

At this I laughed, rolling my eyes, and Dad winked and refilled my glass. He added, with a nod at his wife, "Lanny's right about favors. People don't take them lightly. Ron is as old-school as they come. You can't go wrong on his good side, honey."

I acknowledged this truth. "I'm not eyeing a corner office just yet, but it's good to know there's even a remote possibility."

And I did my damnedest. Both summers, rather than fly home to Landon to indulge in summertime on the lake, I'd completed externships at Turnbull and Hinckley. Ron's firm was elegant and understated, with the prestige afforded one of the top law offices in the city. I'd been so jazzed to step through the revolving doors onto the marble floor of the main entrance, overwhelmed and rabid to prove myself worthy, that it took a few days to realize that everyone around me was enmeshed in competition. Sharks in a goldfish tank, far too confined, constantly eyeing the gleaming promise of the ocean just beyond reach. Sharks that offered sincere smiles but would sink their teeth in any exposed flesh the second your back was turned.

What did you expect? I had reminded myself countless times upon collapsing in my dorm room after midnight, rising before dawn to shower and hit the sidewalk running. I thrived on competition. I was tough. Never mind that a part of me, deeply buried, quivered with fear that I would do well enough, be successful to a degree, but perhaps never achieve real greatness. Never truly matter.

What would it take? Partnership? Your own firm? Rule over the entire city? I giggled at this thought, envisioning a sleek black cape and designer shoes with heels as sharp as icepicks, rubbing my hands together before I ensnared all of Chicago in my power. *That's what sleeplessness does to you. Creates delusions of grandeur.*

The rain seemed unending and I lit a second cigarette with the ember from the first. I would graduate Northwestern in two days, the first major goal accomplished. Mom and my stepdad, Blythe Tilson, were coming for the ceremony and I planned to fly home with them the next day, for a well-deserved rest in Minnesota. My heart swelled at the picture of Shore Leave, of my family waiting there for me; Grandma promised that half of Landon would be at the celebration thrown in my honor. After three weeks at home, I planned to return to Chicago for good, pass my bar exams in July, and then (hopefully) accept a position at Turnbull and Hinckley.

I pressed my forehead to the chill of the window glass. It was humid outside, muggy with springtime, but cold as a meat locker in our air-conditioned apartment. Grace's father paid our utility bill; I never took for granted that one of my roommates was a trust-fund baby. And yet here I sat with the window open, wasting energy even now.

Camille, I thought. *I want to talk to my sister.*

My phone was lying on the windowsill and I snatched it up. Camille answered on the second ring. "I knew you were having a bad day. I had a feeling."

"Hi," I whispered, inundated with gratitude that she knew me well enough to understand this even before I spoke a word. Suddenly I missed her so much that I ached.

"What's going on?" she asked and I imagined her sitting on the porch of the homestead cabin that her husband, Mathias Carter, and his father, Bull, had refurbished. They'd added a whole new wing, two bathrooms, and a loft where the six-year-old twins slept.

My older sister had four children and was currently expecting a fifth in late October; Mathias basically just had to look at Camille to get her pregnant. They hadn't let Aunt Jilly tell them if this latest baby was a boy or a girl, wanting to be surprised instead. I pictured all the kids running loose around Shore Leave these days—Aunt Jilly and Uncle Justin had Rae, Riley, and Zoe; Mom and Blythe had Matthew and Nathaniel—realizing I would hardly recognize my nieces and nephews, let alone my half-brothers, these days. I was not a very good aunt or big sister.

"I'm just…blue," I muttered, without elaborating. I studied the rain streaking my narrow window on the outside world, picturing Landon, no doubt bathed in the dusty-gold glow of the setting sun. My body craved that sunlight, the liquid embrace of the lake water, the natural sounds I'd missed here in Chicago the past three years. Wind through the leaves, water lapping the shore, birdsong.

"Do you have Clinty's calendar?" Camille asked, attempting to lighten my mood.

"Oh my God, yes," I said, giggling. "Ina and Grace have it displayed front and center, just to torture me. They think he's the hottest thing *ever*. I told him if he ever shows up here they'll have him out of his fireman's uniform before he can say 'threesome.'"

My sister laughed; in the background, I could hear nine-year-old Millie Jo fighting with one or both of her brothers. I turned to look at Clint's picture, attached to the front of our fridge with two magnets shaped like chocolate chip cookies. Clint was more like my brother than my cousin and I snorted a laugh at this image of him; every December the Landon Township fire department produced a calendar featuring their firefighters as a way to raise money for the upcoming year—the calendars never failed to sell out within an hour.

"He *has* filled out," I allowed, feeling better just joking around with my older sister, like the old days. Clint was six months older than me, having turned twenty-five last November; he was the July Fireman of the Month and had posed wearing his work pants, suspenders, helmet, and a wide grin. Nothing more. He stood with a heavy-duty ax braced over the top of his shoulders, wrists caught on the handle on either side, nicely featuring his muscular biceps.

"We've all been teasing him," Camille said. "He's so embarrassed."

"Oh please, he loves the attention," I argued. I knew this was true, even having been apart from Clinty for three years. At least back when I attended the U of M in Minneapolis for my undergrad degree I was able to journey home to Landon whenever I wanted; here, in Chicago, that was out of the question. Fortunately Dad and Lanny lived just across the city and were gracious enough to take me to dinner when I was able to emerge from beneath the stacks of law books and petitions and counter-suits which had filled my waking hours for far too long.

But it's been worth it. All those hours you'll never get back, all that sleep you've lost, will be worth it to have that degree.

"I'm sorry we aren't coming to Chicago for the ceremony, Tish. We'll celebrate next weekend," Camille promised, but in the next second her voice moved away from the phone as she hollered, "Kids, quiet down! I can't hear Auntie Tish!"

There was a crash and a shriek, followed by the twins declaring that it wasn't their fault.

"*Dammit,*" Camille muttered. "I'll call you right back!"

I sat there after she'd disconnected, realizing my cigarette had burned out and that my sister would be unavailable for the rest of the evening. I sighed; probably this was a sign that I shouldn't be smoking at all. I tapped the screen on my phone and checked out my text messages; Grace and Ina were at Howie's, our neighborhood bar, and insisted that I get my ass down there as soon as possible, which was a better idea than moping about our dim, empty apartment, but I wasn't sure if I was in the mood for company.

What the hell is wrong with you? Go have a drink. Relax!

Howie's had been our perpetual hangout since living together all of this past year; our lease was up next month, we would go our separate ways, and so I should probably spend one last evening there. It was just that I struggled to relax; my shoulders had been in a perpetual anxious hunch for the past three years. My screen flashed with a picture of Ina and Grace sitting on either side of an empty barstool, both pointing to it. I giggled, heartened by this evidence of my friends having fun; as the image faded out, I texted back, *Be right there.*

I flushed my cigarette butts, washed my hands, and inspected my reflection in the bathroom mirror. My eyes had been shadowed by sleepless smudges for so long that I didn't even notice anymore; I kept a concealer stick in my purse. I supposed the shadows wouldn't disappear anytime soon. I pressed both palms to my belly, thinner than I'd ever been while living in proximity to Grandma and Aunt Ellen's delicious cooking; lawyers didn't eat, we drank—black coffee for breakfast, protein shakes for lunch, vodka shots for dinner. I'd heard variations of this joke since first year.

Counselor Gordon, I thought, and a thrill went all through me.

I removed the clip from my curly hair. It was in desperate need of being cut and styled; surely I could manage a visit to Lanny's stylist before graduation. I reapplied lip gloss; I still loved my old raspberry-flavored dime store brand and even if I someday managed to pull down six figures, damned if I would ever waste money on expensive cosmetics. I changed into jeans, heeled boots, a short-sleeved sweater, and clipped two pairs of gold hoops in each ear before collecting my purse from the heaps of stuff on the kitchen table. I grabbed an umbrella from the rack beside the door and hurried to the elevator.

Howie's was one level below ground; I could hear music pumping as I descended the familiar rickety steps to the front door. Pushing inside, I was flooded with the familiar scents and sounds; I spied my roommates at the bar, sipping from martini glasses, joined by another friend of ours from school, Robbie Benson, my main competitor for top honors. I felt my spine straightening as though about to face off with him in mock debate. Robbie grinned at the sight of me.

"Gordon, where the fuck have you been?" he demanded, already into what was probably his fifth beer. But shit, we deserved it; we'd scarcely seen the light of day since the autumn of 2010, as our pasty complexions clearly attested.

"Tish, I already ordered you a drink," Ina said. She elbowed Robbie, complaining, "You just brushed your arm against my breast and I don't think it was accidental."

I giggled at their usual bantering, claiming a stool as Amy, the regular bartender, slid an icy gin and tonic my way.

"Thank you!" I called, restraining the urge to guzzle it.

"God, where's your cousin when we need him?" Grace asked, bumping her shoulder against mine. "I'm drunk. I need a muscular backwoods firefighter *right now*."

"I'm texting him that you said that," I told my roommate, setting aside my drink to do just that. I reflected, "You'd eat him alive."

"That's about what I feel like doing." Grace sighed, smoothing a hand over her sleek blond hair.

"You know, I have a plastic fire helmet from Halloween. It's right in my closet." Robbie leaned over the bar beside Grace and offered up his best Kennedy-brother smile. He was slickly handsome, entitled as only a boy raised in a household with two successful litigators could be; though he wouldn't have full access to his trust until age thirty, he already possessed more money than I could probably even dream.

"Jesus, I'm not *that* drunk," Grace returned. Robbie was unfazed; he had gamely taken our shit for years now; he grabbed her cocktail and licked the rim of the glass. Grace shrieked, slapping at him. He ducked away, closer to me, just as my phone flashed with a return message.

Tell her I'm free after work, Clint had responded, and I held up the message to show Grace. She shrieked again, snatching the phone from my hands as Ina crowded close. Giggling, they began composing a response.

"So, Gordon, have you talked to your dad today?" Robbie settled on the stool to my right, studiously ignoring Ina and Grace.

I finished my drink in two swallows and nodded when Amy held up the bottle of gin. I told Robbie, "No, actually I haven't. Why?"

"Then you haven't heard about Ron's offer," he mused. "I've success-fully one-upped you. Damn, I feel pretty good about that."

I squeezed a lime wedge over the ice cubes of my second gin and ton-ic. I cautioned, "Don't get too comfortable with that feeling." Curiosity overtook my attempt to play it cool and I demanded, "Ron's offer about what?"

"He needs a housesitter this summer. Well, more like a cabin-sitter. You know how he owns all that acreage out in Idaho or Montana or somewhere? Apparently his regular guy isn't available this August."

I knew Robbie was jockeying for a position at Turnbull and Hinckley, same as me. That Ron Turnbull had approached him with such a request suggested favoritism of an unparalleled degree, and my stomach tight-ened with a cramp. "So he asked *you?*"

"He did indeed," Robbie replied, beaming and smug. "But your dad said he offered you a little something, too."

I looked toward my phone; no hope of getting it back in the near future. Why hadn't Dad called me the moment he was privy to this information?

"So fill me in." I used my best attorney-at-law tone.

"Apparently Ron wants both of us out there to do some kind of long-range externship at a little firm in…shit, I don't remember the town. Let's call it Po-Dunk, for now. A former associate of Ron's went rogue two decades ago and left Chicago. This guy has trouble filling positions out there in Cow-Shit, go figure."

"Po-Dunk," I reminded him.

"*Right.* Ron volunteered us to lend a hand. 'Field work' was how your dad put it."

My shoulders had already resumed their customary hunch, despite two cocktails. "You've got to be kidding me." No wonder Dad hadn't called yet; he wanted to avoid the confrontation he knew was headed his way. The Wrath of Tish. "Did you agree?"

"I'll be in Europe for the first half of the summer, remember?" Robbie said; his parents had gifted him with two months there. I pictured him lounging on the beaches in Spain and France, drunk day and night, charming the bikini bottoms off of local girls while I slaved away back in the States. God help me, I would do that slaving in Illinois, not out west. Robbie prattled on, "Luckily for me, Ron needs the housesitter in August, when I'm available. You, my lovely, get the field work experience starting next month."

"What do you fucking care about a job, anyway?" I bitched. "It's not like you ever have to worry about money."

"Baby girl, that *wounds* me."

I drained my third drink without reply. Robbie knew me well enough to sense the gathering storm and drifted back to Grace and Ina. I closed my eyes, bundling my nerves like cordwood, willing myself to calm. At least until Dad could clarify what this was all about. Ron Turnbull was my future boss; at least, that was how I would continue to regard him until proven otherwise. If Ron wanted me to work outside the state for him, I would have to shoulder arms and do so.

But next month?

I'm supposed to be in Minnesota then.

What the fuck?

This is so unfair.

"Girls, I don't think Tish would approve," I heard Robbie say, catching my ear. I realized the girls were debating sending Clint a picture of Grace's right nipple and leaned to pluck my phone from Ina's grip. Wails of protest met my ears, along with drunken laughter. The phone buzzed then and I saw that Clint was calling; his caller ID picture, from two Christmases ago, appeared on the screen. He was crossing his eyes and blowing out his cheeks in his best chimpanzee face and I showed this gem to the girls, who were undeterred.

"Hey, I just wanted to tell you to bring your friends home with you next week," Clint said as I answered. My cousin's voice was so welcome; it conveyed the sound of home, the familiarity of people who loved me. I could almost smell fried fish and perking coffee from the open windows of Shore Leave, could nearly feel the grain of the dock boards beneath my bare feet.

"God, I miss you, Clinty."

"So when are you coming home?"

"Is that him?" Grace gushed.

Clint heard and laughed. He said, "Tell her yes, *yes* it is."

I snorted a laugh. "Are you seriously trying to sound *seductive*?"

Grace leaned close to the phone and purred, "Hi there, handsome. When are you getting your ass to Chicago?"

I ordered a fourth drink.

Later, I carved out a spot to sit at the kitchen table in our apartment and proceeded to call my dad. He answered on the third ring. "I suppose you've heard."

Dad knew me well enough to realize that I didn't call this late in the evening without being upset or occasionally needing money. Dispensing with any pleasantries, I asked, "What is this about?"

He sighed. "I intended to tell you tomorrow, at lunch. You must have seen Rob Benson this evening."

"Dad, quit evading."

He chuckled. "That's my girl."

"Idaho?" I pressed. "Are you kidding me?"

"Montana," Dad corrected. "Ron has property out there, thousands of acres. He has a local man manage the place, usually, but he's unavailable this August."

"So, enter Robbie. What about me? How do I fit into all this?"

"Ron's friend, Al Howe, operates a small firm out there, in the same county where Ron owns land." Dad sounded mildly stressed. I imagined him pinching the bridge of his nose as he explained, "I remember Al from the old days. He was never much suited to life in the city. He was raised out west and came east for school."

I restrained the urge to snap, *So what?!*

Dad continued, "The closest place that's actually on a map is Miles City. Al's firm is in a town called Jalesville. I believe you've even mentioned this place."

He was right; this town's name chimed in my memory and disjointed images flashed across my half-drunk mind. A big, loud, musically-inclined family comprised of all boys, friends of my sister and Mathias who'd traveled to Minnesota for their wedding seven years ago. This family, the Rawleys, was from Jalesville. Camille and Mathias, and their kids, had stayed out there a few times over the years since first meeting them.

"It's not appreciably bigger than Landon," Dad was saying. "Al's partner is about to retire and leave the firm, and Al has his hands full." Dad hesitated, which suggested extreme reluctance; my father was never at a loss.

"Dad?" I persisted.

"I told Ron you'd be more than happy to help out."

"Help out in Montana?" I cried, cupping my forehead as though I could restrain a headache by sheer force of will. "For how long? I'm supposed to go to Landon! Do you know how long it's been since I've had a vacation?"

"Patricia, it doesn't suit you to whine." Dad sounded more like himself. "It's just for July and August. Eight weeks. Through Labor Day, tops. Think what this goodwill bump will do for you, honey."

"I'll go out of my mind," I muttered, stung that he'd call me out for whining.

"You'll have plenty to occupy your mind," Dad disagreed. "Al's working on a decent-sized case. Land dispute, from what I can tell. Sounds rather interesting."

"I'm listening," I grumbled.

"Just this past April a Chicago-based company began buying up acreage in Rosebud County, where Jalesville is located, and it seems that half the town is ready to sell out and the other half, roughly, refuse to sell. Al's brother-in-law already sold his campground to this company."

"What's the problem with that?" I tugged a notebook from a stack of papers a good foot high. I fumbled for a pencil, my notetaking urge still deeply ingrained.

"Nothing on the surface. Capital Overland has a habit of buying up prime real estate in lower-income areas, where people are tempted with offers. Then they doze these little towns and expand their own business, often reselling the acreage to the highest bidders, people who want vacation homes or timeshares, this sort of thing. If you don't sell out, you're out of luck."

"That sounds like business in the modern world," I muttered, but my heart grew cold at the thought of someone doing such a thing to Landon, where most of my family still lived. As though any business owner in Chicago gave a rat's ass about what they would view as a speck on a map. I imagined everyone in Landon being displaced; no dollar amount could compensate for such a thing.

"Al thinks he can rally enough of the population so that it's no longer worth the while of Capital Overland," Dad said. "He's trying to save his town, and it's a noble effort."

"Capital Overland?" I repeated; it sounded familiar.

"That's the company Al is dealing with," Dad explained. "It's a subsidiary of Yancy Corp. In fact, I believe T.K.'s younger son runs it."

Even I recognized the name Yancy and jotted additional notes as Dad kept talking.

Yancy Corp
Capital Overland
Jalesville
A noble effort

Dad said, "If Capital Overland can finagle enough of the population into selling out, there isn't much of a chance for Al and the others who don't want to lose their town. Ron doesn't have a vested interest in the town itself but he doesn't want to lose his property out there."

My mind was spinning and it wasn't from the gin. "Isn't T.K. Yancy a friend of Ron's?" More spinning. "And yours?"

"You're correct, though 'associate' would be a more apt description."

It seemed strange to think of Ron Turnbull, armored with steely layers of power and intimidation, having friends.

I clarified, "And it's just for the summer?"

"Yes, dear," Dad said in a tone clearly meant to be understood as condescending.

"All right, I'll do it." As though I had a choice. "But Ron better make this up to me this fall. I'm just saying."

Dad laughed. "I'll tell him you said so."

Chapter Two

"CLARK IS *SO* EXCITED TO SEE YOU NEXT MONTH," CAMILLE gushed. "He absolutely adores you."

I was seated at a red picnic table in my sister's yard, which was a cleared quarter-acre in the woods surrounding their cabin. I'd just finished my third beer and was as close to content as I ever felt, surrounded by my family, loud and rowdy as always, the kids tearing around. It still stunned me how much everyone had grown while I was away, as though I was vain enough to think that they remained in some sort of stasis, simply awaiting my return.

Mathias, Blythe, Rich Mayes, my Uncle Justin, and Justin's dad, Dodge Miller, were crowded around the propane grill on the deck. Mathias held Lorie, his and Camille's youngest, in his arms, while little Zoe clung like a monkey to Uncle Justin's back. Millie Jo and Rae, both nine years old, were huddled on the far side of the yard, plotting together as only girls that age are able; the boys, ages eight to six, were in their own group near the girls.

Mom, Aunt Jilly, Ruthie, Grandma, and Aunt Ellen were also seated at the table with Camille and me; Clint and his best friend, Liam Gallagher, were stretched in full-length lawn chairs a few yards away, resting up after a day of working with the fire crew. I considered Grace and Ina, giggling at the thought of what they would do at the sight of Clint and Liam (though they would have to fight Ruthie for Liam). Despite my offer, neither of my former roommates could find the time to come to Minnesota for a visit, much to Clinty's disappointment. I wasn't disappointed at all; I knew they would have hated Landon after the first few days away from Chicago.

"Tish, I was hoping you'd work around here this summer," Mom said. She sat to my left and I rested my cheek against her shoulder, surprising myself almost as much as her; I was not typically given to affectionate gestures. But I had missed my mother. She smelled just the same as always, like peaches, her tanned skin soft as down against my cheek. Her long golden hair, which I'd always wished I'd inherited, brushed my face.

"I know," I whispered.

Ruthie, directly across the table, leaned forward. "You look like you could use a rest. You work too hard."

"You always have," Mom added, tucking her arm around me. I felt like a beloved little girl and allowed this feeling to soak into my soul for later, when I would have zero access to it.

"I'm so happy to be here for June, at least," I said.

Aunt Jilly was studying me, her cobalt-blue eyes intent. She was given to precognitive flashes and I wondered if she was seeing something right now; a tingle shivered along my spine, but she smiled and said, "I was just thinking how grown up you look, how sophisticated. You used to be such a tomboy."

Everyone laughed at this, including me. I declared, "I could still out-run Clint." I looked over at my tall, strong cousin and amended, "Well, maybe not anymore. But I could win an argument with him now, any day."

Grandma said, "We're so proud of you, honey. We just miss you around here so much. It's not the same without you and Clinty bickering about something. Not a day goes by when someone doesn't ask when you're coming back to work at the cafe."

I saw the wistful expression flicker over Ruthie's face; I knew she wished I would move home for good, even if she wouldn't admit it. My little sister was twenty-two and still dating Liam, as she had been since her senior year of high school; certainly they would be married by this time next year. Neither Ruthie nor Camille had ever been to college and a secret part of me was jealous because apparently I hadn't inherited that particular ability to be content; I was always on the lookout for the next horizon, restless with latent energy. I'd been restless for so long now.

I said to Ruthie, "You and Liam are so cute. Who'd have thought, huh?"

She smiled a little, her eyes roving his way. Liam lifted his sunglasses and gave her a low-key wave, and she blew him a kiss.

"No one special for you these days, love?" Aunt Ellen asked me. "We haven't heard about anyone since Randy."

"I've been in law school. Relationships are strictly forbidden." I didn't even have to sigh my tone was so desolate. Randy was the last of my longer-term boyfriends. Yes, I'd slept with men since him but I tended not to get too attached. I was in favor of the weekend hook-up, squeezing sex between rounds of studying and petition preparation. On that front, I was not proud of my behavior.

"You look as though some hot lovemaking would do you good," Aunt Jilly observed, totally stone-faced, the only one of us who could get away with that sort of statement. Ruthie choked on her beer and Mom shot Aunt Jilly a dirty look.

"Laugh it up," I muttered, taking their ribbing at my expense. Directing my words at Aunt Jilly and Camille, I added, "*I'm* not the one attempting to double the population of Landon."

Aunt Jilly lifted both hands, her pixie face alight with amusement. "Not since Zoe! I told J if he wanted to keep having sex so often, he better get himself in for a vasectomy."

Camille's cheeks flushed and I turned to her, on my right, to rest both palms on her warm pregnant belly, round and firm beneath the faded cotton of her t-shirt. It seemed like only yesterday that I'd been cupping her stomach while she was pregnant with Millie Jo. At my words, Camille's gaze touched Mathias and I looked over my shoulder to see the radiant grin he sent my sister's way; the color in her cheeks deepened. In keeping with my old habit, I rolled my eyes, though I was glad to see Camille so happy.

"*Mo-om!* Henry hit me!" Millie Jo yelped from across the yard. I was ashamed to admit that I could not keep the twins straight; they so exactly resembled each other with their curly brown hair, tanned skin, and dark blue eyes. They were each a mini-Mathias.

"Henry, apologize to your sister," Camille ordered calmly.

"All right, Mama," said one of the boys, presumably Henry, before snatching something out of his sister's hand and darting away, the soles of his bare feet flashing.

"God, it's like we have Huckleberry Finn times a hundred," I observed. Millie Jo shrieked and raced after her brother, the other kids hot on her heels. I expected to hear a brawl of epic proportion in the near future.

"Do you need me to whip them?" Mathias called over.

"No, but come give me a kiss," Camille said.

"Oh, dear God," I muttered, taking a long pull from my beer. "You two still make me sick."

"You should have seen your sister this week," Mathias told me after he'd reached the picnic table, gently bouncing Lorie on his forearm. "She's been so excited for you to get here."

To my surprise, little Lorie reached out her arms and I took her into my own, with pleasure, cuddling close the diapered, chubby-cheeked toddler. Her dark curls were arranged in two pigtails that stuck out from behind her ears. She regarded me with serious, gold-tinted green eyes, looking just like Camille, her tiny hands resting on my collarbones.

"I've been excited to get home, too," I confessed, shifting so that Lorie fit between me and the table. "I miss it here so much."

"Are you ladies ready for us to serve you?" Uncle Justin asked, balancing a tray of grilled food, his dark eyes going right to Aunt Jilly; even I could see how their eyes held and spoke in ways only they understood.

"I've got steaks, brats, burgers, the whole works," Blythe said with an easy grin, carrying two loaded platters. I thought back to the first summer Blythe came to Shore Leave, ten years ago now, when he was a stranger to us; or, as Mom liked to say, when fate brought them together. He was thirty-three now, father to five kids (counting my sisters and me), and it was hard for me to imagine a time when he hadn't been a part of our lives. He loved my mother so much, and had been unfailingly kind and patient with Ruthie and me; we'd lived in their house all through high school. He was also an insanely good-looking man but I hardly noticed that about him anymore; I just saw my stepdad.

As Ruthie rose, stretched, and then headed straight for Liam's lawn chair, probably to make out with him, I muttered, "I need a drink," and handed Lorie off to Camille to go in search of the beer cooler.

We ate outside as the sun sank and painted the clearing with saffron light. The kids elbowed and horsed around at their designated picnic table, spilling food all over the place, until Dodge threatened to drag the entire thing, them included, to the lake.

"See how you like eating when you're in the water!" he bellowed, though he was such a big teddy bear that no one believed him anyway.

Rae said, "Grandpa, you wouldn't do that!"

Riley said, "Grandpa, Rae's calling you a liar!"

"You tell him, son," Uncle Justin teased.

Aunt Jilly muttered, "Oh, for the love."

It was every bit as loud and rambunctious at the adults' table; Clint had to lean way over so I could hear him. "So, there's no chance your friends are making it up here?"

I shook my head, mouth full of corn on the cob. "No, they can't take the time, not even to meet Mr. July." Clint flushed beneath his tan, with a grudging smile, and I pestered, "Aren't there plenty of girls around here? What about Claire, or Erica?"

"Tish, seriously, they're both married now."

"Even Claire?" I was surprised; Claire Henry always had eyes for Clint.

"Yeah, but she wasn't the one for me."

"Trust me, Grace isn't either. She may be my friend but she's a materialistic city girl. She'd drive you crazy and not in a good way."

Clint rolled his eyes, as true-blue as Aunt Jilly's, and mine; Aunt Jilly used to joke that the stork brought me to Mom by mistake. He grumbled, "I wouldn't have minded a little craziness this week."

Camille commandeered my attention from the other direction, poking my ribs with her index finger. "The Rawleys are so excited to see you,

Tish. I wish I was going with you. They're all set to show you around Jalesville the minute you get there. You'll love it so much. It's beautiful. The mountains, I'm telling you. The air smells amazing."

"You sound like a travelogue," I teased, before admitting, "I'm excited to see them, too. Remember that first morning you called me from Clark's kitchen, when you and Mathias had just met them at The Spoke? All I could hear in the background was music. And guys, singing."

Camille grinned. "Of course. We all met the night before because Case bumped his guitar into the back of my head trying to squeeze through the crowd. If not for that, he wouldn't have sat at our table and Mathias would never have sung with them. We might not have known them at all." She held my gaze, grin fading as she said quietly, "Fate."

I was irritated by the sudden cold ripple in the region of my tailbone, trying not to squirm under her speculative gaze; I knew my sister well enough to sense that she was debating whether to say something more.

With caution, I allowed, "That's one way of looking at it, I suppose."

She changed the subject. "Where are you staying out there? I know you told me last month, but I forgot…"

"Dad said that Ron—you know, who I'm hoping to work for—is going to provide me with a fully-furnished apartment. I'm actually pretty thrilled about that." I'd never lived in my own space, without so much as a roommate or a pet. "And Uncle Justin fixed up that old Honda of Aunt Jilly's for me to drive out there, so I have a way to get around."

"You'll be busy," Camille recognized; I'd given her the short and sweet version of what was happening in Jalesville. "But be sure to get out to The Spoke to hear the guys play. It's so worth it. Clark will show you around, and so will the boys."

"They're hardly boys anymore. And besides, I can find my way around just fine. The town is smaller than Landon, right?"

Camille studied me for a long moment and again I wondered what she was thinking; the set of her eyebrows and lips communicated such seriousness. But then her entire face softened as she smiled, leaning to kiss my forehead. Exasperation and affection mingling in her tone, she muttered, "Same old Tish."

In my old bedroom that night, in Mom and Blythe's house that was nestled in the woods near Shore Leave, I lay naked and edgy, hearing the muted murmur of Ruthie on the phone in her own room, Matthew and Nate snoring from the bunk beds in theirs; it was almost like being back in high school, though I shuddered at the thought. Not that high school had been so terrible. It was just so far removed from the person I was now.

You're a graduate of Northwestern Law. You have a future at Turnbull and Hinckley. Ron won't refuse you anything after this. Just get through the summer and you're golden. What's one summer? Besides, it's beautiful out there in the mountains, like Camille said. You've never been farther west than Minnesota, after all. It will be a good experience.

I rolled to the other side, my eyes tracking to the open window. I imagined throwing on a sweatshirt and my shorts and then sneaking outside, feeling the damp lawn under my bare feet, following the lake path into the familiar woods where the pliant grass gave way to a sharp carpet of fallen pine needles; exactly three cigarettes were stashed in my purse, if Aunt Jilly hadn't "borrowed" them, and I craved a smoke. I reminded myself I was an adult, that no longer did I have to skulk into the darkness to sneak a cigarette. I remembered bitching at Mom for smoking when I'd been a teenager.

My, how things change, I thought, with only a touch of irony. *You should get some sleep instead of running around outside. When will you have a chance to sleep anytime soon?*

But restlessness wrapped around my mind the way a damp sheet would my body. I had been trying to avoid the thought that kept surfacing for attention, the one lingering uncomfortably in the background since I'd learned I would be spending the summer in Jalesville, Montana. And it was here, in my old room, that I finally allowed the memory free reign.

Camille's wedding.

I hadn't given that October afternoon more than a passing thought in years, but right now it was effectively destroying all chances at sleep. Sighing, I relented, sitting up and tugging on my jean shorts, shrugging into a hoodie sweatshirt. Humidity wrapped me in a sticky embrace the second I stepped onto the porch; the sky was blanketed by a gray cloud-quilt, blotting out all trace of any appreciable illumination. The flame of my lighter nearly blinded my eyes, remaining impressed in red-yellow on the backs of my eyelids as I blinked.

Shit, no more smokes after these last few.

Camille and Mathias had been married in October of 2006. I'd been a freshman at the U of M that crisp autumn, as arrogant as my father at his worst. Big city girl, I'd felt, gracing Landon with my worldly presence.

Oh God.

I exhaled smoke, cringing at the remembrance.

The weekend before the wedding I'd had sex for the first time in my life, with another freshman, a guy from my literature class. I thought at the time that we were headed for serious couple-hood; now, almost seven years later, I could hardly remember his face. I'd been dying to tell Camille all about it and wanted the focus of the attention to be upon me, especially from my older sister, whom I worshiped, even though I would never openly admit this.

It was her wedding weekend and you were acting like a selfish brat.

Of course Camille was a little preoccupied. The intention had been to keep both the ceremony and reception small and sweet, but with all of the Carters, their numerous relatives, the Davises and the Millers, and then the addition of the out-of-state arrivals, the guest list swelled quickly beyond original proportions. Shore Leave and White Oaks almost burst at the seams. The Rawleys, a family that consisted of one father and seven boys (two sort-of adopted; I didn't know all the details) arrived from Montana the Thursday before the wedding. Although Camille and Mathias were all gangbusters at their presence, I'd only been annoyed; here was yet another loud and overpowering distraction to pull the attention away from me. Years later, alone in the dark, I blew smoke rings, wincing as I recalled my behavior on that long-ago weekend.

Were these things in my mind tonight because it was likely that I would run into those people...*that person*...fairly frequently this summer? Surely that was why I was torturing myself with these memories.

I thought of his name then, studying the tops of the pine trees, outlined in sharp relief against the gray velvet of the overcast sky; my eyes had adjusted to the darkness by now. The air was energized by a coming storm and I shivered in the damp, electric chill, thinking of what Camille had said earlier at supper, about fate.

Case Spicer.

I really hadn't known he existed until that Thursday, back in October of 2006. Even when Camille and Mathias related the pretty damn amazing story of what had happened on their trip out to Montana the preceding summer, I hadn't paid strict attention to names and details, my mind overloaded with college plans. Besides, my sister failed to mention one critical piece of information, assuming that I would only be angry. And I was. This guy, this Case Spicer, came to Minnesota carrying a picture of me in his wallet. Apparently he had decided without so much as meeting me that I was the one for him. As in, *the woman* for him. Even now, at age twenty-five, I felt that this notion was absurd; it smacked of romantic nonsense for which I had zero tolerance. To my eighteen-year-old self, it had bordered on insane and stalker-ish.

But did you have to be so fucking rude to him?

I lit my second-to-last smoke, thinking of that particular Saturday night. Autumn in Landon was a sensory overload, the trees blazing with fall colors, nothing half-assed in the north woods. Scarlet and maroon, orange so rich you could taste it, brilliant yellow-gold; Flickertail Lake a solemn indigo beneath a crisp sky. Mathias's oldest sister had begged for red to be our bridesmaid gown color; we'd looked like a crew of vampire princesses, as I'd joked (God, what a mouthy little bitch I'd been), but nothing could deflate Camille's buoyancy that day.

The wedding took place at White Oaks Lodge, Mathias's family's gorgeous hotel and a longtime fixture in Landon, built during the nineteenth century on the shores of Flickertail Lake. I'd been vaguely aware of the red-haired guy from Montana, but only peripherally; at the groom's dinner on Friday I'd caught him looking my way a time or two, but he did not venture within ten feet of me. Saturday, however, he loaded up on some liquid courage and it was a different story. Mathias took the stage at their reception in order to sing to Camille; it was his thing, completely romantic; I could appreciate that today, but at the time I had actually been *texting*, for Christ's sake, sitting at the head table texting the guy I thought I was in love with back in Minneapolis.

Everyone was completely focused on what a wonderful, sweet man Mathias Carter was, singing "Amazed" to his new bride, when someone sat next to me and leaned on his forearms over the creamy table linen.

"Can I tell you something?" he'd asked, with no other introduction or invitation.

I turned to regard this intrusion with eyebrows knitted in aggravation. My hair had been twisted into a series of complicated knots, my make-up meticulously applied, my satin dress as red as any sin, a spectacular gown currently hanging in a dry-cleaner's bag in my old closet. The guy sitting near me was in a state of dishevelment that spoke of the end of a hard night—reddish-gold hair standing on end, bowtie missing and collar undone two past the top button. His breath smelled like pine trees; whatever he'd been sipping for the better part of the night was about fifty-proof.

"Can I?" he'd asked again, and I gave him about one-third of my snotty attention; my phone flashed on the tabletop, indicating a new message.

"*Well?*" I prompted. Even in the dim, candlelit ballroom, I could tell this guy was drunk.

"God, your eyes are so blue. And so beautiful. I can't take it." He spoke hoarsely, and with a tone I had never before heard from a man. Reverent, almost.

My eyebrows lifted at these unexpected words, almost into my hairline. Instead of thanking him for the compliment I responded with an inarticulate, "Huh?"

"Your eyes," he whispered, studying me the way you would a painting in a museum. "Seeing you in person is so…it's just so…" He plunged both hands through his messy hair and muttered, "Oh, my God."

I gaped at him.

"I wrote a song about you," was the next unbelievable statement from his lips.

"What are you *talking* about?" I cried, recovering my wits with a vengeance; the sounds of merriment and music in the surrounding ballroom rushed back to fill my ears, as though I'd been swept momentarily behind a thin gray fog. "You don't even know me. We've never met before this second!"

"I know, I really do, but see…the thing is…" He stumbled over the words, covering his face with both hands before gathering himself together. He lowered his chin and looked steadily into my eyes. "The thing is, I know you're the one for me. I know this with all my heart."

I was stunned into speechlessness, stunned into forgetting my flashing cell phone. He swallowed hard, his throat bobbing; it obviously required a certain amount of bravado to speak these things. Immediately I suspected two things—alcohol was contributing tenfold to these words and/or he was outright fucking with me. Both suspicions did nothing to endear him to me in any way.

"You are *drunk*."

He shook his head. His words fell on top of each other. "No. I mean, I am, but that's not why…that has nothing to do with…"

I decided being forthright was the only way to go. I turned to look him full in the face and said meanly, "Well, you're wrong."

I might as well have punched him in the gut; even as unperceptive as I was at that age, I could see this. He blinked, owl-like, and opened his mouth to say something else, but I stood up and shoved away from the table, intending to hide out in the bathroom until he left me alone. I was embarrassed and angry, however unfairly, for him to be saying such stupid things and putting me in this uncomfortable position. To my dismay he followed me, and though he was drunk he seemed to have no trouble keeping up.

"Wait, please wait," he implored.

I quickened my pace in spite of the heeled shoes I would never wear otherwise. At the bathroom door, when it was apparent he might actually trail me into the ladies' room, I spun to look up at his flushed face. "Leave me alone!"

He lifted both hands in a gesture of apology. "Please, just listen…"

"No, *you* listen!" I felt hot and tight, as though my dress might have shrunk. "I don't know you and I don't *want* to know you! You think I like being followed by some drunk moron?"

Ouch. Now, rocking gently on the porch swing and drawing on my smoke, separated by seven years from that moment, I reconsidered the use of this word. At the time I was irate enough that it seemed appropriate.

When he spoke, his voice was low and full of pain. "I don't understand how I know we belong together, but we do. I *know* this."

My heart had responded oddly to these words, and to the intensity in his eyes, but before he could say anything else I shoved into the restroom, ready to lean against the door so he couldn't follow; I needn't have worried, as he was nowhere in sight when I reemerged minutes later, my heart not yet having resumed a normal, non-frantic pace. I hadn't caught a glimpse of him the rest of the night. And they'd all returned to Montana the very next day.

Of course I'd demanded the entire story of Camille, who somewhat unwittingly related the tale of what had happened regarding Case and my picture, out in Jalesville that July when she and Mathias first met him and the Rawleys.

"Case is actually really sweet," my sister insisted. "He's a honey! You just don't know him."

"And I never will! God, Milla, how could you keep something like that from me? He had my *picture?* God, that's so creepy!"

Camille couldn't resist needling me. "I'm sure he still does."

"You didn't get it back from him?!"

Since then I'd heard only marginal information regarding this guy, Case, who kept in contact with Mathias. Camille and Mathias took their kids out to Montana for summer visits, and all of the Rawleys (just them, not the Spicer brothers) came for a two-week stay during July of 2010. I'd been home for the summer then; it was just before I started law school in Chicago and I'd been floating near the clouds with elation, so proud of myself for earning acceptance into Northwestern Law School.

The Rawleys were great, I could not deny. Camille called them the Peter Pan tribe and Grandma and Aunt Ellen spoiled them the entire visit, plying them with food and drinks and hugs; it was their favorite thing after all, caretaking. The oldest brother, Garth, brought along his wife, a woman named Becky; there were four additional brothers, all looking so much alike that I'd joked they should wear nametags, but after the first few days I'd been able to distinguish between Marshall (who was a drummer, part of a band that included Garth and Case, as he explained), Sean, Quinn, and Wyatt (nicknamed Wy), the youngest. We'd all gathered on the porch on clear evenings during those two weeks so that Garth and Marshall could play their guitars, the music drifting over Flickertail; they favored old songs, cowboy songs, and we all sang along on those still, starry nights.

"Case told us he'd break bones if any of us tried anything with you," Marshall told me when a bunch of us were out swimming one evening.

I laughed over this ridiculousness. "You tell him that he's *funny*." A spurt of ire flared as I treaded water. "Besides, if I wanted to try anything with any of you, it would be my business. No one else's!"

Marshall, who was very good-looking but not really my type (as in, he wasn't bound for a high-profile corporate law career in Chicago), had grinned at my angry words. "Is that a hint?"

"You wish," I groused, splashing him.

"I'm jealous as hell over her anyway," Marshall said then, in a completely different tone. He indicated Ruthann, who'd been riding on Liam's back near the dock, both of them giggly thanks to the schnapps bottle making the rounds, unable to stop laughing about Ruthie's bikini top, which had slipped down around her waist; she compensated for this by keeping her bare front side pressed tightly to Liam's shoulder blades. Her wet curly hair, long enough that it hung nearly to her waist, made her look more than ever like a naughty mermaid. Marshall watched them with his jaw all but bulging. At last he shook his head, muttering, "I hope he knows how fucking lucky he is." His hands, near the surface of the lake as he treaded water, were in fists.

"I hate to say it, but you're asking for it," I couldn't resist.

"I know, I know, 'I wish,' right?" Marshall grumbled, and that was the end of that.

And so it had been nearly seven years since I'd last seen Case Spicer. I was flattering myself to think it mattered to him one way or the other, if at all, that I would be working in his hometown for the summer.

Probably he's married. Maybe he even has kids.

I'm sure he's sorry for all of the things he said at Camille's wedding.

Shit, maybe he was so drunk he doesn't even remember.

I ground out the last of my smoke and sighed, dragging my fingers through my tangled hair. I was exhausted but knew myself well enough to realize sleep would continue to remain a stranger; I was too accustomed to forcing myself to stay awake for studying. I recalled a poster in one of my old law professor's classrooms—Sleep is Overrated.

Right, I thought, heading back inside. In my room I clicked on the bedside lamp, caught my long hair back in a clip, and finally dug the Capital Overland file from one of my travel bags on the floor. I'd spent my last week at the apartment in Chicago poring over all the information I could gather about this company and its parent affiliate, Yancy Corps.

Capital Overland was established in 1993, capitalizing nicely on the dotcom boom. Yancy Corps had been around much longer, established in Chicago in 1893, exactly one hundred years earlier. These days the corporation seemed to specialize in real estate markets around the world, dabbled in stocks, and had apparently earned fortunes for the Yancy family over the past twelve decades. I'd collected numerous data before leaving Chicago, on my own and in contact with Al Howe in Jalesville, relating to the current managers of Capital Overland, two brothers named Franklin and Derrick Yancy; the younger, Derrick, was in Montana as of this moment. He was the company front man in Jalesville, a dark-haired, smooth-browed looker perhaps thirty years old. I would have bet money his hands were equally as smooth, just like Robbie Benson's; men who considered manual labor to be what happened when they went to the gym at their club.

I had no trouble imagining Derrick Yancy charming his way into potential sales; that look practically oozed from him. Charming on the surface anyway, sharp as the knife he'd no doubt plunge into your back, beneath. I couldn't pinpoint exactly what it was about him that bothered me, but coldness settled in my gut the moment I saw his picture. It had yet to dissipate. As of today, Sunday the ninth of June, sixty-eight of the projected two hundred eleven potential sales had been made to Capital Overland. Al Howe provided me with a list of surnames of Capital Overland's targets, three of which I recognized—Rawley, Turnbull (which would be Ron's acreage), and Spicer. None of these families had yet agreed to the sale. According to Al, Capital Overland offered fair market value for each of the properties they were vying for, hoping for fast sales, and there were enough people in the area struggling to make ends meet that they'd been willing to sell their land.

"It's like the town is crumbling apart," Al told me during our brief phone conversation, earlier this week; he sounded close to defeat. I almost considered telling him I'd be there before my projected arrival date of July sixth. He added, "I'm so grateful that you'll be another body out here to work. I mean that, Patricia. I'm beside myself here."

And I'd promised him I would do whatever I could to help.

Chapter Three

THE DRIVE SOUTHWEST THROUGH MINNESOTA AND NORTH Dakota seemed endless, but as of three in the afternoon I had cleared the Montana state line, reenergized by a rush of adrenaline. Aunt Jilly's old Honda ran like a champ but didn't have air-conditioning or a CD player, let alone a port for my phone, and so I'd made do with the radio and Mom's dusty shoebox of old cassette tapes from the 1980s.

Before leaving the cafe this morning I'd clung to my sisters, to Clint and my mother; Grandma and Aunt Ellen each kissed my forehead and admonished me for being too thin. I promised that I would eat bigger meals and that I would sneak back to Minnesota before I returned to Chicago this fall. I tucked directions to the Rawleys' house in my front pocket; I would be dining at Clark's this evening and they'd promised to show me to my new place afterward. I'd found the small apartment complex online before leaving Minnesota; it was just outside of Jalesville, perhaps five minutes from downtown, a newer building called Stone Creek, constructed of beige stucco. The view from my laptop showed mountains in the distance, sending a distinct and unexpected thrill down my spine.

Even now, having driven through Miles City under the late afternoon sun, I was deeply moved by the scenery flashing past. Camille called this area the foothills, a place of odd, towering rock formations and low, scrubby brush. I found the rocks gorgeous and mysterious, a stony palette painted with infinite colors of brown. I marveled that I'd ever found brown a plain color; the sunlight tinted it into shades as dazzling and varied as the nail polish selection at Lanny's favorite salon. I giggled at myself for comparing one to the other.

What I had a harder time acknowledging was the stirring in my soul. It had to do with the very scent rolling in my open car windows, the wildness of the landscape, the sense of something *untamed* in the air, beyond my control. I was a control freak, by nature, and found this sensation both exhilarating and startling. I didn't so much welcome it as I recognized it; I thought, *The country here doesn't care for you at all. It's utterly impassive.* I'd never felt this way, even in Landon; there, the tall trees that ringed Flickertail and whispered in the wind offered a distinct sense of comfort. Here, there was none of that. I crossed over from Custer to Rosebud County in the early evening, pulling into a gas station to refuel and attempt to calm my fluttering nerves. I had never been around the Rawleys without my own family nearby. Would it be awkward? Was I too underdressed to greet them? Pumping gas, I tipped forward to examine my travel outfit: jean shorts, a faded blue tank top, bright green flip-flops. Chipped toenail polish, zero make-up. My hair in a sloppy ponytail.

It's all right. You're just fine. You've been on the road. They're hardly judgmental. You may not look it right now but you're a graduate of Northwestern Law, soon to be employed at a top Chicago firm.

Just as I formed a mental picture of the impressive main lobby at Turnbull and Hinckley, my eyes drifted to the Montana sky, stretching endlessly above the little gas station. I blinked, not quite able to reconcile the sight before my eyes with the one in my brain. The sky was laced with fair-weather clouds as the sun drifted westward, warmed by tones of both blue and copper. A breath of wind fluttered against my cheek and the lobby dissipated.

You'll have the rest of your life to think about Turnbull and Hinckley.

For now I inhaled the spicy, invigorating air; I felt a rush of belonging just before the gas pump clunked, signaling that my tank was full. No more than ten minutes later, I braked on the interstate, seeing the sign for my exit—Jalesville, three miles away. My heart took up a rapid thundering but I was used to this anxious rush. Hadn't I just spent the last three years in law school? Though, my current anxiety was tinged with excitement as I slowed the Honda on the exit ramp. Jalesville appeared on the horizon moments later as I descended a steep hill, the landscape on either side reminding me of old movies, the kind about wagon trains and outlaws.

Jalesville, population 823, I read on the faded sign welcoming visitors, slowing to a crawl as my tires rolled over a pair of train tracks bisecting Main Street. I'd passed the campground that Mathias and Camille had told me about, the one which had already sold out to Capital Overland— Tomlin was that family's name; I'd memorized all two hundred eleven names on my list, mentally dividing it into two separate categories, Sold and Unsold. My curious gaze roved over the buildings; most were weathered, locally-owned shops, wood construction with metal roofs, awnings jutting over the sidewalks. Hanging planters attached to the streetlights, dripping with blossoms. A lone stoplight a few blocks down Main, just like Landon, a series of side streets webbing out from this central artery.

I caught sight of the bar and grill where Mathias and Camille had first met the Rawleys back in 2006, when Mathias sang with their band, a little place called The Spoke. It appeared busy this evening; I reflected that it was Saturday. In the violet tint of approaching dusk, Jalesville was quaint, charming. It felt sheltered by the line of low-lying mountains on the western horizon. The air near The Spoke drifted in my open windows and I caught the scent of grease; my stomach groaned in pain, as I had been too revved up to eat a thing all day. People stood around the parking lot there, beers in hand, smoking and laughing; I almost pulled over to bum a smoke.

There was some foot traffic on the sidewalks, a few inquisitive looks directed my way; people here knew one another's cars and trucks and recognized me for a stranger. The stoplight caught me and I took the time to covertly study my surroundings. My heart jumped as I spotted a little building on the right side of the street, with wide glass windows announcing *Howe & James, Attorneys-at-Law*. The sign in the door was flipped to CLOSED, the interior lights extinguished. It was all I could do not to pull over and press my nose to the glass.

The light changed and the person driving the truck behind me gave a couple beeps on the horn, so I waved apologetically out the window and then drove forward. I needed to catch Cartersville Road to take me out to the Rawleys' place, and it took me two wrong turns before I was headed in the right direction. I cleared Jalesville, back in the gorgeous, wide-open foothill country, gazing out my car windows with a great deal of pleasure. The melting sun was a caramel glow along the edge of the mountain range in the distance when I drove up to what I believed to be the correct residence, my heart fluttery and my stomach tangled in knots. There were no other homes in sight, so I hoped this was indeed Clark Rawley's homestead.

Holy shit, what a beautiful place, was my first thought.

Seconds after I put the Honda in park, nervously gripping the wheel with both fists, the door of the main house banged open and I saw people in the rearview mirror. A bunch of people, and dogs, spilling out of the house and toward my car. Laughter, chatter, exclamations of excitement. Almost before I could wrap my fingers around the door handle, I was surrounded.

"There she is! Tish, welcome!" cried Clark, closest to the driver's side. Grinning widely, he opened the door for me; I was swept summarily into a warm embrace. He smelled strongly of peppermint and faintly of tobacco and looked just as I remembered, sparse silver hair lifting from his head in the light breeze. A mustache dominated his face, along with wire-rimmed glasses. His four youngest boys crowded behind him, Marshall, Sean, Quinn, and Wy. I thought of the two weeks they'd spent with us in Landon, grilling out, singing on the porch, swimming and having fun; I smiled, concern evaporating.

Truly, though, 'boys' wasn't the proper word to describe them any longer, as I'd told Camille; only Wy was still a teenager. The Peter Pan tribe had grown up and I was surrounded, almost overwhelmingly, by a rowdy group of handsome, twenty-something men. I thought of Grace and Ina, a little smug as I considered what my former roommates would say about this fortune. Though it was apparent that a couple of them had girlfriends; either that or Clark had adopted two daughters. Everyone offered hugs; I was swept from one pair of arms to the next.

"Tish, you remember me, don't you?" Wy asked, dancing from foot to foot. He was tall and gangly now, with the same shaggy, dark-brown hair and a long nose shared by all the Rawley men.

"Of course I do," I said, curbing the odd, tender urge to ruffle his hair. He had only been a little kid when his mother died in a car wreck, and I thought of that as I acknowledged, "You're just a little bit bigger now."

"Garth and Becky couldn't make it this evening but they'll be over this Friday for supper, as will you, I hope," Clark said as he led me inside.

"That would be lovely, thank you," I said, charmed by the warm welcome. Flames roared in a stone fire bowl on the back deck and I could smell a charcoal grill. My shoulders relaxed; this house felt something like home.

"Come on out, honey, have a chair," Clark invited. "What would you like to drink?"

Probably I should have said water, but the air was intoxicating and as I sank onto a plushy patio chair near the fire, I heard myself respond, "A gin and tonic would be great."

"Coming right up," Clark promised.

I was joined by the whole bunch, truly enjoying their company as they peppered me with questions about Landon and my family. Clark and Quinn resumed grilling beefsteaks and there were appetizers spread across the patio table, but I was content to sip the icy, delicious gin and tonic, my perennial favorite. Clark's back porch boasted one hell of a view. The cocktail went down a little too well and Wy was quick to refill my glass almost the second I downed the last swallow; I crunched an ice cube as I studied the mountains on the western horizon, which were backlit by lavender clouds and reminded me of a dinosaur lying on its side. I spoke this thought aloud, then giggled.

Marshall, seated on the glider nearest my chair, snorted a laugh and commented, "Wy, I think you're mixing Tish's drinks a little too strong."

"I'm just making them how you guys like," Wy defended. He had found a cowboy hat somewhere and settled it over his unkempt hair. From beneath the too-big brim, he regarded me with a flirtatious smile.

"*Shee-it*," Marshall said, drawing out the word, and then everyone was laughing, me included.

"I'm not drunk," I assured them. "Just…relaxed."

I was surprised to realize this was true. It could be the gin, the company, the scent in the air, the guitar music on the radio; I couldn't exactly define it and decided not to try. I settled my shoulder blades more comfortably into the cushions. Marshall was using his thumbs to drum along with the beat.

"This is us," he said.

"Hmmm?" I didn't follow what he meant.

"One more?" Wy asked, nodding at my empty glass.

Shit, is that already gone?

"Sure, thanks," I said, and Wy disappeared at once.

"Me, Case, and Garth," Marshall explained. "We got in a few recording sessions at a studio in Billings two years ago, when we still played regularly."

"You guys don't play anymore?" I had to concentrate more than usual on my words. I saw Marshall's eyebrows lift in amusement.

"Too busy, mostly," Marshall replied. To Wy, who was approaching with a fresh drink in hand, he complained, "Where's mine?"

"I only wait on beautiful women," Wy said, smooth as whipped cream, and I giggled as I accepted the glass, accidentally sloshing some onto my hand. It wasn't until I was licking gin from my wrist that I understood I was pretty damn toasted.

Sean's girlfriend, Jessie, said, "Hey, in that case, grab me a beer!"

"Camille told me you guys are really good," I said to Marshall, who grinned at the compliment.

"We'll play at the local fair next week. And sometimes in the bars around here. Especially The Spoke, since our aunt owns it. But we all have day jobs now. Can't be out on the town quite so much."

"Oh, *whatever*," Sean contradicted. "You're out on the town as much as you ever were."

"No, sir," Marshall disagreed, but there was a teasing gleam in his eyes. The song switched from a fast-paced guitar to something sweeter and slower; though I was no musician, I recognized a fiddle.

Indicating the music by lifting my glass, I said, "This is *so* pretty. You guys play a lot of old-time music, my sister said."

"We do, but original stuff, too." Marshall seemed to be watching me carefully as he said, "Case writes most of our music, including this song. He wrote most of the CD that's playing now."

I heard myself ask, "Is Case coming for supper?"

Was I a little curious to see him?

Maybe, I allowed.

"Not tonight," Wy answered, returning with Jessie's beer. "He's over in Miles City tonight. But he said —"

"Bud, go get me a drink," Marshall interrupted.

Wy responded, "No *way*."

"You want a beating? Besides, Tish needs a new one now, too."

Wy huffed a long-suffering sigh and I said, "Maybe just a soda this time." He nodded, kicking Marshall's ankle as he walked past.

"You'll be working for Al Howe, right?" Jessie asked.

I nodded. "Yes, for the summer. I saw his office on the way here. I'm supposed to meet him tomorrow so I can get my apartment keys."

"He's a good guy," Jessie said, sipping her beer. "My grandpa just retired but he worked with Al for years." She clarified, "Grandpa is the 'James' of Howe and James. He was just saying at Sunday dinner last weekend that he's so glad someone is coming to help Al. He said what we need around here is some young blood."

"I'll do my best," I promised, picturing the two lists of surnames I had memorized. Even as fuzzy as my thoughts were at the moment, I recalled a family named James on the Unsold side.

"Watch out for Derrick Yancy," Marshall startled me by saying. He rocked the glider into gentle motion. "He's been working on Al for a month now, trying to convince him to sell. He's such a big-city bastard. He'll look at you as a prime target."

I sat a little straighter. "Prime target for what, exactly?"

"Wheeling and dealing," Sean said, cupping his hand around Jessie's thigh. "He'll see you as someone he can use to convince folks around here that they are better off selling to his company and moving elsewhere."

"Some people seem to think he's right about that," I said, as Wy returned with a beer for Marshall and another gin and tonic for me. I murmured, "Thanks," conveniently forgetting that I had asked for soda, no alcohol.

"Ever since the power plant closed down last year, times have been tough around here," Sean said. "It was so unexpected. Just at Christmas, for God's sake."

"Al was saying something about that." My thoughts were pinwheeling. *Shit, lay off the drinks.*

"Dinner, everyone," Clark announced; he held a platter of steaks.

It was then that I attempted to stand and instead stumbled, my drink spilling straight down my tank top. Wy and Marshall caught me, almost as though we had choreographed it, each of them grasping an elbow, one on either side.

"You guys, I'm so sorry," I babbled. My entire front side was soaked with gin. "I'm drunk…"

Everyone was laughing then, to my relief, rather than staring in stun at my ridiculous behavior.

"It's just that I haven't eaten all day…" I mumbled.

Reassuring and decisive, just like a dad, Clark invited, "Hon, how do you feel about being a houseguest this evening?"

"I think that sounds great," I told him.

Sunday morning I woke to see sunlight striking wooden beams, creating a honey-colored glow. I blinked, my mouth so dry it was impossible to swallow, a headache sprouting from the nerves of my right eyeball. I heard noisy activity downstairs, the Rawleys probably having breakfast and marveling at how unprofessional I was, up here in their guest bedroom after having been too loaded to join them for supper. Dear Clark had escorted me upstairs while Wy fetched my travel bag from my car; I'd summarily collapsed on the bed and now here I lay in the unforgiving morning light. Smelling bacon and perking coffee, hearing laughter and chatter, embarrassed as hell.

My phone chirped from somewhere nearby. I rolled to one elbow, groaning at the effort, and spied it on the small sheepskin rug beside the bed; Camille had texted.

Drunk on your first night there. LOL.

For fuck's sake. I supposed I deserved this. Grimly I tapped the screen to respond, *I know. It's totally pitiful. Don't need your shit right now too.*

I heard my sister laughing all the way back in Minnesota.

They think it's hysterical. Don't worry.

Talk to you later, I wrote, then dropped my phone and flopped to my spine, crossing my forearms over my eyes. I knew I couldn't stay up here, hiding out, but I needn't have worried; Clark and the guys gave me a bunch of good-natured ribbing when I cautiously descended the stairs and shuffled to the kitchen ten minutes later, after a cursory examination in the tiny adjacent bathroom. I looked like shit but that was my own fault. What I wanted right now was a hot shower, preferably in the privacy of my own apartment.

Clark was kind enough to call Al, asking him to meet us at Stone Creek Apartments in fifteen minutes with my keys. I was able to get down a few slices of bacon and a piece of toast, and then Clark and Wy elected to escort me to my apartment; they led the way in their big diesel truck, Wy driving. Back through downtown, right at the stoplight, past a grassy fairground and over a wide stone bridge that spanned the distance across Stone Creek; just beyond stood the building I recognized from the pictures I'd found online.

Wy parked and hopped down, hurrying to the driver's side of my car. "There's a spot for you, Tish, right over there." He indicated. "See, it's got your name on it. And that's Al on the sidewalk."

My heart jumped at the mention of my boss, Ron Turnbull's former associate, the man who'd left Chicago for Jalesville almost two decades ago. I parked in the spot labeled 'Gordon' and climbed out under the hot midday sun, terribly conscious of my messy hair, last night's clothes, and un-showered state. Clark and a small, balding man stood chatting on the sidewalk in the shade of the building but they interrupted themselves as I approached, pasting a smile on my face despite my headache.

"Patricia! How are you?" Al Howe beamed, offering his hand, as I took cautious stock, noting his observant blue eyes, confident stance, and casual dress clothes—khaki pants, button-down shirt, no tie. He looked like a grandpa come to visit the grandkids. I recalled everything I had learned about the proper way to shake a hand to indicate that you meant business.

"It's good to meet you," I said.

Al pumped our joined hands twice, then patted the back of mine, offering what I believed was a genuine smile; I knew enough lawyers to be wary. Even my own father's face was rarely graced with a non-calculated grin. He said, "I am *most* pleased to meet you. You come highly recommended, I hope you know."

"Thank you," I murmured, hiding overt pleasure at this statement, wanting to appear professional. "I'm happy to be here." I meant this more than I would have guessed even two days ago.

"You're needing a day or so to settle in," Al recognized, releasing my hand and digging a couple of keys from his breast pocket. "Though, I would like to invite you to dinner this evening, if that works for you. My wife is excited to meet you."

"That would be wonderful. Thank you again."

Clark said to Wy, "Son, grab Tish's bags. Let's get her into her new place."

Between the four of us, all of my things were carried up the stairs to the second floor with one trip; my apartment was 206, and Al unlocked and swung open the door.

"Oh, I love it!" I exclaimed. I set down the two bags I'd hauled up the steps and spun in a slow circle, admiring the sunlit space.

"Brand new building," Al explained. "This is a nice little place."

"I like your porch!" Wy called, darting across the living room with its well-used couch, small TV set, recliner upholstered in faded denim, and lone bookshelf, empty of any reading material. Wy unlocked the sliding glass door and stepped out into the sunshine, absorbing the view from a narrow balcony overlooking the parking lot. But the mountains were visible in the distance and I pictured sitting right there tonight and smoking a couple of celebratory, welcome-to-my-own-place cigarettes.

The living room was to the right, the kitchen straight ahead, both with west-facing windows. The entire place proved small but it was mine, and I felt a delicious thrill. Already I was envisioning where I would put my things—my radio, my files, the plants I would have to buy for the windowsill and the top of the fridge. A round wooden table with four mismatched chairs was stationed beside a patchwork quilt displayed on the wall; Aunt Ellen and Grandma liked to display quilts in the same way. There was a wooden shelf graced by a framed picture featuring mountains at sunset. Stacked atop the table was a set of four canary-yellow placemats and matching dishes.

"Where do you want these things?" Clark asked. He was burdened with two more of my bags.

"Oh, right on the carpet there is perfect," I said, and threw my arms around his waist in an impulsive hug, surprising myself nearly as much as him. "Clark, thank you for your help."

He winked as he set the luggage on the floor. "I'm already looking forward to dinner this Friday. I can't wait to hear all about your week."

Al said, "Patricia, here are your keys, and directions to my house. We live just off of the old highway, about a mile out of town. Can't miss it. Should we say dinner at six?"

"That sounds wonderful. And please, call me Tish. I don't usually go by Patricia."

"Tish," he said agreeably. "You'll have to explore Jalesville this afternoon. The grocery store and the bank are a block over from the law office, which is three blocks from the town square and the courthouse."

"I will, and thank you again."

"Until this evening, then," Al said, taking his leave.

Clark called to Wy, who was still on the porch, "Let's give Tish a chance to settle in, son."

Wy caught me in an exuberant hug on the way out the door. "I work at Nelson's Hardware right near Al's, so come see me if you want. Maybe we can have lunch sometimes!"

Clark said, "Call us if you need anything this week, won't you?"

"I will," I promised. Since Al was not in earshot I felt compelled to add, "I'm sorry about getting drunk last night…"

Clark laughed. "Never you mind about that. You'd obviously had a long day."

A minute later I was alone in my own place. Feeling like the little girl in *The Secret Garden*, I explored both tiny closets, prowled down the short hallway and checked out my bedroom, which featured a full-size bed (I'd brought along my own pillows, sheets, and blankets from Minnesota) and a chest of drawers, but no mirror. The adjacent bathroom was itty-bitty, hardly large enough to turn in a full circle, with tiles the color of old daisy petals. The shower stall was a stand-up; apparently there would be no long tub soaks this summer.

I was exhilarated to be here. I dug out my portable radio first thing and placed it on the speckled Formica counter, finding a country station on the dial—a type of music I had not listened much to during the past three years, but I found myself craving a steel guitar and the sound of a fiddle. Cranking the tunes, I opened the kitchen window and the glass door to the porch, leaving only the screen between me and the scent in the air. The porch featured a solo canvas chair, angled so that someone sitting on it could prop his or her feet on the waist-high railing. Back inside, I spent a good hour unpacking, arranging and rearranging my things, making up my bed, exploring the outer hallway in the building, which led to a communal, coin-operated laundry room.

Remember to get quarters, I thought.

I hung up my five 'lawyer' outfits, which consisted of a standard jacket-and-pencil skirt combo, one jet black, the others no-nonsense neutral tones. I could mix them up with the array of colorful linen and satin blouses I wore beneath the jackets. I loaded all of my casual summer clothes into the dresser, lined up my shoes on the floor of the bedroom closet, and stuffed my panties and bras in the top-most drawer. Then, feeling a swell of accomplishment, I stripped to my skin and showered, determined to make a trip to the grocery store. I needed milk, a few rolls of quarters, orange juice, chocolate ice cream, coffee, and cigarettes. Just one pack. I swore I would make them last the whole summer.

By quarter after six that evening, I was seated at Al and Helen Anne

Howe's dining table. The two of them lived on an acreage—also in the crosshairs of Capital Overland—that had been in Helen Anne's family for three generations, where Al had moved his family after they decided to return west and leave Chicago for good. Their home was quietly impressive, a rambling, ranch-style constructed of native stone, as Al informed me on the grand tour. He and Helen Anne had three grown children, all of whom now lived in southern Colorado, with no interest in returning to their native Montana.

"They've moved where the jobs are," Al lamented as Helen Anne served broiled pork chops smothered in onions, mashed potatoes, crusty white bread, corn pudding, and fruit salad with whipped cream. Pure heaven. Butter and luscious gravy and salt, all combining to make my stomach cramp with hunger; I hadn't eaten since breakfast. Al continued, "I did hope that one of them would go into law and take over the firm someday. But I'll retire long before that happens." He chuckled. "Probably be dead, actually."

Helen Anne, taking her seat, scolded, "Bite your tongue, Albert, goodness." She looked my way and invited, "Dear, please do eat. You're as thin as a whippet, I hope you don't mind my saying so. We'll fatten you up out here, mark my words."

I took up my fork and admitted, "I haven't eaten such a good meal since I was home in Landon."

"Law school," Al sighed, buttering a thick slice of bread.

The three of us were settled intimately at one end of a cherrywood dining table, a fire crackling in the stone hearth. I felt much more comfortable with them than I would have guessed, as though I was seated with my doting grandparents; for a second I imagined what dinner with Ron Turnbull and his wife would be like, and repressed a shudder. Assuming I would ever *be* invited to dinner with Ron and Christina. Certainly it would take place at one of Chicago's top ten restaurants—formalwear and crystal, escargot and champagne and proper cutlery, and my internal guard on all speech firmly in place. Ron's wife would drink vodka martinis, exclusively; she was only a few years older than me, possessed of the kind of outrageous beauty that very few can actually achieve, the kind that Ron's money attracted; she couldn't have been legitimately attracted to *him*. I almost giggled at my uncharitable thoughts.

"I remember well those law school days," Al said. "I must have weighed a good forty pounds less than I do now."

Helen Anne dished more mashed potatoes on my plate without asking, but somehow this only warmed my heart and sharpened the comparison I'd been making between her and Christina Turnbull. Dining in Al's home, wearing a linen sundress and casual sandals, my hair in a loose bun low on my nape, I realized I would never feel this sort of comfort with any boss in Chicago.

Enjoy it while you can, I thought, ladling gravy over my pork chops.

"Tish, we practice primarily family and bankruptcy law, and serve most all of southeastern Rosebud County," Al explained as the meal progressed. "I'm a jack of all trades, to be honest. I know in the city," and I understood he meant Chicago, "there's more exclusivity in what you'd practice on a daily basis. Here, I have to be everything for everyone, so to speak, but it makes the days interesting. Rupert James and I worked together for the last twenty years. I'm close to retirement myself and none of mine or Rupert's children intend to take over the practice. And now all of this business with Capital Overland has cropped up. I've been beside myself."

"In your opinion, what prompted the company to turn its eye to Jalesville?" I asked. "I mean, I understand their basic motive, snapping up land and reselling. But why Jalesville? They've been almost exclusively purchasing in Wyoming for the past five years."

"It has to do with the closing of the power plant," Al said. "Coal mining is a big industry around here, and when the plant closed it put half the area out of work. Companies have ways of smelling opportunities, that's what. Here's cheap land that they can buy, develop and resell as vacation property, knowing that plenty of folks will agree to sell because they need money now."

"Can the plant be reopened?" My mind clicked along. "Why did it close?"

"They claimed bankruptcy at the time," Al explained, his mouth full. "I drafted motions for more than one worker, but the plant did everything by the book. Because they were laid off, the workers were able to file for temporary unemployment. Problem is most of the ranches in the area are no longer working ones, meaning they don't have the livestock anymore. Instead, there are families sitting on hectares of property that have been in their family for generations, just like ours here, and I'm afraid they see this as an opportunity to make money on something that's arguably useless now."

"Never mind that the town will no longer exist," I said. No one in Chicago would give two fucks about it, a truth that offended my sensibilities. This was home to hundreds of people. Where would they go now? Who would care?

"According to Derrick Yancy's exact words, that is not his problem," said Al. "He's very much like his father, aggressive and calculating."

"He's trouble," Helen Anne agreed, eyeing me intently. "You're a lovely young woman. He'll try to manipulate you, mark my words. Albert, you don't let that happen."

I felt my spine straightening, ready to inform her that I would not let that happen, but then I wisely bit my tongue; she was offering the kind of commentary that Grandma and Aunt Ellen would. She was only worried about me, not intending to patronize. I would prove that I could hold my own, and then some.

Al said, "You'll meet plenty like him in your career, Tish, I hate to say. He's a typical big-city businessman, unfortunately. This will be good experience for you."

"Field experience," I said, repeating Dad's words.

"Indeed," Al said, with a wink. "Tomorrow, why don't you head to the office around eight and I'll show you the ropes, introduce you to Mary, my secretary. She baked a half-dozen loaves of banana bread for you."

"And I'm sending you home with two more of sourdough," Helen Anne added. "Just came out of the oven a few hours ago."

"Thank you." I was overwhelmed by their kindness. "Everyone has made me feel so welcome."

"That's our job," Al said. "Small-town nice, right? Now, eat up and let's chat about non-work-related things, shall we?"

Chapter Four

EXHAUSTED, I SLEPT DEEPLY AND DREAMLESSLY THAT night, one pillow tucked against my stomach in my customary sleeping position. At some point in the night it rained, as the sharp, pleasant scent of it was in my nose as I woke; the square of sky framed by my bedroom window faced south, showing lingering cloud cover. I snuggled a second pillow beneath my jaw, thinking about everything I'd discussed with Al and Helen Anne last night; I'd left their house feeling like a beloved granddaughter, gifted with loaves of bread, a container of leftovers from dinner, and an entire pan of spinach quiche that Helen Anne had baked for my breakfast.

Don't get used to this. This is way beyond what you should expect.

I showered and applied make-up appropriate for a day appointment, the amount I would have worn to try a mock case for appellate court in school. I twisted my curly hair up high on my head and pressed both hands to my stomach, drawing a fortifying breath. I was dressed in bra and panties only, and eyed myself critically in the bathroom mirror. As a teenager, I had been so self-conscious of my growing breasts that I'd worn sports bras until my first year at the U of M in Minneapolis, when it finally dawned on me that maybe I shouldn't be so quick to hide what some people would consider an asset.

Standing before the mirror I turned to the side and sucked in my belly, sticking out my chest and wiggling my shoulders. I rolled my eyes, giggling; I was hardly wearing seductive lingerie, the kind appropriate for such a pose. My bra was a serviceable nude-tone from Victoria's

Secret, my non-matching panties a flowered, department store pair that
a girl of twelve could wear. I giggled again, clearly already beginning to
go crazy here in Montana. I quit fooling around after a glance at the
clock on my phone display; it was 7:36 and Al was expecting me by
eight. I dressed in a hurry slipped on my favorite indigo blouse, sleeveless and with a subtly-ruffled v-neck, and my ivory jacket-and-skirt set.
With these I paired my nude heels and buttoned my jacket with only a
little tremble in my stomach.

There. You look good. Professional and polished.

Not a bit frightened or uncertain.

I locked my apartment, having foregone breakfast, determined to start
a better routine tomorrow, and drove across Jalesville under the morning sun. The town was bustling as I braked to a stop at the streetlight
where I would turn right to get to the law office. I realized there wasn't
any traffic and that I didn't need to wait for the green, but advanced
slowly, peering at shops and wondering about the people walking along
the sidewalks. Would I get to know any of them? *Well*, that is? I saw an
appliance store, a diner, the hardware store where Wy said he worked…
and then my eyes roved over a shop with a front window adorned by the
words, *Spicer Music.*

Is that…

I wonder if…

The door sign was flipped to OPEN. I couldn't see anyone through
the window; the sun was at the wrong angle, gilding my vision. I realized the Honda was crawling at an inchworm's pace and that there was
a truck behind me, surely wondering what the hell I was doing, so I
accelerated and drove on to the law office, where I parked beside Al's
rusted-out pickup; I assumed that around here people knew him well
enough not to judge his legal abilities based on his vehicle.

Heart at a clip, I entered the law office to the tinkle of a bell above
the door. The room smelled of coffee and old books. Al was bent over a
desk, pointing out something on a file folder to a woman who appeared
old enough to be his mother. Both of them looked my way and grinned
as though I'd appeared to inform them that they'd won the state lotto.

"Tish, good morning!" Al welcomed. "Mary, this is our new associate, Patricia Gordon."

New associate.

I liked how that sounded. I went directly to her and offered my hand. She reached, with care, to remove her carnation-pink reading glasses, which were linked to a bejeweled chain, lowering these to her ample bosom. She took my hand into both of her soft, wrinkled, and much-spotted ones, patted me twice, and then proclaimed, "If only my youngest grandson wasn't married! Albert, you didn't tell me our new girl was so beautiful."

I blinked, observing Al's mouth twitch with a restrained smile. The woman at the desk released my hand and continued to peer at me. She was eighty if she was a day, wearing a pink dress with pleated sleeves, lace at the collar, and matching lipstick; auburn eyebrows were drawn upon her face with great deliberation. She smelled of a delicate, floral perfume.

"Tish, this is Mary Stapleton, our dear secretary."

"I've been at this firm since I was a girl your age," Mary explained. "I worked for Rupert James's father before him, God rest him now. Rupert's retired just recently. He wasn't as good at his job as Albert here, however. Don't be fooled by Albert. He's sharp as a little tack. He just looks absentminded."

I choked back a giggle and nodded seriously. "I'm happy to meet you. And thank you for the compliment." I had never been one for comfortably accepting words about my looks, so I added, "I take them where I can get them."

"Bosh," Mary said. "Those eyes of yours, blue as a spring-fed lake. You've had compliments by the dozen, or young men these days don't know their rears from a hole in the ground!"

I did giggle then, looking helplessly at Al.

"Now, if you've got the brains to back up the looks, you're a force to be reckoned with," Mary continued. "You've the look of it, somehow." She gave me the kind of eagle-eye worthy of a Northwestern Law School professor, and my shoulders squared in response.

"I do, and I am," I said, and she smiled wider.

"Thatta girl," Mary said. "Give this young lady something to do, Albert, for heaven's sake."

Al showed me around the office while Mary began clickety-clacking on a computer keyboard, reading glasses back in place, pink lips pursed. My desk was to the right, just beside the front window, with a view of the activity on Main Street. I saw a computer, file cabinets, an old-fashioned phone with a long corkscrew cord, and a wheeled desk chair upholstered in cracked brown vinyl.

"You can bring whatever you'd like to spruce up the space," Al said, leading me behind the counter that ran the length of the main room; his desk was toward the back, near a closed door labeled CONFERENCE ROOM. "There's one bathroom, just over there, and a storage room down that hall. We haven't redecorated in some time." He grimaced apologetically.

"No, this is great," I countered, recalling the lack of any personal space I'd ever been afforded during my summer externships at Turnbull and Hinckley.

"I'll have you start researching right away, if you would," Al said. "This next Tuesday, a week from tomorrow, there's a city council meeting at the courthouse. An information session that I requested, and at which Derrick Yancy has also requested to present. He wants to argue why people should sell to him, why it's in their best interest. I want to prove him wrong, and that's where you can help."

I nodded, tucking stray hair behind my ears. "Just point me in the right direction."

Four hours later, I had shed my jacket. Al left an hour earlier to attend a hearing at the courthouse, and Mary just a second ago, for lunch. She addressed me as 'Patty' when she bid me farewell but I felt impolite correcting her. I looked up from my notes to watch her make her way down the sidewalk under the brilliant noon sun, which sparked in her jeweled glasses chain, nearly blinding me. I took the opportunity of being momentarily alone to stretch, twisting at the waist and rubbing the back of my neck; this office was not air-conditioned, not that I was a complainer, but the only window that actually opened was on the opposite side of the room, near Mary's desk.

I had been engaged in gathering information all morning and was proud of the stack of notes I'd already assembled. Al tasked me with looking into Capital Overland's activity over the past five years, specifically the fates of the people displaced from the towns the company had purchased, and then typically dozed and resold. What I discovered wasn't a pretty picture. The families I found information about had not fared any better after selling and relocating; so far, dozens had since declared bankruptcy.

"Draft up an argument," Al instructed. "We want to rally all the locals at the meeting. We want solidarity. Point out that they aren't assured of finding a better circumstance by selling and relocating."

I was thinking about getting a batch of t-shirts made that read *Save Jalesville!* since this had been my mantra for the last month. All kidding aside, I felt I was doing something worthwhile, a feeling I had not experienced in some time. I was just about to bend over my notes when a movement out the window caught my eye and I received a jolt of pure and unrefined adrenaline. A man who was unmistakably Case Spicer was approaching the law office from across the street, and my heart stuttered, kick-started, and then surged, fueling the rush of angst in my entire body.

Oh my God. Oh my God.

Is my picture still in his wallet?

All those things he said at Camille's wedding.

He said he knew we were meant to be together.

That's long gone now, for fuck's sake, Tish.

Wow, he looks different than I remember…

The bell above the law office door tingled as he entered, his gaze scanning the otherwise empty room before coming to rest on me. Maybe I imagined that his eyes held all of the attraction and longing I remembered from years ago.

Of course you're imagining it! Jesus Crimeny, Tish.

My heart thudded so hard it was probably audible even as I rose and offered what I hoped was a professional and impersonal smile. Case was stone-faced and serious, no trace of a return smile or even recognition. I had been imagining anything else in his expression.

"Hi," I offered, my voice embarrassingly husky. I cleared my throat and continued, "How have you been?"

"Great," he said shortly, and his deep voice sounded just like I remembered. "And you?"

"Well," I responded, tight in the chest as he came to a halt on the far side of the hip-high counter. "Very well, thank you."

Case nodded without saying a word, while our eyes held and I tried not to appear to be marveling at him as much as I actually was. The guy I remembered from my sister's wedding had been drunk and hesitant. The man before me could not have been more different; he regarded me with a solemn expression as I studied him, both of us silent.

He was taller than I remembered, lean but with broad shoulders, and close-cropped auburn hair. I vaguely recalled at the wedding that it had been longer, almost curly. His eyes were a rich brown, like cinnamon, and held no trace of apparent humor, hardly even seemed to acknowledge that we knew one another, at least marginally. I did a quick calculation and determined that he was now about thirty years old. My gaze dropped to his lips, crisply sculpted above a strong, clean-shaven chin, and realized I was staring, very non-professionally. Almost moronically.

I opened my mouth to say something, anything, to fill what was becoming a tense silence, but then he said, a little more softly, "You got in on Saturday night, Clark said. You were still sleeping when I was there yesterday morning."

"You were there?" I asked weakly. "I was…I was a little…"

I couldn't tell if he seemed amused, if that's what was subtly present in his voice as he said, "Clark explained."

I swallowed, mentally cringing at my own foolishness. What a lovely impression to make after seven years, hungover and sleeping it off in someone else's guest room. When I had accused *him* of being a drunk moron, years ago.

"Oh," I stumbled, embarrassed and flushing, fidgeting with the bottom hem of my blouse, self-conscious of my less-than-completely-professional appearance. To change the subject I said, "Clark invited me to dinner at their place on Friday."

"It's been a long time," Case finally allowed, still holding my gaze prisoner. He seemed to be trying to get a read on me, to discern who I was now versus who I had been; or maybe that was simply what I was doing to him. "You're a lawyer now, just like you wanted."

I flushed even worse, feeling hot, bright blood descend from cheeks to chest. I affirmed, "Yes, I just graduated this past spring."

"Clark said you were out here to work for the summer."

"Yes. It's more a favor for my future boss, who owns land out here. Apparently there's a buyer snapping up acreage, who wants —"

"Capital Overland," Case interrupted, and his face grew more animated. "They've approached everyone in the area. They want quick sales, no trouble."

"That's what I've heard," I said. "Actually, this is good. I mean, not that they want your land, but that you have information. I need all the info I can gather on them." I gestured at the paper mess sprawling across my desk. I turned back to his eyes and my heart continued to kick at my ribcage. I ignored this and asked, even though I was fairly certain I knew the answer, "What is your position on the sale?"

"Over my dead body." For the second time a hint of a grin lifted the right side of his lips. "Those were my exact words. I doubt they appreciate me much."

A small, crooked smile tugged at my mouth.

"Turnbull is your future boss?" he asked.

I nodded affirmation.

"We share a border with him. He's only on the land in the autumn, for a month or so."

I nodded again. "Yes, he lives in Chicago. I'm planning to work at his firm starting this fall."

"He has a local guy who manages the property. I could put you in contact with him, if you'd like."

"Thank you. You also share a border with the Rawleys, isn't that right?"

"We do." He held an envelope in one hand and tapped the edge of it against the counter as though restless.

"Your family?" I asked, not sure why a small, sharp hook inserted itself in my flesh at the thought that he might be married. Of course he probably was, and I was incomparably vain and immature if I thought he still carried a torch for me after seven years. To compose myself, I turned and riffled through the papers on my desk to extract a notepad and pencil.

Case stood watching me. As I turned back around he affirmed, "My family has been on the land since the late nineteenth century, yes."

"You and..." It didn't matter one bit who lived with him, but I used my most professional tone of voice, implying that this was a business question.

"Just me, these days. Dad passed a few years back. And Gus lives with his girlfriend in town."

"No one else?" I pressed, keeping my eyes on my notepad. Seconds ticked past and a trickle of sweat skimmed between my breasts. He was still studying me as though attempting to read my mind.

"Not since Lynnette and I divorced." He spoke calmly and I realized he recognized my transparent attempt to fish for personal information that was absolutely none of my ever-loving business.

I dared to look up at him, curious to know more. I wasn't at all relieved that he was no longer married. *Not one bit.* There was no logical reason for me to feel that way. I noticed that his skin was tanned and freckled. Freckles were scattered all along his arms, disappearing under his black t-shirt. He had strong, wiry arms, corded with muscle and dusted over with red-gold hair.

"Any children?" I asked, as though just making conversation.

Just a hint of a smile as he replied, "None that have ever been brought to my attention, anyway."

"Do you still play guitar?"

"Couldn't live without it," he said in response, and I damned my heart for responding to those words. I was about a step away from tachycardia. His smile had vanished and he looked hard at me for a second before seeming to gather himself together. He said, "I stopped out to drop off something for Al."

"He's out," I murmured, stating the obvious. "But I'll be sure he gets it straight away."

"Much obliged." Case set the envelope on the counter that separated our bodies and seemed to hesitate, as though unwilling to leave even though his errand was complete. I tried to conjure up a reasonable excuse to keep him a little longer, too.

"This is a beautiful area." *Great, Tish, talk about the weather next.*

"Isn't it? Although where you're from is gorgeous, too. I was only ever there the once, but I've never forgotten it. Mathias and Camille are still having babies, huh?"

I knew he and Mathias talked frequently. "Yes, they're like bunnies."

"I never saw two people so happy," he said, smiling a little at my wording. "So I'm glad for them."

"Me, too," I admitted. A strand of hair slid down the side of my face. I tucked it back behind my ear but it wouldn't stay put. Case's eyes followed the movement of my hand as I messed with it again.

"There's something..." he said, and a small bomb burst in my chest as he reached and used the tips of his fingers to carefully extract something from my hair. He explained, "I think you had a piece of tumbleweed," showing me the wiry little stick. He set it atop the counter. He had inadvertently tugged free another piece of hair from the clip at the back of my head, and I felt disheveled and sloppy.

"Thanks," I muttered, tucking both loose strands behind my ears. My face was about a hundred degrees.

"Well, I better get back to work," he said. Somehow we had ended up much closer than we'd been when he first came into the office.

"It was good to see you," I said, surprised by how much I meant this. "Will I see you around?" I hurried to explain, "I mean, to talk about Capital Overland, and all of that..."

"Friday," he said, heading for the door. "Gus and I always eat dinner at the Rawleys' on Fridays."

But before I could reply he was already back outside, the bell tinkling as the door closed. I sank to my desk chair and watched as he climbed into a well-used maroon truck and drove away, east along the dusty street. A second later I turned to my computer and typed his name into the search engine. Ignoring both my conscience and my workload, I scrolled through hit after hit, glutting on the info dump at my fingertips.

In short order, I discovered that his full name was Charles Shea Spicer. I cupped my chin in one palm, staring out the window at the sun-drenched street, wondering how 'Case' had come from that. Born December fifth, 1983, to Owen and Melinda Spicer. He'd mentioned that his father had passed away but I discovered that his mother had been gone much longer, dying back in 1991. His dad, Owen, had never remarried.

He must have loved her too much to find someone new, I thought, and continued scrolling.

Case was something of a local celebrity; there were dozens of articles featuring him singing, songwriting, and performing in area festivals. I clicked on each photo I found, some professional-grade, taken for a newspaper, and others informal, posted by friends. In most, he was both singing and posing with Garth and Marshall Rawley.

Charles Shea Spicer. He is really good-looking, I acknowledged, almost unwittingly. He looked so at home on stage, in complete enjoyment, grinning widely in some shots, cradling his instruments—he favored the guitar and the fiddle—eyes closed with concentration in others.

This is what he was doing all those years you never gave him a thought. He was out here living his life. So what does he do now? Surely he can't make a living performing on weekends.

Owned an instrument repair shop, I discerned minutes later. Spicer Music, which I saw just this morning, a few blocks from where I sat right now. Lessons offered.

A woman with shiny brown hair, large breasts, and tiny shirts kept appearing in pictures with him, and I assumed that this was his ex-wife.

Who wears shirts that small on a regular basis? That much cleavage is tacky anywhere outside of Las Vegas.

I finally found a captioned picture; Tiny Shirt was indeed Lynnette Spicer.

Aren't they divorced? Why does she still have his last name?

When the bell on the door rang again I jumped as though prodded in the kidney, closing the search screen at once; I felt like I'd been surfing for porn. Al held the door for Mary as they entered.

"Hello, Patty!" Mary was cheerful and beaming. I didn't bother to correct her; if that's what she felt like calling me, I supposed she had a right.

"Holding down the fort all right?" asked Al, giving me an indulgent wink that acknowledged Mary's misuse of my name.

"No fires or famines," I assured him. "I've got quite a pile of notes here. And Case Spicer dropped this off about a half hour ago."

"Oh great, thanks." Al collected the envelope. "Did you get out for lunch?"

"I brought a sandwich," I lied. "I usually eat on the go."

Mary disappeared into the employee bathroom and Al ducked behind his own desk. He said, "I've got a second hearing over at the courthouse at two-thirty. Would you like to accompany me?"

"Yes, absolutely," I responded.

Al and I spent the afternoon in the county courthouse, a dignified brick building on the east side of a well-groomed town square. I refastened my hair and made sure my jacket was buttoned properly into place before we met with the client, a man in the midst of a custody battle over his two children. I simply observed and took notes, letting Al do the talking; Al was soft-spoken but he meant business before a judge, I saw right away. The hearing was brief, over before the dinner hour, and we ambled together across the town square in the late afternoon sunshine, toward Main Street. Al favored walking and I was reminded of Landon, where all the downtown businesses were a block from Flickertail; the only difference was that Jalesville boasted mountain scenery rather than lakeshore.

"Tish, you've worked hard today," Al said. "I hope you've had a good day."

"I've learned a lot," I said, which sounded lame but was true on two fronts; I'd gained knowledge of both Capital Overland and one Charles Spicer.

I was on high alert as we strolled along, taking special notice of people; was that a part of me hoping to catch a glimpse of Case? I realized that my eye had been caught twice now by maroon-colored vehicles, and mentally slapped the back of my head.

Stop looking for him!

At the courthouse Al had introduced me to a number of people, including the city clerk and the mayor, both of whose names appeared on my mental Unsold list. Many others offered greetings as we walked, prompting Al to introduce me as his newest associate. We had only a block to go before reaching the law office when a voice behind us declared, "Mr. Howe, I don't believe I've had the pleasure."

Al and I turned at the same moment. Immediately I was aware of a big white smile and glossy dark hair. I found myself thinking that I could very nearly see my reflection in his teeth as a tall man approached us, suit jacket slung casually over one shoulder.

"Derrick Yancy," he offered in a cultured voice that spoke of educated, privileged pleasantry, though I'd already recognized him from his picture. A chill seeped through my gut. He stopped *just* too close to us and I battled the urge to lean away from this calculated intrusion into my personal space. Instead, I lifted my chin and met his gaze.

"Patricia Gordon." I extended my hand, which he gripped.

His eyes held hints of innuendo. "It is indeed a pleasure, Ms. Gordon. I know your father of course. I understand you represent Turnbull and Hinckley's interests here in Jalesville?"

Not exactly, though he wasn't about to get that out of me. I withdrew my hand. "At this moment, I represent Howe and James."

"You're not planning a long-term residence here, though, isn't that correct?" he pressed.

Al said mildly, "Derrick, you know well that my associate is only here for the summer," but his tone implied, *Quit wasting our time.*

"I'll settle in Chicago this autumn." I was not about to be intimidated.

"Myself, as well," Derrick replied. "I look forward to bumping into you in the city."

"You may not as much as you think." I kept overt challenge from my tone but could not, however, repress a flare of anger in my eyes. Here was the man attempting to destroy this town, a place he cared nothing for; it was a matter of capital for him, money and more money. Capital Overland, acquiring land for capital. Their name was an apt descriptor.

Derrick flashed his teeth again, openly amused now.

Al said, "Good-day."

"Oh, to you, as well." Derrick tipped his head to the side and studied my face, the kind of look that was meant to induce obedience, the kind of look you might give a dog you were training. I repressed the instinctive, violent urge to shove him backward—and therefore away from me.

Back at Howe and James, Al said, "Yancy believes he has the upper hand, as you can see. Spoiled little bastard. His father is a bastard of epic proportions, so I guess I shouldn't be surprised, though T.K. won't show his face out here. Too far from the city, so he sends his son in his stead. Derrick is staying over in Miles City at some fancy hotel. Tish, don't let him get to you."

"I won't," I replied, with more assurance than I felt. I was all sweaty again, this time with outright discomfort, and shrugged from my jacket; I couldn't help but consider that my father and Ron both ran in T.K. Yancy's circle, back in Chicago. "I think I might take off a little early, if that's all right with you."

It was approaching five and Mary had already left for the day. Al said, "Of course, you go on. You've had a productive first day and I appreciate it. It's hardly early!"

"See you tomorrow," I told him, and collected my purse.

Driving up to the single stoplight on Main a minute later, I suddenly realized, from a block away, that I was approaching the back bumper of Case Spicer's big truck. New tension seized my body and caused additional sweat to form on my temples and under my arms; I had the unpleasant realization that I'd neglected to apply deodorant today and my car was scorching. In light of how I had spent the afternoon online, digging up information about Case, I felt more like a spy than ever, and tried to sink lower in my seat.

There's no way he could know your car. He doesn't realize you're behind him. I eased to a stop a good ten feet away, scrunching down behind the steering wheel. My windows were lowered and I could hear country music emanating from Case's truck; I recognized the Eli Young Band and peeked cautiously at his back window. Case wore a cowboy hat and seemed to be messing with the radio, his left hand hanging from the top of the wheel as he leaned toward the middle of the dashboard. My throat felt tight and I looked away, my gaze flickering to the tailgate. A grudging smile overtook my face as I observed the detailing present there: the top edge of a black horse, scrawled as though in mid-stride, leaping over an acoustic guitar; beneath these images were the words *Gotta Ride, Gotta Play.*

So he's cool. So what?

"Tish! Hey there!" I heard someone holler to the left, and my attention snapped that direction to see Wy Rawley emerging from the hardware store, waving and grinning, backpack slung over his shoulder, probably just getting done with work. He jogged toward my car, which could only happen in a town as tiny as Jalesville.

In front of me, in his truck, Case straightened as though poked in the side.

"Hey, Case!" Wy called, such a friendly little shit. "How's it going?"

"Wy, you're gonna get run over!" I scolded as he reached my idling car; I felt like I'd been caught peeping into Case's bedroom window.

"Are you coming for dinner Friday?" Wy leaned down to ask.

"I sure am." I really liked the kid but I was flustered as hell right now, not up to conversation. The light turned green and I indicated with my left hand, but I couldn't move unless Case drove forward and at present he wasn't moving an inch, peering over his shoulder at Wy and me.

To my consternation, Wy reached in the open window and honked my horn, holding it down for extra emphasis.

"Hey!" I squeaked, horrified. I wanted to sink right through the dusty ground; Case already thought I was rude. In front of us, Case lifted his right arm in a wave and then drove away. I sat there with my foot on the brake, hot and irritated and ready to take it out on poor, unsuspecting Wy.

But he only shrugged and said cheerfully, "See you Friday!"

"Friday," I muttered as he headed back to the sidewalk with a spring in his step.

My little apartment was lit by the evening sun as I stepped inside and turned in a slow circle, indulging in a space that was completely my own. No roommates, no sisters, no parents. Just me. To illustrate the freedom of this, I tossed my keys to the floor, kicked out of my heels, tugged the clip from my hair and shook out its length. Then I clicked on the radio, still tuned to the country station I'd found yesterday, and cranked it loud.

And in the next second I stood in my empty kitchen debating who I could call to alleviate my loneliness. I ran through the list of my family; Camille would be serving supper for six; Ruthie, Mom, and Aunt Jilly would be out on the lake, probably, since it was a gorgeous summer evening. I could no doubt drive out to the Rawleys' place, certain they would welcome me, but I felt awkward imposing upon them like that, especially since they'd hosted me Saturday night and would again on Friday. I had no real desire to talk to Grace or Ina, or my dad. And I had no friends in Jalesville; maybe I could get a hamster.

I went outside and sank to a seat on the lone patio chair, bracing my bare feet on the railing. I shaded my eyes against the glare of the setting sun, catching the scent of supper from someone's nearby apartment; my stomach growled. I closed my eyes, finally letting myself focus on the thoughts that had been clamoring for attention since noon today.

So…what's Case doing right now?

Does he play somewhere tonight?

He said he can't live without playing guitar.

Maybe he's at the Rawleys' house right now.

My heart sprouted fluttery wings at this notion. I knew that Case and his younger brother, Gus, were like family to the Rawleys. Maybe Case had stopped there on the way home from work; he lived right by them. He said he ate dinner there on Fridays.

That's four whole days from now.

But still. Maybe he's there, maybe right now…

I was holding my phone almost before I realized I'd moved. I swiped through my contacts, finding the one for Clark and pressing the icon to call him so I couldn't second-guess my motivation. Clark answered on the second ring. "Tish, hi! How was your first day?"

My heart was thrashing but I maintained calm. "Great! It was really productive."

"Good, good. Have you had a chance to go grocery shopping? Camille warned me that you aren't good about cooking for yourself."

Bless my big-mouthed big sister. It wasn't that I didn't know how to cook; many summers past, back at Shore Leave, I'd begged Blythe and Rich to let me help them on the line. I just hated cooking for only me. I admitted, "She's right on that count."

"Why don't you stop out for a bite, hon? I have a couple of chickens baking. Wy said he saw you this afternoon and I told him he ought to have invited you for supper right then."

"You're so nice." I wanted to beg, *Will Case be there?*

As though reading my mind, Clark said, "Case said he saw you today, too. He came by on his way home. Just left."

Just left?

No...

"He did?" I asked, hoping for any additional snippets of information. My voice sounded reedy but Clark didn't know me well enough to realize this meant I was all jacked up.

"He wanted to see if Marsh was able to play drums on Thursday night," Clark said. "Lee Heller, my niece, asked the boys if they would play at The Spoke, as it's been a while. It'll be a good show. I meant to ask you to join us there."

"I will plan on it," I said, a little stunned at the level of anticipation this invitation induced.

"And how about some baked chicken in about an hour?"

Clark was such a dear. I said, "I would love that."

Chapter Five

Tuesday and Wednesday passed in a blur. By Thursday morning, I had established a tentative routine—up at seven to shower and dress, grabbing a slice of banana bread from the incredible supply that Mary gifted me with, toting my empty coffee cup along to the office where a large pot was brewed every morning, again courtesy of Mary. Maybe I drove a little too slowly past Spicer Music on my way to work. Possibly I kept watch for big maroon trucks. If my back was turned when the office door opened, my heart became a firecracker that burned my ribs.

Despite everything, I had not set eyes on Case since Monday, when I'd been behind his truck at the stoplight. I was far too chicken to walk down the street past the front windows of his music shop. But I thought about doing so almost constantly. Meanwhile, I drafted legal documents as directed by Al, made phone calls to families who had not yet sold to Capital Overland, encouraging them to come to the informational meeting next Tuesday. According to Al not all of the sales were final, and he tasked me with contacting these folks, in addition. By the second day of phone calls, people were referring to me by name even before I'd introduced myself.

"You're Patricia Gordon, that new lawyer of Al's," I heard more than once. It seemed my presence was feeding the town grapevine.

"I am, thank you," I responded crisply.

One woman said, "You're the one taking over for Al, aren't you? When he retires?"

"No," I was quick to inform, hoping she'd spread the word. "I'm only here for the summer."

"Oh," she said, but her tone implied that she knew otherwise.

I'd built the beginnings of a pretty decent case—argument, really, as the informational meeting hardly amounted to a hearing, for next Tuesday. I was, however, mentally gearing up as though it was indeed a legal proceeding, considering Derrick Yancy opposing counsel. *My enemy.* I planned to point out that selling now for quick cash was not in the best interest of individual families, not to mention the entire town. I had also been reorganizing the office itself; the files were in shit shape. Al told me about seventy times a day how he couldn't imagine what he'd done without me. I thanked him just as often, privately hoping that this would also equal a glowing recommendation to Ron Turnbull, come the end of summer.

"I'm serious as a heart attack," Al said.

"Patty just brightens up this whole space," Mary agreed, before harping, "Helen Anne wouldn't like to hear you talking about heart attacks in that fashion, Albert. Considering your own father, God rest him."

I ate dinner with the Rawleys again on Tuesday, fended for myself on Wednesday, and planned to meet them at The Spoke this evening. I was all quivery with nerves an hour before. I showered for the second time that day and blew out my hair, then stood in bra and panties in front of my bedroom closet. Despite my best intentions, I had not yet done any laundry; I eyed the roll of quarters sitting on my dresser.

This weekend, I promised.

I ransacked my clothes for something that was right. Suitable for listening to music in a bar called The Spoke.

Jeans, I decided, tugging on my favorite faded pair.

Too cutesy? I held up a ruffled yellow blouse, something that Camille had lent me. I tossed it to the bedspread, where it slid down an ever-increasing pile.

Too deliberately sexy? I considered a red-and-black striped tank, one with a neckline that fell pretty low between my breasts. Especially when paired with the bra I was currently wearing. I glanced down at my boosted cleavage and reconsidered my lingerie choice.

Quit! It's fine. But…maybe pick a different shirt.

I finally settled on a blue tank top, a soft cotton one with silver detailing around the collar and hem; I'd always liked it but never found an excuse to wear it in Chicago.

Not because Ina once said that this shirt matches my eyes perfectly.

Not because Case once said I had beautiful eyes.

Not because of that at all.

But then I found myself applying an extra coat of mascara and understood I wasn't above a little flattery. Things Case said in the past clearly still affected me. Maybe they had always been in the back of my mind, still very much there, unacknowledged until recently. I left the windows down on the way to The Spoke, vibrating with anxious energy as I pulled into the parking lot there, already packed with vehicles; immediately I spotted Case's truck, tailgate down. Which meant he was probably outside somewhere.

Oh my God…

Calm down, Jesus Crimeny, Tish.

I climbed from my little car. The evening air was soft and warm. I could already smell deep-fried food and hear music, the subtle thump of it through the walls, and my heart began to match this heightened pace. I settled my purse strap over my shoulder and hadn't taken six steps before I spied Case, striding through a door near the back of the place, wearing jeans, his cowboy hat, riding boots, and a belt with a silver buckle.

My feet stalled.

He caught sight of me and paused for a fraction, about twenty paces away, before lifting his right arm in a casual wave, giving me the sense that he was about to go right back to what he was doing. Though, when I headed in his direction he waited, watching me, the evening light striking the bottom half of his face. The top half was in the shadow of his hat brim.

"Hi." I stopped five feet away, suddenly embarrassed. I felt like I'd just done something unimaginably bold and my face was hot. Hot all the way back to my ears.

Case resettled his hat and said in his deep voice, "Hey there. Clark said you were coming to the show." He looked good in the sunset light, so damn good that my fingers tightened around my purse strap and every pulse point in my body grew hot. At last he explained, "I'm just unloading the truck."

"You need any help?" I asked, moving closer, indicating the truck bed.

He seemed to gather himself together, resuming his original course. He said over his shoulder, "It's all heavy stuff."

I followed right behind. "I'm pretty tough."

He sent me a half-grin. We were at the open tailgate then, our hips no more than two feet apart. I could see his eyes better now without the distance between us. He studied me for the space of a breath, amusement fading away, his face becoming unreadable. Lightning-flash quick, his gaze detoured to my lips, then lower, before he turned to the truck and became very businesslike. "I feel like a jerk asking you to carry something for me."

I thought his voice might possibly be a little hoarse. And I would be a liar through and through if I didn't admit that I had just felt his eyes upon me like a touch. The feeling was strong enough that my nipples swelled, as though he'd actually cupped his hands over my breasts. I was breathless and electric, slightly stunned by the intensity of this.

It's just been too long since you've had sex, that's all.

"Well, that's just silly," I said, referring to him being a jerk for asking me to carry something.

He sent a questioning look my way this time, shouldering a huge black bag. He had great hands, strong and wide through the palm, long-fingered and brown from the sun. The hair on his wiry forearms was as red-gold as that on his head, and there were cinnamon-tinted freckles on the back of his hands. He settled the strap over his broad right shoulder and reached to grip the lip of the tailgate, in order to slam it closed; I stepped back so he could.

"My fiddle is in the truck. If you wouldn't mind grabbing that…" He nodded at the passenger door.

"I think I can maybe handle a fiddle," I said, drippy with sarcasm, earning another half-grin.

The cab of his truck smelled fucking good. Spicy, somehow. The fiddle case was black and well-worn, resting on the right side of the bench seat, and I closed my fingers around the handle, thinking of how many times his fingers had been wrapped around this same spot. I cradled it against my breasts; somehow the pressure of the instrument case alleviated a fraction of my increasing desire to be caressed.

Case watched me approach, again stone-faced.

"We can sneak in back here," he said, indicating the door at the rear of The Spoke.

He led the way, allowing me the chance to study the back pockets of his jeans, the way his t-shirt subtly hugged the lean shape of his back. Burdened as he was with gear, he still held the door for me, watching me pass in front of him, holding close his fiddle. Once inside, we were surrounded by the excited, contagious buzz of people ready for a good time, as addicting as anything you could inhale or shoot up. Case leaned close to my right ear and said, "This way," and I shivered as I followed him.

We cut through a back hallway to a small storage room, where Marshall was sitting on an old keg, a black cowboy hat pulled low over his eyes, tuning a guitar. He looked up as we entered and drawled, "Well, howdy."

I was still clutching the fiddle case as though I didn't intend to relinquish it. Case set his armload on the floor and nodded toward the instrument. "That fiddle has been in my family since around the time of the Civil War."

"No kidding?" I asked. "Can I see it?"

Marshall grinned at the eagerness in my voice. "I hate to tell you, but it looks just like a fiddle made today."

I surrendered it to Case's hands and he said without looking up from the instrument, "Now that's where you're wrong, little bro." He dropped gracefully to a crouch and I joined him, my right knee very close to his left. Case balanced the black case over his thighs and eased it open, revealing a beautiful piece of craftsmanship; even my untrained eyes could perceive this. It shone honey-brown in the single light fixture.

"Did someone in your family make it?" I asked, watching his face, rewarded as he looked into my eyes. He studied me no longer than the time it took for me to grow slightly breathless.

Tracing a thumb over the strings, he said, "I'm not entirely certain. I only know that an ancestor of ours brought it to the Civil War. Later, it came west with the family. Years ago Mom found it in one of Dad's trunks, along with some old letters. I learned to play on it."

I was thrilled that he was telling me these sweet, personal things. "Can I touch it?"

My question prompted Marshall to snort and then laugh, the guitar in his hands whining with a discordant note as he turned one of the little handles connected to a string. Case only smiled, the half-smile I was already beginning to anticipate, and nodded. I smoothed gentle fingertips over the buttery woodgrain; Case's thumb was still on the strings.

"I love imagining all the people who played it before me," Case said.

"That is something to think about," I agreed. "How many songs does it know, you know what I mean?"

He nodded in understanding.

Wy's head appeared around the open door; catching sight of me, he said, "*There* you are."

There was such a sense of relief in his tone that I giggled. "Were you worried about me, buddy?"

"Well, we saw your car but you weren't in the bar anywhere," Wy explained. His brown hair flopped over his forehead and he swiped at it, with impatience. "C'mon, we got seats right in front."

This meant I had no excuse to linger. Case's eyes followed as I stood, even though he remained in a crouch. I held his gaze, feeling all quivery and warm inside my clothes, and said, "Good luck. I mean, break a leg… shit, one is bad luck, isn't it?"

Case was grinning. "Nah, that's only if we were performing in a play."

"Well, good luck all the same." I wanted to tell him that I could hardly wait to hear him in action. But I could be just as much an expert at hiding my emotions as he; three years of law school had at least taught me that.

"Thanks," he murmured, as Wy stepped into the room to appropriate my elbow. Seconds later we entered the main floor of the bar and grill, where the scent of the deep-fryer made my stomach growl. Neon signs lent the space a feeling of easy welcome. There was chatter and laughter everywhere, country music from a jukebox, people milling about with beer bottles and cocktail glasses, servers in black aprons weaving expertly through the crowd.

"God, I've wanted to see these forever!" I told Wy, pausing by an empty two-top, admiring the wagon wheel beneath the glass. "Mathias made one for his and Camille's cabin. But these are original wheels, aren't they? Not reproductions, right?"

Wy nodded, smiling, navigating to a pair of round tables placed alongside each other like pool balls and surrounded by the Rawleys, their girlfriends, Case's brother Gus, and an older man I didn't recognize. The men all tipped their hat brims as I approached.

Yes, a girl could get used to that.

"Hi, guys," I said to the table at large, thankful that there was still an empty chair facing the stage. Damned if I was going to miss even one second of watching Case play. Clark introduced me to the older man, whose family ran the hardware store where Wy worked.

"Something to drink, hon?" asked a server in red cowgirl boots.

"Just water, thanks." I planned to pace myself this evening.

"Tish, this is Lacy," Sean said, leaning over the table to be heard. He indicated Gus's girlfriend, who flashed me a smile. "Lacy, Tish."

I hadn't seen Gus since Camille's wedding, back when he'd been a teenager. "How are you doing?"

"Good," he said, smiling, too. He had the same coloring as Case. "Welcome to town."

Sean's girlfriend, Jessie, leaned toward me, setting her beer aside to do so. "How was the first week with Al? Grandpa said he heard you've been kicking some ass already?"

I flushed with pleasure. "Well, that's very kind of him to say so. I've been doing my best."

"We heard you met Derrick Yancy," Sean added.

I nodded; I'd told Clark and Wy all about it at dinner on Monday. "What did you think?" Sean pressed.

"He's rude and arrogant," I said, earning nods and murmurs of agreement. "Smooth talker. Everything is an opportunity."

There was a sudden burst of applause and people scrambled to take seats; we all turned to see Marshall and Case, cowboy hats in place and carrying their instruments, coming from the back of The Spoke. My heart seemed to be on a trampoline. The guys mounted the steps to the little stage with the ease of familiarity; there was a set of drums, two stools, and two microphones on stands. Shrill whistles greeted their ascent. I couldn't pull my eyes from Case, who was grinning under the warm glow of the neon lights, totally comfortable, totally sexy. I could not deny this any more than I could deny that I noticed. A lot. He took a seat, placing his fiddle in its case upon the stage, his guitar on a thick leather strap that diagonally bisected his chest. He took a second to lower the mic stand so that it was nearer his mouth, while Marsh claimed the stool behind the drums and skimmed a quick riff, earning more whistles.

"Evening, everyone," Case said into the mic, and I felt his voice vibrate through my entire body.

"Hi, Case!" called a woman, excited and eager, and Case laughed, joined by about half the bar.

He responded easily, "Hi, there. It's been a while since Marsh and I played here."

People clapped and cheered; Wy hooked his pinkies in his mouth and let loose with a whistle.

"We thought we'd start off with a couple of old favorites, if that's all right," Case said, and I wanted him to look our way, *my way*, toward the table to the right of the stage. He collected his guitar closer and strummed a few notes, and my eyes dropped to his hands, his strong hands that curved so knowingly around the instrument. He turned to Marsh and asked away from the mic, "You want to join me for this one?"

Marsh nodded twice, collecting his guitar from its stand near the drums, and dragged his stool to the front of the stage. The two of them exchanged a look, timing their first notes, and then Case leaned forward and took up the song. I knew they were into old-school country and this first song was no exception, an old Willie Nelson standard. Case closed his eyes as he sang. I clasped my hands beneath my chin, caught up in the beauty of his rich, true voice. The melody was sweet, almost haunting; there was an instrumental measure in the middle, both men strumming their guitars. Just before Case took up the final verse his gaze flickered briefly to me, sending a hot jolt down my spine; a sudden realization struck me just as soundly.

No, it's just a coincidence.

This is not about you.

But the song was called "Blue Eyes Crying in the Rain."

When it ended, there was raucous applause. Case strummed a straight G-chord and grinned out toward the crowd. "Are we mellow tonight, people? Mellow out there?"

Whistles and more cheering, and the two of them laughed.

Marshall asked, "Should we keep some Waylon and Willie going?"

They did, and people began dancing to the second song, "Luckenbach, Texas." I sat as one entranced, watching Case on stage, where he so clearly belonged. He enjoyed every second of it, as I could plainly see and hear, was so natural, sitting with his shoulders relaxed, one bootheel caught on the bottom rung of the stool. His voice rippled over my skin. I hardly took my eyes from him, feeling drunk though I had not sipped a drop of alcohol. I knew the number of times his gaze flashed my way—twice now, counting the first song, and only for an instant each time. But again I felt those looks as tangibly as if he'd cupped his strong, sexy hands around my face.

He was singing "Neon Moon" right now, about an hour into the show, while Marsh did impressive duty on the drums. Couples were whirling and waltzing; just about everyone wore a cowboy hat. I tore my gaze from Case to observe, rather surprised, that I was nearly alone at our table; everyone else was dancing, even Clark. Wy was sneaking the last of an abandoned beer but I didn't have the wherewithal to stop him, because just as Case sang the line about *your one and only*, our eyes held for a full two seconds, or, if I was keeping time with my heart, the equivalent of about twenty beats.

I swallowed hard.

He closed his eyes as he continued singing.

Wy said, "Tish, you wanna dance?"

I shook my head, unwilling to do anything but sit here and watch.

"But I feel guilty if you're here alone."

I looked at the boy then. "Huh?"

He explained, "I wanna dance, but if you're here alone I feel bad."

I almost giggled at his earnest expression. "You go and dance, buddy. I'm just fine."

Wy stood, then immediately stooped to kiss my cheek. "Thanks, Tish."

Alone, I leaned on my forearms, resting my breasts atop them, just watching. I didn't care if Case realized I was staring at him as though hypnotized. He sang the next two songs without looking in my direction; was I imagining that he was still watching me from the corner of his eye, or was I just flattering myself?

"Casey, do some of yours!" someone called from the dance floor, and he grinned at this request, resettling his hat over his hair. I saw shiny lines of sweat trickling from his temples to his jaws. He grabbed a bottle of water from the stage and took a long drink, tipping back his head. I watched his throat move as he swallowed. He blew out a breath and then nodded acceptance. Marsh tapped the drumsticks together before setting them aside and rejoining Case up front. Case shifted his wide shoulders, lifting the guitar strap over his head and placing the instrument on its stand; he caught up the fiddle, to loud whistles.

"Maybe one," he agreed, and I shivered as he lifted the fiddle to his chin, poising the bow over the strings. And then my heart ached for reasons I could not explain as he drew the first notes. I felt bruised, suddenly thinking of everything he had said at my sister's wedding, seven long years ago.

I wrote a song about you.

The thing is, I know you're the one for me. I know this with all my heart. I don't understand how I know we belong together, but we do. I know this.

I knew all those words were in the past; I knew he had more than moved on from anything he'd said back then…

Case played with eyes closed. Marshall joined in on guitar; the music reminded me of something from the original era of the fiddle, achingly lovely. I realized that I recognized this song; it had been playing at the Rawleys' on Saturday night, when I'd first arrived in Jalesville.

Case wrote this.

It's beautiful.

The song ended much too soon and I felt like someone had kicked me in the heart. The crowd surged with cheers and whistles, begging for more, but Case shook his head, smiling, good-natured.

Look at me, oh God, Case, look this way…

But he kept his eyes away. He lifted his hat to swipe the back of his wrist over his forehead. Everyone wanted his attention, and Marshall's; there were three women in particular, young and pretty and clutching drinks, crowding the stage, and one of them actually reached and tugged at Case's jeans as he collected his guitar, making him laugh.

I didn't even say good-bye to the Rawleys; I was out in the parking lot no more than fifteen seconds later, where it was dark and I could hide the flames consuming my face. I felt shaky and weak-kneed, suddenly terrified that I hadn't remembered my purse, meaning I would have to go back inside; but no, there it was bumping along on my hip.

Thank God.

Go home, Tish, you're just tired.

And so I let myself believe that as I drove home, leaving the windows down so I could hear the crickets.

Chapter Six

I THREW MYSELF INTO WORK THE NEXT DAY, MORE THAN usual, determined to impress Al on this last workday of my first week in town. Never mind that I couldn't think of anything but the fact that it was Friday and Case would be at the Rawleys' house for supper. But I did a good job keeping that thought basically unacknowledged, poring over my research, calling people to invite them to the meeting next Tuesday, looking through backstories from the local news affiliate that served the Jalesville area, motivated by the occurrence of the power plant closing and Derrick Yancy's company sweeping in, vulture-like, not long after.

There was a connection that went deeper than business savvy, I was certain.

It was after four when Al returned from court. "Tish? What are you still doing here? It's Friday."

I looked up from my notepad. My neck was cramped, along with my right hand; Mary had left over an hour ago. "Hey, Al."

Al came to the far side of the hip-high counter, where Case had stood on Monday. He set his briefcase atop it and regarded me with a fondness that reminded me of my dad. "Listen, I know your experience is in the city, but here, we don't work fourteen hours a day, we do what we can in our workday. We make it a priority to enjoy our beautiful land, our families and friends. All work and no play…might I remind you? Plus, aren't you supposed to be heading to the Rawleys?"

"Yes, sorry," I mumbled, not meeting his eyes. I was quick to add, "I promise to get outside this weekend. I'll hike around the foothills, or something."

"I'm holding you to that," Al said.

I sat on my porch after I got home, just staring, watching the sun strike the mountains in the distance, listening to the sounds of people through the open windows of other apartments—the ringing of a phone, a mother calling to her kids, a distant radio. I pressed the base of both palms to my eyes. Pressed hard, until all I could see were patterns of swirling color against the backs of my eyelids.

Not long after, I parked in the yard at the Rawleys' place, determined to bury away my more vulnerable and uncontrollable emotions. Instead, I appreciated how the Rawleys' homestead appealed to me the same way that Shore Leave did. Warm with firelight and laughter, crowded with people who talked over one another, food lining every horizontal surface. I felt the pull of family, though they weren't exactly mine; but I pretended, indulging myself, missing my own. It was a gorgeous time of night. I climbed out of the car and stared westward for a minute, imbibing the magnificent view. Case's truck was not in sight, as I was one hundred percent aware, and so my heart had calmed a little.

I had tried really damn hard to look good without *appearing* to have tried hard. I was wearing a sundress of the palest blue, casual but really pretty, which fit like a tank top with a knee-length skirt. I'd left my hair pinned up, added silver hoops and a single silver bracelet. A little mascara and my favorite raspberry lip gloss—and that was that. I studied the sunset, wondering when he would get here, inhaling the herbal scent in the air, distinctly different than the lakeshores of Landon.

"Pretty out here, isn't it? I haven't gotten tired of it yet," he said from behind me, and I jumped as though he'd fired a gun, spinning to see him approaching with the sun gilding his wide shoulders.

Oh, holy shit.

I was a fool to think I could be around him without experiencing this tidal-wave of attraction. Case kept his eyes on the sunset, as though he didn't realize I was staring speechlessly at him. He joined me at the side of my car, where I stood still enough to put roots in the ground, and rested both hands on top of his head, linking his fingers. He may or may not have been aware that this defined his biceps *really* well. He wore faded jeans and a faded red t-shirt, his bone-colored cowboy hat, boots, and a belt with a fancy silver buckle, the same belt from last night.

"I didn't see your truck," I babbled. I wanted to tell him that I had loved every second of watching him play last night, that I was sorry I hadn't stuck around to say good-bye, because I was chicken and madly jealous, and I had less than no right to be jealous over him.

"Gus stopped by and we rode over on the horses," he explained, not meeting my eyes. I stared up at his profile, crisp against the blue of the sky. He had a stubborn-looking chin, a straight-edged nose that had probably taken a punch or two. The sun shone in his irises, its beams angled low enough to sneak beneath his hat brim, creating a color I'd never seen in someone's eyes, a rich auburn. His lashes were as red-gold as his hair.

Oh, I said, inaudibly.

"You want to meet them?" he asked, at last looking at me.

Thinking he meant the Rawleys, I said, "I've met them plenty of times."

That half-grin again, just like last night. "The horses, I mean, you want to meet them?"

Oh for the love, Tish. This time he was openly tickled by my fluster, I could tell. *You are a graduate of Northwestern Law School. Pull it together!*

I straightened my shoulders like it didn't matter much one way or the other. "Sure."

He led me to the split-rail corral that surrounded one of the barns; there were two barns on the property but I favored this one, which looked like something out of an old-time western. As we walked, Case kept a very appropriate distance between us; he hardly afforded me a spare glance. I felt foolish and vain; vain as a peacock as Gran, my dear great-grandmother, would have said, over the fact that I had been hoping he just might compliment me on how I looked.

At the fence he leaned on his forearms; I too short to do the same, so I climbed up on the bottom rung to mimic him. A light breeze kicked up my hem but Case didn't seem to be paying attention; he made a low whistling sound in the direction of a cluster of horses. A caramel-colored one eased away from the group and clumped our way.

"This," he said, with fondness, "is Cider."

I reached out cautiously and patted the horse's sleek neck. She was warm and solid beneath my hand. I rubbed my palm over her more firmly, stroking her hide. There was a small white patch between her nostrils and I wanted to touch it but held back, uncertain if this would be acceptable.

"She's beautiful. She's a girl, right?" We stood in the shade afforded by the house and I studied Case as I asked, my heart beating too fast. I told myself I was flustered by memories of things he'd said in the past, by how many times I'd repeated those words last night, alone in bed, restless and tossing half the night.

He met my eyes and nodded affirmation, scratching her neck on the opposite side. "I've had her since she was just a foal, only a few weeks old."

"How old is she now?"

"Almost five years," he said, stroking the backs of his curled fingers along her jaw, with clear affection. My hand stalled on her neck, motionless as I watched his hand move.

"Is that old for a horse?"

"Not at all," he said easily. "Her brother Buck is a little older. I've had him from the time he was a foal, too."

"Is Buck with the other horses?" I asked, wanting to linger here, with Case.

"Over there, on the right." He indicated. "Gus rode him over."

"Is he a buckskin? Not that I'm an expert or anything…"

"He is. Cider is what you'd call a sorrel."

"What does that mean, exactly?"

"It has to do with her coloring, just like a buckskin," he explained patiently. He laid his hand flat against Cider's neck. "Usually sorrels have a reddish-yellow undertone."

Behind us I heard the door to the house open.

"Thanks for introducing me to her," I said.

"Evening, Tish!" Clark called. "You were in an all-fired hurry last night!"

Unsure how to answer, I stepped down from the fence, taking care in my sandals; I sensed more than saw how Case reached as though to assist me. His hand didn't make contact, and in any event Clark was there, gathering my arm in a gentlemanly gesture, tucking my hand around his elbow.

"I was just tired last night," I said lamely, aware that Case was listening.

"Understandable," Clark reassured, leading us toward the back porch, patting my hand. "As soon as Garth and Becky get here, we'll eat. I've got drinks out already," and he looked down at me, teasing, "But maybe you better not go there this evening."

"Ha, ha."

"Bar's open, you guys!" Marshall hollered as we came around the side of the house. "Tish, you gonna get bombed again?"

"I haven't the past few nights I've been here, have I?" I grumbled at Marsh as I scaled the porch steps. Marshall blinked a couple of times at the sight of me; I saw his eyes flash to Case, who was, as I was vividly aware, climbing the steps just behind me.

"You look nice, Tish," Marshall said, almost wickedly.

I rolled my eyes at him, all fluttery that he was saying so in front of Case; I just wished that Case would notice.

But why?

To what end?

I was so confused.

"Hi, Tish!" Wy heralded from the picnic table, where he stood loading a plate with appetizers. "Where'd you go so fast last night?"

"Can I get you a drink?" Marshall asked. Everyone was probably on their second round; Sean and Quinn and Gus, and their girlfriends, all of them sitting in chairs close to each other. Gus had his hand on Lacy's thigh as she said something that made him laugh, and he looked so much like Case that a lump of jealousy lodged in my throat—I wanted to be sitting here on this same porch with Case touching my leg that way, with such tender intimacy.

That can never happen, I thought; my imagination was a real bitch sometimes.

"Sure, a gin and tonic would be great," I told Marsh, suffering his knowing look. I defended, "I'll just have *one*."

"Coming right up," Marsh promised smoothly, winking; he had a good wink and I could tell he knew it, which almost made me giggle. He asked Case, "How about you?"

"I got it, little bro," Case replied, delivering what seemed like a playful little punch to Marshall's midsection as he walked past him, though Marsh released a surprised *whoosh* of breath.

Wy caught my elbow and hauled me to a seat near the fire, then claimed the chair on my right. I tried to pretend I wasn't watching, observant as a spider, for Case to grab a drink and come sit down. There was an unoccupied chair just to my left.

"Tish, wasn't that fun last night?" Wy leaned forward to claim my attention.

"It sure was," I said, peeking at Case from the corner of my eye. I saw him take my drink from Marsh, who muttered something to him that it was too noisy for me to hear, but Case ignored this and paused near my chair to hand me the drink. He held a can of cola in the other hand.

"Thank you." The sun was in my eyes, backlighting him so he appeared haloed in gold.

Case sat just where I'd been hoping he would as Wy prattled on, "Tish, for real, Dad says you're calling up everybody to get rid of Capital Overland. Everyone is saying that you're gonna run them out of town!"

"People love to make things larger than life," I reminded Wy.

"No, really!" Wy insisted earnestly. He cried, "Super Tish!" and I giggled, almost spitting out a mouthful of gin in the process.

I shook my head, aware of Case watching me from the corner of his eye.

"They know something they aren't letting on," Case said then, sitting forward as though restless, curving both hands around his can of soda. His words were just what I had been speculating. "I'm worried the offers might prove too tempting for some people."

"Not all the sales are final," I confirmed, feeling comfortable in this knowledge after my week of research. "Unfortunately, Derrick Yancy is a good salesman. I'll give him that."

"You've met him then?" Case asked. I felt such heat whenever his eyes touched mine, as they were now, but I didn't let any of that show on my face.

I nodded. "I know his type. He reminds me of the spoiled rich kids I went to law school with. The same entitled arrogance. But he's also smart. I'm considering him a mortal enemy at this point."

Sean said, "He doesn't give two fucks about our town."

"Language!" Jessie scolded.

"Well, he's right," Marshall said, shoving at his brother to gain a seat on the glider. Sean obligingly scooted over.

"I agree with Case. I think Yancy knows something he's not letting on," Quinn said. "I think he's a criminal."

"He's a businessman," I corrected. "Same difference, in his case. I wish he *was* a criminal. Then I'd have something concrete to attack him with."

"You've met a bunch of people around here this week," Marsh said, sipping his beer.

"And you've made quite an impression," Clark added, joining us. "I mean that in the most complimentary way, you realize."

"I do," I assured Clark, flattered that he thought so; Case was still looking at me as though concerned, but when I turned his way he looked out toward the horizon.

"This guy won't get our land, will he, Dad?" asked Wy.

"Not while I can still draw breath," Clark said.

"And not yours either?" Wy asked Case.

"Hell, no," Case said, and Gus nodded vigorous agreement. "There's that info session next week at the courthouse and I'm hoping to talk some sense into people, Hank Ryan included."

"Next Tuesday, right?" I asked, my fingertips twitching for my notebook and pencil. "Al wants me there, too. Hank Ryan is a councilman, right?"

"And a former rancher," Case said. "He chairs the council now. He's been considering selling, I've heard."

"I've heard the same," Clark affirmed. "Damn, that would be a real score for Yancy."

"Why here?" I asked again, not yet having found a satisfying explanation, even in theory. "Why Jalesville in particular?"

"We're ripe for the picking, that's why," Case said. "Power plant goes belly-up, everyone out of work. It's almost too good to be true from Yancy's standpoint. And I don't get the sense that they're here in Montana just to buy vacation property." He was turning the soda can in slow circles between his strong, long-fingered hands, the hands I had watched for hours last night.

I took a long drink of my gin and tonic.

"Enough business talk," Sean insisted. "Ease up, you-all. I'm trying to get a little drunk right now."

I admitted, "Sorry, I have trouble relaxing."

"We're here! The party can start!" Garth called from inside the house. He and his wife, Becky, appeared on the porch, and I jumped up to give them hugs. Garth was carrying their son.

"You look so grown up," Becky said, gathering me close for a second hug. She was as curvy as a pinup model, a lovely woman with wheat-blond hair gathered in a ponytail.

"I'll take that as a compliment," I said, happy to see her; I'd gotten to know her the summer the Rawleys had visited Landon.

"Don't work too hard while you're here," Becky said. "I wish I could offer to take you out on the town but I have my hands so full with the baby these days."

"You playing later?" I heard Garth ask Case, settling near him with a beer. So far I hadn't observed Case have even one drink; he stuck to cola or water.

"Not tonight," Case said.

"Maybe we can get to the fair next week, though," Becky was saying, and I refocused on her.

"The fair?" I repeated.

"The county fair and music fest. It's a good time." She smiled at Wy and said, "Be a honey and go get me a beer, will you?"

Dinner was incredible; I was getting far too accustomed to being spoiled in this fashion. I hadn't yet attempted to cook in my little apartment and dreaded the thought; I despised anything domestic. We ate on the deck as we had the past few nights, at an enormous picnic table. Case sat on the opposite end and I tucked away all hints that I minded being displaced from him but when it was apparent he was planning to leave, no more than a few minutes after dinner ended, I couldn't suppress a sharp pang of disappointment. He and Gus had a conversation about Case bringing Buck with him, so that Gus could ride home with Lacy, and then Case bid everyone farewell; the next thing I knew, I was watching his back as he descended the porch steps, heading to the barn to collect his horses.

Wait.

Before I even concocted a good excuse, I rose to my feet and threaded through the chaos on the deck, ducking inside and scurrying across the living room, just beating Case to the front yard. I startled him as I opened the screen door, I could tell, though he buried that away at once. He was nearly expressionless as we stared at each other. He'd donned his cowboy hat since dinner, leaving his eyes in partial shadow beneath.

"I just…" I was slightly out of breath, holding the screen open against my forearm. *Jesus Christ, Tish.* And then, even though I hadn't planned to, I said what I'd been longing to all evening. "I just loved hearing you play last night."

He continued to watch me for a long moment, in which I felt increasingly foolish, but then he said quietly, "Thanks."

I was suddenly in the yard with him, though I didn't recall moving. I wanted to reach and pluck the hat from his head so I could see his eyes without the shadow over them. "You're very talented."

His face remained unreadable; I saw his chest rise with an indrawn breath. "Thank you."

"Well…good-night," I mumbled, self-conscious as hell, having so obviously chased after him.

"You want to meet Buck?" he surprised me by asking. "I have to saddle up Cider, so I have a minute." So casually, as though it didn't matter to him one way or the other.

A smile stole across my face but he was already heading for the corral, resettling his hat as he walked. I followed in his wake, catching up with him at the gate.

"On second thought, those shoes won't protect your feet enough," he said, nodding at my sandals. "You better stay on this side of the fence."

I nodded acceptance of this and climbed up one rung so I could lean over the top beam. The air was chilly now that the sun had faded and indigo shadows were gathering. Case disappeared into the barn, reemerging a few seconds later leading the two horses. He walked them right up to where I waited on the fence, not meeting my eyes until he drew near.

"This is Buck." He tilted his hat brim toward the larger of the two, a gorgeous animal with a creamy hide and a thick black mane. He patted the horse's solid neck.

"Pleased to meet you," I said formally, leaning to stroke Buck between the eyes. Case was close enough that I could have reached and done the same thing to him. I admitted, "I always felt like these bangs tickled their faces," indicating the clump of hair that hung down between Buck's ears, almost to his eyes.

"That's the forelock. It doesn't seem to bother them much, as far as I can tell."

"How would they scratch it if it did itch?" I persisted. I stroked Buck's forehead. "There you go, boy. How's that?"

"They rub their faces against each other, sometimes," Case said. "Or on the fence. But I'm sure he likes that best by far."

Cider made a whooshing noise and nudged Case's side with her long nose. He cupped her big square jaws and planted a kiss on her nose, on the white spot I had noticed earlier. He asked her, "Are you a little starved for affection, huh, girl?"

I almost said, *Yes, very much so*, before biting my tongue. I continued to scratch Buck's nose and Case said, "I'll be right back. I have to grab her saddle from the barn."

He reemerged carrying it against his waist; his arms were taut with muscle, which I observed from the corner of my eye. He drew Cider to the side and settled the saddle on her, next draping the stirrup over her back and bending to adjust a strap beneath her belly. He was facing away from me and I studied him openly, the way his wide shoulders shifted as he saddled his horse with efficient motions. By the time he straightened and turned around, my attention was completely focused on Buck.

Now there seemed to be nothing to say and we studied each other in the growing dusk. I could hardly make out his eyes beneath the hat brim. At last he asked, "Do you have a jacket? It gets cold out here at night."

"In the car, I do." I was embarrassed by the husk in my voice.

He nodded and ran a palm along Cider's flank, almost unconsciously. She shifted and nosed his ribs again, seeming to bring him back to reality. "Well, this girl wants her stall. I better head out. I'll see you around."

Not quite a statement or a question, instead somewhere in between. I nodded and my breath caught as he moved toward me, but I realized he was just gathering Buck's reins. He climbed on Cider with easy grace and adjusted his hips in the saddle. My chin lifted to continue looking at him. Silhouetted against the darkening sky, he looked right back at me.

"Good-night," he said, and nudged Cider with his heels. She responded to the gentle motion by tossing her head and heading out of the corral, Buck trailing them.

"'Night," I responded, just as quietly, and he tipped his hat brim. Without another word he set Cider into a faster pace, and disappeared down the road.

Back inside, I rejoined the activity and poured myself a drink. Gus and Sean, along with their girlfriends, were just leaving, calling farewells.

Probably to go somewhere and have hot, hot sex.

Not that I was jealous or anything.

I added another glug of gin to my glass.

"Tish, you wanna play a little cards?" Wy asked. Everyone other than Clark was settling around the dining room table. The baby was snoozing in a playpen; Becky was mixing up a pitcher of margaritas.

"Maybe in a bit, thanks," I said, wanting to sit outside a little longer.

"Tish, there's a couple old sweatshirts just inside the door there, on the coat rack," Clark said as I joined him. "You'll freeze otherwise."

The night air was thin and cold, so I retrieved a sweatshirt and then snagged the chair beside Clark's. "Thank you for dinner. I really appreciate it."

"Well, you're most welcome." He nodded toward the horizon. "Would you look at that?"

I shivered with delight at the sight of the western sky, alive now with stars; a slim, saffron band of afterglow rimmed the mountains. I agreed, "It's beautiful." And then I amended, "But it's more than just beautiful. It's...majestic somehow. I can't explain it exactly. Everything out here feels grander in scale."

"I know just what you mean. It's all the open sky. I couldn't imagine living anywhere else, though I've loved visiting the lakeshore in Landon."

"I miss it there," I whispered. In the starlight the mountains appeared more mysterious and romantic than anything I had ever seen, and I found my gaze roving to the chair Case had vacated only a little while ago. Was he still riding home? How long did it take to ride the distance between here and his place? Was he admiring the sky at this moment, too? Wouldn't I love it if Case was the one out here with me, instead of Clark?

Stop.

Clark and I sat in companionable silence for a time; the gin warmed my blood and blurred the edges of my tension. But then everything within me sprang to awareness at Clark's unexpected words.

"It's Case I'm worried about," he said.

"Worried?" I repeated cautiously. "Why's that?"

"He told you pretty plain how he felt for you, back when," Clark said, without preamble, and my heart seized. "It's been years now and he's not the same person he was, I'll be the first to admit. But I've watched him this past month, ever since Mathias told us that you were headed our way for the summer, and he's been hoping again."

Even though I was far from ignorant to the matter, I whispered, "What do you mean?"

"Case won't come out and admit it, not now, but I've known the boy since he was born. He's stubborn as hell. And he's hoping again, I can see it the way you'd see lightning on the horizon."

I didn't know how to respond; I found my voice and spoke quietly.

"Clark, with all due respect, I think you're reading too much into it. I really do."

Clark released a soft sigh. "Let me tell you about Case, honey, because he's not like other men. He won't talk about his past. Don't let on that you know anything, promise me?"

"I promise," I whispered, trembling in the chill air; I wished I was wearing jeans and not this stupid sundress. The rowdy laughter in the house seemed far removed.

"Case's mother was named Melinda," Clark said, in a storyteller voice that reminded me at once of Dodge. "She was the one who gave the boys that golden-red hair. And she gave Case her talent for song. Melinda sang in the church choir, and in the choir at school until her father stopped that, thinking she was getting too social. Melinda's father, Case's grandpa on the Dalton side, was a preacher, and not a kindly one who spends the week pondering his Sunday sermon. He was the type on the lookout for sin, morning and night. And when you're looking for trouble that hard, it doesn't take much to find it. Old Edwin Dalton was a widower. Melinda was his only child and what do you know, she got pregnant just out of high school, without even a boyfriend to blame."

"With Case?" I was hugging myself around the ribs, and loosened my hold.

"Yes, indeed. Her father locked her away until she confessed the truth and no one could quite believe that Owen Spicer, who was a good ten years older than Melinda, was the child's father. Even then Owen drank far too much, and gambled, lived in a trailer out on the old Spicer property. And here, beautiful little Melinda Dalton was going to have his baby. Go figure."

"Melinda must have loved him a great deal," I speculated, submerged in the romance of this notion, which was not like me at all.

"I wish I could tell you that was the truth," Clark said, and I looked his way. His gaze was trained on the far horizon. "Owen married Melinda, very nearly at gunpoint insistence from old Edwin, and she went to live on the Spicer homestead out on Ridge Road, about a mile from here. The Spicers were hit hard in the 1930s, see, and never quite recovered.

Reputations for being drunks and laggards, I hate to say. Case and Gus broke that mold. They're good men, the both of them, and I'd like to believe I've had a hand in that. The family house burned down back in 1971. Owen's pa hauled a trailer out there, in which they've lived ever since. It's rundown. Case keeps the barn like it was his home, instead. He cares more about his horses than just about anything."

I thought of Cider and Buck, how I'd been able to touch them, to put my hands on something that mattered to Case more than just about anything.

I gulped a little.

Clark continued, "I knew Owen, of course, though we were never close. It was through my Faye that I got to know Melinda, as she and Faye became fast friends. Melinda brought Case over here to play with Garth and Marsh, when they were just little sprouts. I would never have guessed anything was wrong. I was too busy ranching at the time, as we still had sheep in those days. But my Faye knew something wasn't right, knew that Owen was abusive. I wish now, God, how I wish now, that I would have done something more about it. A part of me felt as though I was imposing, that it wasn't my business. And I regret that very deeply. That's a part of why I tried so hard to care for those boys once Melinda passed."

"How did she die? She was sick, wasn't she?" I set my drink aside.

Clark nodded. "She was, for a long spell before she passed. Case would have been about eight years old, Gus just a few months. Owen was a rotten son of a bitch, though I wouldn't say so in front of the boys. He was their father. But Owen was worse than Edwin. He was meaner than a snake to them when he drank. When Melinda died, Case rode out into the foothills on his horse and didn't come back for three days, until I saddled up and went after him. I rode out the moment I heard he was missing. Owen, damn him, didn't tell anyone at first, probably didn't even notice for a day or so. I was worried as hell. I love Case like my own kin. I found him huddled in a cave where the boys all played once upon a time. Took my best talking to get him to come with me. Little fella was so weak from hunger he could hardly even stand up. His horse had long since hightailed it for home. Case said he wanted to die so that he could go to heaven and find his ma."

My heart constricted into a tight, aching fist.

"I could hear exactly what Edwin, Case's grandpa, would have said. He would have told the boy not to set his heart too much on earthly things, that's what, but that's always been Case's way, for better or worse. I told him how much we'd all regret it if he went to heaven so young. I told him that his little brother needed him. And sure enough, Case has cared for Gus like a father all these years. Fed him, clothed him, made sure his homework was done, all the while taking the brunt of Owen's tempers. Case tried to hide it when Owen would beat on him. I'll never forget the night I found out the truth. Owen had made Case shoot a dog earlier that day, a dog that Owen didn't want, one that wouldn't run off, and he made his son do it. Case was only ten years old, couldn't quite handle a pistol, but Owen called him a pussy and told him to do it or he'd whip him. So Case did it, shot the critter, and cried his eyes out. Owen gave him a beating anyway, for crying."

I listened with the knuckles of one hand pressed hard to my lips. In law school I had been presented with all manner of depositions, statements, testimonies, all for the purpose of study and speculation, the building of imaginary cases. I had been privy to information that would make anyone curl up with horror. And yet nothing had ever affected me this way, as though I'd been slammed in the gut with a baseball bat.

"I could have kicked myself for not acting sooner. I rode over to their place and made it clear, in no uncertain terms, that if Owen ever laid a hand on the boys again, I would shoot *him*."

"You did?" I whispered, suddenly hard-pressed to recall that this was 2013, well into the twenty-first century. People didn't behave that way any longer. Yet here sat proof that they did, indeed.

"Yes, and I don't regret it a minute. Long story short, Owen cleaned up a little after that. Never heard about him beating on the boys again, but I would imagine he still did. Case is a great one for keeping secrets. He and Gus very nearly lived here most of their teenage years. Faye adored them. My boys and them may as well be actual brothers." He looked my way and said, "I don't tell you any of this lightly, honey. I just want you to have a little insight. See, Case won't admit to anything anymore, won't admit that he feels a thing for you. But I know him well enough to see the hope in him, now that you're here for the summer. Making excuses to be near you. Thinking it might be different this time."

"What about his ex-wife?" I could hardly bear to ask.

"Lynnette," Clark affirmed. "They wed in 2009. Lynnette claimed to be pregnant, that's what sparked the whole thing, ironically, just like Melinda back when. But Case is nothing like his pa. He did right by Lynn and married her without a word of protest. Then she claimed a miscarriage a month or so later. I don't know. Never felt right to me. They fought a great deal. She hated that he worked late nights, performing. They split about a year and a half ago."

"He was married that summer you came to visit Landon?" I asked. When Case told Marshall he'd break bones if any of them tried anything with me.

"That's the only reason he didn't join us. He wanted to come, something fierce, but Lynn said *no sir*."

"Where is she now?" I asked, I hoped casually.

"Remarried and living in Idaho, last I heard," Clark said, and my shoulders relaxed; I hadn't realized they were hunched with tension.

"Clark, I don't know what to say," I whispered at last. A sense of emptiness had been stalking me and I shivered as it pounced.

"Honey, you don't have to say a thing," Clark said, kindly. "I just worry about my boys. Be his friend if you want, but that's where it has to end. He can't have false hope, I can't watch him go through that."

I closed my eyes, shutting out the stars. "I think he's beyond all of that, I do. It's been a long time, and we're older now. And I'll be so busy while I'm here, we probably won't see much of each other at all."

"Dad! You and Tish still out here?" Wy yodeled from the house. I looked over my shoulder to see him silhouetted in the open door.

"It's late," I noted. "Thank you for supper, and for telling me everything."

Clark rose as I did, cupping my shoulder before holding out a polite hand, allowing me to walk first. "I'd like it very much indeed if you'd come back on Fridays as a matter of habit. And any other night you'd like."

"I'd like that too," I said.

In my car, heading home a little while later, I felt as tiny as an ant crawling along on the ground, and just as insignificant. All of the information I'd just absorbed swirled in my head, certain words and images standing out from others. I pictured Case as he'd looked last night on stage at The Spoke, and how he'd looked tonight, grinning as he stroked Cider's neck, introducing me to her. I thought of him as a vulnerable little boy, shooting a dog, hiding out in a cave and nearly starving to death. Marrying a woman he believed carried his child.

He's obviously a passionate man.

And if Clark's right, you can't encourage any sort of attention.

Even if you want Case's attention, really badly.

Something caught my gaze, a road meandering to the left, and I braked fast enough that my tires squealed, fishtailing in the gravel. Clutching the wheel, my knees jittering, I read the words on the road sign for the second time. *Ridge Road.* The Spicer place was just down this road, Clark had said.

What are you doing?

Are you crazy?

It's late. He's in bed.

I just want to see his place, that's all. Just see it.

I turned left onto a gravel road.

What is this about?

Are you a stalker now?

Tish. Seriously.

There was nothing but empty land for a mile or so, stretching to the mountains on the horizon. Dark as hell, nothing to illuminate the black except for my headlights. Then I saw a looming structure on the left side of the road and hit the brake. A barn, huge and imposing. And then I spied a trailer tucked into the side of a small ridge south of the barn. White and green, shitty-looking, spared total desolation by two strings of red chili-pepper lights stretched above the door. These were glowing; I realized I had a white-knuckled grip on the steering wheel.

As though to highlight the fact that I was indeed staring at Case's home, the headlights picked out a mailbox to the right, silver and faded, the word *Spicer* stenciled in black upon it; somehow I knew, *I knew*, Melinda Spicer had been the one to stencil the word there, long ago. I wasn't considering how conspicuous I was, in a car out here on a remote road, and my heart went shooting right through my ribcage as a light toward the back of the trailer, maybe a bedside lamp, clicked out.

Shit! Go!

I felt low and despicable and criminal; the barn and the chili-pepper lights and the stenciled mailbox were receding before I could think twice.

Now you're going to get lost! You have to turn around.

You have to go back that way or you'll never find your way to town.

Shit, shit, shit.

Perhaps a half-mile from Case's front yard I pulled to the side of the road, killed the engine, and climbed out. I was amped up, my thoughts darting like minnows; too restless to return to the car, I paced the deserted road. After a few minutes I had calmed enough to stop pacing, and leaned against the Honda's warm hood. I felt strangely engulfed by the Montana night and lifted my chin to the stars.

God, it's beautiful out here. Like Landon, but wilder somehow. Even the air smells wild. It could be any year right now, hundreds of years ago. Montana doesn't realize or care what year it actually is, I get that now.

I cupped both hands around my temples and studied the sky, the way I used to as a little girl when we'd visited Landon in the summers, before we'd moved there for good. Shutting out the world this way, I could pretend I was able to rise from solid earth and fly up to the stars; the sensation was both heady and slightly terrifying.

What if you can't get back to the ground?

What then?

I dropped my hands and took stock of my surroundings. The sky was black silk, teeming with crystal stars. Wizened scrub brush on the edges of the road appeared pagan and wholly mysterious. A particular rock formation to the east snagged my gaze because it was so large and distinct, shaped like an uppercase T. It reminded me of a wizard with arms outstretched, spell-casting. I felt like I could stand here all night, inhaling the air and studying the landscape; I liked the sensation of being embraced by the night itself.

I had just turned to reenter my car when something hooked my senses, stalling my intent to leave. I squinted into the distance, sure I had imagined it, but there it was again—the flicker of a voice somewhere out in the foothills. Even though no one could see me at such a distance, I crouched near my car's front bumper and peered toward the faint hint of distant activity. I realized that a voice didn't necessarily justify concern, but some instinct warned me to pay attention. Something felt off.

Trespassers?

I wonder if this is still Case's property.

Something's happening out there by the wizard rock, I know it.

Men. At least two men.

Hunters, maybe? Is it hunting season?

Why else would a couple of men be out there at this time of night?

I have to tell Case.

I cut short the thought, knowing I could do no such thing. What would I say? Would I openly admit to having been skulking about his property like a stalker, looking for trouble? Hadn't Clark just delivered a cautionary tale involving that very idea? Looking for trouble only led you to it that much faster.

But something's not right, I can tell.

Fifteen seconds ticked by; I could no longer hear the voices and had almost convinced myself I was imagining things when I heard a car engine start. I watched, breathless, as taillights flared to life out there on a road not visible from my vantage point; the vehicle was pointed in the opposite direction of mine.

Follow them!

Hurry!

I leaped into the Honda, starting it but keeping the headlights off, then cranked a U-turn, not so much following as driving parallel to the other vehicle. The rutted road jounced my tires as I drove back the way I'd come. Case's yard appeared on the right, the red chili-pepper lights still glowing, all other lights extinguished.

I don't know what's going on but I will find out, Case, I promise.

Charles Shea Spicer.

For whatever reason, I liked the sound of his full name.

The vehicle to my distant left moved slowly, taillights bouncing as it passed over rough terrain; I was not about to let them get away. They reached the main road, the one that led back to Jalesville. I turned onto the same road, keeping my distance.

You better turn on the headlights.

Not yet.

You'll get a ticket! Worse, you could hurt someone.

I clicked the button on the dash and the vehicle I was tailing accelerated. They were a good half-mile ahead but I interpreted this action as their suspicion. I sped up, too, keeping them in sight without closing the distance too fast. They drove into Jalesville ahead of me and it was my luck that they were momentarily hung up at the stoplight; I pulled behind them, leaving ten feet between our bumpers. Black GMC 4x4, tinted windows, Colorado plates. Interesting. I couldn't tell how many people were inside. I memorized the license plate, knowing I had to quit tailing them.

Probably none of this means a damn thing anyway.

The light turned green and the GMC pulled forward. I turned left, toward my apartment, deciding to research the car in the morning after a good night's sleep.

Chapter Seven

LATE MORNING SUNLIGHT WAS SOFT AND WARM AS A mother's hand on my cheek. I stretched, not fully awake, and my first thought was to find my sisters and Clinty and tell them what I'd done last night. But they were in Minnesota. And I had work to do on this sunny Saturday, intent upon living up to my growing—and at this point, thoroughly undeserved—reputation as the hero of Jalesville.

You have a real complex, you know.

I brewed coffee, biting into a banana as I reworded my argument for Tuesday night. As much as I tried not to acknowledge it, my attention kept getting swept away by the notion that Case would be at the meeting; not to mention about half the town, but Case's opinion, as I was quickly discovering, mattered to me. I moved out to the porch with my notes and woke hours later with sunburned shoulders when Clark called to tell me that they were having a bonfire at their place this evening; I had dozed off on the porch chair.

"Supper, too," Clark added.

"You spoil me."

Clark laughed. "I won't deny that I love having a woman around *to* spoil, that's God's truth."

I dressed in jeans and my tennis shoes, a faded yellow t-shirt, and brought along my jacket for when it got cold later, embarrassed that I had gone too far with the sundress last night. I felt small and petty, wanting to attract attention that I had no business attracting. I left my hair loose and held off on any make-up, only dashing some gloss over my lips.

Will he be there?

He might not even be there.

He will. He'll ride Cider.

I was somehow certain of this as I drove through Jalesville, suddenly overwhelmed by an intense vision of riding Cider along with Case, sitting in front of him, his chest bracketing my shoulders, his thighs aligned with mine, his hungry kisses on my neck.

Oh my God.

I shuddered hard, mentally banging my forehead on the steering wheel as I turned into the driveway and parked. I noticed right away that Case's truck was absent, trying to appear casual as I walked straight to the corral fence and peered at the barn doors, thrown open to the evening. I saw the edge of a stall and heard numerous horses, but could not tell if a certain sorrel with a white spot between her nostrils was among them. I pretended that Cider would clomp over to the fence if she was here, just to greet me.

It was Clark, Wy, Marshall, and me for dinner; I ate as much as I was able with a ball of disappointment wedged in my gut, though we talked easily and I enjoyed their familiar company. When the sound of a truck entering the yard rolled through the open windows, I almost jumped out of my seat to race to the door—but it was just Sean and Quinn, returning from a roofing job, sweaty and starving. I was debating which excuse I could use to beg off and leave early, intending to go home and curl up on my bed, when Clark said from the kitchen, "I told the boys eight-thirty. I wonder where they are?"

He means Case and Gus!

My eyes flew to the grandfather clock in the living room; it was quarter to nine and we were lingering around the table as Sean and Quinn finished eating. At Clark's words my energy was all at once restored; I felt buoyant, there was no denying.

"Gus had dinner at Lacy's folks tonight," Sean said around a mouthful of food. The Rawleys had accepted me as a sister; I knew this because they acted just like brothers or cousins around me. I might as well have been a boy for the level of comfort they displayed in my presence, belching and telling off-color jokes, unconcerned if their hair was messy or their clothes stained with a day's work. Instead of repelling me, I only felt the warmth of acceptance and security; I knew they wouldn't hesitate to stand up for me if the occasion ever required.

"What about Case?" I pestered Sean, who was elbowed up to his plate on my left, sopping cornbread through gravy, using his fingers instead of a fork. At my question I felt Marshall's curious gaze from across the table.

"He's probably on the way right now," Quinn answered, snatching the last pork chop before Sean could. "He joined us shingling today. Said he had to go home and clean up quick."

I beamed at this news, unable to help it; I happened to be looking at Wy, whose eyebrows lifted as he returned the smile. I grew flustered then, rising and finding an excuse for my restless movement by helping clear the table; I'd insisted upon loading the dishwasher each of the nights that Clark had invited me for supper, feeling as though it was a small way to repay him for making me a part of the family this summer.

"*Shit*," I muttered as gravy splashed across my t-shirt; I was carrying too many dishes for one armload and made the mess on my shirt worse by scrubbing at it with a damp towel. Of course right then I heard the dogs barking in a friendly, excited way.

He's riding up!

He's here, he's here!

I darted down the back hallway to the bathroom and clicked on the light, shutting the door and regarding my reflection. My cheeks were on fire, as though I'd downed a couple bottles of wine rather than the single beer I'd sipped with dinner. I ran my fingers through my hair, which was extra curly and tangled in the humidity. It appeared that maybe I hadn't even brushed it today and here I stood in a gravy-stained shirt. There was a small window in this bathroom, open a few inches, and even though I was on the opposite side of the house I distinctly heard Case asking Sean to grab Garth's old guitar.

"It's still here, isn't it?" Case's deep voice carried right to me. I fantasized that he was going to ask if I was here; but of course he would have seen my car. My belly was on a roller coaster, currently at the peak of a steep hill, poised to fall into open space.

"Yeah, I'll grab it," Sean said.

"Guys, help me with this wood!" Wy called plaintively, from farther away, probably around the barn.

"Buddy, you gotta help yourself with your *own* wood," Marshall teased his youngest brother. "Ain't nobody gonna help you with it, unless maybe you get a sweet little girlfriend."

They were all laughing then and I couldn't help but giggle; it was such a welcome feeling, this unexpected surge of happiness in my blood.

Wy fired back, "At least I *have* wood," and then there was more laughter, and the sounds of scuffling, and I realized I couldn't keep hiding out in the bathroom.

The first thing I saw upon stepping outside, my senses on high alert, was Cider nosed up to the corral fence. I smiled at this sight, pausing to caress her warm jaws; because no one was looking I pressed a quick kiss to the white spot on her nose, the exact place Case had kissed her yesterday. Marshall and Quinn had constructed a kindling tepee in the stone fire pit beyond the barn, which was already blazing away, and right then I spied Case, lounging in a lawn chair, plunking the strings on the old guitar. As I approached the fire he looked over at me and grinned, wide and warm. He nodded at the seat beside his and my heart executed a complete backflip.

"Hey," I said, tamping down the urge to touch his hair, which I could tell was freshly washed, so soft-looking in the firelight. The orange flames played over the angles of his face, his firm chin and jaws, his cinnamon-brown eyes. I sat and angled my knees toward him.

"Hey there," he said softly. He began picking out the tune of the song with which he'd ended his show at The Spoke two nights ago; I recognized it even though he was using a guitar rather than his fiddle. He strummed the instrument almost unconsciously as he asked, "You have any requests?"

I do, oh God, I do.

But I can't request any of those things of you.

I continued to study his eyes, thrilled to be this close to him; he usually kept a subtle distance between us. I could not for the life of me figure him out. Last night he'd been aloof except when we'd talked about the horses. Tonight he seemed relaxed, approachable. So much so that I was considering displacing the guitar and climbing right onto his lap.

I wanted to say, *I drove by your place last night, Case. And something was happening out there.*

I had to find a way to tell him.

He raised his eyebrows, certainly wondering at my silence, and I blurted, "That song you were playing is really pretty. I liked it the other night, too."

Is that satisfaction in his eyes?

"Thank you." He spoke quietly, stern-faced again.

"Did you write it?" I pressed, even though I knew he had.

He strummed a G-chord, eyes now in the fire, and nodded.

"That's so impressive." I wanted him to know that he impressed me greatly. I wished we were alone out here; I was so greedy of my limited time with him, longing to stockpile it. I wanted to ask him a thousand questions. I wanted him to look at me again.

"We're on for Wednesday at the fairgrounds, right?" Marshall asked, flopping down on my other side, and I could have kicked him for interrupting.

Case nodded. "And Lee asked me to fill in on Tuesday night but I told her not until after the meeting."

"I can join you Tuesday," Marsh said, and bumped his shoulder against mine. "Lots of hot girls come to the fair."

"Hot girls like musicians," I agreed, bumping my shoulder against Marshall's, with slightly more force than necessary. "*Lucky you.*"

Marshall caught me in a playful headlock and knuckled my scalp, messing up my hair even worse. God, he was just like Clint. I elbowed his ribs and Case reached behind me and slapped the back of Marsh's head, hard.

"Ouch!" Marshall complained, releasing his hold.

"*Dammit*, Marsh," I grumbled. "Now my hair is all tangled!"

"It already was," he shot right back. "I didn't do anything that wasn't already done."

I had to giggle at this logic, but not before punching his shoulder.

Case returned to strumming the guitar. His arm had briefly touched my back and I wanted to beg him to put his arm around me, this time on purpose, and for much longer than a second. Marsh saw Wy approaching with a tray of s'mores supplies and jumped up to snatch a marshmallow.

"He's such a *child*," Case said in mock exasperation. Before I could respond, he added, "And your hair is beautiful, by the way, all down like that."

My cheeks erupted with heat at this unexpected compliment. Case studied me for the space of one more breath before looking back at the fire, strumming the guitar strings; I felt their vibrations deep inside.

"Thank you," I whispered.

Wy claimed the chair Marsh had abandoned.

"Here, Tish," Wy said, passing me the tray. "Will you be in charge of making the s'mores?"

"Sure." I settled the tray on my thighs. "I'll make a little assembly line here."

Sean passed around roasting sticks.

"I can roast you one," Wy offered, since my hands were full unwrapping Hershey bars and breaking graham crackers in half.

"I got it, buddy," Case said easily, setting aside the old guitar and reaching to take two marshmallows from the tray on my lap; he murmured to me, "I roast a pretty good marshmallow, just so you know."

"I'm holding you to that. I can never get the right balance. Either too burned or too raw."

Case said, "One time Garth had a marshmallow catch on fire out here, so he starts waving it around, freaking out, and it flew off the stick and landed on his nose. We were maybe twelve or so."

"It sounds like you guys have a lot of good memories," I said as Case aligned the marshmallows on the stick, mesmerized watching his hands perform this little task. He nodded acknowledgment of my words.

Everyone else was joking around, drinking beer and laughing, allowing us a small, fire-lit slice of privacy. I studied the side of his face as he leaned forward to put the marshmallows near the flames. His right elbow was close to my left thigh, the fire playing over his hair and his right ear, the skin of his neck exposed by his t-shirt; a solid line of muscle ran along the tops of his shoulders. Before I could stop myself, I touched his back. He was so warm and hard beneath my fingertips, and looked immediately over his shoulder.

Jesus Christ, Tish.

I withdrew my hand as quickly as if it had been in the flames; I lied, "There was a mosquito on you…"

"Oh." He looked back at the fire. "Thanks."

"No problem," I whispered, a catch in my throat.

Everyone crowded their chairs closer in order to get the marshmallows in the flames and I followed suit, gazing around the fire at my surrogate family. The Rawley boys all looked so much alike, with their dark hair and merry eyes, their long noses dominating their lean, handsome faces. Wy especially had yet to grow into his nose and I hid a smile, remembering how he'd been kind enough to worry that I would be alone at the table on Thursday night if he went to dance.

"First kiss," Sean said, and everyone started laughing while I stared at him, mystified by these words in this context.

"Oh yeah," Marsh agreed, and Case shook his head, smiling, as he turned the roaster stick with our marshmallows in a slow, continuous circle.

I looked at Clark for an explanation; he sat with one ankle caught on the opposite knee, regarding his boys with fondness. "It's an old rule. New people around the bonfire have to tell the story of their first kiss."

And then they all looked at me, with varying degrees of speculation and teasing. Case was the only one who kept his eyes on the flames; our chairs were so close together, my (I hoped subtle) doing, that I was chicken to look his way.

I stalled for time, protesting, "But I don't know any of *your* stories."

"Ladies first," Marsh insisted. "Then we'll tell ours."

"What girl has ever kissed you?" Wy blustered. "I bet you've never *had* a first kiss."

Everyone laughed uproariously; Marsh was the scapegoat of his family but he totally asked for it. Marsh retorted, "Katie Nelson, seventh grade, behind the bleachers after school."

"Tongue?" Wy asked, adding to the general hysteria. He concluded, "I bet no tongue."

"The real question is has there been anyone *since* then?" Case said, sending Marshall a wicked grin across the fire. Marsh flashed a lazy, raised middle finger at Case.

"Clark, what about you?" I asked, fascinated.

Clark tipped back his head as he laughed. He said gamely, "My first love was also my first kiss, my Faye, mother of five of my boys. Junior year of high school, October, her mama's front stoop."

"That's so sweet," I said, steeped with wistful sincerity. "That's so romantic."

If my sisters could hear me, they wouldn't believe it; I never said things like that. Romance was simply not in my vocabulary. And here I sat, close to tears.

"Way better than bleacher-kissing with Katie Nelson," Quinn agreed, everyone still taking potshots at Marsh. "Katie with her braces that had two different colors of rubber bands."

"Did your braces get tangled with hers?" Sean asked, almost laughing too hard to ask.

"Y'all can screw off," Marsh muttered.

At that moment Case finished our marshmallows, leaning back. I was ready with a graham cracker/chocolate bar sandwich. He plucked them, perfectly roasted, from the stick and presented them to me with his half-grin.

He said, "See there?" with an air of teasing confidence. We were no more than eighteen inches apart and I realized he was politely waiting for me to take the marshmallows; I did, our fingers brushing together. We both got all sticky and I had the distinct notion that if we were alone he would have taken my hand in his big, strong, sexy one and licked every last bit of melted sugar from my fingertips. Wy and Sean crowded close with their own toasty marshmallows, forcing me to abandon my fantasies and turn to the task of passing out chocolate and graham crackers.

I finally bit into my delicious marshmallow concoction and so it was then I had a large, gooey mouthful when Wy ordered, "Tish, you're up!"

Shit.

I shook my head, indicating my full mouth.

"No getting out of it," Wy insisted. He peered more closely. "You've got marshmallow all over your lip, like a mustache."

That was me, super sexy at all times. I swiped at my top lip and made it worse.

"Eighth grade, Kayla Murray, her basement," Case said, sitting forward with his forearms on his thighs. He was saving me, I realized. He grinned as he added, "We were watching some horror movie, I can't remember exactly, but it was scary enough that I took advantage. You know, like, 'It's all right, you can come closer' kind of thing."

"Tongue?" Wy asked, sounding truly curious, and then we were all dying with laughter.

"What has gotten into you, buddy?" Quinn demanded, roughing up Wy's hair.

Case nodded affirmation of Wy's question, still smiling.

"Eighth grade, Marni Fraser, in her garage," Sean said. "Dang, I almost got to second base that same day." He winked at Wy as he said with salacious glee, "*Lots* of tongue."

"*Boys*," Clark reprimanded, but he was laughing, too. I loved their easy camaraderie.

Quinn said, "I was old. Ninth grade, Emily Inman, my bedroom after school. We were working on algebra but I couldn't think of anything else after she put her hand on my knee."

I had finished chewing and knew I needed to be a good sport. Probably there was still marshmallow on my lip. God, and gravy on my shirt. I sighed and admitted, "No, I was older than that. Summer between junior and senior year." They all gaped at me with what I supposed I should consider rather flattering disbelief. Self-conscious as hell,

I finished, "My cousin's friend, Jeff Worden, baseball field in Landon after their game." Before he could ask, I told Wy, "Yes, a *little* tongue." And then I was laughing again, shaking my head, wanting to cover my face with both hands.

"You were almost a *senior?*" Marsh demanded. "What's wrong with the boys in your town? Are they nuts?"

"I didn't want a boyfriend," I said. "Not then. I was too much of a tomboy."

Case was watching me with warm amusement in his gaze. "I can see that."

I was full-body flushed and my clothes felt too tight, so I redirected everyone and put Wy on the spot with, "Ok, Tongue Man, you haven't told us *yours.*"

There was too much laughter for anyone to say anything. Wy shook his head until his hair flopped, and finally managed to gasp, "I tried…I tried to kiss Hannah Jasper, last summer, at a party, but I…"

His brothers were almost in tears, holding their sides.

Wy cried, "But I missed and kissed her ear! She turned her head at the last second, I swear! I got a mouthful of *ear.*"

"Oh, buddy," I laughed. "Did you try again?"

"No," he admitted. "I see her all the time at school and all I can think is that I tasted her ear!"

"So there was tongue involved," Case said.

By the time the fire died down a half hour later, my stomach hurt from laughing. The air grew steadily colder but I hadn't noticed at all until Case got up to duck inside. I realized too late I was staring after him and snapped my attention back to the fire only to observe that Clark had been watching me watch Case. I pretended to be preoccupied with finishing the last of a chocolate bar, probably my third or fourth of the evening.

"You have plans for tomorrow?" Clark asked. "You want to come for lunch?"

"Just working on my argument for Tuesday. I spent the week researching what happened to families displaced by Capital Overland buyouts.

And it's not good."

All of the guys were somber now, the boisterous mood having fizzled out, echoing the dying fire. Wy was munching a marshmallow while the others sipped their beers.

"If we can convince enough of the people around here to avoid selling out, it might be enough to drive Yancy's interests in another direction. If only we could somehow reopen the power plant," I said.

Clark nodded agreement. "That was a damn shame. I've lived here my entire life, as have most of the other locals. And now it seems that people are willing to pull up stakes and move on, without a fight."

"It's hard to fight when you're being offered a chunk of change," Case said, reappearing from the house. He walked in front of me to reclaim his seat while I concentrated on breathing normally. It seemed as though my hands wouldn't obey me when he was near. I shifted and slipped both beneath my thighs, one on either side.

"You're right," Clark agreed. "But what's the alternative? Moving to an unfamiliar place? Leaving behind land that's been in your family for generations? Most of us have been here since the late 1800s."

"We'll do our best," Case said, settling in his lawn chair and leaning forward. He spoke with quiet confidence, the sound of someone who wouldn't be budged from a certain position.

Though it had lingered at the back of my mind along with everything Clark told me last night, I suddenly thought of the story of Case hiding out in a cave, wanting to die so he could get to heaven and find his mother. He was so powerful and capable-looking now, far removed from that devoted little boy with a broken heart. To my horror, tears spurted into my eyes, causing everything in sight to starburst.

I stumbled to my feet. "Excuse me."

Inside the empty house I darted to the bathroom—I had walked as calmly as I could manage from the fire, praying that no one noticed my tears—and barely managed to shut the door behind me before I gave over to weeping.

What in the hell is the matter with you?

My period must be starting.

I sat on the closed lid of the toilet and sobbed into my palms, smothering all sound, though I didn't think anyone had followed me inside demanding an explanation. I cried so hard my shoulders shook, further stunning me; I was not a crier. Camille and Ruthie were the emotional ones. Even Clint choked up more often than me; I could think of multiple times I had made fun of him over the years for being too sensitive. God, I was mean. And yet here I sat, bawling with my throat aching.

You need to go back to your apartment and have a smoke.

And you have to stop thinking about what Case said at Camille's wedding. It doesn't matter anymore. It's in the past...

To my relief, I didn't hear the sound of the screen door opening, indicating that someone had followed me inside; I could claim to be tired and steal away. I tried not to think about how much I hated the thought of relinquishing my spot beside Case at the fire. I liked being close to him, so much that it scared me, quite desperately; further, it meant I had to go. Letting anyone see I had been crying this way was out of the question. I splashed my face, thankful I wasn't wearing mascara. I shook my hair around my face as a sort of protective barrier and gathered my nerves together. Back outside, I kept my distance, calling over to the fire, "Hey guys, I'm headed home! I'm tired. Thanks for supper, Clark!"

There were multiple sounds of protest at my words; I hadn't heard Case's voice and couldn't bear to look that way. Clark, ever the gentleman, strolled over from the fire to wish me good-night; I couldn't tell if he was observant enough to see that my eyes were red and swollen.

"Give us a call if you're bored tomorrow, honey," Clark murmured. I pretended to be busy, this time digging for my keys so I wouldn't have to meet his eyes.

I forced a cheerful tone. "I will. And thanks again for everything."

Clark patted my arm and he knew something was wrong, I could tell, but he let it be, saying only, "You're more than welcome."

I drove home, with tears again washing over my face and blurring my vision.

Chapter Eight

I didn't see Case or the Rawleys at all on either Sunday or Monday. My period started on Sunday, to my relief, giving me something upon which to blame my uncontrollable tears. I spent most of the day lying in bed in a half-headachy funk, pressing a pillow to my belly in an effort to alleviate my cramps, too out-of-sorts to drive to the grocery store for a bottle of aspirin. I stared alternately at the ceiling fan above the bed and out the window at the sky, which was padded with dense gray clouds until early afternoon, when I shuffled to the kitchen to brew a pot of coffee and eat some banana bread.

The sun peeked out as I drove over to Al and Helen Anne's for dinner; they had also invited Mary and her husband, Joe, a tall, stoop-shouldered man with blindingly-white false teeth, whom I quickly discerned let Mary do all the talking. Al was excited about Tuesday evening, getting himself worked up enough that both Helen Anne and Mary scolded him. I reassured Al I would present the best argument I was able, using the evidence I had at hand, and that we would work together to convince people to stay in Jalesville.

"I don't know what I'll do if we lose out to Yancy," Al said, unbuttoning his collar as Helen Anne served coconut cream pie. I wondered where my fiery feminist spirit had been misplaced; in college I had scoffed at traditional male/female roles and would have been unduly troubled by a wife serving her husband this way, along with their guests. And yet I didn't get the sense that Helen Anne felt demeaned by these unspoken expectations; she rested her hand on the back of Al's neck as she refilled his coffee cup, and he winked at her in response.

If you fucking start crying right now…

"We won't lose," I said, taking my third bite of pie. Helen Anne's desserts were always incredible. "I just wish there was a way to make up the jobs to people around here. Al, if I was wealthy I would just buy the plant and reopen the doors. According to what I read last week, it's still basically operational. It's just sitting there empty and unused. Why?"

"The plant closing was terribly ill-timed. People didn't know what to think," Helen Anne said. "There's no explanation."

"It's not the first time Jalesville's been out of work on a large scale," Al said. "Back in the early seventies, times were just as tough."

"We've always pulled through," Mary said. "But nowadays the kids are getting seduced by the big cities. They aren't settling around here anymore."

"My own included," Al said. He looked my way, his expression softening. "Tish, I know better than anyone that this isn't your problem. You're a trooper and I can't tell you how much I appreciate all your effort here."

"Thank you. I really do want to help." I genuinely liked Al, not only as my boss but as a person, certainly another rarity in the cutthroat world of legal service.

"Don't think this means I'm not going to try to convince you to stay with everything I have," Al said, pointing his fork in my direction, narrowing his eyes in mock severity.

Mary nodded emphatically and nudged her husband's elbow, interrupting his next bite. "Joseph, wouldn't it be lovely if Harold wasn't yet married?"

Joe touched a finger to his hearing aid. "What's that, dearest?"

"Our grandson, Harold! If he wasn't married to that Denise, he could court Patty!"

Al hid a laugh behind a sip of coffee and I snorted, unable to help it; Harold had appeared at Howe and James to bring his grandmother something, just last Wednesday. He was fair and plump, dimpled as a baby, shorter than me by a good six inches; his nose was level with my breasts and he'd flushed pink as a June rose when I walked over to shake his hand. Undoubtedly Mary had also informed him that she wished he was still single.

I pointed my fork at Al this time, holding it like a judge's gavel. "I appreciate your compliment, a great deal. I just can't imagine living outside Chicago. I've been planning that since I was eighteen and first attended the U of M. My dad is so proud of me…"

"As he should be," Al acknowledged. "I remember Jackson, of course. Handsome devil. But not a bad sort, unlike most lawyers." As though offhandedly—but I was well-trained enough to spot a calculated question—he asked, "What do you think of Ron Turnbull?"

"I consider him my future boss," I said carefully; I suddenly envisioned sitting on a witness stand. "He wasn't around much when I worked at Turnbull and Hinckley the past two summers. My father respects him."

Al pursed his lips. "You'll think this is a ploy, but I promise it's not. I'm not positioning here, just being truthful. He's fairly despicable."

I was more than a little stunned. "What makes you say that?"

"Just a feeling. Nothing that would hold water in court, I assure you. I can see that now—Judge, may I present the evidence? A gut feeling, Your Honor, a gut feeling."

I was more troubled than I let on; I was astute enough to understand that men didn't ascend to Ron Turnbull's level of position and prestige without a certain amount of ruthlessness. *All justifiable, right?* I finally allowed, "I know it won't be easy. But I'm ready. Dad thinks I can climb the ladder relatively quickly."

Helen Anne leaned forward to implore, "Just consider the toll it will take on you, Tish."

I had, and then some. "I'm ready for that."

Al took up the reins. "You'll be exhausted. You'll be constantly jockeying for position. No one will support you because they all want the same prize."

"I'll just want it most, that's all."

"I believe you," Al said, making a steeple of his fingertips.

Mary set aside her empty pie plate. "Albert, let the girl alone. Let her eat her dessert, for heaven's sake."

That night I lay in bed, staring at the ceiling fan, which was motionless in the chilly room. I kept the window open so I could hear the sounds of night; I listened to crickets and the whisper of a breeze, seeking comfort in these familiar noises, and debated calling my sisters. For the first time in my life, I didn't know how to talk to them. I couldn't give words to the feelings crashing like breakers on the shore of my consciousness; I'd already delivered a good show for Dad, who'd called shortly after I arrived home from Al and Helen Anne's. I could be as false-cheerful as anyone; whereas Mom would have asked within five seconds why my voice sounded funny, Dad bought everything I sold him about feeling wonderful.

I rolled to my other side, swiping heavy, tangled hair from my face. I thought about what Al had said about Ron Turnbull. I thought about the way Case's hands looked as he held his fiddle and drew the bow over the taut strings. I thought about the way he touched his horses, with such subconscious love. The way his eyes looked in the glow of the sunset light, and in the orange of the fire. The way his deep voice sounded and how I wished he would say my name. The way his lips curved into that half-grin when he teased me. I thought of the story he'd told, about learning to play music on the beautiful instrument his ancestor had carried to war, and then westward. How he cared about his land, his town.

I flopped to my spine and crossed both forearms over my eyes; my jaws were clenched, my nipples at attention, which infuriated me. And at some much later point, I finally fell asleep.

I was a certifiable wreck by Tuesday, noon, running on perhaps two hours of sleep. I'd spent the morning agonizing over my research, scrawling notes with sharp slashes of a pen. I chewed the ends off two pencils, fully deserving of the woods shards between my teeth, and was considering walking over to the grocery store for a pack of smokes. I was alone in the office when the bell above the door sounded and my heart absolutely detonated. I turned as calmly as I could, but then my heart stuttered for a completely different reason—pure alarm. For there stood Derrick Yancy, dressed as though for a court appearance, dark hair shining and front teeth bared in what was meant to be a smile.

"Counselor Gordon," he greeted, his eyes moving fast as a hand flicking aside a mosquito, down over my breasts and hips and then back to my face.

I kept my tone neutral, clutching a stack of file folders more securely against my chest. "Mr. Yancy. How can I help you?"

"Oh, there are numerous ways you could help me, I have no doubt," he murmured, all innuendo; his gaze dropped for a second time, lingering on my thighs.

So you want to play this game, huh, asshole?

"I'm busy," I said, level as a tabletop.

His lips widened with a smile that sent shards of glass through my blood.

"Busy planning for tonight?" He stepped closer and I resolved to hold my ground, grateful for the counter serving as a barricade between our bodies.

I refused to respond or look away from him. My tongue hurt, pressed so tightly to the roof of my mouth.

He shifted position and my belly jumped, my limbs tensed; his tone changed as he said, "I know you think you're doing these people a favor, but you're mistaken. I offer them cash for property that is essentially useless to them. Your little champion act isn't going to serve them well when they can't pay their property taxes."

I drew a subtle deep breath, blood still hopping, not about to let him observe my discomposure; I'd actually thought he was going to leap at me. I lifted my chin, having achieved solid ground. "I'd prefer to address the topic this evening, at the meeting. You'll be there, of course."

"Of course." His smile vanished, mouth becoming a hard line as he stared at my face. I almost dropped the folders when he suddenly invited, "Would you care to join me for lunch? My treat."

I blinked at this question. Was he kidding? What was he playing at, shifting gears this way? Did he actually think he could change my mind with a seduction act? His slick good looks, not to mention his real estate fortune, had no doubt padded the way for many a one-night stand, I was certain. Awareness suddenly dawned; he was bored, I realized, bored in a place he considered the armpit of the earth. Second son, sent here by the elder Yancys to charm his way into easy sales for them while Daddy and older brother remained in the comfort of Chicago; major potential chip on his shoulder. I recognized that he was waiting for my response and cleared my throat before responding, "No, thank you."

He shrugged. "Suit yourself."

"Good-bye," I hinted.

"I'm already looking forward to tonight," he said, and took his leave.

That evening I drove across town with my heart feeling like a bird in a painfully small cage. I'd spent an hour getting ready and looked as lawyerly as I could manage; I felt like I was on the way to argue before the appellate court from first-year, green as spring leaves, wet behind the ears, all of that.

Stop this. You're a graduate, summa cum laude. You're smart. You're prepared. You're tough. You...you need a better mantra.

I had chosen my outfit with greater care than usual—my favorite silver-gray jacket-and-skirt combo, the skirt of the strictest pencil variety above nude silk hose and ultra-respectable nude heels, all chosen for me by Lanny's personal shopper in Chicago. The jacket was fitted perfectly to my waist, latched with a single hook-and-eye at my navel. The blouse beneath it was crystal blue; a man I'd dated for a few weeks second-year told me that it made my eyes glow. The tasteful diamond studs Mom and Blythe had gifted me with upon acceptance into law school, each gem an emerald-cut quarter-carat, my hair twisted high and neat at the back of my head. My make-up was appropriate for an evening appointment and I was wearing Dad's graduation gift for the first time, a beautiful, understated Cartier pendant timepiece, pinned to my left lapel, just above the fullest part of my breast.

I fussed with a loose strand of hair after I'd pulled into the parking lot of the city offices, noticing Case's truck among dozens of others. *Gotta*

Ride, Gotta Play. I hadn't set eyes upon him since Saturday night, eating s'mores and hearing about his first kiss. When I'd left so abruptly. Since then I had seen him only in my very vivid and near-constant imaginings, in which he slowly licked melted marshmallow from my mouth, parting my lips with his tongue as he unbuttoned my blouse with those strong, capable fingers…

Stop! You can't afford to lose focus right now!
But he's right in there! He's right in there, so close.
Quit wondering what he'll think of what you're wearing!
Shut. UP.

But it was too late; I'd already started sweating.

I took my sweet time gathering files from the passenger seat before entering the brick building; by night, it appeared stern, intimidating and decidedly unfriendly. There were dozens of people gathered in the wide foyer, most of whom I recognized, talking excitedly, sipping coffee from Styrofoam cups, kids darting between elbows. I noticed immediately that I was way overdressed and felt more than a few curious stares directed my way. I pasted on my most pleasant expression, the one that people who knew me well realized masked complete self-consciousness, and threaded through the throng to room 105, where the meeting was scheduled to be held. It was stuffy and crowded, scented with a melee of brewing coffee, aftershave, cologne, and sweat.

I noticed that Derrick Yancy had set up at a front table, briefcase and laptop and a black-as-death suit. As I emerged from the hallway he extricated himself from two men I didn't recognize, surely his henchmen, and made his way directly to me, all the while offering the smile that I was sure had spread many pairs of legs for him in the past. *Ick.*

"Counselor Gordon." He offered a hand and I stalled, transferring my briefcase to the opposite hand; I kept my grip firm.

"Derrick," I returned, determined to bring him down a notch or two.

His smile widened as he ascertained my obvious intent but he was all manners on the surface. "You're looking particularly well this evening. Breathtaking, really."

I tried to withdraw from our handshake but his fingers had tightened.

If this bastard thought he could intimidate me in this fashion, he didn't know who he was messing with. Never mind that my gut was sloshing. I bent slightly closer and hissed, for his ears only, "*Fuck you.*"

He laughed, totally unperturbed, and I knew that if we were alone he would have done something grossly out of line to assert his assumption of power over me, like squeeze my ass. He did, however, release my hand. "As expected."

I stepped around him, feeling his eyes follow me, and set up at the front table to the right, where Al had clearly already arrived, though he was nowhere in sight. I saw a pamphlet placed beside Al's briefcase, not something I recognized as belonging to him. I picked it up, realizing it was an informational brochure for Capital Overland; there was Derrick Yancy and another man, probably his brother, shown at a groundbreaking ceremony somewhere, smiling for the camera with their wingtips braced delicately on shovels. It was the kind of thing designed to encourage goodwill toward a bloodless business entity. I very nearly chucked it to the floor but that would be the ultimate display of immaturity. Instead I set it to the side, facedown.

I glanced at the large, schoolhouse-style clock on the wall, which read 6:51, only nine minutes until the meeting would commence, but I was far too restless to sit. I needlessly rearranged my things before deciding to return to the lobby, intending to mingle if it killed me, when I turned and my heart stopped. It just plain stopped for the space of a regular heartbeat, and then surged to life as though delivered an electric charge.

Oh my God. Oh. My. God.

Don't stare, don't stare, don't stare…

But it was too late; besides, he was staring right back at me and though his face was not hidden in the shadow of a hat brim, it was just as unreadable as ever. No jeans and t-shirt in sight this evening. The man before me, the length of a room away, dozens of residents of Jalesville milling obliviously between us, was so formally, intimidatingly handsome that I felt kicked in the gut. His hair caught the lights, almost throwing sparks. He was clad in smoky-gray dress pants that fit him as well as his faded jeans, belted at his lean waist, a shirt of palest lavender tucked in beneath an open sport coat of the same shade as his trousers. His top collar button was undone and he was not wearing a tie, as though this would prove too much a concession to formalwear.

Before I realized I had taken a step, I was walking up to him. He watched me approach with no change of expression, his auburn eyes steady and totally inscrutable.

"Ms. Gordon," he acknowledged, as though our first names were too casual for this particular moment. Not that he'd yet spoken my first name, as I was one hundred percent aware. He was freshly shaved, his lips appearing full and soft above the strong lines of his chin, which was marked with a narrow white scar I'd noticed before. His eyelashes were long, remarkably red-gold, creating a sharp contrast with his brown eyes. The freckles lightly sprinkled over his cheekbones were muted by the deep tan of his skin; I would bet money in the winter they became more visible.

Bowing to his lead, I responded, "Mr. Spicer. How are you this evening?"

You sound giddy and stupid!

Snap out of it!

"Well, thank you," he said. Just a hint of a smile graced his lips as our gazes held fast and I beamed in response, radiantly. It came out of nowhere, my real smile, and he blinked and inhaled a deep breath through his nose, slamming me straight back to that moment outside the bathroom at Camille's wedding. I seized control of my face. I could not think of one damn thing to say. Right at this moment Case seemed far removed from the person with whom I'd roasted marshmallows on Saturday night.

Thank God for Al, who bustled through the door, eyebrows raised in perfect, worried arches. He caught sight of me. "Oh, thank heavens, Tish, I'm glad to see you. I didn't think you were here yet."

"Al, are you all right?" I reached to catch his elbow.

"Yes, yes, just fine." He tucked my hand politely to his side. "Spicer, good, you're here, too. People listen to you. Isn't Clark coming? Oh, there he is, thank heavens. And there's Hank…" He indicated the councilman, a wiry, darkly tanned man wearing a string tie and faded jeans along with his sport coat. "Tish, are you ready?"

Al was going to have a coronary. I said to Case, "We better sit…"

He nodded, studying me as though trying to read my thoughts, but Clark came near and commanded everyone's attention. I was heartened at their presence, each ready to talk sense into the crowd; Garth, Marshall, Sean, Quinn, and Wy were on their dad's heels. There was a shifting in the crowd as Hank Ryan strode to the front of the room and then a rush of organized chaos as everyone attempted to find a seat. I led Al to the front, towering over him in my heels, and lost sight of Case until we were seated; it was only as I turned, covertly, to scan the murmuring crowd, some people fanning themselves with Capital Overland pamphlets, that I noticed he and the Rawleys were three rows back.

"Good evening, friends." Hank Ryan tipped his hat brim. "I'd like to thank all of you for finding time to come out this evening. I know you all have questions and I would like to allow time for those." He possessed a commanding voice and wore cowboy boots that had been around a very dusty block. I sat straighter, a trickle of sweat gliding between my breasts. "Now, we all know each other well. I don't see an unfamiliar face in the crowd, with the exception of Albert's new associate, whom I've not had the pleasure of meeting." He looked my way and I lifted my chin, heart throbbing. Hank Ryan continued, "Ms. Gordon, welcome. And I believe most of you know Mr. Yancy, who represents his father's business dealings in Jalesville."

To our left, I saw Derrick shift in his chair and knew without a doubt I was correct about the chip on the shoulder notion. *His father's interests*—how subtly demeaning, as though he was a child dressed in daddy's clothes, playing at business.

"My longtime friend, Al Howe, asked for this meeting, so we'll leave it up to him to begin." Hank Ryan looked to Al, raising his eyebrows.

"Mr. Yancy may have the floor," Al said in his lawyer voice, with a gracious gesture at the podium. He may have looked like a kindly grandfather but he was nobody's fool; I suspected that people often underestimated him, but he used this to his advantage.

Derrick looked our way and nodded, rising smoothly and moving to shake Hank's proffered hand. He faced the crowd as Hank took a seat to the side.

"Good evening, folks," Derrick said, smiling at the assembled faces. It was so quiet in the room I could almost hear the ticking of the secondhand on the wall clock above his head. The room was stuffy with so many bodies wedged so close; a little kid giggled and there was a subsequent, sighing murmur through the crowd, displacing the tense silence. Derrick continued, in a tone meant to reassure, "I know that many of you have heard from me before now, and have had a chance to read through the literature I've provided in the past few weeks. I know many of you by name. I have felt welcomed into this community, to be honest." He sounded so sincere I nearly believed his ass. "I would like to maintain a positive relationship here, as I've said from the get-go. Highland Power closed its doors six months ago, leaving many of the residents of this area unemployed. I empathize. But, admittedly, I see this as an opportunity. It's win-win. You get money up front, the ability to then relocate to a place with greater employment opportunities."

"What if we don't want to move? We've lived here for three generations," said a man from the back of the room.

Derrick clasped his hands, nodding as though he truly cared about this question. I noticed he had neglected to mention just how *he* would win in his little scenario. He said, trying for a reasonable tone, "I understand. I even empathize, as I said. But staying on land that will continue to drain your finances, with so many out of work as it is, will only hurt your family in the long run. I'll purchase your land, pay you, and then you'll have choices again. The ball is back in your court."

Here goes.

"Mr. Yancy, I have a question." I was proud of the way my voice emerged with a confident edge that in no way hinted at my leaping anxiety.

His eyes flashed to me; he maintained a smile, holding out a palm in open invitation. His entire posture suggested that I bring it on.

"Explain your rationale for choosing this particular area of Rosebud

County, if you would. Prior to this year, your land purchases have been primarily in south central Wyoming."

"That's quite true, counselor."

My notebook was open but I had memorized all of the names and dates, information swirling through my mind. "Your first inquiry to purchase property was on January eleventh of this year, via email, to Hoyt Church, who has since sold to your company. Interestingly, only three weeks prior, Highland Power closed its doors with no intent to reopen in the near future, leaving well over a third of the residents of Jalesville without employment."

"My offers are even more a godsend then," he responded, without a flutter of discomfort.

"How fortunate for your company." I paused for a beat and then leaned forward to ask, "What are your intentions for the property you're purchasing?"

"I can't see how that's your business, but our plans include resale." He sustained a smile.

"What of the town itself?" I insisted.

"The town will be unchanged."

"Unchanged?" cried someone from the crowd. "When more than half of our residents have moved away? It will be a ghost town."

Derrick couldn't quite contain a shrug. "Consider the fact that in a more populous locale you'll have greater opportunity."

"That's an easy claim for you to make," I said, wondering if he realized he wasn't winning any points with such pretentious language. Al looked between Derrick and me, resembling a spectator at a tennis match. I pressed, "Former residents of Parkton and Cedar Gap, Wyoming, which represent only two of the nine towns your company has purchased in the state of Wyoming since 2009, have not fared well since their relocations. Thirty-eight, and these represent only the families I was able to find since last week, have since declared bankruptcy."

"Surely, as a lawyer, you can spot the fallacy in that logic," Derrick said. "As though you could prove that they wouldn't have declared bankruptcy had they refused to sell to our company."

"You're right," I conceded. "I can't yet unequivocally prove that. But that's not my point. The bottom line is that these people were relocated from acreages similar to the ones you're attempting to buy here in Jalesville. Relocated from their homes. Many of them had lived on their property for generations, also similar to this area. And for what?" I stood abruptly, the legs of my chair scraping along the floor. I braced my fingertips on the table, bending forward in what was an unmistakably aggressive posture. "You are failing to grasp the real issue here, Mr. Yancy. This place *matters* to the people gathered here tonight. To you, this place is a speck on a map, a potential for profit. But this is their *home*. Their community."

There was a ripple of murmured commentary at my words. I felt a small spurt of pure righteousness and held Derrick's increasingly less composed (though he veiled it well) gaze. His mouth compressed, a subtle flash of anger he quickly submerged. I knew I'd found a weak spot with the timing of the power plant's closing and Capital Overland's immediate presence in the area. There was more to this situation than I knew; I had seen how Derrick's expression tightened at the mention of the January inquiry, but I couldn't press this advantage until I learned more.

"But I need money *now*," said someone else, in the void left behind after my words. "I can't wait around for the plant to reopen. It might be years!"

"What if I've already sold? Is it too late?" asked another.

"Capital Overland paid up front," said a woman. "I'm happy to have the money."

"As you should be," Derrick said to this woman. "As should all of you."

I sensed more than saw Case stand up, three rows behind me. Derrick's hostile gaze moved at once to him. I turned to see Case, who stood with shoulders squared and eyes steady. Not quite threatening, but close. The crowd quieted as Case spoke and I felt a swell of pure gladness; his act of standing seemed to suggest that I had his complete support.

"Mr. Yancy, where are you from?" Case asked. He sounded truly curious.

"Chicago," Derrick snapped. "How that matters is hardly —"

"It is relevant," Case interrupted. "Were you born there? Do you have roots there?"

Derrick remained stubbornly silent, regarding Case with an expression of arrogant distaste that suggested this wasn't worth his time. After a tense silence he barked, "I was born in Manhattan, Spicer. What of it?"

"Nothing, to you perhaps." Case stood with his hands caught loosely on his narrow hips. My heart was wild in my chest at just the sight of him. Case continued, "I was born here. In this very town. My family has lived on our acreage since long before my grandfather was born. Since it was homesteaded in the late nineteenth century. I have roots here, that's *what of it*. That land is all my brother and I have in the world, and you would have to shoot me where I stand before it would be for sale."

Without glancing at Derrick, I had the horrible sense he was even now plotting that very thing, more than willing to shoot Case where he stood. I couldn't tear my eyes from Case, who held Derrick's gaze unwaveringly, his face stern in its intensity. Despite everything, I felt a pulse low in my belly, the insistent pull of my raging attraction to him.

It's all my brother and I have in the world, that's what he said.

Oh, Case…

I wanted to tell him, *You have me. You have me in the world.*

But of course that was absurd.

Clark rose, and in his wake his five sons joined him, aligning with Case, shoulder to shoulder. Garth glared at Derrick. Marsh folded his arms, biceps bulging. Their quiet dignity, their combined strength, sent a warm, shivering sense of pride through my center. Tears blurred my view but no one noticed, watching with varying degrees of awe as the seven men stood together.

Case acknowledged the Rawleys with a small nod, then looked around at his town, at all of the people he certainly knew by name. He spoke earnestly. "We have to see this through. Jalesville means something to all of you, I know it does. I know it to the bottom of my heart. Think how you'd feel if it was gone, bulldozed for some fancy goddamn vacation homes. Can you imagine never seeing each other again? What of that?"

There were a few grudging laughs, and a man muttered, "That might not be a totally terrible thing. I mean, my ex-wife still lives in town…"

More laughter, but then someone else said, "Spicer is right. We can't give up on our homes. I can't imagine relocating. It's the last thing I want."

Al faced the crowd and said mildly, "The sales don't have to be final, people. We call that in the business the 'weasel clause.' I can help to rescind the agreements, if you're willing."

There was a burst of startled chatter. Derrick Yancy had turned a pale shade of red.

"Folks," said Hank Ryan, lifting his hands in a call for attention. "Let's come back together."

"You people are buying into something that doesn't exist," Derrick said, having regained tentative calm. "Money is what you need, not romantic nonsense. It's the modern era. Keep in touch on social media. It's not as though you can't make a phone call. What you can't make is your next mortgage payment."

There was a sobering slack in the chatter. Sensing his advantage, Derrick pressed, "Don't mismanage your money. Save it, invest it, move to a place where you can find work."

"Such as?" I demanded. "Name a place where there's work, at this very moment."

"Am I the Chamber of Commerce for the state of Montana?" Derrick snarled, in a tone so riddled with anger it seemed he'd struck my face. Three rows back, Case stood tense and watchful; I sensed his extreme dislike at the way Derrick had just spoken to me. Derrick looked out at the crowd, his face adopting an expression of calculated appeal. "I have roots here, indirectly, more than you could know. An ancestor of mine was cheated out of his land."

This was interesting; maybe not so calculated, after all? I made a mental note to add this to my Capital Overland file as the crowd grew noisy with chatter at this startling news. I looked over my shoulder, seeking Case, who was looking at me. I fought the need to elbow people from between us and run to him. Would he collect me close against his chest, if I dared to do such a thing? He sent me the briefest hint of a smile; was that admiration on his face?

The official meeting disbanded shortly thereafter; I tried to be patient, talking with Al and Hank Ryan, and the many people that mobbed us to ask endless strings of questions. I kept tabs on Case without appearing obvious, taking minute note of his position in the room, concerned that he would leave before I did. Nearly forty minutes rolled past before the room began emptying. Derrick had already vanished.

"Tish, you did a great job tonight. I'm officially impressed," Clark said, wrapping an arm about my shoulders; he'd finally managed to get close enough to Al and me for actual conversation.

"Thank you. I'm so glad you were here tonight." I tried not to let my gaze rove past Clark but I'd lost sight of Case. Would he avoid me? Where was he? Had he really left without saying good-bye?

"We're homeward bound. Have you had supper?" Clark asked.

"Yes." It was a true statement if you counted a handful of crackers.

"We'll plan to see you Friday," Clark said, kissing my temple before taking his leave.

Case is gone.

I didn't get to talk to him.

I can't believe he left without—

Wait!

There he was. I couldn't suppress the giddy swell of happiness any more than I could jump and snag a couple of stars from the night sky. In a frantic rush, I scraped my things together, stuffing notebooks and manila folders in my briefcase; pencils fell to the floor but I left them. Case was chatting with the Nelson family but appeared ready to leave; he stood near the door, his gray sport coat folded over his forearms.

"Al, I'll see you tomorrow!"

"Great job tonight, Tish!" Al called after me.

There was a jam in the flow of people and I tried not to appear as concerned as I felt, that Case would leave before I reached him. I couldn't see him through the crowd. A folder slid from my partially-unzipped briefcase and loose paper spread across the carpet like an old-fashioned lace fan.

"*Dammit*," I muttered, shuffling things in order to attempt to stoop delicately in my heels and skirt to gather up the strewn notes. The briefcase strap slipped from my shoulder and thudded to the floor, spilling additional contents; I felt like crying and hated myself.

"That was some courageous work." And Case was suddenly beside me, crouching down to help collect the mess.

"You're here." I stared foolishly at him, suddenly motionless.

"Can I walk you to your car?" he asked. He grinned at my obvious fluster, his arms full of my notes. Meanwhile my skirt was riding up my thighs. With as much grace as I could manage, I stood, unable to peel my eyes from him as he rose to his full height.

"Of course," I whispered.

"Here," he said, amusement coloring his tone. A smile lingered in his eyes, crinkling them at the outer corners. He indicated my briefcase with a tilt of his head and stashed the papers inside. We reached for the zipper at the same moment, hands colliding; the bag bumped my hip and I laughed, taut with heady tension.

"Thank you," I muttered, face scorching.

Case rolled back the cuffs of his dress shirt as we walked along the hall leading to the foyer, looking more like the cowboy musician I knew with each step, but I liked this. I liked it far more than I could even begin to admit. I loved the way he'd spoken so calmly and yet with such controlled fire, going after Yancy along with me; I wished I was brave enough to tell him so but my tongue was currently tied in a tight knot. I thought about what I had learned tonight, not the least of which that Case was a man of conviction. He was forthright. He stated his opinions with dignity, though I suspected he would be more than willing to take the gloves off, if push came to shove.

I respected that immensely.

And, if I was totally honest, it made me hotter than fucking hell.

At the heavy double doors leading outside, he moved ahead and opened them for me, and I used this as an excuse to look up at him. I found my voice. "Thank you."

"My pleasure," he said easily, as we were immersed in the balm of the summer evening. The sky was crystalline with starshine and I took a moment to inhale the sweetness in the air; I was close enough to Case as we descended the stone steps that I could smell his aftershave, something rich and pleasantly spicy. I fantasized about putting my face against his neck and my breasts against his chest.

The parking lot was emptying of vehicles, taillights flashing as the residents of Jalesville headed for home. I thought of all the people who were worried, worried deep in their bones, that the homesteads where their families had put down roots and carved a life for them generations earlier were now threatened. How many of these people were driving home tonight thinking about the fact that they may be displaced by this time next year? That they would have no choice but to sell to Capital Overland, in the end.

Case and I reached the sidewalk in front of the courthouse and I paused, watching people climb into their vehicles, hearing the muted murmurs of conversations through open car windows. Had I done anything to help them this evening? Case remained at my side and I had the sense he was watching me from the corner of his eye, even though he was gazing at the parking lot.

"I wish I felt like I'd done some good tonight," I said, unhooking my jacket at the waist. I was sweaty and my jacket felt too tight so I shrugged out of its confines; beneath it, my sleeveless blouse was limp with sweat.

Case turned to me. "Hey. You were incredible in there, if you don't mind my saying. Yancy was doing his best to take you out at the knees but you didn't let him push you around. That's impressive."

His words buoyed my stomach and charged through my heart; had I been fishing for a compliment? I curled my jacket around my right forearm. "Well, you were pretty damn impressive yourself. You care, and people sense that."

He shrugged, looking into the distance, at the outline of the mountains on the western horizon; it was so difficult to tell if my words had any impact upon him at all. At last he said quietly, "I do care. Jalesville is my home. I know it doesn't mean shit to someone like Yancy, but it's all I've got. It's all most people around here have. We have to stick this through, together."

He means himself and the other residents, not you!

Tish, you idiot.

"You're right," I whispered. The air grew quiet as cars and trucks vanished down the road, raising a fine, silty dust in their wakes. My heartbeat seemed amplified, as though I had my ears plugged. Case turned his chin back in my direction and tipped it down to look in my eyes. His shoulders, clad in the pale shirt, were wide and strong against the dark sky. He stood with his jacket caught over his wrists, held to his stomach. He was wearing his stone face again. I couldn't draw a full breath.

He said, "This was a worthwhile evening and you should be proud of yourself."

"Thank you," I whispered, the third time I'd thanked him in the past fifteen minutes.

More time crept past as we couldn't seem to look apart or find an excuse to say good-night. He lifted his right hand from beneath his sport coat and my heart leaped, but he was just fishing the truck keys from his pocket. "I play this evening, so I better get going."

"Out at the fairgrounds?" I asked, even though I knew damn well that's where he was headed; I was concocting shallow excuses to keep him a little longer. I wanted him to ask me to come listen to the music, too shy to do so otherwise, even though the fairground was very near Stone Creek.

He nodded.

I was pulling at strings to keep him here. "I'll have to text Camille and Mathias about this evening. They'll want to hear about it."

He smiled then, his gaze moving up and to the left, backward through time. "I wish they lived out here. It seems like yesterday that we all met. That was such an incredible night." His eyes flashed again to mine as he said, "For a number of reasons."

"They miss it out here."

"Yeah, I miss them, too. I felt so at home with them, the both of them." He seemed in a hurry then, shifting his jacket over his left shoulder and holding out a polite hand to let me lead the way. I did, feeling as deflated as a leftover party balloon. It was only a handful of steps to my car; there, I fought the terrible urge to catch his shirtsleeve.

I filched my keys from my purse and forced a cheerful tone. "Have a good evening, then."

"Good-night." I was probably imagining I heard a note of regret in his voice. Yes, clearly I was imagining this, as Case barely paused before continuing toward his truck, several rows over. I stood there in the parking lot watching him go, disappointment crushing my breastbone. But then he paused and turned back—my heart flared with hope.

"See you at the Rawleys' on Friday?"

"I'll be there," I responded.

Three days away, I thought as I drove home to Stone Creek.

Friday is three whole days away.

You're crazy as a jaybird, girl, I heard Gran say, my dear great-grand-mother, who'd died almost ten years ago now.

Crazy as a fucking jaybird, I agreed.

I showered in scalding water, then donned a long pajama t-shirt and curled up on the couch to look over my notes on Capital Overland; I added the bit about the alleged Yancy ancestor who'd been cheated out of land, deciding I would research this particular vein of information instead of taking Derrick's word. Finally, I closed the notebook and pressed both hands to my face.

I wish I was watching him play right now.

I could hear the tinkling sound of a guitar across the creek, from the fairgrounds.

I want to be near him.

I have no right to want these things.

When would he get home tonight? Would he go straight there after singing? His home, his family's land; it was all he and Gus had left in the world, Case had said. Were the chili-pepper lights strung over the door glowing? Did Buck and Cider come from the barn and poke their noses over the top of the corral to greet him when he pulled into the yard? What if a black 4x4 was even now prowling his property? I sat straight at that thought, knowing I had to tell him.

Why were you driving past his place on Friday evening, anyway? How would you explain that to him?

Miserable, I tossed aside the notebook and wrapped into my own arms.

Hours later, deep in the night, a storm rolled over Jalesville, the thunder grumbling a low-pitched threat, rain spattering the windowpanes. It wasn't quite enough to wake me, instead incorporating into my dream. And in my dream, I held Case's head to my breasts, my fingers in his hair as he plied his tongue over my nipples. My breath came in panting gasps. I couldn't get enough of his hot, caressing kisses. The growl of the thunder was my desire; my head fell back and I begged him for more as he held me close with both strong hands spread wide across my naked back.

I woke to an especially frightful crash and fell off the couch. Heart hammering, I lay flat on my spine and tried to make sense of what was happening. My body was rigid with tension; I'd come awake in the middle of a powerful orgasm. I could hardly move for the sensations rioting through me. Lightning sizzled, backlighting the curtains, followed by another tremendous, building-rattling burst, and I jerked to a sitting position, a wave of dizziness blurring my vision.

"Holy shit," I gasped as my apartment was inundated by unearthly blue-white light. "Oh, holy Jesus."

My dream was still happening in my head and I closed my eyes, desperate to return to it, shaking as I cupped my breasts; my nipples felt like gemstones. I shuddered, bending forward, and somehow understood that I would see Case before Friday. I knew it, and this knowledge filled me with enough strength to climb back onto the couch and sleep until morning.

Chapter Nine

I SPENT THE ENTIRE NEXT DAY BATTLING THE URGE TO run straight down the sidewalk to Spicer Music, where I had not yet been brave enough to venture, and burst through the door to see Case. Just see him. That was all. Just put my eyes upon him. Then I would unbutton my blouse...

Tish, you are crazy. Cra-zy.

But it was such a realistic dream...

At the law office, Al was so proud of how I'd presented myself last night that he couldn't quit remarking; he might as well have been my father. I thanked him repeatedly, honored by his praise. Evidence of my good work bore fruit even before noon; three different families called the office to say that they had officially turned down prior offers from Capital Overland.

"Minor victories are still victories!" I crowed, toasting Al with my coffee mug.

"None are minor in this instance." Al beamed. "I'm scheduled in court at one. You hold down the fort for me, all right, counselor?"

"Aye, captain," I teased.

By the time I finished work at six I was rabid to see Case. I drove home and frittered around the apartment for two hours before making up my mind. Resolved, I changed into a soft, daisy-print sundress (an old one of Camille's that I may have borrowed without her knowing) and strappy sandals. I intended to wander the fairgrounds on the off chance that Case would be done performing and looking for me, too. I knew he was playing on the main stage tonight, along with Marshall, but I had no idea what time.

Dressed and ready, I debated driving versus walking. It would likely be late when I came back home but it was a beautiful, mellow evening and the fairgrounds weren't far; minutes later I was strolling along the gravel path that led to the bridge spanning Stone Creek. Beyond the creek stretched the county fair, the sounds of which had played in the background while I brushed my hair and applied mascara. I could smell mini donuts and popcorn from a hundred paces out. At the main entrance, two older men with orange vests and pocket aprons waved me inside the gate.

"Have fun, honey," said one of them. "Your fee is on us."

"Good work at the meeting last night," said the other, and I blushed with pleasure.

"Thank you," I told them.

There was just no such thing as a county fair in a place the size of Chicago. I was taken back to my high school days in Landon as I walked along the midway, drinking in the sights and sounds. Food vendors in trailers painted with brilliant colors and decorated with flashing bulbs. Music blasting from the bigger rides, like the Ferris wheel and the Zipper, the intermittent clacking of the roller coaster. Carnival games, where you could win huge stuffed animals and t-shirts with neon slogans. I was surprised by the amount of people who called me by name, and whose names I knew in return; I might as well have been at Trout Days, back in Landon, warmed by this notion.

Despite the growing sense of familiarity, I was too shy to ask anyone when Case and Marshall would be playing. The main stage was located through the grandstand arches, not visible from the midway, and the crowd was increasing now that the sun had set, the mood ever more boisterous. I began to feel like a stalker, scanning groups of people at first covertly and then less so. As my heart was literally palpitating, I decided I needed to quit walking in circles and that a drink was in order. Fortunately I spied the striped awning of the beer garden. Two women were working the counter of a small building open to the outside, lit by candle lanterns. Though I could have ducked inside to what was surely a bigger bar, I claimed a stool at the outdoor counter, where I could continue to observe the action on the midway.

"Hi, hon," said a curvy woman with a deep tan, lots of eyeliner, and long hair held back in a clip; I recognized her as a server from The Spoke. She leaned her palms on the counter opposite. "What can I get you?"

"Whatever you have on tap." I was in the mood for beer. "Thank you."

"Coming right up."

I heard excitement ripple through the crowd seated on the grandstand risers, just beyond my sight, and someone using a microphone drawled, "Good evening, Jalesville!"

I sprang to attention—but it wasn't Case or Marshall.

"Here you go," the bartender said. "Can I start you a tab?"

"Isn't Case playing tonight?" I asked, subtlety be damned.

"He and Marsh played the early set. Traded spots with the guys on now."

I would *not* ask if Case was still here. I would not.

Don't you dare start crying! Jesus, Tish...

But you just walked around for an hour and he already left.

"Speaking of the devil," the bartender muttered, nodding at something over my shoulder. I dared a look, fidgeting with my hair as if that was my excuse for movement.

Case was headed our way from a distance, guitar case in hand, black backpack slung over his shoulder. He was wearing his customary jeans and t-shirt combo this evening, cowboy hat in place, chin lowered a little as he listened to the guy he was walking with, who was also carrying an instrument.

"Dang. He is *such* a sexy man," the bartender murmured and my gaze flew back to her face.

It would not be in your best interest to tear out her eyes, I told myself, taking a long pull of my beer.

She smoothed both palms down the front of her server apron and thrust out her breasts as she continued watching Case. My hackles rose, sharp as spikes. As though I was a good friend instead of a virtual stranger, she confided, "I told Lynnette she was crazy to let him go. I've heard he's incredible in bed, and I believe it. Takes his time on all the right spots, if you know what I mean." She looked at me and winked.

I hid behind another long swallow; my nipples became hard pearls and a burst of heat smashed through my lower body. Goddammit, of fucking *course* she would say such a thing to me right now. Just what I needed to hear.

"Another, sweetie?" She nodded at my now-empty glass.

"Sure," I muttered. My voice was hoarse.

She filled a second beer and set it in front of me while I used every bit of willpower I possessed to remain facing away from Case, determined not to turn and watch him approach; never mind that I was dying for him to come and sit by me. Probably he would walk right past.

But then the bartender smiled in an undeniably warm welcome. "You guys ready for a drink? Sounded good earlier."

"Yes, ma'am," said a man I didn't recognize. "And we're plenty thirsty."

I turned on the barstool to see Case with his eyes on me.

He's here, he's here, he's here!

I rejoiced at this fact even as I played it cool. I hadn't seen him since the parking lot at the courthouse last night. Well, unless I counted my thunderstorm-induced dream.

"Take a load off, guys," the bartender invited and my heart shot up somewhere near the stratosphere as Case claimed a stool to my left, leaving one empty between us. He braced his guitar case beneath the edge of the bar. The other guy sat on Case's far side, grinning at the woman behind the counter.

I tilted my chin to peek at Case, who looked my way at the same moment. Candy colors flashed over our faces and there was a chorus of screams as the Zipper rattled to life across the midway. Music from the main stage played in the background.

"Hey," he said softly.

"Hey," I whispered, eating him up with my eyes. The candle lanterns spun gold in his hair. "I guess I missed your show."

"We traded spots," he affirmed, accepting a beer from the bartender with a polite thank-you; she smiled, tugging the brim of his hat, and I thought my glass might just shatter in my grip.

"Lee, this is Patricia Gordon," Case said then, surprising me. *My first name!* He hadn't ever spoken it in my presence.

The bartender leaned her hips against the counter. "So you're the new lawyer in town working for Al. Well, nice to meet you, Patricia."

"And this is Lee Heller. Her family manages The Spoke. They're cousins with Garth and those guys," Case explained.

I reached to shake her hand. "I'm pleased to meet you."

"Dad was saying that the new lawyer at the meeting seemed like a little pistol," Lee said, eyebrows lifting as she regarded me anew. "I see Case has already recruited you to his side of the land debate."

Case laughed a little at her words. "I did no such thing. And watch who you're calling names, now."

"It's a compliment!" Lee insisted. "Means you impressed him, and my dad isn't easy to impress. Means you're getting the job done, just like a pistol would."

"What Lee's dad didn't mention was that you're gorgeous," said the guy on the far side of Case. He rose and came to stand closer to my barstool, extending his free hand. "Since Casey obviously isn't going to introduce us, I'm Travis Woodrow."

Case took a long drink from his beer as I shook Travis's hand. Travis was about my age probably, stocky and cute, with a black cowboy hat and a dark goatee; he added, "Nice to meet you, Patricia."

"It's Tish," I explained. "I mean, that's what everyone calls me."

"That's all kinds of cute," Travis said smoothly, reclaiming his seat. "You see our show, Miss Tish?"

"No, I got here too late."

Travis said, "I happen to have a roll of tickets right here, in my pocket."

Lee burst into laughter. "Watch out, he'll want you to reach in his pocket, next thing."

Travis grinned, leaning around Case to insist, "I've been crazy to ride that Ferris wheel tonight. You want to join me, little lawyer lady?"

" 'Lawyer lady?' " I repeated with just enough bite in my tone, to which

Travis was totally oblivious, and Lee laughed even harder. Case might as well have been deaf to everything we were saying, barely reacting at all.

"Yeah, you sure know how to win 'em over, Trav," Lee giggled, refastening the clip holding back her hair.

"Come on," Travis wheedled. "It'll be fun. I'll keep my hands on the bar at all times."

"I need to unwind for a little while." I held up my glass to indicate, and was surely imagining the satisfaction that flickered across Case's expression.

"Later?" Travis pressed.

"Maybe," I allowed, as Lee moved down the bar to wait on an approaching group. As though a floodgate somewhere had released a burst of thirsty people, the bar grew busy. A man jostled my elbow, apologizing even as he crowded closer.

Without questioning the action, I scooted over to the left, freeing the space for the group to my right. Case acknowledged the proximity of our bodies with the faintest flicker of an eyelash. Determined to engage him in conversation, I leaned forward. "Have you been here long today?"

Travis filled in, "Since the early set. We're done for the evening now."

Case angled just slightly toward me; his right knee and my left were only about four inches apart. My leg was bare, his in jeans, and I wondered just what would happen if I pressed my skin against the denim on his thigh.

Your mind is clouded by lack of sex, I tried to rationalize. *It's fucking up your judgment.*

Takes his time on all the right spots...

Goddammit to hell.

"Did you walk over?" Case asked. He looked so damn good that I needed to take another long drink before I could answer this simple question. His jaw appeared chiseled, lightly stubbled with a day's growth of beard, his gaze holding mine as he waited patiently for my response. I noticed then that there were slight shadow-smudges beneath his eyes, as though he hadn't slept well. He sat with his forearms lining the bar, a posture which emphasized his wide shoulders. The lanterns created a warm glow around us and highlighted the hair on his arms.

"I did," I said. I had taken a good five seconds to respond, which was weird, I realized. He probably thought I was drunk. There were so many things I wanted to ask him, not the least of which what he thought of Derrick Yancy's claim about his ancestor's land. But I couldn't seem to form coherent sentences, caught up in studying him.

"Wy was saying something about how you wanted a cat," Case said. I felt as though we were encased in our own little private bubble, the laughter and chatter, the hard-rock music from the main stage, distant from us.

"Yeah, I told him that the other night at supper," I admitted. "It's a little lonely at my apartment. I mean, I'm so used to the company of other people. I shared a room with my younger sister forever. I don't have enough time to take care of a dog, but Clark suggested that maybe a cat would be perfect."

"One of my guitar students has one he's been trying to get rid of, that's why I brought it up," Case said. "I can tell him that you'd like it, if you're interested. Otherwise I thought I might keep her."

I thought suddenly of Clark's story, about Case's abusive father making him shoot a pet dog. What kind of despicable bastard would do such a thing to his son? My eyes flickered to Case's lips and the scar on his chin, to the evidence of shadowy sleeplessness beneath his eyes, and then I looked entirely away, back to my beer. I felt hollow and strange. I realized I hadn't answered his question.

"You can tell him I'm interested." My voice was hardly more than a whisper.

"I'll see him tomorrow. Will do."

"Thank you." I was unable to keep my eyes from him. He was thoughtful. He didn't take people's shit, but he was thoughtful, and kind.

Travis, who had been joined by a noisy group of people, mostly girls, leaned around Case to order, "Time's up! Tish, lawyer lady, let's go ride that Ferris wheel!"

I could tell Case wanted to smile at my irritation over the stupid nickname.

"You go ahead," I told Travis. "I'm still having a drink."

Travis held up a crumpled roll of tickets and declared good-naturedly, "Don't make me beg!"

On inspiration, I asked Case, "You up for a couple of rides?"

He finished his beer with two more swallows and said, not meeting my eyes, "I need to get home and feed the animals."

He set a five dollar bill on the bar, then stood and collected his guitar and backpack from the ground. I watched all of this with a sickly feeling of desolation in my gut. For a second I thought he was just going to walk away without so much as a farewell; he'd shouldered the pack, guitar case in hand, but then he said, "Please be careful walking home."

Stone Creek was close enough it would have been visible, were it day rather than night. His tone was casual but his eyes were momentarily intent, holding fast to mine as he spoke these words. My heart lurched.

"I lived in Chicago for the last three years." I spoke with the same casual tone, trying to tease. "I think I'm good to go."

He continued to study me, somber and unsmiling.

Offer me a ride, please, oh please, I'll go right now.

"See you around," he said, then nudged Travis's shoulder. "See ya, buddy."

"Casey! You gotta go already?" Travis complained. "You're getting old!"

Case smiled and said, "Shit happens," and then walked away without a backward glance. I watched him until all I could make out was his hat, before he disappeared into the crowd.

Travis asked merrily, "So how about that ride?"

I joined their group for a while; we rode the Ferris wheel and the bumper cars, the tilt-a-whirl, and I enjoyed myself to a degree. But I begged off early, despite Travis's protests, and made my lone way across a plowed dirt field currently in use as a parking lot. Stone Creek was in sight as I wound between the rows of cars and trucks. My shoes had caused blisters and I had just slipped out of them, carrying them by the heel straps and proceeding barefoot, when someone said, "Counselor Gordon. I thought that was you."

I smelled cigarette smoke, startled by the sound of a voice where I was not expecting one. I turned to see Derrick Yancy leaning against a black 4x4 with tinted windows, one row over, smoking and watching me.

Not sure exactly how to respond, I heard myself say, "I thought you were from Illinois."

He narrowed his eyes, questioning what I meant.

I explained, "Your plates say 'Colorado.'"

"Observant," he said, drawing on his smoke. He was dressed much less formally this evening than last night. He skirted a couple of cars and walked over to me, darkly attractive and undeniably intimidating, not that I would dream of letting him see that I felt intimidated. He blocked my path and made an observation of his own. "No shoes this evening?"

I held up my sandals by their straps.

Why the fuck were you on the Spicers' land last week at night, you slimy bastard?

I wished I was brave enough to grill him.

You have to tell Case about this. No more excuses.

"I meant to offer you my compliments last night," Derrick said, catching me off guard, and I reprimanded myself. I couldn't afford to be caught that way, not with what amounted to be my opponent. I drew the mantle of the last three years' worth of training over my shoulders.

"I'm good at what I do," I said briskly, imitating my father at his most lawyerly.

Derrick chuckled, letting his gaze glide down my front, lingering on my breasts. "I'd offer you a job right here, right now, if I thought you were at all inclined."

"Not in a million years, but thank you all the same." I would not fidget, no matter how much my stomach churned with unease, hearing a former professor in my mind, one who had maintained that the downfall of young lawyers was the unconscious tendency to fidget and therefore project uncertainty. I kept my shoulders back and held his increasingly familiar gaze.

"You're much too lovely to be in a career as brutal as law," he murmured. Did he actually think he could win points with such condescending flattery? I realized he wasn't so much complimenting me as he was pressing his assertion that I was less-than, inferior to his experience and gender.

"And you're far too presumptuous," I responded, maintaining a friendly playing field.

"Just calling things as I see them." He edged one shoulder closer to me, really studying my face. I sensed he was moving in for the kill. Hoping I was maybe just drunk enough to figure it was worth it to do something really stupid, like accompany him back to his fancy hotel. He struck me as a big fan of one-night stands.

"Why are you here, anyway?" I asked. "At the fair. It all seems so *beneath* you."

"Maybe I was hoping to run into someone specific."

I refused to take this pathetic bait. "Then I'll let you find him."

I moved to step around him but he caught my upper arm in a hard grip.

"It's early, you don't need to go," he whispered, very close to my ear. He smelled overpoweringly of expensive cologne and cigarettes.

"Get your fucking hand off me," I ordered, not about to let him see my fear. At least, so I hoped.

In what was obviously a nonverbal taunt, he ran his thumb over my skin before obeying and letting go. I released the breath of air I'd withdrawn, prepared to scream for all I was worth, and the sounds of the fair rushed back to my ears.

"See you around, *Patricia*."

I ignored this, forcing myself to walk rather than run as I resumed my barefoot journey toward Stone Creek. At home behind a locked door less than five minutes later, I paced my little balcony, tense with this latest information. I debated calling Case, not that I had his number. I wanted to tell him about the 4x4 driving on his property. I wanted him to come over, though that was out of the question. I comforted myself with the thought that I would perhaps see him tomorrow.

No more stalling over telling him about Derrick.

Agitated and energized, I stalked back inside, clicking on more lights and the radio. I changed into a long pajama shirt and situated myself on the couch to reread my notes, adding the new info.

Capital Overland—potential trespassers

Derrick Yancy—possesses a GMC 4x4 from Colorado, uncertain if he was driving it on 7/12 when it was on Case's property

Yancy ancestor—possibly cheated of land?

I chewed the end of my pencil, staring at the silver square of my laptop. I leaned to grab it, opening it over my knees, intending to research the Yancy family but instead typing *Case Spicer* into the search engine. At least I was in my apartment, no one to catch me spying. Still, my hands trembled as though I was committing a crime as I clicked on the Images link and pictures of him spread like a checkerboard across the screen.

More than thirty minutes passed, but I only realized when I glanced at the toolbar clock and saw that it was after midnight. And still I kept clicking on images of Case, punishing myself somehow, especially drawn to the photos of him playing his music. There was one in which he was holding the fiddle (and it was always with the fiddle that he closed his eyes), bent just slightly forward, such an expression of concentration on his face and yet joy was present, too, an aching joy. I could tell this just from the set of his lips, the angle of his head, the way his eyes were shut.

What was he playing that night, in that particular picture? I wondered. Then I saw a small triangle in the center of another image. I clicked this and cranked up the volume, and heard laughter and chatter; the video was poor quality, grainy and jerky, as though held in the hand of someone who'd been drinking, but I could tell it had been shot at The Spoke. Case and Garth were both on the stage, laughing together before the audience quieted and they lifted their instruments, Case on the fiddle. He closed his eyes the moment it was positioned under his chin.

I tried to zoom in but it wouldn't let me. I could hear the Rawleys murmuring in the background; Sean seemed to be the camera operator. I full-screened the video and restarted it; when the music began Garth was singing lead and I recognized the song as one we'd sung on the porch that summer the Rawleys visited Landon, "Red River Valley." Case played the violin with so much skill, such obvious love, each note with its own haunting sweetness. He sang harmony with Garth, his beautiful voice that made tears form in my eyes. It was the late hour, the lack of sleep, it was the homesickness in my heart…it was all of these things.

The song ended to raucous whistling and applause and I was about to start it over when, in the video, a woman appeared in the shot—I realized, with a start, that it was the woman named Lynnette. Of course she'd been sitting with the Rawleys, watching the show. She approached the stage and Case grinned. As I watched, he leaned down to kiss her, catching the back of her head in one big hand, holding his fiddle to the side so it wouldn't bump her. She put her hands on his shoulders and it was a long kiss, a good ten seconds. My stomach surged, my throat tightened; I clenched my jaws.

I scanned for the date the video was posted, seeing that it was from November of 2009. Newly-married then. Was this taken when Lynnette was still pregnant? What had I been doing that November? Last year at U of M, frantically prepping and reviewing for the looming LSAT exam, sleeping occasionally with Randy, the last of my longer-term boyfriends. In the video, Case hopped from the stage and collected his wife to his chest. He murmured something in her ear and they rocked side to side as they hugged.

I slammed the laptop closed.

Chapter Ten

THE NEXT DAY I WAS THE ONE WITH SLEEPLESS SHADOWS beneath my eyes. Despite a dull headache I worked like a champ, drafting minor things for Al, reorganizing files; Dad had always joked that a lawyer's primary work was paperwork. The clock hands swung around to noon; Mary and Al went home for lunch, as usual, but I had neglected to bring anything to eat. I sighed and decided to take the time to drive home, too, not that there was anything edible in my fridge. But I was restless as hell. Remaining alone in the office was not an option; I would go out of my mind. Outside under the hot, dry sunshine I climbed into the oven that was my car and turned over the engine, only to hear a grinding chug.

"Dammit," I muttered, trying once more; the Honda didn't start, instead issuing a pathetic wheezing. I slapped my hands on the steering wheel. "*Dammit!*"

Back at my desk, I debated what to do about the car. Clark would certainly help me, or maybe Al could recommend someone. Just what I needed right now. I reached for my cup of coffee, without looking, and bumped the edge of a picture of Camille, Ruthie, Clint, and me, knocking it to the floor and shattering the glass in the frame.

"Dammit," I said for the third time. My headache intensified. I wanted to cry.

I knelt down to check out the damage, glancing around for a broom. Shit, I knew Al kept one somewhere. I grabbed an empty file folder, intending to create a makeshift dustpan to scoop up the shards. I collected the biggest pieces and was holding a large, jagged handful when

I heard the bell above the door. I looked up and received what felt like a lightning bolt straight to the heart. Ironically, Case, holding a white cat in his arms, was standing right beside the AED box on the wall. He was wearing a blue t-shirt and sunglasses braced over the top of his head. His eyebrows lifted.

"You're bleeding," he said, dropping the cat and coming at once behind the counter.

The glass in my hand tinkled back to the floor as I opened my fist—he was right, blood dripped over my palm like a gory instance of stigmata, running down my wrist.

"Here, let me see." He was calm and reassuring, crouching beside me, grasping my forearm to inspect the damage. "I think it looks worse than it is. There's no glass stuck in there that I can see."

I hadn't yet located my voice. His fingers were warm on my skin. He was close enough that I could smell him, aftershave and soap and dusty denim and sweat, a heady elixir. He seemed to find my speechlessness amusing; I watched a smile start in his eyes and move to his lips.

"Does Al have a first-aid kit?" he asked.

"I don't know," I said miserably, and then couldn't help but giggle, a nervous huff of sound. "Some professional lawyer I am."

He grinned, gently releasing my arm. "Why don't you go wash your hand and I'll get this cleaned up."

I found a first-aid kit in the bathroom, but it was empty of anything but a fingernail clipper. Blood spiraled down the sink and the liquid soap stung; my face was a thousand degrees. I wadded up a bundle of paper towels and pressed them to the cuts, then rejoined Case, who had located the dustpan and made short work of the broken glass. The cat prowled near and twined around my ankles.

"Who's this?" I asked, bending to scoop her up with my uninjured hand. The cat was glossy white, with translucent green eyes.

"That's Peaches," Case said, emptying glass shards into the garbage. "She's a sweet girl. Do you think you might want to keep her?"

She began purring, rubbing her soft, rumbling face against my ribs. "I do. Thank you. Thank you so much."

He stashed the broom and dustpan and came near; I kept my eyes on the cat, pretending I didn't feel my heartbeat everywhere in my body, including my injured palm. I couldn't banish the picture of Case cupping his wife's head and kissing her, the tender possessiveness his touches conveyed.

It's none of your business!

Never mind that you focused on it half the night.

You're jealous as hell.

I'm not!

Case ran one hand over the cat's sleek fur. "I have all the things that my student left for her, including a bag of litter. You want me to put them in your car? I'll bring her back to the music shop with me until this evening. I just thought you might want to meet her right now."

I looked up and simply drank in the sight of him, observing that his eyes still bore traces of sleeplessness. He was hatless, his red-gold hair appearing soft, his eyes holding fast to mine. I wanted to lean closer, even though he was close enough that I could almost feel his breath on my cheek.

I stumbled over an explanation. "My car isn't running right now. I'll probably get a ride home from Al and then try to figure out what's wrong with it. And thank you, that's sweet of you."

"I hate to tell you, there's blood on your skirt." He nodded toward my legs.

"Shit!" I muttered.

Peaches squirreled free of my arm and leaped to the floor, where she proceeded to walk with mincing little steps, fluffy tail aloft.

Case said decisively, "Why don't I run you home right now? You can change and then we can leave all her things at your place."

"You don't mind?" I asked, trembling at the thought of him in my apartment.

"Not one bit," he said easily, leaning to collect Peaches. "You look like you just committed a murder."

I glanced at my sleek gray skirt, now blood-smeared. "Thank you. You don't have to do this."

"It's no problem," he insisted, maddeningly polite, as though I was his little sister. Or a family friend.

You are a family friend!

I grabbed my purse from the bottom desk drawer and flipped the sign in the window to CLOSED.

That's exactly what you are. Jesus, Tish.

Case held the door, which I locked behind us, and then opened the passenger door for me at his truck, parked across the street. The interior smelled as it had last week when I'd retrieved the fiddle case, herbal and spicy, just like him. His truck was dated but well cared for, the bench seat upholstered in smooth beige leather. His cowboy hat lay on the seat and really quickly I ran my fingertips over it. I watched him round the hood, sunlight glinting off his hair, Peaches prowling along the floor at my ankles. He climbed in, replaced his sunglasses over his eyes and donned his hat, with naturally graceful motions that reminded me of the way he'd saddled Cider the other night.

"It smells so good in here," I said as he shifted into first and executed a quick U-turn.

He tapped a bundle hanging from the rearview mirror, which I hadn't noticed. "Sagebrush. It grows all over in the foothills."

"Case." I spoke in a rush, before I completely lost my nerve. "Last night I ran into Derrick Yancy at the fair. On the way home. He was in the parking lot. He stopped me, and tried to feed me a bunch of shit about how the law was too brutal a career for me—"

"He said that?" Case interrupted, low and quiet. "He spoke to you that way?"

"He was being an asshole. Asserting his sense of power." Never mind how he'd grabbed my arm. I didn't feel compelled to mention that particular detail, nor how much Derrick frightened me; I didn't want to seem like a coward.

"He's a bully," Case said, grit in his tone. His hands fisted around the steering wheel. "No better than a fucking junkyard bully. He might dress well and have money, but that's all he is. He didn't try anything else, did he?" His voice was carefully neutral as he asked, but his shoulders were tense.

"No," I said, too quickly. "But he drives an SUV with Colorado plates."
Case looked my way. "I'm missing something here."

"I have to backtrack." I felt hot and squirmy, my injured palm aching and sweat collecting on my hairline. I stared out the windshield at the sunny day. "Last Friday, after dinner, I drove out past your house. I wanted to see it." I sensed his surprise like a third person in the truck, but plowed ahead. "I drove about a half-mile past your place and then I felt like I was going to get lost, so I parked. And then I paced for a while…"

Case was staring at me rather than the road; he probably thought I was crazy. I interrupted myself to say, "You missed the turn to Stone Creek…"

"Shit," he muttered, pulling to the curb, his hands hanging from the top of the steering wheel as he regarded me. Slowly, he lifted the sunglasses from his face and I braved a look at him. He was utterly stone-faced, an expression I'd already learned that he'd perfected.

I actually stuttered as I said, "P…pacing helps me collect my thoughts. I'm sure I was still on your property and it's important to tell you that because then I heard voices, way out in the foothills. I realized at least two men were walking out there. They got in a car and drove back to Jalesville, so I followed them, at a distance. And I realized just last night that it was Derrick Yancy's SUV I was following. I don't know if he was driving that night, or not. But they were trespassing on your property."

Case opened his mouth to say something but then seemed to think better of it, as he chewed his bottom lip for a second. He knitted his eyebrows, trying to process what the hell I'd just said, while hot sweat pooled between my breasts. Ignoring for the moment just why I had been, for lack of a better term, trespassing on his property, too, he finally said, "That was probably dangerous of you."

"They had no idea." I spoke with more assurance than I felt. "What do you think they were doing out there?"

I could almost see his thoughts whirling; he looked out the windshield and said, "I knew there was something more to this. I *knew* it. There's something they're not letting on."

"What can we do? Should we tell Clark? Hank Ryan?"

Peaches stuck her nose in Case's side and purred. He stroked her absently with his right hand. "Not just yet. I have an idea, though."

"What's that?" I demanded, excited despite everything.

"How do you feel, professionally, about a stakeout?"

"You mean out on your property?"

"Where else?" A smile had already started in his eyes.

"I better dig out my hiking boots."

My words prompted his full grin and I swallowed hard at the sight, my hands curling into tight fists because I wanted to touch him and I knew I could not. The clenching motion drove nails through my injured palm.

"We better get you home and then back to work," he said, growing very businesslike all of a sudden, driving around the block to get back to the right street.

"What could be out there worth prowling around in the dark for?" I pressed, trying to forget about how much I craved another sight of his smile.

"There's a local legend about gold that was buried back in the 1800s somewhere around here. It's been a tall tale in our area for over a century, so it's plausible that Yancy may know the story. My pa—" He paused only slightly but I knew enough, thanks to Clark, to have at least a context for understanding this hesitation. Case went on, more quietly, "My pa believed in it. When I was a boy he used to spend nights out there in the foothills, searching for it."

"He did?"

Case's jaws tightened, almost unconsciously, and again I restrained the urgent desire to touch him, his hand or his shoulder...his face...

"He was a drunk," he said, softly and without rancor. But I could hear pain in his voice, no matter how deeply buried. "We were poor and he believed in that gold. After my mom died, he spent even more time out there, searching."

I wanted to ask why; I especially wanted to ask him about his mother, Melinda, but we'd reached the gravel parking lot at Stone Creek, so I shelved the urge. "You can park in my spot, right there."

Case did so and I collected Peaches, tucking her against my side as he jogged around the hood to open the door for me. After I climbed out he leaned back in the truck to grab a few things from behind the front seats.

"I can carry something else," I said. He was juggling an armload but shook his head, hat and sunglasses in place. Holding Peaches, I readjusted the purse strap on my shoulder and dug around for my keys as we walked into the cool interior of the apartment building.

"Second floor," I said, leading the way up the carpeted steps. We were silent on the way to 206, just down the hall. I unlocked it, vividly aware of him close behind me, and let Peaches jump to the floor. "You can put that stuff anyplace. I'll be right back."

I retreated to my bedroom, all hopped up, hardly able to breathe. I leaned against the closed door and pressed both hands to my blazing cheeks, hearing him out in my kitchen. I was very conscious of my almost-nude body as I slipped from my bloody skirt and limp blouse, and stood in non-matching lingerie at the edge of the closet. I hadn't done laundry in days. My heart would not slow its pace. My skin felt feverish. I could hear Case out there, murmuring to Peaches. My nipples rubbed against my lacy bra and I cupped my breasts, bending forward.

You're taking too long!

At last, growing desperate, I grabbed a casual cotton sundress that I would never have dreamed of wearing to work at a law office in Chicago; not that Al wouldn't mind or probably even notice, one way or the other. I couldn't tie the lacing that wrapped around the waist, one-handed as I was at present, and fantasized for no more than a lightning flash about calling Case to come in here and help me.

Family friend, I thought, gritting my teeth. Case hadn't alluded to a word of the things that he'd said at Camille's wedding, leading me to the conclusion that he'd been drunk enough that the entire conversation had faded, if not fully evaporated, from his memory. Or, more likely, he'd reconsidered his youthful position on those matters.

You're the one who can't forget what he said that night.

You're the one who reads too much into things.

I gathered courage and emerged from my bedroom; Case and Peaches were on the balcony and I made my way to the open screen door.

Studying the mountains, his back to me, Case observed, "It's a great view out here. This is a nice little place."

"Would you mind helping me for a second?"

He turned around at this request; he was still wearing his cowboy hat and sunglasses, so I couldn't tell what he was really thinking; his mouth remained unsmiling.

"Sure," he said.

I stepped onto the balcony, the concrete warm under my bare feet. "Can you maybe help me tie this? I'm sorry…my hand…"

"Sure," he said again, sounding the slightest bit hoarse.

I turned and felt his hands take up the ties, just at my waist. It took effort to breathe normally; he was so tall and immediate behind me. He asked, "Knot or bowtie?"

To cover my bursting nerves, I griped, "A knot? Are you kidding me?"

"Bowtie it is then," he responded easily. His fingers brushed my waist and it took everything in me to repress a shiver.

"Thank you," I mumbled the second he was done, hurrying back inside and to the bathroom to inspect my palm. I washed my hands and slapped a couple of bandages over the cuts. My face was so flushed I appeared sunburned, my hair windblown from its clip. I refastened it; out in the living room, Case asked, "You want to leave Peaches here, see how she likes it?"

I rejoined him, all fluttery and butterflies-in-the-stomach at the sight of his eyes; he'd removed his sunglasses in the apartment.

"Sure, that's a good idea. Thank you again."

"Anytime," he returned. "We better get going…"

I bent to speak to my new cat. "Be good until I get back, all right?"

Outside the sun was edging toward afternoon, hot on our heads. Case opened the passenger door for me and I felt compelled to tell him, "You're such a gentleman."

"That's all my mom's doing," he said. "She was insistent. Gus was too little when she died, he doesn't remember her at all, but the one thing she wanted was for us to be polite. To treat ladies well, she said."

Probably because she was married to such a lowlife, I thought, watching Case's profile as he drove us back downtown. I said, "That's no small thing. And I'd say you learned well."

He changed the subject. "The fair is in town for two more nights. What are the odds –"

"Good, the odds are good," I interrupted, understanding exactly what he meant. I was afraid he would suddenly reconsider asking me to join him on a stakeout and was not about to let that happen. "What better time to sneak onto someone's land, when the whole town is preoccupied?"

"That's just what I was thinking," he murmured. I was watching his forearm as he shifted gear, the way the muscles along its length tightened. "You want to plan for tomorrow night, after dinner at Clark's?"

I wanted to be near him. I understood this with sterling, razor-edged clarity. I further understood that I could not let on that I felt this way.

It wouldn't be right.

Tish, it wouldn't be right.

Do you want him?

Yes, I fucking want him, but he's not the sort that you can have a fling with.

Half-kidding, I asked, "Do you have night vision goggles and all that?"

A flash of his grin. "No, but that would be a good idea."

"They were probably about a half-mile from your front yard, on the east side of the road."

"You'll have to show me where you saw them. Do you remember well enough?"

"I do," I said, thinking of the T-shaped wizard rock.

"How about if I pick you up after work today and we'll drive out there? While it's daylight, I mean. You said your car wasn't working…"

I refused to acknowledge the bursting bloom of joy this suggestion triggered. I said offhandedly, "I can be done by three, I'm sure Al wouldn't mind. How about you?"

"I have one last lesson at two. I'll take a look at your car when I'm done."

"You don't have to do that."

He shrugged. "No big deal."

We'd reached Howe and James. Case drew the truck to the shoulder and put it in park. Not wanting him to go to the trouble, knowing he would take the time to climb out and open my door, I hurried to say, "I got it this time. Thank you, for everything."

"See you later," he said, and I resisted the urge to look back as I stepped to the sidewalk and entered the little office as he drove away, I turned and all but pressed my nose to the glass to watch his truck roll down Main Street.

"See you later," I whispered.

At quarter to three I was replacing files in the conference room when I heard Mary say brightly, "Well, if it isn't Charles Spicer. What a nice surprise!"

"Afternoon, Mrs. Stapleton," he said. I pressed my knuckles to my lips, studying the slanted bar of sunlight gilding the dusty file cabinets, blood surging. I composed my face before stepping around the corner into the main room. Case's eyes held me tight. There was nothing on his face but politeness. His eyes didn't flash with a pulse of heat...

Not one bit...

He was wearing his hat, sunglasses hooked on the collar of his t-shirt, creating a little gap that exposed the line of his collarbones along the top of his chest. I wondered if he had red-gold hair there, too, and if his freckles continued downward on his body...

"Is young Mr. Spicer your beau, Patty?" Mary asked, clearly delighted at the prospect, clasping her be-ringed hands and smiling between the two of us.

Case, angled away from her, asked without sound, *Patty?*

I hid a giggle by biting my bottom lip. "He's helping me out with my car." And then I couldn't resist adding, "Charles and I are just friends."

Yes, friends. We're friends.

Nothing more.

"Ha, *ha*," he muttered, narrowing his eyes as he couldn't quite contain a smile. He explained, "I came to get your keys."

"They're in my purse." I moved to grab them.

Al breezed through the door just then, smiling and merry. "Afternoon, everyone! Tish, my dear, I just had three separate people tell me they think it's wonderful that you're taking over Howe and James when I retire."

I giggled at this news, digging through my purse. "Could it be *you* who started that rumor?"

"Oh, it was me," Mary declared, unashamed. "I've been telling everyone that very thing."

"*Mary*," I complained. I could just picture her, like a woman who operated one of those old-fashioned switchboard telephones, the kind where you could listen in on any conversation in town, fueling the rumor mill. I found my keys and Case collected them, seeming to study me with extra speculation before he tipped his hat once more to Mary and headed outside.

"Well, you tell me the minute you decide that very thing," Al said, winking as he shed his sport coat and headed for his desk.

I shook my head at the idea of them putting any store in such a notion and returned to work. I was, however, so terribly conscious of Case out in the parking lot that I was useless. No more than ten minutes ticked by before I asked Al, "Do you mind if I take off a little early?"

He was on the phone and nodded distractedly. Covering the mouthpiece, he murmured, "That's fine."

I rounded the building to see Case bent over the open hood, the lowering sun glowing in his hair. I barely curbed the urge to race to his side and slide my arms around his waist, bury my face against the scent of him.

"So, do I need a new car?"

"It's just your battery." He straightened to his full height, leaning one thigh against the side of my car, his hands dirty from checking the oil. "You left the headlights on. Don't worry. The battery is an easy fix."

The sun cut across my eyes. "Thank you. Apparently I'm a moron. I really appreciate the help."

"Sure thing." He wiped his hands on the sides of his jeans. Echoing my words from earlier, he said, "Besides, you could very well be saving my property and that's no small thing."

I shaded my eyes to better see him. I wanted to grab his face and make him look at me. I whispered, "It's my job."

"Here, I'll close the hood," he said, which forced me to step back. "Let's get you a battery first, and then we'll drive out and you can show me the spot."

We walked across the street to the hardware and auto parts store, where I recognized the clerk, Ken Nelson, from last Tuesday's meeting.

"Fine afternoon, ain't it?" Ken asked us. "Patricia, how do you like Jalesville?"

"I love it here," I said, quite honestly.

"We need a battery for that little white Honda across the street, the '97 Accord," Case said, leaning his hip against the counter. He looked all lanky and sexy, his jeans dirty with motor oil.

"I'll see what I have," Ken said, and went to look.

Case leaned a little closer and murmured, "His daughter is Katie."

I giggled. "Of the bleacher-kissing fame?"

Case nodded and my eyes detoured to his lips; with no more than a few inches I could have been hardware-store-counter kissing him.

"Here we go!" Ken heralded, and I snapped my eyes to safer terrain.

Back outside, Case carried my new battery. "I don't have my tools here. I'll get them from my place when we head over there."

I felt incomprehensibly happy at this gift of extra time with him, and did not want to squander a millisecond. But I felt like I had to say, "You really don't have to do that. I mean, I feel guilty...can I at least pay you?"

We reached his truck, parked in front of the law office. "That's just plain insulting."

It wasn't the first time I'd insulted him but he politely refrained from saying so; I was thinking of what I'd said at Camille's wedding and even though his eyes were hidden by his sunglasses I was somehow certain he held the same evening in mind. I wondered if he would ever mention any of that; I was far too chicken.

"I didn't mean..." I faltered, and then jumped ahead to open the driver's side door for him. "Here, it's the least I can do."

He wore his impassable face again but said, "Thanks," as he deposited his armload behind the front seat and I hurried around the hood. Already I felt much too at home settling onto the leather of the seat.

Case started the engine and I asked, "What do you think about Yancy's claim that he had an ancestor who was cheated out of land?"

"I was hoping to talk to you about that. I had all these things I wanted your opinion on the other night."

You did? I marveled. "Same here, with you."

"I'm curious just what he's using to make that claim. Documents, letters, family stories, what?"

"That's a good question. I wasn't expecting him to dish out such a claim. But, Case," and I loved saying his name so much I almost said it again, "I know there's a connection between the timing of the plant closing and the company sweeping in here."

"I agree with you, but it may just be that they caught wind and smelled an opportunity. It could be nothing more than a sharp business sense."

"But I know it's not. I promised Al I wouldn't rest until I found evidence."

Case angled a look my way. "You're dedicated. I respect that very much."

Pleasure that he would say so rippled all through me, warm and sweet as melted chocolate. "Thank you. I appreciate that."

There was a beat of something between us, the awareness of a powerful, thrumming connection. I thought I might die—and there was no exaggeration in that notion—if I didn't touch him at once. I knew he felt the same, I knew it to my bones; his hands tightened on the steering wheel. Yearning clamped my body in a stranglehold.

And so it was that I asked something totally ridiculous to cover the intensity of my emotions. "So, how long is the winter out here?"

He answered in the same quiet tone. "The old-timers have a saying: when summer heads back up the mountains, it meets winter coming down."

"Sounds like northern Minnesota. Do you ski and snowmobile, all that stuff?"

"Some. The worst part is that I can't get out and ride as much as I'd like. It gets a little claustrophobic."

"I remember feeling that way in Landon," I said, as we cleared the town and the landscape stretched to the horizon on all sides, gorgeous and somehow secretive. "That's when it's great to have the cafe, especially. Everyone gathers there and hangs out and passes the time."

"It sounds like you have a close family. That's such an important thing. Gus and I are pretty far apart in age. I know he thinks of me as a second dad as much as he does Clark."

"But you always took care of him, so that makes sense," I said without thinking, and could have bitten through my tongue. Case didn't know that Clark had told me about his past.

"Yeah, I suppose that's pretty obvious. Our dad was not the world's best role model. And Faye Rawley was the only mother Gus ever knew. I loved her dearly, but she couldn't replace my mom."

"How did she die?"

"Faye, or my mother?"

"Yours," I said.

"She was sick. To be quite honest, I don't know all the details. Dad never talked much about it. I know she had some kind of genetic abnormality that her mother passed to her, a defect in her heart valves. It was how Grandma Dalton died, too. Even though we didn't go much to the doctor, she made sure Gus and me were checked for it."

"*And?*" I could hardly speak the word.

"They didn't find anything wrong."

His heart…

He had once tried to give his heart to me and I'd not only handed it right back, I'd thrown it across the ballroom at White Oaks Lodge. My own seemed as tiny and shriveled as a raisin at the remembrance of my behavior.

But you didn't know him then.

And besides, he doesn't feel the same way anymore…

"Well, that's a very good thing," I told him, my voice low and hoarse.

"Aw, shit! Look at that!" he said in a completely different tone. To my surprise, he braked and pulled to the left side of the road, taking the truck well onto the scrubby edge. He shouldered open his door and invited, "C'mon!"

He was already headed for the ditch as though drawn by a tractor beam. I hesitated at the edge of the road, in my sundress and heeled sandals. My goddamn ridiculous shoes. Case stood about twenty feet away, fingers linked together and braced on the top of his hat, looking out toward the distance. And then I saw it—a herd of horses, running fast enough to kick up giant dust clouds.

"Oh *wow*," I breathed, and forgot all about the inappropriateness of my footwear. I was winded as I reached his side; he looked down at me, the sun refracting from his sunglasses, painting his face in amber. He appeared reverent.

"You don't see them too often. Isn't that a sight?"

"Are they wild?" I shaded my eyes from the glare.

"They are. God, it makes me happy that something still is, you know what I mean? That not every wild creature is locked up in a goddamn zoo."

"No one tries to round them up? Control them?"

"No…occasionally a rancher's horse gets mixed in, and that calls for saddling up, if you want your horse back. Usually the mares, during mating season," he said, so very matter-of-fact, studying the horses as they receded into the distance in a haze of golden dust.

A hot pulse beat between my legs; I peeked over at him as he remained in the same position, fingers laced atop his hat. His biceps were also amber-tinted in the sunbeams, solid and strong and sharply defined. My jaws ached as I gritted my teeth, trying to smother all feelings of raging attraction.

No use.

"That makes my whole day," he said, turning back towards the truck.

"Mine, too," I muttered, picking my way along the uneven ground, with care. Just behind me, Case stooped to break a twig from a nearby plant.

"Here, for your car. It's sage."

"Thanks." I was terribly unsettled; desire skimmed my skin like the tips of knife blades, just as keen, demanding my attention. I took the sprig of sage, as charmed as though he'd offered two dozen roses. I held it under my nose and inhaled. "Oh, that smells so good."

At the truck, I clambered in the driver's side door ahead of him. A minute later we drove past the Rawleys' place, and then Case took the left on Ridge Road, out toward his property. I could tell he wasn't going to ask why I had been out here the other night; I was glad, as I couldn't explain why either, even to myself. I recognized the stenciled mailbox, the tall barn cast now in sunlight, the trailer as rundown as ever.

Why are you so judgmental? Jesus Crimeny, Tish.

He parked near the barn and Buck and Cider loped from its depths, hooves clomping and stirring up dust. The barn was in far better repair than the trailer, appearing to have new shingles. It was constructed of stained wood, unpainted, a split-rail corral circling outward from the west side. A pair of fluffy black and white dogs bolted from behind the trailer.

"Get down, guys," he said, laughing as the dogs jumped around the truck, mouths open and tails wagging. He climbed down and bent immediately to one knee to knuckle their heads. The second my feet touched the ground the dogs raced around the truck and crowded my legs, tongues lolling, wiggling to displace each other for full attention. I leaned to rub their heads; they reminded me of Grandma's old labs as they tried to lick my face.

"Guys, come on. Down!" Case ordered, pulling off his sunglasses and then his hat, swiping the back of one wrist over his forehead. The dogs obeyed but their brown eyes remained bright with excitement at this new body in their yard.

"So, who are these two?"

Case indicated with his sunglasses, pointing to one and then the other. "That's Mutt and that's Tiny. They're Border Collies. Poor guys need sheep to herd."

A sleek orange cat leaped atop the highest rail of the corral and walked precisely along, while Cider and Buck stuck their noses over the top rung, whooshing big breaths through their nostrils in a clear demand for attention.

"What are you talking about? You have a zoo right here," I teased, moving to cup Cider's nose. She made a whickering sound and I laughed, patting her warm neck, one hand on either side of her face. I'd never known how good it felt to touch a horse.

Case joined me at the corral, scooping up the cat and rubbing a thumb over its head; it began purring as though equipped with a motor. "You know, as a kid I wanted to be a vet more than about anything."

"That's funny, I wanted to be one, too, for a long time." I nodded at the cat. "Is this everybody?"

I swore a flush stole over his cheeks but it was difficult to tell, as he was already so tanned. He used his free hand to scratch Buck's neck as he murmured, "No…"

"Who else?"

"I have a rabbit in the barn. And a few chickens…"

"You do?" I giggled at his expression. He looked like a kid, sweet and endearing. I couldn't resist teasing, "Do you have a shoebox with a turtle, too?"

"No, thank you very much." He grinned anew. "I like animals, what can I say?"

"So that wasn't just an excuse to leave last night. You really *did* have to feed all the animals."

He studied me in complete silence; my heart hammered my ribs. Only Cider swinging her head in annoyance broke our absorption with one another. Case said, "Whoa there, girl, I'll get you fed."

"Can I use your bathroom?" I felt intrusive asking but it was either that or find a place to squat out among the sagebrush.

"Of course," he said, tucking the orange cat under his arm. "Just to warn you…I wasn't exactly expecting company…"

I rolled my eyes.

He clarified, "Your place was so clean today…"

"I just don't have a lot to do in the evenings," I said. "Normally I live in complete squalor."

His yard was in shade at this point in the afternoon, only the top half of the barn bisected by the bright, slowly-sinking sun. Case led the way to his trailer, a green and white doublewide with metal siding; the chili-pepper lights were strung in two rows above the screen door, which sang on its hinges as he opened it, reminding me of the porch doors at Shore Leave. There was an undeniable intimacy involved in seeing someone's home in this fashion. I might as well have peered into closets and underwear drawers while I was at it.

Case said, "On the right, down that hall."

He retreated to feed the animals; I watched him out the window before moving in the direction he'd indicated. The windows were all open a good six inches, allowing in the scent of sage. The walls were paneled in wood, the carpet in the living room a burnt-orange in color. There was a small television, an old leather couch with a bed pillow at one end; did he sleep out here? The small kitchen contained one table, three chairs, and dishes stacked in the sink, probably a week's worth. I trailed my fingers along the yellow counter as I moved slowly through his house, picturing him leaning against it drinking coffee in the mornings. Blinds, but no curtains. Pictures on a lone shelf; I was drawn to these as though they were magnetized.

A couple of shots of him performing with the Rawleys, one from a long time ago; he looked the way I remembered him from Camille's wedding. And then, my heart seizing, I spied a small wallet-sized photo, tucked like an afterthought into the edge of a larger frame, of him and Lynnette. Before I could question the wisdom I lifted it from the shelf and studied the image. An engagement picture, maybe. Lynnette stood facing him, hands on his shoulders, his jaw against her temple, and they were both smiling for the camera, outside somewhere, sunlight dusting their hair. She was pretty. Really pretty, with soft brown eyes and full pink lips, and I hated that I cared. He seemed to be smiling genuinely; he appeared happy.

God, you are a selfish, selfish little bitch, I thought, harshly reprimanding myself, tucking the picture back in its original place, feeling as though images of my fingerprints covered its surface, my rudeness on display. Of course Case hadn't spent all these years longing for me.

But he wrote a song for me.

I bet he wrote plenty of songs for her, too.

Grow up, Tish.

I found the bathroom and could hardly meet my own gaze in the small oval mirror. The space was tiny and cramped, tiled in greens that spoke of the 1970s. It wasn't really messy, just full of the evidence of the man who lived here alone. The shower curtain was drawn aside, a single bottle of two-in-one shampoo/conditioner lying forlornly on a built-in shelf. I flushed the toilet and then found myself lifting the plastic bottle to my nose; it smelled spicy and just like him, and I closed my eyes.

A straight-blade razor on the counter, a can of shaving cream, a large dark blue towel hanging from a single towel rack, a curled-up bottle of toothpaste...and, to my chagrin, a pair of black boxers scrunched in the corner behind the door, as though carelessly tossed aside. Near these was the t-shirt he'd been wearing last night at the fair. I bit my bottom lip, hard enough to leave dents, and carefully washed my hands, in a hurry now, feeling more like a trespasser than ever. But then, after I used his towel, I bent, scooped up his soft old t-shirt, and brought it to my face. Again I was inundated by his scent; I stood there inhaling him, heart quaking, blood beating at my forehead. It was only as I heard the screen door sing on its hinges that I snapped to motion, letting the shirt fall back to the floor and hurrying from the bathroom.

Case barely looked at me as he stepped inside, moving to the fridge and extracting a can of mineral water, which he held to the side of his neck. He was even more disheveled than he'd been checking my oil, bits of hay clinging to his jeans and t-shirt, his hat on the kitchen table. Sweat trickled along his temples as he cracked open the can and drank about half of it, then backhanded his lips. I had never wanted to throw myself into someone's arms more desperately in my entire life. Sweat snaked down my spine in a hot, wet line.

Still without a glance my direction, he asked, "Are you thirsty? I've got my tools in the truck, so we can head out anytime."

So casual, so polite. Of course he had no idea what I'd just done in his bathroom, taking ridiculous liberties. He had no idea that I was vibrating with desire and he would not know, because I had less than no right to feel this way. I'd nearly convinced myself it was because he had once flattered my vanity, that no one before or since had said such things to me—that I was meant for them, that they'd written a song for me.

You don't deserve him. He's way too good for you. You have casual sex with men you hardly care about, men you've never considered loving, just for the orgasm. Just because. And he's someone who loves with his whole heart.

I was beginning to fully comprehend this.

I had lost my chance with Case Spicer, many years ago.

And it was clear he no longer felt the same way about me that he once had.

Besides, he belongs here. And you belong in Chicago.

"Thanks." I spoke around a husk in my throat. Case handed me a can of mineral water and it was all I could do not to hold it to my temple. He collected his hat from the table and let the orange cat inside as he went out; there was nothing I could do but follow, looking over my shoulder at his kitchen, one last time, before the door creaked shut behind me.

Rumbling along in his truck a minute later, I sipped the can of bubbly water and watched the foothills in the distance. "The other night, standing out here, I felt like Montana doesn't know what year it actually is."

He angled a glance my way. "I know just what you mean. When I ride, it could be a hundred years ago, more than that. Sometimes I even imagine that it is, for whatever reason."

"Mathias said he felt like you guys had known each other forever. I know he wishes you could hang out more often."

"Yeah, that very first night we all met, when he sang with us at The Spoke, I had that feeling. Like he'd been my friend before I even knew him. Garth and Marsh felt the same. I don't know how to explain it. I guess some things you can't explain."

My heart broke rhythm at these words—a desperate thought screamed through my head.

You just need to remember, Patricia, just remember!

My own voice answered—*remember what?!*

I realized we were approaching the wizard rock. "There, out by that big rock formation shaped like a T!" Case drew the truck to the shoulder and I indicated with my can. "Out that way, that's where the SUV was parked last Friday."

"There's the old access road," he said, peering out the passenger window. "Garth and Marsh and I used to play out there, by that rock, all the time. It was kind-of like our clubhouse."

"So this is still your property."

"Yes, for another mile or so," he affirmed. "What the fuck were they doing out there?"

"Something lowdown and dirty. That would be my first assumption, given what I know about Derrick Yancy."

"Let's drive out there," he decided. "Hold on."

He turned the tires onto the shoulder and we bumped over the uneven ground, avoiding the larger clumps of brush. I braced one hand on the seat between us, not daring to sip from my water for fear of inundating my clothes. We came to a gravel road and he drove slowly, both of us scanning the landscape.

Case spoke with a touch of self-deprecation. "Am I stupid enough to think that Yancy would have left a sign? He's careful. Whatever he's looking for, it won't be obvious."

"I'd bet he wasn't even out here the other night. He seems like the kind who'd have others do his dirty work."

"You're a good sport," Case suddenly said. "Like you don't have better things to do on Friday night than stake out this rock."

I kept my voice very neutral as I replied, "This is the kind of thing I will never get a chance to do back in Chicago. And I *don't* have better things to do, believe me."

His eyes held something deep within but he was so damn good at hiding things. It was nearly impossible to tell what he was really feeling. He studied me, only a few feet away on the bench seat, and then his gaze lowered to my lips for the length of a breath.

Damn, damn, damn you, I thought, not certain if I was addressing myself or him.

"Well, your car isn't getting fixed with me sitting here," he said, all business again.

"You're right," I muttered, and this time really did hold the cold can to my temple as we drove back to the law office.

Case swapped out the battery as the sun sank and decorated the sky. I leaned against the hood and took great pleasure in covertly observing him. My cotton dress was grimy, but I didn't care. I handed him tools; I knew what was what in a toolbox, thanks to Uncle Justin, who'd taught us to change a tire and drive a stick shift. Clint and Ruthie had been eager, while I was a reluctant student at best; I liked it better when Uncle Justin took us out in the boat, letting Clint, Ruthie, and me take turns driving.

"You know what, I wish we were close enough to Flickertail Lake to jump in."

Without looking up, Case asked, "That's the lake by your family's cafe, right?"

"Yes. God, this time of night is perfect for swimming."

"You sound homesick," he observed.

"Maybe a little," I admitted.

"But that's not where you plan to live, in Minnesota?"

I shook my head; realizing he wasn't looking at me, I said, "No. I hope to get a good job offer from Ron Turnbull's firm. And I've put in my time at his firm already, the past two summers. It won't be easy, but I'm a fast learner. And I know how to work." I paused, feeling like I was trying too hard to convince myself. "I really do love Chicago. I'm flying back next week to take the bar exam. Shit, that came fast."

Bent over my open hood, Case seemed to ignore this information; he requested quietly, "Can you hand me the smaller pliers?"

"Sure," I whispered.

"But you'll be back out here, after that? Through August, you said?"

My throat felt tight. Our fingers brushed as I passed him the small, pointed tool. "Through Labor Day weekend."

I watched him absorb this news.

I prattled on, "I don't have a place to live yet, so I'll probably stay with my dad and his wife, Lanny, for a while. You should see her, she's like a caricature. Everything fake. Fake lips, fake breasts, fake nails, hair extensions, but classy ones at least." I didn't know why I was babbling like this. I didn't know why all I could think about was how fucking much I was going to miss Jalesville. And how much I wanted Case to stand up and curl me against his chest.

Case said, "Your dad must be into appearances."

"Yeah," I reflected. "He's materialistic. But he's not a bad guy. I mean, there are worse things than that."

"That's for sure," Case agreed, and I thought of Owen Spicer. My father may be shallow, but at least I knew he loved me, in his own way.

"There's Derrick," I hissed, spying the black 4x4 rolling down Main. Case straightened and together we watched as the big vehicle, with its tinted windows, halted at the stoplight.

"He's a weasel," Case said grimly. "He's a weasel and a bully, both, and damned if I'm going to let him fuck us over around here."

Case was so reassuring, confident of his position, and I loved that. No one would push him around. I was glad I could help him, at least for this summer.

This one summer…

The 4x4 was headed our way now, on the opposite side of the street, and the driver's side window lowered at the touch of a button inside the vehicle. Slowing to a crawl, Derrick called over, "Lovely evening, isn't it?"

When neither of us responded Derrick grinned, flashing white teeth, and accelerated away.

"What an asshole," I said.

"You can say that again," Case muttered, wiping his hands on an old towel he'd stowed with his tools. He changed the subject, nodding at my car. "You want to fire her up? You should let it run for about thirty minutes, let the new battery charge."

I knew he meant to leave now that there was no logical excuse to stick around; he'd drive back to his place and care for his animals, make supper, maybe eat while he watched TV. Would he take Cider or Buck for a ride? Would he sleep on that lonely pillow on the couch? Or would he prowl his yard, restless in the dark, waiting for a sight of the black 4x4 with Colorado plates?

Let me come back with you. I can't stand the thought of you leaving without me. I want to wrap your towel around my wet, naked body after we make love in your shower. And on all fours on your bed. And then on the kitchen counter and the living room rug…

I felt just shy of outright crazy. A ruthless fist squeezed all sense from my brain; my nipples were nearly jutting through the material of my dress. I realized I was staring at him with all these thoughts rioting out of control, and almost jumped in my haste to move to the driver's side door to break the intensity of my imagination.

Get a fucking hold on yourself.

I leaned in the window and turned over the key; the engine sputtered and then caught, and the Honda growled to life.

"That's a good little four-cylinder in there," Case said, closing the hood. "Once you get home, let her run for another fifteen minutes or so."

I nodded inanely.

He said, "I'll see you tomorrow night, at Clark's."

The time between this moment and that one was twice an eternity. I found my voice; I'd lost track of how many times I'd expressed gratitude today. "Thank you again, for everything. You're a lifesaver."

He shrugged as though it was nothing; was that a pleased expression in his eyes? I hoped so. I squelched the aching need to touch him and instead curled my hands around the top edge of the open window.

"Do you play tonight?"

"Not until Saturday," he said, collecting his tools. He regarded me for just a second longer, then slipped his sunglasses into place, toolbox in hand.

"See you tomorrow." I wasn't quite able to offer a smile.

He tipped his hat brim and then left me standing there beside my idling car, alone.

Chapter Eleven

It was sometime after midnight when I awoke to both the grumble of thunder and Peaches as she jumped on me. The living room was chilly enough that goosebumps broke out along my arms and I shivered, stumbling from the couch to close the sliding glass door to the porch, effectively shutting out the cold draft. Rain wasn't falling but the scent of it hung in the air, heavy as a threat. On second thought, I grabbed the blanket from the back of the couch, where I'd fallen asleep yet again, and went outside onto the porch.

I curled up in my solo chair and watched the sky; even in the darkness it was fearsome-looking, a looming anvil cloud intermittently backlit by sizzles of lightning. I wrapped more securely into the blanket. Thunder growled, ever increasing, as though a vindictive giant was dragging its feet in the direction of Jalesville, intent on smashing the town to jagged bits. I thought of sitting on the dock at Shore Leave with Ruthann and Clint, watching storms roll across Flickertail Lake, pockmarking the water and creating whitecaps. I'd always experienced a thrill at the sound of thunder; something within me that longed for danger found it appealing.

Case.

I hugged my bent legs, bare heels braced on the chair. There was no point pretending I wanted to think about anything other than him.

Are you awake right now?

I wish you were here with me.

I want to be in your arms.

Oh God, I can't think of anything else…

Obsessively, I tallied up the times we'd touched—at the bonfire last weekend, my forearm in his hands just today. I thought of inhaling the scent of him from his shampoo bottle and his abandoned t-shirt, the insanity of that.

Where is this coming from?

Was it loneliness? Lack of physical contact? Maybe this meant I needed to get back to Chicago that much more quickly. Maybe after the bar exam next week I could find an excuse to stay in the city.

No.

Oh God, no…

I pressed my fists to my eyes and thunder exploded, closer this time. I stayed motionless for long moments, blocking my vision. I had no right to long for Case. Not when I was returning to the life I was supposed to live come the end of summer. Rain began striking the ground, lifting the sharp scent of dust. I wrapped into my own arms, thinking of everything I had learned about Case since arriving here and reentering each other's lives. I thought of the things he'd told me about his family. How he stood up for what he felt was right. I pictured his lonely trailer, his barn full of animals he so obviously loved. How he played his guitar and his fiddle with quiet passion.

I squeezed until my ribs hurt.

And even knowing all of these things about him, he still confused me terribly. There were times, like today, when I was certain he was every bit as attracted to me, but in the next moment he came across as though trying to convey that he was concerned about me in the vein of a good friend.

Do I want his friendship?

Yes.

I want a hell of a lot more than that.

I spoke his name, whispering it aloud so that I could feel it on my tongue and taste it in my mouth. I thought of him telling the story of the first girl he'd ever kissed, and was unreasonably jealous of her. I couldn't even think about Lynnette, who'd been his wife. She'd left Case, not the other way around, Clark had said; he'd also said they fought about his late nights; could there have been a deeper reason for their split?

Don't even, Tish, you're wrong. You're dead wrong.

Go to bed.

It was raining so hard that there was splash-back on my face as I sat there under the ceiling that formed the bottom of the balcony on the floor above mine. I let the rain strike my skin, hugging with all my strength, and still it wasn't half enough.

I spent Friday at the law office with two tasks in mind. First, I investigated the closing of Highland Power. Second, I asked Al about the Yancy ancestor, the alleged former landowner in Jalesville. Al told me that I should visit the courthouse on Monday, when the records office was open. He said it was a musty basement room but it contained microfiche files for all of the newsprint articles that had been published in the greater Jalesville area since 1893, when the town had been founded.

"Microfiche?" I repeated.

"I know, you'd think it was three decades ago down there," Al joked.

"No, it's not that I'm complaining. I'm just surprised. I'm embarrassed to admit that I don't know how to use that type of machine." My eyes swept to the clock, which I had been checking all day.

Four hours until I can see him, I thought.

Al appeared speculative when I glanced back at him, but he refrained from commenting. Instead, he said, "I was going to ask you to come in for a few hours tomorrow to help me do inventory, but now I'm reconsidering. You look exhausted, counselor. I've been working you too hard."

"Al," I reprimanded. "No such thing. I'm happy to come in tomorrow. What time?"

"I'll bring us chocolate cream pie, Helen Anne is making some as we speak. Maybe five or so hours, tops. You're my angel, kiddo, no joke. Let's say about two?"

"I'll be here," I promised. "You can count on me."

Driving home, a few hours later, pure anticipation spiked my blood. I would see Case at the Rawleys' and later we were staking out his property. I kept envisioning us in black jumpsuits with guns strapped to our hips, prowling through the foothills. I giggled, realizing that I did not care one bit how we looked or what we did, as long as it meant I could be near him. At Stone Creek I dressed in my darkest jeans and a black t-shirt, and grabbed a black sweatshirt. I left my hair loose (*your hair is beautiful, all down like that* may have been echoing in my head) and allowed one concession to femininity in a pair of silver hoop earrings. I laced my heavy-duty hiking boots and then drove too fast to Clark's.

I pulled up and saw Wy hanging on the corral fence, lavishing both his horse, Oreo, and Buck with attention. My heart tripped over itself to see this evidence of Case having already arrived; I put the car in park and nearly skipped to the fence.

"Hey, Tish!" Wy was all smiles. He was wearing his cowboy hat and I grinned in response, cupping Buck's face and kissing him between the eyes.

"They like it when you blow your breath into their noses," Wy explained with an air of all-knowing. "See, like this." He leaned to demonstrate, exhaling gently near Oreo's nose; the mare nickered and brushed her lips against the boy, as though bestowing a kiss. Wy ordered, "Now you try."

I giggled, muttering to Buck, "I hope you don't mind, buddy," before pursing my lips and directing a breath between his nostrils, keeping his big, square jaws in both hands. He whooshed and nudged my chest, and I laughed all the more.

"Now he'll never forget your scent," Case said from just behind us, and my heart detonated like an explosive charge.

I turned to look over my shoulder at him, unable to keep from grinning. He was hatless, in a black t-shirt and his customary faded jeans. Sunglasses hanging from the collar of his shirt, like usual. He observed, "You found your hiking boots."

"Why, are you guys hiking somewhere?" Wy asked, hooking his elbows over the fence and leaning forward. "Like, into the mountains?"

My gaze flashed to Case; by unspoken agreement, neither of us mentioned our plans for later in the evening. Slightly breathless, I said, "No, I just got sick of wearing dress shoes all the time." Everyone else was out back, I could hear them, and on inspiration I asked Wy, "Hey, will you grab me a drink?"

"Sure," he said at once. "What'll you have?"

"My usual, but not quite so strong."

Wy darted inside and I demanded, "What is it? I can tell there's something…"

Case's grin deepened. "You had the same thought as me, about the ninja look," nodding at my black shirt and dark jeans; his eyes stroked over my breasts subtly, but it was enough that my nipples swelled. Case returned his gaze to my eyes but there was a flash of heat in his, scorching heat that burned straight to my tailbone.

"What else?" I whispered, knowing there was more. I was stroking Buck's neck as though it was Case's chest, I suddenly realized, and stilled my hands.

"After supper we can meet over at my place. It's less than a ten-minute ride by horseback. I'll head out when you do. And I found something just this afternoon, out by that rock." He came closer and put his hands on Buck's neck, on the opposite side. "It's the strangest thing. Someone was digging out there."

"Digging?"

He nodded. "I took Buck for a ride out there and explored all around, like a kid, not exactly expecting to find anything. But then, near the base of the rock, I saw that the earth had been turned. I could tell. A couple of scrubs uprooted. And there were boot prints, not my own."

"Did you grab a shovel?" I cried, ready to drive straight there and put one to use. My imagination was firing on all cylinders. "Do you think they buried something? *A body*? Maybe Derrick had someone killed!"

Case didn't make fun of me, didn't scoff or even laugh. He admitted, "I felt the way I used to when we were kids, Garth and Marsh and me trying to find mysteries to solve, the legend of the gold all up in our heads. But, Tish, I don't think they were burying something. I think they were –"

"*Unburying* something," I finished. Then it struck me and I babbled without thinking, "You said my name!"

He knitted his eyebrows and I was not imagining the flush over his cheekbones; I suddenly realized I threw him into a tailspin just as much as he threw me. His voice was soft as he contradicted, "I've said your name."

"Not 'Tish,'" I disagreed.

Buck's long nose was the only thing between Case and me, and our invisible connection sizzled and throbbed, stronger than ever. I knew he felt it, even if he wouldn't acknowledge it. I studied his eyes and had the strangest flash of what felt like a memory surfacing—Case coming to me while I sat up high on a wagon seat, his shoulders near my ankles. His hand gliding along my bare right leg, hidden beneath the heavy layers of my long skirt, his eyes burning into mine. The strength of this vision was like a striking fist—and then it blinked away as quickly as a mirage.

What was that?

Did I just have a Notion? I wondered. *Like Aunt Jilly?*

"Here you go!" Wy announced, popping out the front door, a gin and tonic in hand.

"Thanks," I whispered, flustered and sweaty. Wy passed me the drink and some spilled over my hand. I wiped my wrist against my thigh as we walked around the side of the house, to the porch. I knew Case and I would have to shelve our discussion until later; I was dying to ask him if he'd had the same sensation of the wagon, of touching my leg…

Clark and Wy had spent the day hickory-smoking about ten pounds of pork, which smelled incredible. It was a full house tonight, all the girlfriends in attendance; I couldn't help but pretend that Case and I were a couple, too. I fantasized about this, watching him as he chatted with Clark near the grill; to my delight, Case set his eyes on me every so often, just so. Once he smiled, the kind of private and intimate smile that lovers exchange, and I lost complete track of what Sean was saying; luckily he was a little drunk and didn't notice.

By the time dinner was over I was resonating with impatient

excitement. When Clark asked if I wanted to play cards, I said, with what I prayed was a casual tone, "I'm so tired tonight. I think I might head home."

"You've had a busy week," Clark allowed. "Come back for dinner tomorrow, if you have a craving for pulled-pork sandwiches."

I went on tiptoe to kiss his cheek. It was so easy to love Clark.

I bid everyone good-night, keeping my eyes from Case with every ounce of effort I possessed. In my car, which smelled of sagebrush thanks to the sprig on the dashboard, I drove out to Ridge Road with the radio off, imbibing the night. The almost-full moon was so distracting that I almost drove into the ditch before I reached Case's house. I inched the car through his yard, mindful of the animals; already Mutt and Tiny were crowding the vehicle. I parked on the far side of the trailer; the chili-pepper lights were lit, throwing cheerful red-orange light in a circular splash across the yard.

The air was so still that I could hear the fair back in Jalesville, tinkling music, the faint swell of delighted screams from people on a ride, and the sounds of someone speaking through a microphone, bouncing off the foothills to my ears. I bent and hugged the dogs, letting them lick my face. Cider came out of the barn to greet me and I climbed up one rung to throw my arms around her neck. I kissed her nose and blew a gentle breath into her left nostril, murmuring, "Now you'll remember my scent, too."

I kept near the mare, resting my forehead on her warm neck, the dogs wriggling around my knees. I closed my eyes and pictured Case out there in the night, riding toward me on Buck, coming closer even now. Waves of heat sliced through me and I clung to Cider, who nickered and let me hold her. I wasn't sure how much time passed before I heard hoofbeats thudding on the ground, matching the pace of my heart. And then he rode into view.

"That is a hell of a moon," Case said, riding Buck into the corral. He dismounted with a graceful motion and patted the big buckskin before turning him loose. I could not tear my eyes away as he walked over and hung on the fence beside Cider, inside the corral. His face appeared silver-white in the milky moonlight.

"It seems twice as big as I've ever seen it," I agreed, my breath shallow.

Cider belly-bumped him and he elbowed her firmly away. "No crowding, you know better."

"I'm nervous, now that we're here," I admitted.

"Likely no one will even show up," he said. "I wouldn't let you come with me if I thought it was going to be dangerous, I hope you know. And if we see or hear anyone, I'm calling the police, first thing. Our local sheriff is Travis's dad, Jerry Woodrow."

"Will we walk out there?" It seemed too conspicuous to take the truck.

Case was watching me and didn't seem to hear my question; I promptly forgot what I had just asked. He stood on the opposite side of the fence, hardly more than an arm's length away.

Oh God, kiss me, please, just one kiss so I have something to remember...

He blinked then, and refocused his attention on Cider, rubbing her neck. He answered me by saying, "No, we'll ride. I'll saddle up Cider for you. She's a little calmer than Buck, even though she's younger. You'll be all right on horseback?"

I nodded, not trusting my voice, and he pushed off from the fence with both hands. I followed him into the barn, not about to waste a moment in his presence; he clicked a couple of bare, overhead bulbs to life and I turned in a slow circle, admiring the space. It was large and cavernous and pleasant-smelling, with a second-floor loft stacked with bales of hay. I heard a muted clucking somewhere beyond the stalls, one of which was occupied by Buck, crunching loudly on something as he intermittently stomped his back hooves.

"Can I see the chickens?" I begged, and Case, who was lifting a saddle from its holder, grinned and shook his head, teasing me.

"You really are a city girl, aren't you?"

I felt an uncomfortable twinge at those words. "It's not every day you get to see where eggs come from, firsthand."

"They're back here." Case led the way. "I made them what amounts to a chicken coop."

I followed close behind, studying the slope of his shoulders, taut now as he continued to carry the saddle, the way his hair caught the light and how the bottom edge, at the center of his nape, was shaped into a comma. His jeans fit just so; I was gazing at his back pockets when he stopped abruptly and I plowed into him. Case looked over his shoulder, shifting his grip on the saddle, but I had already composed my face into a look of polite interest.

He said, "There they are."

"Do you have a rooster?" I was truly fascinated by all these animals. The hens were roosting in an enclosure surrounded by chicken wire, their feathers a combination of burnt-orange and black.

"No, just these three."

"*Can* you get eggs then?"

He snorted a laugh. "Of course. Just not fertilized ones."

I couldn't help but laugh, too, latching both hands on my hips. "It's not like I grew up on a farm!"

"Didn't you take biology in school?"

"Well, it's been a few years," I defended. I caught sight of the rabbit, a floppy-eared gray one in its own cage; it appeared to be sleeping.

"Oh, man," I said. "My twelve-year-old self just went to pieces. I begged for a bunny that year. My birthday is right around Easter, so I thought it might actually happen."

"That's Penelope. You can hold her if you want. Just lift the latch on the top there."

I stepped around him and opened the top, reaching to scoop up the bunny. She was about as big as Peaches but a thousand times softer. She struggled at this intrusion on her nap, kicking with long hind legs, so I let her go; she darted to the far side and turned her rear toward me.

"You'd think rabbits like to be cuddled, but they don't," Case said, as though in apology. He shifted the saddle again.

"Next time," I muttered, supposing there was a next time.

Back under the night sky, Case whistled to Cider, who trotted right over. He saddled her up while I sat on the top rung of the corral, watching. When he was through he asked, "Have you been horseback before?"

"Just once," I said, hopping from the fence.

"You'll do fine. Come here and I'll help you up. Just step into the stirrup, on the left there." He stepped back to allow room and I gripped the saddle with one hand on each of its curves, fitting my boot in the dangling leather foothold. Cider jostled a little, nickering, and Case took her face between his hands and spoke to her.

"There's a good horse, good girl," he murmured, while my insides sizzled and melted, by turns. With determination, I settled atop the saddle but couldn't get my other boot situated.

"I can't quite reach the other stirrup," I said, and Case moved to his horse's side, where, with the lightest of touches, he took my ankle in one hand and guided my foot to the stirrup. Fire torched my leg. I couldn't suppress a small sound.

"Here's the reins," he said, stepping away, handing me the two leather straps that looped over Cider's head.

I gripped the reins, begging silently, *Look at me, please, Case, acknowledge that you just touched me...*

As though hearing my thoughts he looked up at me, his eyes luminous in the moonlight; he explained quietly, "Hold them with just a little slack. I trained Cider myself, so she responds well. She'll follow Buck and me pretty easily. Just say if anything is wrong, all right? Does the saddle feel secure beneath you?"

I nodded.

"You'll get cold. Did you bring a sweatshirt or jacket?"

"In my car," I whispered.

"I'll grab it," and he jogged to do so. He ducked inside his trailer and in his brief absence I patted Cider, rubbing her neck, adjusting to the sensation of her beneath me. She seemed taller than ever from this vantage point but didn't appear to mind me on her back; I noticed that her ears twitched around like radar. She kept making little nickering sounds and lifting up her right front leg to paw at the ground. Was she trying to communicate with me somehow?

"Here," Case said, handing up my sweatshirt.

"Thank you." I slipped it over my head as he climbed atop Buck and brought the big buckskin to my side. Cider nosed Buck and then danced sideways; I overcompensated, yanking on the reins.

"Oh shit, sorry, girl! I didn't mean to do that."

Case nudged Buck forward and scratched the top of Cider's head, between her ears. "She's just fine, don't worry. She has to adjust to you, too. Your weight is a lot lighter than she's used to. No one but Gus or me has ever ridden her."

"Not even your wife?" I asked without thinking and could have bitten off my tongue.

Without missing a beat, Case said, "She wasn't much for animals, one way or the other."

His words hung in the air and I let them be; I whispered, "Do you ride much at night?"

"I do. It's peaceful." He looked so natural astride a horse. Deep in my mind was that strange flickering, a movie projector crackling to life, wanting me to *see*. I thought of Camille and Mathias, how they believed that they had known each other before this life, in another. I was skeptical about such things, and had teased my sister time and again. But here I sat, knowing that I'd ridden horseback with this man long before tonight.

What in the hell?

"Shall we?" he asked, ever the gentleman.

We set out at a steady walk, keeping to the wide left shoulder of the gravel road. There was enough room for the horses to walk abreast, though Case insisted that he and Buck take the outside edge, closer to the road itself. Our knees, his left and my right, were very close as the horses plodded along, their hooves crunching gravel.

"I was telling Clark the other night that the air out here feels wilder than back home," I told Case, lifting my chin to study the sky. In the scope of this landscape, especially beneath the cloak of night, I felt as tiny as a speck of dust. It was awesome in the truest sense of that word, inspiring complete awe. The moon was close to a silver-dollar, lifting higher with each passing minute. It was spectacular, so immediate, creating within me the sense that I could reach up and cup my hands around it.

Case said, "I haven't been many other places in my life, I admit, but I've been away from Montana long enough to realize I *can't* be away. Call me a redneck, but my heart shrinks up in a city."

I thought of Chicago, the noisy urban splendor sprawling in all directions. The place where I planned to live and work and spend the rest of my life after this summer. My voice was hoarse but I could pretend it was from the crisp air as I replied, "I think if I'd been raised out here, I would completely agree."

"You didn't grow up in Landon, right? But your family is all there now?"

"It's a long story."

"I'm a good listener," he promised.

"I grew up in Chicago." My gaze prowled the dark landscape, the rock formations in the foothills gilded by the pale glow of the rising moon. "I was fifteen the summer that Mom moved us to Landon for good, because my dad had been having an affair with a woman from his law firm. Actually, he's married to her now, the woman I was talking about yesterday."

"With the fake everything?" It sounded like he was smiling.

I giggled. "Yes, fake to her core. I don't know, I guess my dad loves her. But that summer, ten years ago now, Mom brought us to Landon in May, much earlier than usual. She was in a bad place, even though I didn't know it at the time. I mean, I didn't acknowledge it. I was too young and immature. And besides, I loved it in Landon, where we went every July. Our family is there, and the lake. I was glad to leave school and go early."

"Did you know your dad had a girlfriend?"

"Not at the time. I knew he and Mom fought a lot, but once we got to Landon I conveniently forgot about all of that and just had fun. My cousin, Clint, is my best friend in the world, even to this day."

"He's a good guy, I remember him," Case said. "What's he doing these days?"

"He's a fireman in Landon. My old roommates thought he was so good-looking and always tried to convince me to get him to come to Chicago for the weekend. They wanted to seduce him ten ways from Sunday."

Case teased, "And he never showed up? What the hell?"

"No, he's actually really shy. Plus he has the same attitude as you about the city. He loves Landon too much to leave, even for the promise of a threesome in Chicago."

"I know Mathias and Camille love it on the lake. Their cabin and all."

"They do. They've put so much work into their home. It's gorgeous. You'll have to see it someday." *With me*, I longed to say, but didn't. I thought of seeing Case after this summer, down the road, years from now…

He said, "I used to have this plan to build a cabin, get rid of that old trailer. It's such a piece of crap. When Lynn lived there with me, after Dad died, she hated it so much. I wanted to build a beautiful place. I had this vision of it…"

I looked his way, unable to help it, hearing the note of regret in his tone. I hadn't, in my all-consuming vanity, considered that maybe he still longed for his wife. That maybe he wished she was still with him. Jealousy stabbed my heart, creating gashes. It hurt so much that I had to lift my hand from the reins and press it against my chest. I hated how he'd called her 'Lynn' in that tone of voice, thinking of the wallet-sized picture of them still in his kitchen.

With more asperity than was probably appropriate, I said, "Well, I would bet that you still have this vision in your mind. What's stopping you?"

His half-grin sent my aching heart to pinwheeling. "That's a good point."

"Clark said your family's original homestead burned down, back in 1971."

"Dad always claimed that it was an arson fire but it was never proven one way or the other. Knowing my Grandpa Spicer, it was probably a cigarette that got left unattended because he was shit-tanked drunk."

"When had the house been built, originally?"

"Late 1880s, can you imagine? I've seen pictures. What a goddamn shame."

"Is that why you don't drink much these days?" I felt as though I could ask him anything right now. "Because of your grandpa and your dad?"

"That's the main reason. I used to drink all the time, thought I could handle it all right. I always used to wonder if Dad would have been a different man if he hadn't been lost in the bottle all the time." He paused and studied the distance. "What am I saying? Of course he would have been different."

"Did your mom love him?" I asked quietly, before admitting, "Clark told me the story of how they married. I feel strange knowing that from someone else."

"No, it's all right. Everyone around here knows that story anyway." He released a quiet sigh and I wanted to touch him so much that the puncture wounds in my hand and heart all started throbbing. "My mom was like this beautiful, fragile little bird. My memories of her are so clear, even now. She sang to me. I was protective of her but I was too little to do any good. Dad was mean as a fucking goddamn rattlesnake when he drank. I learned to avoid him. I don't know how Mama ever could have loved him, even though she claimed she did."

He'd called her 'Mama' unconsciously, I could tell, and tears were pulsing in my eyes and in the back of my throat.

Case continued, "After she died it was hell for a long time. I don't know what I would have done without Clark and Faye. God, they've helped Gus and me so much I could never begin to repay them. And now Faye is gone, too. Sweet Faye. Clark has never been the same since she passed. They were so in love."

We had left Case's homestead far behind. I blinked back tears as fiercely as I was able. "I'm so glad you have him. All of the Rawleys. They're such a loving family."

"They are. It's what I —" But he cut short the sentence.

"What you..." I prompted.

He looked toward the distant horizon. "What I always wanted."

Oh, Case...

Why are you making me feel this way?

I knew if I didn't try to tease him I would start crying in earnest, but it came out sounding all wrong. "It's not as though there isn't time, you know. You're not exactly an old man."

He muttered, "You tell it like it is, as I well know."

Was that a jab or a compliment? I thought the latter but I couldn't discern from his tone. At that moment I caught sight of the T-shaped rock and pointed. "There's the wizard."

Case looked east, toward the rock and the rising moon. "It does have that look, doesn't it?" He took Buck in that direction. "Here, let's cross the road."

I led Cider after them, watching Case's broad shoulders just ahead, overwhelmed by the vision of the two of us riding double. Right now I would have given about anything. I thought of holding his shirt against my face. I thought of the single pillow on his couch, the way our eyes had met time and again at the Rawleys' house earlier this evening, the way he'd cupped my leg with his strong hand, fitting my boot to the stirrup. I thought of the effortless way his hands curved around a guitar to draw forth music.

My heart seemed to be bleeding out.

Case led Buck down the gradual incline of the ditch and there drew on the reins, waiting for Cider and me to catch up. Once we were beside them, he pointed east. "We'll head straight over there. The ground is more uneven off the road but Cider is used to it. We'll take it slow. You doing all right so far?"

"We're just great," I said, leaning forward to rub Cider's warm neck. The moonlight leached the color from everything around us, creating a surreal, otherworldly landscape. Buck nickered and tossed his head, sidestepping, and Case drew him back in line. The two horses touched noses, nickering to each other, and I couldn't help but laugh. "I think they're plotting."

"They want to run, but I would never run them at night, especially not with you on Cider."

"We could handle it." I saw the way Case smiled at my words. Cider danced forward and I let her, straightening my spine.

"I have no doubt," he said. "But it's still dangerous. In the day, after you've had more practice."

I could just picture Case riding Buck at a full-out gallop; I could probably reach orgasm just watching.

Dammit, don't think that word right now…

"You're on," I said.

Again we rode side by side, our knees in proximity but not touching, and there was a part of me that wanted us to keeping riding like this, for always. In less than an hour, I'd determined that I loved riding Cider beneath the moon, Case and Buck at our side. It was so right that I battled the urge to tell him so. He rode with his wide shoulders squared, hips relaxed, holding the reins loosely in one hand.

"Do you believe in past lives?" I suddenly asked.

Case shot a glance my way. "I think I do. I can't explain certain things, otherwise." He was silent for a second. "What about you?"

"My Aunt Jilly believes in them, and my sisters. So does Mathias."

"But what about you?" he pressed and the entire landscape held its breath. I concentrated on my own breathing, wanting to tell him that I'd had a strange memory of him just earlier this evening—but I wasn't sure if that's exactly what it had been.

"I think I do, too." My voice seemed unnaturally hushed out here in the wide open. I peered at the sky, feeling the moon beam over my face, a pleasant and familiar sensation; moonlight on my skin reminded me of swimming in Flickertail at night. "Out here, especially, I can believe that they're real. I was pumping gas the first night I got here, just outside Jalesville, and I had this sense of—I don't know, exactly—of recognition, I guess. Like something here was…*waiting* for me to arrive. Does that make sense?"

"Perfect sense."

I knew he wasn't just saying that. I whispered, "Thanks for letting me ride Cider. This is the best evening I've had in a long time."

Maybe ever, I acknowledged, but I didn't need to be that specific.

Case was bathed in moonlight, its light decorating the angles of his handsome face.

"It's my pleasure," he said quietly.

"How'd you get that scar?" I indicated by pointing at his chin.

"Falling off a horse, back in third grade."

I clutched Cider's reins; I had to say something. "I bet that's not like falling off a bike."

"No, it's not, and I've fallen from a bike plenty of times." He cleared his throat, a low, soft sound. "I wanted to ride my dad's horse and she didn't want a rider just then. She stopped short, bent her front legs, and I sailed over her head like a kite. Bashed my face on the gravel and a piece dug right into my face."

"Were you near home when it happened?"

"I was, but I walked over to Clark and Faye's since I knew Faye would take care of me. Dad and Gus—he was just a toddler then—were both sleeping. That's what made me think I could sneak off with Dad's horse." He laughed at the memory. "That horse's name was Whiskey Belle. Isn't that great?"

I was stuck on the picture of him as a little boy, walking with blood dripping from his face. I demanded, "Were they home? Did Faye take care of you?"

"She picked the gravel out of my chin and patched me right up. But my shirt looked ten times more like I'd committed a murder than your little gray skirt yesterday."

We reached the base of the T-shaped rock and Case halted Buck; as Buck stopped, so did Cider, she and I about a dozen paces from them. Before Case could dismount to help me, I leaned forward and eased my right boot free of the stirrup. Damned if I was going to seem like a city girl, unable to figure out the process of dismounting. It didn't seem all that difficult; I felt balanced but when I swung my right leg over the saddle my left boot remained lodged in the stirrup. Cider neighed in alarm, sidestepping as I fell with a thud, flat on my ass.

Case was at my side in an instant.

"Tish," he said, concerned but also laughing, as though unable to help it. I'm sure I must have looked ridiculous. Before I could move, he bent and hooked both arms around my waist, helping me to my feet, running both hands carefully over my shoulders and along my sides, inspecting for damage. "Are you hurt?"

I *don't care how stupid I looked, it's worth it for this*, I thought, shaking my head to answer his question. I was wreathed in the scent of him, his warm strength and tender concern; ten thousand times better than holding his empty t-shirt to my face.

"I would have helped you down," he reprimanded, still laughing. He seemed satisfied that none of my bones were broken, his hands cupped around my elbows—the thrill of sparks this light touch sent through me almost took me back to the ground. "Next time wait for me to help you."

Cider nickered and stepped closer, nudging her long nose against my breasts. Case eased back and caught up her dangling reins. I rested a palm on her neck and muttered, "Sorry, girl."

"Come on, I'll show you where I think they were digging," Case said, collecting Buck's dropped reins and looping both horses' leads securely around a stand of brush.

This close to the base of the towering formation I felt almost microscopic. I stuck beside Case, craning my neck to peer at the horizontal rock ledge far above; my vision swam with a rush of dizziness. The rock appeared to soar against the sky and my ears rang to a high, shrill frequency.

I've been here before.

But when? How?

"Right here." Case crouched a few yards away. I scurried to kneel at his side. "See, there's turned and re-turned earth all around here. What the hell?"

"It's a good marker. A way to remember where you put something in the ground. Millennia could pass and it would never change."

"That's true. It's got a permanence to it, it's recognizable from the thousands of other rocks. That's part of the reason we were always drawn to it as kids."

"You think that maybe gold has been buried here?" I asked. "Gold that Yancy knows about?"

"You'd think the bastard has enough money that he wouldn't trouble himself, even if he did know. It's a local story, infamous enough that he could have heard of it."

"And he's bored," I said, thinking of how he'd looked at me that day in the law office.

"That's a good point, too," Case said. "Jalesville isn't what he's used to, and thank God people haven't been rolling over and selling to him as quickly as he anticipated. But it means he's stuck here for the time being."

"We have to keep that momentum," I agreed. "What's the chance he'll get tired of waiting and go back to Chicago? Some people can't survive long outside of the city…"

I was actually thinking of Grace and Ina with that comment but Case's silent gaze told me he figured I was referring to myself. I opened my mouth to say otherwise when he suddenly murmured, "Headlights."

Both of us looked the way we'd come to spy a vehicle moving along the access road, headed in our direction. My heart kicked up another ten notches, this time in fear. Cider nickered and Buck stomped the ground. Instinctively, Case put me behind him, angling in front of me.

"What should we do?" I asked, all jacked up at the sight of the headlights gliding slowly toward us.

His voice low and adamant, Case murmured, "If these fuckers think they can come onto my land with no explanation, they have another fucking thing coming." He added, "Pardon my language."

I straightened my spine and moved to stand beside him, rather than behind. I could sense the rigid tension in his strong body; he was ready to fight. The car was close enough now that I could tell it wasn't the SUV from the first night. It was small, much like my Honda, and Case suddenly relaxed. With annoyance and affection mingled in his tone, he said, "It's all right, it's just Gus."

"Your brother?" I clarified, disappointed that we weren't going to confront Yancy or his dirty workers at this moment, here under the moon-drenched sky. I'd been envisioning making a stand beside Case, the two of us together, like at the town meeting.

The car came to a halt and through an open window Gus called, "Damn! You guys beat us here! Casey, what the hell?"

Lacy and Gus both climbed from the car and I looked up at Case, stunned that he'd invite other people to our stakeout. "You were *expecting* them?"

"No," he said at once. "They come out here sometimes to —"

"Make love," I finished, interrupting him as understanding dawned.

Case was studying me again, so intently that I dared not look at him. Gus and Lacy reached us; they were both grinning and had probably consumed too much alcohol for any sort of driving.

"Shit, I didn't know you two…" Gus let his voice trail away.

"We took the horses out," Case explained, offering nothing more by way of explanation. He roughed up Gus's hair. "And you shouldn't be driving right now, little bro, I hope you know."

"Hi, Tish!" Lacy chirped.

I was so jealous at what they were coming to do that I felt as fragile as an eggshell.

"Don't you two have your own apartment?" I snapped, and they both started laughing.

Case's expression was unreadable in the moonlight. I couldn't tell if he was even one-tenth as disappointed as I was right now.

Gus said, "We do. We just left Clark's. Thought we might…you know…"

Lacy giggled and buried her face against his shoulder.

"But we'll get going," Gus said, wrapping his arms around his girlfriend.

"Not driving, you won't," Case said. "You're shitfaced. You should have called me for a ride."

"Aw, Casey," Gus wheedled. "I'm fine."

I realized what had to be done and said, with a sigh, "I'll drive you two back to the house. You can lead Cider, right?" I implored Case, willing him to show what he was feeling. I could have punched Gus for ruining this evening. What if I didn't get another chance to hang out with Case before I left?

The insidious feeling of desolation crept back into my soul.

"I can lead her," Case said. I could not tell exactly what was present in his tone.

Disappointment weighted my body so heavily I almost bent double as I led the way to Gus's idling car. I ordered, "Let's go," with an edge in my voice that could have carved a Thanksgiving turkey. I somehow sensed that Case was smiling.

"I'll see you at home," he called, and though he was addressing all of us I indulged in a little fantasy that he was talking just to me, that I was heading to *our* home. And that he'd come galloping to find me and we'd make love until I couldn't walk, until I couldn't possibly take any more, and then I would beg him to make me take more. I released a shuddery breath, looking over my shoulder to find Case standing with his hands caught on his hips, like he'd stood at the meeting on Tuesday, just watching.

And once again I was struck straight through the heart with the knowledge that I had been here with him before tonight.

Gus and Lacy were apologetic and giggly, and started kissing in the backseat as I drove the short distance to Case's trailer.

"God, you guys," I complained, driving with my right hand on the steering wheel and the other against my forehead, where I used four fingers to scrunch up my loose hair.

"We're sorry," Lacy said for the both of them, giggling more.

"I didn't know that you and my brother…" Gus leaned forward. "Aw, Tish, that's so great. I can't even tell you."

"No, we're just friends," I was quick to inform, and he sat back again.

"Shit, that's too bad. Damn."

The red chili-pepper lights were glowing when I parked Gus's car beside my own. Mutt and Tiny were excited to see us; Gus and Lacy crouched down to lavish them with affection and I said, "I'll be right back," realizing I could seize this opportunity to see Case's bedroom.

Really quickly. Just see it, that's all.

Jesus, Tish. What is wrong with you?

Talk about a stalker.

The screen door sang on its hinges as I went inside; the light above the sink was on, lending the space a warm yellow glow. I tugged out of my hiking boots before walking down the little hallway, knowing I had only a few minutes, tops. I could hear Gus and Lacy out the open windows; I was listening for hoofbeats coming closer—but what I heard instead was the frantic thrusting of my heart.

There were two bedrooms, but the smaller was crammed full of instruments and other trappings of a musician. I crept to the next room; in the dim light provided by the fixture in the hallway I saw that his bed was unmade. It was a full-size, with one pillow, sheets in a whirlwind. It smelled so much like him in here, spicy and masculine, and a trembling started in my knees. I knelt on the bed and touched his sheets, running my fingertips all over them, pressing my palms flat to the mattress. I took his pillow and brought it to my breasts. I breathed against it, letting my tongue touch the pillowcase. I felt weak, literally weak, with desire, a wild pulse beating at the juncture of my thighs.

I want to wait for him, right here.

I want to strip naked and wind his sheets between my legs.

What has gotten into you?!

Stop this! This is beyond insane.

I released a tense breath and replaced his pillow, in a hurry now, my face hot as the base of a long-burning fire. Case had not returned and I knew I had to go *now*, as much as I loathed the idea of leaving before he got back with the horses. I felt guilty, like a total deviant, entertaining notions that would never have occurred to me in this life, erotic things that rendered me so flustered I could hardly remember where I'd put my keys.

"You want a beer?" Gus asked, he and Lacy headed now for the trailer, holding hands.

"No, I have to help out Al tomorrow." My voice shook but they weren't inclined to notice. "Gus, please tell your brother I said good-bye. Tell him thanks for letting me ride Cider."

"Will do," Gus said amiably.

It wasn't until I was home and stripping naked in my own room, Peaches purring around my ankles, that I reached to unclasp my earrings and realized one was missing.

Chapter Twelve

THE NEXT AFTERNOON, AFTER SPENDING THE MORNING obsessing about my lost earring—it had certainly fallen off near the wizard rock, *not* in Case's unmade bed—I met Al at the office, where he was already busy going through stacks of files, papers sprawled everywhere. The window fan was cranked on high and the radio was playing a country station, the same one that I routinely listened to in my apartment.

"Hi," I said, lifting my sunglasses to the top of my head. My desk was untouched, other than its usual stacks.

"Hi, Tish." Al nodded toward Mary's desk. "There's the pie I promised."

"Yum," I said, gravitating to the paper plate. "Thanks."

"Thank you for coming in today. I hate this sort of thing, going through supplies and cleaning out old files and all of that. Mary would help, but I feel guilty."

"It's no problem. Besides, I won't be here after tomorrow, for a couple of days."

Al looked up; he was sitting on the floor. "Oh, that's right. Bar exam. You'll hit it out of the park, don't you worry."

"Thanks for the vote of confidence. Just tell me what to do, boss man, and I'll do it."

Al put me to work on a stack of files in a cardboard box about as big as a refrigerator. I was glad I was wearing ratty cut-off jean shorts and an old pink t-shirt, my hair in a ponytail. I reflected as we worked, occasionally chatting, sometimes in companionable silence with only the radio in the background, that I truly enjoyed working for Al. He was a kind man, especially for a lawyer. It troubled me more every day that he had mentioned disliking Ron Turnbull. 'Fairly despicable,' Al had said; Al, who was fond of understating, as I had learned. What 'fairly despicable' would translate to if he were to speak forthrightly made my stomach cramp.

By quarter after five the sun was angling over the law office in its languid summertime descent. My neck was aching when something suddenly snagged my eye—a file containing copies of motions drafted by Al this past Christmas when Highland Power closed its doors. I thumbed through these, not sure what I was searching for, and the words *Redd Co.* caught my attention; printed above their business name was a red bull that I remembered only because it resembled the much better-known Merrill Lynch logo.

Where have I seen this before?

"Hey, Al, who or what exactly is Redd Co.?"

"I believe that's the company that purchased Highland Power. Last December. Little bull logo, right?"

"That's the one. I don't know why it seems familiar to me."

At that exact moment, Case's truck glided into view just outside the front window. Heart throbbing, I watched him park at the curb. Everything within me sprang to instant, delighted life as he rounded the hood, hopped up the curb, and then pushed through the office. I was already standing, brushing at my dirty shorts, restraining the urge to jump straight into his arms. I hadn't seen him since last night when I'd left him at the base of the wizard rock.

"Hey there," he said, removing his sunglasses and tapping them against his thigh, cowboy hat in place.

"Hey," I said back, unable to fully suppress the longing in my voice. The song "Just a Kiss" was playing on the radio; for an instant I imagined Case playing it for me.

"You left before I got back," he said, with no trace of a smile.

I didn't know how to respond, my hungry gaze moving between his eyes and lips.

We continued to stare wordlessly at each other until, from his side of the office, Al called, "Hello to you, too, Spicer."

At this, Case seemed to come back to himself. "Hi, Al. How goes it?"

Al crossed the room to shake his hand. "What are your plans this evening, young fellow?"

I tried to appear as though it didn't matter a whit to me what he was doing tonight.

Glancing my way, Case said, "I wondered if Tish wanted to join me this evening. We have a gig over in a bar in Miles City in about two hours." My heart responded like a discharging cannon as Case thumbed casually over his shoulder, toward his truck. "I have Wy out there. He's hitching a ride." And then, softly, "What do you say?"

"I would love to." I spoke calmly, pretending that I didn't feel as though all of heaven had opened up to me.

Tish, for fuck's sake. Wy is right out there in the truck.

But Case is here! He's here to pick me up! He came to see if I wanted to come with him!

Is this a date?! It's not a date!

"We have to head out pretty quick here," Case said. "Sorry, I should have called..."

I was all quivery and warm. "Just give me one second."

I walked with admirable poise to the employee bathroom; once safely behind the closed door I leaned toward the mirror and attempted to breathe. My cheeks were bright, my eyes even brighter. My clothes were not exactly the sexiest things I owned; I smoothed the worn t-shirt over my belly and tugged at my shorts. At least I could take my hair down. I ran a wet fingertip over my eyelashes on either side then hurried to unclasp my hair, tipping at the waist to shake it out. When I straightened, I finger-combed it over my shoulders, feeling like I was taking too much time in here; I could hear Al and Case talking. Stilling the trembling in my knees with a great deal of effort, I reentered the main office.

"Someone might slap a suit on you for looking so pretty, counselor," Al said. "Have a fun night. You deserve it. Working on a Saturday."

"I will. Thank you, Al."

Case held the door for me; outside, in the hot evening air, I couldn't help but tell him the truth. "I'm so glad you came to get me."

I loved how a smile could touch his eyes before reaching his mouth. He replied easily, "I thought you might like a night out. Here, let me get that."

I felt as buoyant as a cottonwood seed; his forearm was very near my waist as he held the door handle.

"Come on, you guys!" Wy called from the truck, leaning forward from the backseat. "I'm starved! Tish, you get the front seat, Case said."

"Thank you," I murmured as I climbed in, smiling at Wy. "Hey there, buddy. You have a fake ID, or what?"

Wy laughed. He looked cute, his shaggy hair combed into something resembling order, wearing an old black Grateful Dead t-shirt. Case slid behind the wheel and happiness punched me in the gut, almost doubling me over with its force. I stowed my purse on the floor at my feet so that there was nothing between Case and me. He tilted his chin to the right, my direction, as he shifted into first, still smiling.

"So, where exactly are we going?" I asked as Case took the truck straight out of town, hooking east onto I94.

"We have a show at a bar in Miles City, called the Coyote's Den." At my laughter, he hurried to explain, "It's a great place, not as bad as the name implies. Garth and Marsh are on the way. Becky actually let Garth out of the house for the evening. I haven't played with Garth for a long time. I'm pretty excited, actually."

I could tell, though I tried to downplay as I said, "Well, thanks for letting me tag along."

"Tag along?" Wy scoffed, leaning so far forward that he came close to obscuring my view of Case. "You aren't tagging along. That's what little sisters do. You shoulda heard Case, he said like twenty times that we had to stop and get you."

Case cleared his throat at Wy's words while pure joy spread upward from my stomach. I hadn't felt this way in so long that I was almost dizzy; I looked away, out the window, to hide my smile. The foothills were gorgeous in the sunset, the scrubby brush sparking with splashes of orange light and intermittent shadows, deep and mysterious and guarded.

I wondered just what secrets were harbored out there that no one would ever discover; the original secret-keepers long since dead. I leaned my elbow on the edge of the window, pondering that thought.

"You know what's weird, Tish?" Wy asked. "I feel like you've been here a lot longer than this month, you know? Almost like you've always been here."

It was strange to hear him speak these words, when the same notion had been circling me for days now, whispering to be acknowledged. It had to do with the feeling in the very air, a sense of being in the right place at the right time. Being near the right people.

These will be good memories when you're back in Chicago. When the city gets to be too much...

I said to Wy, but really to Case, "I've been feeling that way since I got here, to be honest."

Sounding more like a little boy than ever, Wy begged, "Can we get elk steak before the show, huh, Case?"

Case laughed. I loved the sound of his laugh, which I had heard far too few times. The sunset pouring in the back window lit his shoulders, clad in a black t-shirt. I wanted to reach and take off his hat so I could see his hair in the sunlight.

"Sure thing," Case told Wy. "It's a Montana specialty."

"I'll try it," I said. "Camille really liked it when they were out here."

Wy piped up (and I adored the kid, I really did, but I so wished he had hitched a ride with his brothers instead), asking, "What are you guys playing tonight?"

"The Den wants classic rock, that's what they told Garth," Case replied, shifting into fifth gear as we cruised along the interstate, the wind ruffling my hair.

"What's your favorite to play? Country, right?" I asked.

"Country, old-time country," he affirmed. "It's what I was raised playing. But we have a pretty damn good range of material so it'll be fun to play something different tonight. What's your favorite to hear?"

"I've always liked country music. But it's been a long time since I've listened to it like I have since moving out here. In school these past three years, old-time blues relaxed me as much as anything could. When I'd be studying late, or writing a new petition, I would listen to the blues."

Case said. "That's one genre I have not mastered. But I'll do my best, next time we're around the fire."

I couldn't look away, studying his crisp profile against the blue of the evening sky.

"I can play the harmonica!" Wy said; I had almost forgotten he was here, so absorbed with Case.

Case laughed again. "Yeah, you can. I'll give you that. Can't sing worth a shit, though."

Wy boxed at Case's shoulder.

"I can't sing worth a shit either," I said. "Camille can sing, and Ruthie, but those talents skipped me, I guess."

"You got other talents, like kicking butt," Wy said, and I had to smile. "Thanks."

"You worked yourself pretty hard in school, didn't you?" Case asked.

"I would have failed, if not," I acknowledged.

"But I mean you worked harder than you probably had to, pushing yourself. I can still see you doing that."

"It's my job now," I said, my heart catching at the tone in his voice; he sounded concerned, I could tell, even if it was subtle. Sleepless smudges were still visible on the skin beneath his eyes, matching my own. Apparently neither of us were sleeping very well, alone.

"Al is right, you deserve a night out," Case said. "Will you let us treat you to dinner? Wy and me, I mean?" How cagey of him, disguising his buying me dinner in this way.

I addressed Wy. "Sure, but I usually pick the most expensive thing on the menu, champagne, lobster, filet mignon…"

"Or elk steak!" Wy reached to rough up my hair.

I was so used to Clint doing this sort of thing that I evaded Wy and reached behind to get him in a headlock. "*Ha!*"

He struggled and I held, all of us laughing. I knuckled his scalp before letting him free.

"That'll learn ya," I said, echoing Clint, a little smug as Wy frantically inspected his reflection in the rearview mirror, smoothing his hair.

Case took the exit into Miles City and drove us to a bar on the out-skirts of the little town; though in comparison to Jalesville, Miles City was huge. We pulled into the lot of a busy bar and grill with a gigantic howling wolf's head busting through the roof.

I giggled. "Look at that wolf."

Case nudged my arm. "*Coyote*. That's a coyote, lawyer lady." I loved how at ease he seemed, the way he'd been around the campfire roasting marshmallows.

Wy jumped out of the truck as I said, "Right. I stand corrected." I no-ticed a smudge of dust on my t-shirt. "I hope I'm not too underdressed…"

Case was already grinning. "Are you kidding? For a place called the Coyote's Den?" His tone changed and I knew he was teasing because he spoke my full name. "Patricia. You're way *over*dressed for this place." He paused, studying my eyes. "Besides, you couldn't look more beautiful. It wouldn't be possible."

My heart threw itself against my ribs. I wanted to tell him that I had never been so drawn to someone in my life; that I dreamed about him nearly every night, but all I could whisper was, "Thank you."

"C'mon, you two!" Wy yelled from the parking lot; he whooped and took off at a gallop, yelling, "Hey guys!"

"There's Garth and Marsh." Case nodded in their direction and I dragged my eyes from him to see the guys toting their guitars. "We're plugged in tonight, so it's a completely different sound."

"What can I carry?"

"You don't have to carry a thing," he said, and then yelled, "Wyatt! Get over here!"

Wy bounded back, taking the gear Case handed him, including a huge black backpack.

"No fiddle tonight?" I asked, disappointed.

"Not tonight," Case said, effortlessly shouldering another enormous pack. He was so strong. "Maybe you could get the tailgate, though…"

I slammed it shut, smiling at the *Gotta Ride, Gotta Play* emblem. We headed toward the front door, which was flanked by a pair of smaller howling coyotes. Music poured from the place, along with the scent of greasy food. I fantasized again that I was Case's girlfriend and that he would dedicate songs to me all evening, and then afterward…

Afterward, we would…

Stop. Don't torture yourself.

I stooped to pat one of the stone coyotes on the nose on the way past, something I would have done as a kid.

"Ranger," he said, and I looked up to find Case holding the door with one shoulder. He grinned. "I named them when I was a kid. This place has been here forever."

"Then what's this guy's name?" I touched the second coyote's nose.

"Dancer." He shook his head, cringing a little. "It's so original, I know…"

"I love it! Ranger and Dancer. They go together. Who's the big guy on the roof?"

"You'll have to name him. I never came up with one."

Loaded down as he was with gear, he still held the door for me. Inside the Den it was dim and crowded, neon signs brightening small pockets of space, bare-bulb lights strung along the host stand. We had entered through the bar, where the stage was located, but there was another room through a double arch, clearly the restaurant; I saw tables and a roaring fire in a stone hearth.

"We'll stash the gear and then go get a table," Case said.

Marsh and Garth had already collected Wy and after Case unloaded his gear, the five of us went to eat.

"Not too close to the fire, it's too hot," Marsh complained as we all followed the server to a table. He said, "Tish, there's something on your shirt," and indicated with an extended index finger, not touching me, just pointing near the middle of my breasts. When I looked down, he flipped up his finger and flicked the end of my nose, then laughed.

I shoved his ribs, laughing too, at having been stupid enough to fall for that old joke. Wy thought it was hysterical and Case flicked Marshall's ear none too gently, demanding, "You want a broken arm?"

Marsh lifted his hands and pretended to tremble. "Tish fell for it!"

Abbie Williams

Garth said with all sincerity, "God, I miss hanging out with you guys."

Case withdrew a chair for me and then claimed the seat directly across, just as I'd been hoping. Marsh sat on my left and Wy across from him, Garth at what amounted to be the head of the table.

"This would be perfect if Carter and Camille were here," Garth reflected. "What would it take to get them out here for good?"

"They love it back home," I said. "So no chance there. Plus they have twenty children, so it's not exactly easy for them to do anything."

"I know, I was just wishing," Garth said.

"I just talked to them last night," Case said. He was leaning on his forearms over the table, menu caught loosely in his hands. His hat kept his eyes in partial shadow but accentuated the contrast of his soft lips and firm chin, the angles of his jaw and cheekbones. He looked so good that it almost hurt.

"You did? I haven't talked to Camille since I've been here, which is terrible."

"She was a little upset," Case acknowledged. "She said to tell you to call her."

"I will tonight," I said, though I couldn't think much beyond this moment.

"Thanks for bringing Gus and Lacy back last night. They ended up sleeping on the couch."

"Did you go back out to the rock?" Somehow I was sure he had. The Rawleys were busy ordering appetizers and drinks so I felt safe asking, since they weren't listening.

"I took Buck out for a long time, but no one else showed up."

I wished I'd been with him so much that my chest ached. I thought of him sleeping in his bed last night, in the sheets I'd touched, using the pillow I'd kissed—what if he *had* found my earring there? We were so absorbed in staring at each other that I jumped when Garth flicked a piece of breadstick at Case.

"Hey, you two want to go in on a pitcher?" Garth asked, looking between Case and me with thinly-veiled speculation.

"Yes, that sounds great."

Case nodded.

"Can we get some potato skins?" Wy begged. "Remember, Tish, anything you want!"

"You buying? Sweet," Marshall declared.

"Sure, that sounds good, and some mozzarella sticks," I said to the pretty redheaded server who stood waiting near Marshall's left elbow. She was totally giving him the eye but he was playing it cool; cool as a cucumber salad as Gran would have said, and I almost giggled.

"No problem," she said, clicking her pen and fluttering her lashes at Marsh.

"Thanks," Marshall murmured, only checking her out after she sauntered away. He muttered, "Shit, I gotta get her name, dedicate a song or two."

"What a *smooth* operator." Garth reached to mess up Marshall's hair.

"Hey, that's how you first got in Becky's pants, I'm just saying," Marshall fired back, ducking away from Garth's reach.

"Damn, not in front of the kid," Garth said through his laughter. "Shit, he hasn't even French-kissed a girl yet."

Wy grew indignant. "Have so!"

"When and where?" Marsh demanded.

"Other than Hannah's ear?" Case asked.

Wy knitted his eyebrows and admitted with a sigh, "Not yet."

"There's plenty of time for that," I told him. "Remember, I was almost a senior in high school before my first kiss."

"Yeah, I heard that story," Garth said, grinning at me.

"So, judging by this timeline, are you still a virgin?" Marsh kept a somber expression as he asked and everyone laughed harder, including me. I punched his shoulder.

"You are *begging* for a severe beating," Case told him.

"Ow," Marsh complained, nursing his arm where I'd decked him. "It's all right, I still am, too. Maybe we could, like, help each other in this regard…"

"*Oh my God*," I groaned, and my stomach hurt from laughing.

The server returned with our appetizers and drinks, and Garth did the honors, pouring for all of us. Wy had a cola with two cherries stuck on the rim. I snagged a mozzarella stick and leaned toward Case. "So, where's the elk steak on the menu?"

"Second page. I'd order you the nine-ounce with mushrooms, that's the best. I mean, if you like mushrooms."

"I do."

His eyes tracked to my mouth and lingered there. "You have a little bit of mozzarella…" He indicated my top lip by touching his own.

"Dammit," I muttered, and Case's smile widened. "I'll be right back."

I threaded through the growing crowd, noticing that I *was* over-dressed for this particular bar; Case wasn't kidding. I spied a few neon-tinted tube tops, a lot of stone-washed denim and hair-sprayed bangs. I found the bathroom and ducked inside to do a quick check, swiping the sticky cheese from my lip and finger-combing my hair, which was wild in the humidity. I wished I was wearing sexier shorts, maybe my striped tank top that showed off my cleavage.

Why, Tish? To what end?

Remember, you're leaving this place at the end of summer.

Shit, sooner than that—in two days for the bar exam.

I studied my somber eyes in the mirror, noting the shadows darkening the skin beneath. Maybe being back in Chicago would restore me to my senses; remind me what I had been working for since I was eighteen years old.

I shoved out of the bathroom and hurried through the crowd, anxious to get back to Case. Only the unfortunate sight of someone I recognized, elbowed up to the adjacent bar, slowed my pace.

Shit, he saw you.

Derrick was perched on a stool, a highball glass near his folded hands. I could tell he hadn't anticipated seeing me here tonight, because his shoulders straightened and he actually appeared somewhat startled before his natural arrogance reasserted itself. He blinked slowly, in the manner of someone who'd been drinking for hours, then nodded at the empty barstool nearest him. I turned away so quickly I bumped into a heavyset woman with bright red lips but didn't pause to apologize, fleeing for the safety of our table. I remembered Al saying that Derrick stayed in a hotel in Miles City.

I returned out of breath. Garth and Marsh were talking with a guy standing between their chairs; Case had been listening to them but watched as I took my seat. "You got all of it."

"Case," I implored.

The teasing fell from his face as he saw that I appeared concerned.

"Yancy is here, at the bar."

His eyebrows lowered. "Call me crazy, but this doesn't seem like the kind of place where he'd hang out."

"That's what I was thinking. He wanted me to *join* him." I almost shuddered.

I saw the way Case's jaws tightened at this news, though he didn't react in any other way. He said, "We play in about a half hour, but we'll situate you right by the stage and Wy will sit with you."

His protectiveness made my heart resonate like a tuning fork. Because this level of emotion was almost too much for me to bear I changed the subject. "I can't wait to hear you play again."

"Tell me what you want to hear, we'll play it," he promised.

"Your song," I said at once. "The one you played on your fiddle at The Spoke. I can't get it out of my head."

Case went still, almost as though holding his breath. He studied me intently and there were several things I sensed he wanted to say, but didn't. Finally he murmured, "I need the fiddle to play that one right. Next time we're around the fire, I promise."

"It's a deal," I agreed.

The rest of the food arrived and the conversation swelled to include everyone, Marsh and Wy vying for attention, Garth telling Case that they better eat fast and make sure their amps were ready to go. I kept stealing long looks at Case; he took off his hat before eating and I made fists to keep from reaching to stroke his hair. If I was the praying sort, I would pray to Melinda Spicer, his sweet mother, to thank her for the man before me. I experienced physical pain at these thoughts, as though life in the past month had repeatedly punched me in the chest.

"C'mon, Tish, these guys gotta get ready. We can sit and have dessert if you want," Wy said after we'd finished eating. "Hey, did you like the elk steak?"

I hadn't been able to eat much, my stomach in hard knots of confusion, but I said, "Yes, it was delicious."

Case walked close behind me as we all cut through the bar, lightly resting his hand on my lower back, as though to guide me as we maneuvered the crowd; a spasm of sparks blazed across my skin. I stalled, leaning into his touch; it was so packed with people that it wasn't an obvious ploy for him to keep touching me. But he did and I could have died it felt so good, his warm, strong hand on my body.

I couldn't see his eyes, since he was behind me, but I imagined how he looked as he stroked ever so gently, his thumb moving in slow arcs. His other hand joined the first, on the opposite side of my waist, his fingers curling possessively around the material of my shirt, the way he might just before tugging it over my head. I couldn't breathe. The crowd shifted and Case let his hands fall back to his sides. My knees were almost too weak to walk forward. I thought of how I had knelt on his bed last night. How I had licked his pillow and probably left behind my earring.

"We're over here," Case murmured, close to my ear.

In the bar the tables were jammed with people; two men with black bandanas were running cords on stage. The Rawleys claimed a small table that was obviously reserved for us.

"You'll be all right here?" Case asked, still close behind me. I turned and my heart shredded, going all to pieces; he appeared somber, studying me from beneath his hat brim. If I was brave enough, I would have stood on tiptoe and put my arms around his neck. I nodded and he stunned me anew by tucking a stray strand of hair behind my ear. His fingertips lingered briefly on my jaw and my knees gave out; fortunately I was in the proximity of a chair.

"Tish!" Wy snagged a seat to my right as Case, Garth, and Marsh carried their guitars up onto the stage. "You wanna get some dessert?"

"Sure," I whispered, watching Case as he extracted a dark blue electric guitar from its case and proceeded to hook it up to the proper cords, so efficiently, something he'd done hundreds of times. All this time he'd been out here, living his life while I'd been living mine in Illinois. I wanted to sprint backward through those years and shake sense into the old me, the girl from Camille's wedding who had been so selfish and so cold. One of the sound-check guys was saying something that made Case laugh and my heart throbbed.

"Another drink?" asked the redheaded server. She leaned closer to Wy and me and nodded toward Marsh. "Is he your brother?"

Wy and I said, "Yes," at the same time, and Wy grinned at my lie.

"What's his name?"

"Marshall," I told her.

"He's *so* hot," she breathed.

"He thinks so, too," Wy said, and she giggled.

"He's *totally* single," I added, trying to be helpful.

"Your next round's on me. I'm Sara. Nice to meet you."

Just like last night at Clark's, Case would send me a look every so often. I sipped my free beer as I watched him, noticing every detail. He was careful and loving with his instruments, just as he was with his horses. Tender touches on everything, his big hands with their long and knowing fingers that could tune a guitar just as effortlessly as they could saddle a horse, or pluck sage from the brush in the foothills and tuck hair behind my ear.

The bar lights glinted in his hair and played over the angles of his face; he'd left his hat on the chair to my left, where I could reach over and touch it, which I kept doing. He looked so damn sexy, tall and lean, his shoulders wide, his movements unconsciously graceful, simultaneously powerful and lithe. He finished his ministrations on the guitar and sent me a sweet smile, cradling his gleaming, dark blue instrument; I smiled right back.

The guys in bandanas finished up their work on the stage and jogged down the steps. Marsh settled behind the drums while Garth and Case took positions near the two floor mics, their electric guitars held at their hips. So totally sexy. The crowd rumbled and then a few cheers became a round of excited applause; I recognized people from Jalesville here and there on the dance floor.

"Hi, folks, how're you doing this fine evening?" Garth asked. There were raucous whoops and cheers, and he grinned. "*Fuck* yeah."

"*We love you!*" called a woman, and Garth winked at her; all the Rawley boys had good winks.

"I came out of retirement for tonight and it feels pretty damn good." There were more cheers at this, louder than before, and Garth ordered, "So don't fucking disappoint me. I want to see asses on the dance floor, people!"

And with that he played the first few bars of "Welcome to the Jungle," while the crowd went insane. Marsh was wild on the drums and Case tipped his chin, lashes lowered, completely overtaken as his fingers flew to make music, keeping time with his wide shoulders, stroking that electric guitar like it was a woman he could not touch enough.

Oh God, look at him. I can't handle it. I just plain can't handle it.

I held my icy beer bottle to the side of my neck, struggling for composure, afraid I might lose hold of my inhibitions and rush the stage. After the first song they were laughing, the crowd hot for more; I saw plenty of women stalking the stage and my fingers became talons. They played and sang with such effortless joy, leading from one rock song to the next. I could not tear my gaze from Case; he returned my looks every so often, as though to reassure me that everything was all right. Late in the evening, as they led into "Wanted Dead or Alive," he sent me a smile, red stage lights gilding his hair...and everything else in the chaotic bar retreated behind a haze, receding to invisibility as awareness shattered over me, sharp as broken glass.

I've known you. I've known you far beyond this place and this time...

I know it's true. I can't explain it, but I know it.

I saw him on horseback then, astride Ranger, outside in the blazing sun, his hair afire with sparks before he resettled his hat. Looking back over his shoulder at me, where I sat high atop a wagon seat, distant from him.

I'll protect you, he whispered later, in a moment we dared stealing.

We cannot risk this. But even as I spoke the words my hands were all over him, digging into his hair, clutching his shoulders, need overpowering all else. We were not allowed near one another in the daylight hours and if we were discovered now I knew they would kill us. Or, far worse, they would kill him to punish me.

My wedding band caught the glimmer of a nearby lantern.

The night air crackled with urgent heat. His strong hands spread my legs as we kissed, devouring each other.

We cannot risk it.

I will protect you. I swear to you, Patricia, on my life. Trust me, you have to trust me.

I blinked and cold air screamed in my ears as I was abruptly returned from the prairie in my mind to the crowded, noisy barroom; I rose too quickly, stumbling over a chair, and muttered to Wy, "I'm going to the bathroom…"

I sensed Case observing, concerned; as I made my way through the crowd I looked up at him, explaining without words, *It's all right. I just need a second…*

In the bathroom I bent low over the sink and splashed my face with icy water. It dripped down my neck and I let the chill shock my senses into something resembling reason.

What the hell? That was so real. It was too real…

Am I going crazy?

I drew a deep, painful breath.

Case…

We have belonged to each other before now.

I knew this to the interior of my bones.

I realized that I could not stay in here, hiding out; as though to emphasize the point, a toilet flushed. I retreated to the hallway outside the bathroom, shaken and disoriented, and almost immediately a voice behind me asked in a conversational tone, "Are you dating him then? Or just *fucking* him?"

I spun to see Derrick leaning one shoulder against the wall, clad in designer dress pants and a pale shirt. His black hair was disheveled, falling over his forehead, his collar undone two past the top button, no tie or matching suit jacket in sight. He was clearly shit-tanked, as Case had said last night, describing his grandfather.

"You're drunk." I tried for a steady voice. I didn't intend to say anything else, but then heard myself hiss, "Nothing I do is *any of your goddamn business.*"

"You'd think in a hick town like Jalesville there'd be corrals full of slutty girls I could fuck, but so far none I want. Except *you.* You're the slut I can't stop thinking about." He did not take his eyes from my stunned face as he slurred through this nasty little speech. Beside him, the door to the men's room opened to a guy who gave us a curious look. There was a wall separating the bathrooms from the bar and I heard Garth joking with the crowd between songs.

Derrick blocked my path, so drunk he was weaving side to side, and this unkempt, foul-mouthed version of him made my stomach clench with true fear. I adopted my best lawyer voice. "Get out of my way."

"What do you see in that goddamn yokel?"

"Move!" I insisted.

Derrick narrowed his eyes, shaking his head in the manner of someone attempting to clear his thoughts. "He killed him, you know. *Coward.* Shot him in the back. Fucker has it coming now."

My vision wavered and I felt caught up in whatever it was he was blathering about, as though I somehow understood. I demanded, "What are you *talking* about? Killed who?"

"Thomas Yancy," he said, enunciating carefully; his eyes appeared glazed. He looked so alarming that I thought I should call for help, that maybe he was about to have a seizure. But then he refocused, muttering viciously, "*Whore,*" and shoved me out of his way.

I gasped, more shocked than in pain, and Derrick stumbled away, disappearing into the men's room. Not five seconds later, Case strode around the wall from the bar and the expression in his eyes was enough to make any man run for cover. His voice was rough as he explained, "I had a horrible feeling. Are you all right?"

I wanted to tell him what had just happened but was not willing to chance the resultant confrontation; I realized if I told Case what Derrick had just said and done, Case would find him and things would get ugly, real quick.

And so I lied in a whisper, "I'm just fine."

He recognized that I was lying but didn't call me on it. "Do you want to go?"

"No!" I tamed my voice. "No, I want to hear you play. You guys aren't done yet, right?"

"We have another half hour or so, but we can leave if that's what you need."

Oh God, what I need...

"No, I want to stay here," I insisted. *With you.*

He nodded, studying my face as though to make certain I was serious. He sweating from the exertion of performing, his hairline damp, forehead shiny with moisture that tracked down to his jaws. As he turned to head back to the bar I grabbed his arm, allowing myself this indulgence; he shifted and I was afraid he meant to put distance between us, but instead he tucked me to his side. I teetered between this reality and another—a distant prairie where we existed in grave danger; the boundary between these realities seemed thin and insubstantial.

Garth, Marsh, and Wy were crowded around our table, along with Sara, the server, and a few other people I didn't know, drinking beer, laughing, the mood merry. Case led me to my chair and then took the seat saved by his cowboy hat; I hated that we were no longer touching. I tried to listen to the banter all around us, distracted by the image of Case on a horse—not Buck or Cider, but a horse I didn't recognize—riding near my wagon over an expanse of dusty prairie. I sensed danger, sharp as a well-honed blade, both here in the bar and in this inexplicable vision.

I did my best to pull it together when Case left the table to finish the set; he was clearly worried and I was jittery from my encounter with Derrick. I scanned the crowd for a sight of that asshole, but he was nowhere to be seen. Probably he had passed out in the bathroom, but I didn't care enough to check. By the time the guys were allowed to leave the stage after two encore songs, it was edging past midnight.

Case came to our table and told Wy, "Help me load this stuff, all right?"

"Sure," Wy said, sensing no chance to argue, jumping to do as Case asked.

"You're exhausted," Case observed, his eyes on me. When Wy was out of earshot in the noisy bar, he explained, "I have to take the kid home. Garth and Marsh want to stay a little longer."

Oh God, Case, take me home with you, hold me close in your bed.

I can't bear to go back to my apartment without you...

But I knew that if Wy wasn't riding home with us I couldn't trust myself. It was too dangerous. I would beg Case to stay, to make love to me until the sun crested at dawn; his place, my place, even in the truck. I didn't care where.

"I understand," I whispered.

"I'll grab my things and we'll go."

Outside under the stars I inhaled a long breath, trying to steady my leaping nerves; I paused to pat Ranger and Dancer, the coyotes, farewell, prompting Case to do the same, and Wy told us we were weird. We drove back to Jalesville in almost complete silence, only the radio playing softly in the background. I thought Wy might be sleeping as cool night air rushed through the windows. I wanted to tell Case what Derrick had said, and what I'd seen in my strange visions, but couldn't find the right words. Instead we sat in tense, electric silence, so very aware of each other. We reached Jalesville too quickly. I spoke around the growing lump in my throat to remind him, "My car is at work..."

"I'm so glad you came with me tonight," Case said as we approached Howe and James, dark and locked up, along with every other business on Main.

"I had such a good time. Thank you for dinner."

"It was my pleasure." He spoke quietly, parking beside my lonely car, his truck idling.

From the backseat, Wy mumbled, "G'night, Tish."

"Good-night, buddy." It struck me afresh that I was returning to Chicago on Monday morning. What were the chances I would see Case before I got back the following Thursday? I stifled my growing panic, my voice husky beneath the weight of regret as I explained, "I'm flying back to Chicago on Monday."

Case nodded at this information. "Bar exam, you said."

I nodded, wondering how in the hell something I'd worked for so very hard now seemed almost trivial. Insignificant, even meaningless; I knew this doubt would dissipate the moment I touched down in Chicago. I could almost hear my high heels on the city sidewalk.

"You'll kick its ass," he said, as though trying to elicit a smile. But I felt more like weeping.

"Bonfire tomorrow night, Dad said to tell you." Wy sounded more awake. He sat up and murmured, "Tish, don't forget to bring Peaches with you."

The Rawleys were watching my cat while I flew back to Illinois.

"I won't forget," I whispered, still caught up in Case's eyes.

Stop it, stop it, stop it.

Stop looking at me that way when I can't want you like this.

I can't. I'm leaving.

A wailing cry formed at the back of my throat as I reached for the door handle.

"I'll see you tomorrow night, then," Case said.

"Good-night," I whispered.

They waited until I had unlocked and started my car; we turned opposite directions from the parking lot, and I watched his taillights disappearing in my rearview mirror.

Chapter Thirteen

THE NEXT EVENING AT DINNER, CLARK MADE TWO TOASTS in my honor, everybody excited for me to venture forth and prove myself on the bar exam. The food was delicious, the weather sublime. We all sat on the back deck until it was time for the fire. I knew I needed to get home to bed; I hadn't slept a wink last night and my flight left at seven tomorrow morning, requiring a two-hour drive to the airport in Billings. But I couldn't bear to leave because when I did I would no longer be near Case; four days' separation from him loomed like an impassable desert.

Do you hear yourself?! Jesus Christ, what will you do when you leave for good?

I can't think about that right now.

You'll miss him.

A lot.

Oh God, a whole fucking lot.

I took one of the first seats at the fire, watching as Sean, Marsh, and Wy worked together to build it. Quinn and his girlfriend, Ellie, set out more chairs. Case and Garth had promised music and went to retrieve their instruments; I prayed Case would take the chair to my right but instead he ended up directly across the fire.

This, I learned, was both better and far, far worse.

He wasn't near enough to touch but this way I could watch him to my heart's content, all the while pretending to be studying the fire. He looked my way as he took his seat, both of us islands of silence among the laughter and chatter, as we had been all evening. Then he refocused on tuning his guitar, so close and yet so goddamn far away, which only highlighted the fact that he was not mine, and that I had no right to wish *anything* about him. We'd hardly spoken all evening, though I was aware of his every movement, his every breath.

"Tish, you're gonna get cold," Wy observed.

I'd spent an hour getting ready, blowing out my hair and highlighting my eyes, dressing in a soft yellow sundress. I knew Case had noticed; his eyes told me I looked beautiful, even if he hadn't said the words.

"I've got a jacket in the car —" I shifted to rise.

"Here, you can wear mine," Case said, not meeting my eyes as he stood, unceremoniously lifted his jean jacket from the back of his lawn chair, and passed it to me. It was the one he'd worn on Thursday night, when we'd ridden Cider and Buck to the wizard rock.

I felt all shivery and splendid at this gesture. "Thank you."

He barely nodded in response, busying himself tightening a guitar string. I held the jacket to my breasts, feeling the rough-textured denim. I wrapped into it and was embraced by his scent—immediate and in-toxicating. I resisted the urge to turn up the collar and hold it to my nose, as I'd done with his t-shirt, as I'd done in his bed. His glance flickered my way, however briefly, as though he could somehow read my mind.

"You're welcome," he murmured.

Clark joined us, Case finished his ministrations on the guitar and Garth strummed a couple of chords.

"Tish, you choose," Garth invited. "What do you want to hear?"

"The one you said you'd play, last night," I reminded Case. "I love that one."

Case nodded acceptance and exchanged the guitar for his fiddle. I shivered in anticipation. He lifted the instrument to his chin; he played the fiddle with eyes closed, I knew well. I curled my fingers around the cuffs of his jacket as he began to play, his expression intent, so ab-sorbed, the music flowing from his fingertips. The melody was haunting and sweet, as always; I knew it well enough by now that I could have hummed aloud my favorite parts. When he finished there was a hush around the fire; he lowered the fiddle and opened his eyes, and our gazes held while my heart throbbed.

"That's so beautiful," Becky said, breaking the tension in the air. "I love that one."

"You pick now, hon," Garth told his wife, and she chose "Red River Valley."

Requests flew for the next hour and Case and Garth obliged, long-time friends and almost-brothers singing in easy harmony, their voices blending. Everyone joined in when it was a song we knew, even though I was too shy to really sing. Wy kept whispering, "You gotta sing for *real*, Tish," when all I really wanted to do was watch Case, with his rich, true voice. He did not look across the fire again. Finally the late hour began claiming the Rawleys and their women, one by one. I hugged everyone in turn, promising to see them all at dinner this upcoming Friday, like usual, when I'd be back in Jalesville.

"And you'll be a bona fide legal lady by then," Clark said as I hugged him.

Friday seemed more than a century away. I found myself watching Becky and Garth as they headed for their truck, their son in tow, Garth tucking his wife against his side and kissing her hair. A fist squeezed my heart; I had trouble restraining tears.

"You all right to drive?" Clark asked, since I'd had a couple of drinks.

Case was putting away his fiddle, seeming to linger over the task, the last one at the fire.

"I'll just sit for one more minute," I said, offering Clark a smile.

"Let us know when you're safe in Chicago tomorrow, all right, honey?" To Case, he added, "Good-night, son."

Case said, "'Night, Clark," just as I said, "I will."

At the fire, Case hardly looked up. He appeared completely preoccupied, though there was an air of what I interpreted as tension hovering all about him. I took my seat as the outer door of the house closed behind Clark and Garth drove from the yard with a crunching of tires on gravel, leaving us alone with the crackle of the slowly-dying fire. I watched Case as he worked, thinking of everything we had been through since I'd arrived in Jalesville, wondering if he would continue to pretend that I wasn't sitting here, too. He placed his fiddle case carefully on the ground and then sat still, forearms to thighs. I was feverish with tension. When he at last looked my way, a swell of painful longing jammed the space behind my breastbone.

He said quietly, "I owe you an apology."

The fire danced in ever-changing patterns across his face, his powerful shoulders, his boots. When I couldn't manage to respond to this bewildering statement, he clarified, "I used to drink way too much. I was young and stupid, and I owe you an apology for how I acted at Mathias and Camille's wedding. I'm sorry about that, I really am."

I shook my head, stunned into speechlessness that he'd finally mentioned that night. His somber gaze held steady as I whispered, "You don't need to be sorry. I was so rude to you. I'm the one who should be apologizing."

"You put me in my place, and I needed that." His eyes shifted up and to the left. "I can see exactly how you looked that day. That red dress."

I cringed, recalling my behavior. With no small amount of self-deprecation, I said, "I'm so sorry for how I acted. I've grown up a little since then."

I wanted him to know I was sincere; I wanted to talk about last night and the strange vision of us in another time that I'd been unable to erase from my mind. Even now it crowded my thoughts, begging to be recognized; I was dying to ask if he realized that we'd known each other before now.

"And you've done everything you planned to back then," he observed before I could speak. "I admire that a great deal. I just want you to know that."

"Thank you." I had never been more quietly proud of myself. "I worked hard for it."

"I can tell you work hard for anything you put your mind to," he said, again complimenting me perhaps more than I deserved. "I'd hate to come up against you before a judge, I'll say that. And everything you've been working on around here. That bar exam has nothing on you."

I whispered, "I'm still worried," but that was a flat-out lie; I had hardly thought about the exam in days, other than the fact that it was forcing me to leave Jalesville.

"You'll be glad to see Chicago?" He asked carefully, as though it might be an offensive question. Or maybe he just didn't want to hear my answer.

"It'll be good to see my dad," I said, side-stepping his question. Such a goddamn lawyer.

"Will you see the place you plan to work?" His voice was strained; it hurt him to ask this of me. It hurt me just as badly to respond.

"Turnbull and Hinckley." I shook my head, indicating that probably I would not.

"It's much different than Howe and James, I'd bet. It's what you want?"

"For three years now." I closed my eyes. Because I couldn't think any more about Chicago, I whispered, "Thanks for playing that song. I just love it."

He remained silent. I opened my eyes to his searing gaze. I thought of how he'd caressed my back last night; how he'd touched my hair and tucked me close when he was worried. I *knew* he wanted to touch me as desperately as I wanted to touch him; he was holding back for reasons of his own, I was certain.

At last he murmured, "Thank you."

"Do you like making music for a living?"

His brows lowered a little, questioning what I really meant by this; I scrambled through my own floundering thoughts, wondering just what I meant, too. Reading between the lines could suggest I was indirectly asking a number of rather insulting things, such as *it doesn't make you much money, does it?*

"It pays the bills," he responded. He was perceptive, following this with a matter-of-fact tone as he allowed, "I'll never be rich, if that's what you mean."

I let that go.

"How long were you married?" I was pulling out all the stops now and wanted to hear it from him.

As always, his gaze torched my bare flesh, so intense and searching were his eyes; calm and quiet, he answered, "Close to three years."

"What happened?"

"Does it matter?" His voice wasn't sharp but an edge was there.

"No, it's not my business," I admitted. My face was so hot that I might as well have been roasting it on a stick. He linked his fingers. My hair hung loose down my right shoulder and I'd edged up the hem of my skirt. I felt dangerous and reckless and wanton, and all of these things were no secret as I held his gaze. My heart crashed and throbbed, a prisoner rattling the bars of my ribcage. I had never felt as alive as I did just now.

Case, come over here, please come over here. Carry me somewhere and make love to me. Make love to me until dawn…

I begged for this with my eyes, and his darkened. In the firelight he was heart-stoppingly handsome. He returned my gaze, unblinking. And then he shifted.

Oh God, oh God…

Oh my God…

He stood, slow and deliberate, and stepped around the fire. A small sound escaped my lips as he stopped no more than a foot away and reached to place his fingertips beneath my chin. Hot, livid sparks flamed outward as he stroked, his eyes burning down into mine, at long last hiding nothing. He traced his thumb over my lower lip, once, twice, before gently pressing the center of it, and my lungs blazed with repressed breath. My heart was out of control. I gripped my knees, fingernails cutting into my bare skin.

"Patricia." His deep voice shook, despite his outward calm. "No one could ever compare to you. Oh Jesus, not ever."

"Case," I begged, trembling as he caressed my throat. His thumb outlined my mouth a second time and I felt that light touch in a fiery arc all the way to my toes.

He withdrew his hand and stepped away, and I thought a lightning bolt might strike me dead; for a moment he covered his face with both hands. When he spoke, it was with quiet resignation. "But I wrecked myself on you for way too long. You're leaving and I can't go through that again."

"*Case*," I demanded, breathless and shattered.

"I *can't*," he repeated and his movements were decisive. He collected his guitar, his fiddle, and walked away without a backward glance. I sat unmoving in his absence, hugging my ribs as though to keep my heart in place. I felt cold and disastrous and sickly. I was shocked, twofold, at both his words and what they meant, and by my own incredible need for him, which had blindsided me. Even untapped, it felt all-consuming.

Playing with fire. You're playing with fire and Case is not someone you can play with. He doesn't deserve that shit. You're going home to Chicago after Labor Day. And that's that.

What have I done?

Oh God, I want him so fucking much.

No, Tish, not ever.

You can't ever go there.

I heard his truck growl to life but I didn't move. I remained frozen, alone at the fire, his words trampling across my mind like runaway horses, and he drove away.

Chapter Fourteen

DAD MET ME AT O'HARE THE NEXT MORNING, HUGGING me and then drawing back with an ill-concealed wince. His nose wrinkled as he observed, "Kiddo, did you get caught in a fire on the way home, or what?"

I giggled; Dad was as handsome and impeccable as always, his dark curls without a hair out of place, clad in one of his many summer-weight designer suits, gold pinky ring set with a tasteful diamond to match his wedding band, his teeth professionally whitened. He smelled of aftershave and a hint of his cologne, which Lanny handpicked for him. He was dressed for work; he'd taken the morning off to pick me up.

"No, I just haven't had a chance to wash my jacket." Dad didn't need to know it wasn't technically my jacket, I had no intention of washing it, and that last night I'd slept in it—and absolutely nothing else. I wore it over a short red sundress and red flip-flops. I settled my sunglasses on the top of my head.

"Isn't that jacket a little too big for you?" Dad asked, his tone just this side of critical. My dad, the fashion police. But again, I was back in Chicago.

"It's my new look," I said, just to unsettle him, and pointed at the baggage claim to redirect his attention. "There's my bag!"

"So tell me what you have learned, daughter of mine," Dad said as he shouldered my luggage and led us to a taxi.

I filled him in on some of the details and he appeared to be listening attentively, but I knew him well enough to recognize his distraction. He was such a consummate lawyer that his current expression fooled most people, but not me. I finally concluded, "I feel like I've done some good. I really like Al. I've enjoyed working for him this summer." My tongue in danger of further loosening, I added, "I've liked living in Jalesville this summer, if you want to know the truth."

"Hon, I wish you didn't have to worry about it one more minute." Dad tugged at his tie; he hadn't processed any of what I'd just said about enjoying my work in Montana. His gaze wandered out the window. "But I am proud of you for working out in no-man's land for the summer. It is good experience, if nothing else."

I nodded as though I agreed with his condescending words, wondering why he seemed so restless.

"Ron is very appreciative. And that's nine-tenths of the battle, making contacts, doing favors, getting ahead of the next guy. Ron will open doors for you down the road, in return for helping him now."

"I thought possession was nine-tenths," I said lightly.

Dad and Lanny treated me to dinner at Jerome's, one of our old favorites. Dad insisted gently but firmly that I leave the jean jacket at home, and so here I was clad in a sleek black designer dress Lanny kindly lent me. I was tall in my heels and couldn't help but wonder what Case would say to this whole evening—how I looked and where we were dining. In comparison to anything in Jalesville, the restaurant was posh on a scale almost incomprehensible.

Linens and crystal, champagne and new forks for every course; people murmuring in quiet conversations at nearby tables, anonymous as fish in an endless ocean. Lazy jazz from a quartet in the bar. I gazed at the spacious grandeur and felt like my heart might shred apart with homesickness. I wanted to be at The Spoke. I wanted to hear Case playing his fiddle. I wanted to be at the Rawleys' dinner table, around the fire with the guys singing hokey old songs, working in my little office on Main Street and recognizing nearly everyone who walked by out the window.

What in the hell has happened to you? I wondered as Lanny perused the wine list with her plump lips in a slight pout; though I suspected this was due to a recent collagen injection rather than any sort of petulance.

Suddenly Dad rose from his chair, offering his lawyer smile to someone beyond my shoulder. I turned just in time to watch my former classmate Robbie Benson make his way to our table, smiling just as toothily.

For the second time in the last half-minute, I thought, *What in the hell?*

But then I realized he was home to take the bar exam, same as me.

Robbie joined us and shook Dad's hand as though concluding a business deal.

"Jackson," he acknowledged. "Lanny, it's a pleasure as always." His grin was almost fiendish as he said, "Tish, how *wonderful* to see you. You've been getting some sun out west, it appears." Robbie was clad in black tie, just like Dad, and claimed the chair that the maître'd discreetly held out from our table.

"Rob is going to be joining you in Jalesville for a spell," Dad explained.

I'd forgotten this might ever be an option and felt a flash of anger, as though they were conspiring against me.

"I think I have things under control."

Robbie knew me well enough to pick up on my irritation, which tickled him to death, I could tell. He hid a smile behind his copy of the wine list. Lanny glanced up as though mildly interested in the conversation.

Dad sighed. "It's not about you lacking control, Tish, I assure you. He needs summer clock hours and contacts, too."

"I have the distinguished honor of housesitting for Ron. His manager needs time off, remember?" Robbie was perfect-looking, disgustingly so, with polished skin and eyes the blue of robin eggs, teeth from a mouthwash commercial and his Kennedy-brother haircut. He was also sun-bronzed and I recalled that he had just returned from Europe.

"Don't expect me to entertain you when you're there," I warned Robbie, glaring at him, and Dad rolled his eyes.

"We'll have a bottle of the 2003 reserve cabernet," Lanny murmured to the sommelier as he approached our table.

"Oh, I don't expect that," Robbie assured me, eyes on his menu. I could tell he loved torturing me this way; we'd always been competitive.

"Are you flying back with me on Thursday?" I pressed, truly hoping he was not.

"No, I'm driving out. I'll be there by late Friday, early Saturday." Without looking at me he insisted, "We'll have *fun*, Patricia."

I sent Dad a scorching look and he muttered under his breath, "You look just like your mother."

I took this as a compliment; my mother was the best-looking woman I knew.

"For real," Robbie said, cajoling me with his tone. "I won't be in your hair. I won't even be in town for more than a month. I have to be back here before Labor Day. I need the goodwill bump, I admit. I need Ron to know that I'm willing to do what it takes."

"Speaking of the devil," Dad muttered, though his face was wreathed in his most charming smile as someone else approached through the crowded restaurant; he murmured, "Game face, Tish."

I turned just in time to see Ron and Christina Turnbull. My heart snagged on something sharp at the sight of this pair, but I smiled graciously as they paused to greet us.

"Well, if it isn't my two hardest-working interns." Ron was jovial and smiling, though this expression did not detract in any way from his basic air of intimidation. "Glad to be back in civilization, my dear?"

"Yes, but I've been enjoying working for Al Howe." The words 'fairly despicable' blazed unchecked through my mind as I spoke. I squared my shoulders, struggling to keep an edge from my voice. "I've accomplished a great deal in Jalesville this summer."

Ron winked indulgently. "It's a lovely place to spend a month, I'll give you that." He snared Robbie in his gaze. "Just remember, young man, no house parties in the cabin."

"Wouldn't dream of it," Robbie murmured, on guard and at his most deferential. I could tell it was taking everything he had to keep his eyes from popping out at the sight of gorgeous Christina Turnbull, who was perhaps all of twenty-eight, with hair streaked in shades of icy blonde to match the chill of her green eyes and breasts the size of ripe coconuts; Lanny's plump lips pursed and her spine straightened at this imminent threat to her status as the most desirable surgically-enhanced woman in the restaurant.

Christina, appearing bored as always, regarded her nails, the sparkling city view out the window…but then, no mistaking it, she directed a side-long look at my father, quick as a flash.

Interesting.

Dad didn't appear to notice; he said to Ron, "Tish tells me that she and Al are this close to running Capital Overland out of town for good."

Ron's silver eyebrows lifted. "Impressive work. And here I was con-sidering selling to them."

He saw the stun on my face, which I couldn't suppress in time, and reassured, "Only joking, my dear."

"I still haven't discovered everything, but I intend to." I spoke with asperity; maybe it was the power of suggestion, what Al and Helen Anne had said about him, but I quite disliked Ron's patronizing attitude. Or maybe I was just pathetically hoping for praise as I explained, "I'm look-ing into a connection between the local power plant selling to Redd Co. and the Yancys sweeping in so conveniently. The timing is too perfect."

Dad smiled at me with subtle admiration, which did my heart good. Ron's expression didn't change as he said, "Lovely and smart, Ms. Gordon. A *lethal* combination," and Christina Turnbull turned her glit-tery green eyes on me for the very first time. I doubted she even knew who I was before this moment. I held her arrogant gaze and tipped up my lips, but couldn't convince my eyes to likewise smile.

"We'll let you dine," Ron said, and I remembered the way he looked all those times I'd argued before him in appellate court, while attending school, how fucking much I'd longed to impress him. "Good luck on those exams, the both of you."

"Thank you, sir," Robbie said at once.

I nodded my own thanks as Dad and Robbie stood to shake Ron's hand. By the time dinner was over I was more than ready to return to Dad's, despite Robbie's sly coaxing to join him for a drink; Grace and Ina both texted to say they would love to see me but my heart wasn't in it. I was exhausted, and besides, all four of us had two days' worth of testing ahead.

Later that night I lay sleepless in the guestroom in Dad and Lanny's townhome, which they had purchased my first year at Northwestern, a building with sweeping panoramic views of the skyline that glimmered like a seductive promise beneath the matte-black sky. There was far too much light pollution here for a chance to make a wish on any stars. I rolled to my other side, as restless as if staying in an impersonal hotel. My only comfort was curling into the scent of Case's jacket, the only piece of clothing I'd worn to bed, my bare legs chilly under the sleek sheets of the king-sized guest bed.

Case, I thought, over and over.

I miss you, Charles Shea Spicer.

I miss you so much that I hurt.

I thought of his words at the fire last night; I had thought of little else all through my plane ride from Billings, and all the hours of today. He confirmed that he still felt something for me and that he would not allow this to continue.

You're leaving, he said.

I draped a forearm over my eyes and considered the insanity of maybe not leaving. Of staying in Jalesville and working with Al.

Tish. You can't even consider such a crazy thing. You've been working toward a career here since you were eighteen years old.

I flopped to stare up at the ceiling fan, whirring silently above me.

Why the fuck is that thing running anyway? It's freezing in here.

I threw off the covers and stumbled to shut off the fan, then sank to the wingchair near the window, naked beneath Case's jacket, tucking the denim more securely around my body. The rough material rubbed along my nipples, which swelled with longing; my bare skin smelled like Case and his jacket now smelled like me. Did he wonder if I'd brought it with me to Chicago? He probably figured I left it at the Rawleys' place, along with Peaches. I inhaled the scent of him like a drug and at long last drifted into a fitful sleep.

I had survived the bar exam, for better or worse.

Under the hot Montana sun, late Thursday afternoon, I retrieved my car from long-term parking at the Billings airport and drove east toward Jalesville, fracturing the interstate speed limit because I was so rabid to get there. I kept the windows at half-mast, letting the scents of the foot-hills rush inside the car, fumbling my phone from my purse to call Clark.

Wy answered and a smile broke over my face as he cried, "Tish! You home?"

"Almost. I'm so excited to see you guys. Can I pick up Peaches in about an hour?"

"Case has her," Wy said, and my heart accelerated.

"He does?"

"Sean's allergies were acting up so Case took her home with him."

"That was nice of him," I whispered, hesitating only a second before asking, "What's his number?"

Wy said, "I gave him yours, too. You have a pen?"

"Just tell me, buddy, I'm driving. I'll remember it."

Wy rattled off all ten numbers, including the 406 area code, and I committed them to memory. "Thank you. I'll see you guys tomorrow night!"

I tried three times to dial Case's number, with no success; I called Al with no trouble, leaving him a voicemail, and drove through Jalesville with a sense of homecoming, the familiar little town peaceful in the evening light; I parked in my spot at Stone Creek before I knew it, lift-ing a fingertip to my mouth and tracing over my bottom lip, pressing its center, my heart crashing like a breaker against the shore, a force beyond any control.

Inside. I'll go inside and then I'll call him.

I hauled my travel bags up the stairs and unlocked 206. The door bumped against something but it didn't occur to me to worry; I just shoved harder, irritated. I stepped inside and then paused, frowning as my eyes roved over the familiar space. Goosebumps broke out on my limbs. My purse slid from my shoulder and hit the floor. My apartment floor was strewn with my things. Trashed, as though a bunch of teenag-ers had thrown a roof-shaker of a party. My coffee maker in pieces on the kitchen floor, my clothes tossed everywhere, along with all of my shoes, the contents of my dresser drawers overturned in front of the television. The placemats from my table, the picture from the wall, the hanging quilt—all torn from their original locations.

"What?" I whispered faintly. "What the hell?"

Anger overpowered my shock. I stormed through my apartment, finding the sheets ripped from my bed, my underwear and bras littering the hall.

What the fuck?!

I marched back to the living room and retrieved my phone, dialing Case; he answered between the second and third ring.

"Tish," he said, and his familiar voice made my knees weak. I sank to a crouch.

"Hey," I whispered, nothing more, but that one word was enough for him to understand something was wrong.

"What is it? Are you all right?"

"Someone has been in my apartment."

"What?" he demanded.

"Someone's been in here and ripped apart all of my things." Tears leaked over my face, infuriating me.

"I will be right there. I want you to go outside and call 911. Will you do that?" When I was too choked to reply, he said more urgently, "Tish. Will you do that?"

"Yes," I whispered. "Please hurry."

I put his jacket over my sundress, stumbling down the steps and then outside. I sat on the curb and dialed 911; the woman on the line assured me that someone would be right over. Minutes later I spied Case's truck and sprang to my feet, gladness rising so swiftly that I felt dizzy. I met him halfway across the parking lot, crazy for the sight of his face, devouring him with my eyes; his burned a path straight through me. Nothing seemed more natural than to be collected against his chest, where I clung. I didn't care what he thought about that, I simply held him as hard as I could.

"When did you get home?" I could feel his heart beating against me.

"Did you call 911?"

I nodded, reluctant to draw away but wanting to see his face. I felt like I had already taken too many liberties and let my arms drop back to my sides. He cupped my right elbow before releasing me altogether, asking softly, "What happened?"

I tucked loose hair behind both ears; my fingers trembled. "I just got home. When I opened the door, I saw…" I paused to steady my voice. "Everything is torn up or broken, and my clothes are all over the place…"

"What the hell? I'm glad you called me."

"Wy gave me your number," I explained, just as a cop car crunched into the gravel lot.

"There's Jerry," Case said, turning with me to address the man climbing from the white SUV with a revolving toplight.

"Spicer, what's going on?" asked the sheriff, an older, mustached man with black hair going salty-white; he wore a battered gray cowboy hat. He extended a hand to me. "Jerry Woodrow. You're Patricia Gordon, the new lawyer, is that right? I haven't had the pleasure."

I straightened my shoulders and shook his hand. "Yes, that's me. Good to meet you."

"Not the best circumstances, unfortunately. What's going on this evening?"

I told him what I'd found and he said, "I'll go have a look. Did you notice anything missing?"

"It didn't occur to me to look."

"That's all right. You two stay here and I'll be back directly."

"I still have your jacket," I told Case as Jerry disappeared into the apartment building.

A smile shone in his eyes. "I noticed."

"Thank you for coming," I whispered.

"I was supposed to play at The Spoke but I told Lee I'd do it tomorrow night, instead."

"Thank you," I whispered again. "I kicked the bar exam's ass." Another round of tears blurred my vision and I swiped at them with the cuff of his jacket.

"Of course you did." He smoothed a hand over my right shoulder. "I'm so glad you're home."

From up on my balcony, Jerry called, "Ms. Gordon? Would you be so kind as to come up?"

Case and I joined him in the apartment; Case made an angry sound at the sight of the destruction. Jerry met us in the living room. "My first instinct would be a robbery, but there doesn't appear to be anything missing. TV's still here, radio, DVD player. Do you have any valuables, smaller things?"

"Not really. My diamond earrings and pendant watch from my father."

"Will you see if they're missing?" Jerry asked.

I hurried to my bedroom. Oddly, my cut-glass jewelry holder remained undisturbed on my dresser; the diamonds and the Cartier timepiece glittered from their usual places. I called, "Nothing's missing!"

"Strange," Jerry mused. "You told dispatch you've been out of town since Monday, is that right?"

"I just got home from the airport."

"I'll check with the neighbors, ask a few questions," Jerry said. "No one had access to your apartment that you were aware? No one who might be an asshole and throw a party while you were away?"

"No," I said, but the words *Derrick Yancy* flashed through my mind; I needn't be a lawyer to realize I had less than no proof to support this suspicion.

"Can I clean up in here?" I asked Jerry. "Do you need to, I don't know, check for fingerprints or anything?"

He shook his head. "Not typically in these circumstances." He joked, "You didn't find a body or anything, did you?"

"*Jesus*, Jerry," Case muttered.

Jerry chuckled, tipping his hat brim. "For now, I'm going to assume that some kids broke in here and trashed the place. Who knows? Maybe they heard you were out of town, maybe a neighbor has a teenager. Call your insurance company tomorrow, first thing, and get a quote for property damage."

"I will," I said, feeling helpless and therefore angry.

"I'll help you clean up in here," Case said.

Jerry went to knock on my neighbors' doors but I knew they would have no answers; many of the apartments in the building were unoccupied since the building was so new. I straightened a chair and draped Case's jacket along the top, too hot to continue wearing it, and for the next fifteen minutes Case and I worked in almost complete silence, both of us brimming with things we wanted to say, but couldn't. I stuffed all of my lingerie back into its drawer before I did anything else, while Case righted chairs and filled a garbage bag with the broken pieces of my coffee maker and my radio.

Next I collected all of my clothes and threw them in my hamper, then bundled up my sheets and took them to the washing machine down the hall, feeling utterly violated; someone other than me had touched these, had torn them from my mattress. I wiped angry tears on my shoulder as I shoved quarters into the machine, harder than necessary. When I reentered the apartment, Case said immediately, "I don't want you staying here alone tonight."

Everything I wasn't supposed to feel for him stormed my blood; I argued, "I'm *just fine*."

"I think you should stay at Clark's," he insisted, eyebrows lowering.

Stay here with me, oh God, please stay here with me, Case.

I wanted to beg him, but wouldn't. I knew he saw this in my eyes; he inhaled a deep breath, wide shoulders tensing.

Jerry popped back through the apartment door, almost crashing into me. "Ms. Gordon, pardon me. No one seems to have heard anything. I talked to the super and he told me he can't believe this sort of thing could happen, go figure. He said he'll make sure he puts a lock on the door in the lobby sometime soon, as just anyone could come in right now."

I shivered at this unpleasant thought.

"I hate to say it, there's not much more I can do tonight," Jerry concluded. "I don't think you're in harm's way, to be honest. This sort of thing happens. Be sure to latch that deadbolt on your door, as a matter of practice, if you haven't been. And don't hesitate to call if you're concerned about anything else tonight."

"Easy for him to say," Case muttered after Jerry took his leave. My place was reasonably tidied up; my nerves, however, were not. "You're exhausted. I won't let you stay here alone tonight. I'm going to drive you to Clark's."

Anger broiled over. I wanted him so very much and I couldn't want him, and it was destroying me. I insisted, "I'm *all right*. I don't want to needlessly worry Clark."

Case's eyes took on increasing heat. "He would worry more if you didn't tell him."

"I know," I admitted. Our gazes clashed. I could feel the pulse beating in my throat. We stood facing each other, no more than five feet apart; Case was holding a full garbage bag. "I'll latch the deadbolt. I won't be scared to stay in my own place."

"Dammit, Tish," he growled.

My attraction to him seemed to be a living thing that grew more every second I was around him. I would be lying if I didn't acknowledge that his belligerent, authoritative tone made me hotter than all the coals in hell. I latched both hands on my hips. "I appreciate your concern, but I won't be scared to stay here. Whoever did this wants that." Somehow I knew this was true. "Has anyone been back out to your place?"

Gone was the tender concern that had permeated all of our interaction when he first arrived an hour ago, replaced by a red-hot intensity that siphoned all of the air from the room. Throttling down the emotion in his voice, he said, "No. But I know one has to do with the other."

I wanted to tell him everything—what I'd seen in my mind while we were in Miles City last Saturday, about what Derrick had said in the hallway, calling me a whore and blathering about a murder. But I didn't know where any of that would lead. All I knew was that I wanted Case to make love to me right now, to grab fistfuls of my hair, bunch up my skirt, and bend me roughly over the kitchen table. Already I had forgotten everything but him and it terrified me. I was so unprepared to feel this way.

My heart was thrusting so hard I was sure he could hear it. "I won't be scared here. *Damned* if I'll be scared here."

"I'm bringing you to Clark's." There was no room for argument in his dangerous tone.

"I think you better leave," I said, even though it was the last fucking thing I wanted. "I think you better go *right now*." Otherwise I was going to lose all of my thinly-veiled control.

"You are so goddamn stubborn." There was fire in his voice. "You want me to leave? I'll *fucking leave*."

"*Stubborn?*" I yelled.

"You're stubborn as hell!" But there was admiration in his tone, along with the frustration.

"You should talk!"

He dropped the garbage bag and closed the distance between us. The air in my lungs vanished. He took my face in his strong hands and I grabbed his t-shirt with both fists. The expression in his eyes, as though he was touching something unimaginably precious, made me come undone. I threw my arms around his neck and clung. He buried his hands in my loose hair and pressed his lips to the pulse throbbing in my neck. My head fell back as he tasted my skin, groaning deep in his throat. He took my chin between his teeth and red fireworks burst before my eyes, my breath coming in hot, heavy spurts.

He drew away, his heart thundering against my breasts.

"You're ripping me apart," he growled, digging his hands into my hair.

"*Case*," I pleaded.

He released me, turning as though in a fury, grabbing up the garbage bag and saying around a husk in his throat, "I'm calling Clark to come and get you."

I stood speechless, shaking with desire and stun, with the primal need for more.

He didn't look at me as he opened the door. "You are not staying here alone tonight."

He could have slammed it on the way out, but didn't. I brought both hands to my mouth and sank to a crouch. Through the open patio door I heard his truck fire to life and then the sound of him driving out of the parking lot.

Chapter Fifteen

I refused to let Clark see how unsettled I was when he knocked on the apartment door no more than twenty minutes later. I told him what happened, omitting a certain few things, proud of the way I held it together. Clark was outraged that someone had been in my apartment; it took all of my fast-talking skills to convince him I was not about to be scared away from my own place, that I didn't need him to take me back home with him or send one of the boys over to guard the door.

At Howe and James the next day, Mary and Al had heard all about the break-in. I was a wreck, having spent a sleepless night in my unmade bed, unable to think of anything but Case's lips on my skin. He hadn't kissed my mouth, but he was going to kiss it. And soon. Tonight, if I had anything to do with it; it was Friday, and he was playing at The Spoke. This certainty kept me from stalking down the street to Spicer Music to confront him; Case had brought Peaches to the law office before I'd arrived, as though he couldn't bear to see me this morning.

I told Al all about the bar exam once he calmed down regarding my apartment situation, and he insisted that I head out early and get some rest.

"I already called Bill," Al said, referring to my super at Stone Creek. "He is installing a camera system in the entryway, just so you know."

"You're the best," I told him. I could not ask for a better boss or mentor. "Thank you. And I promise to take it easy this evening."

"Don't forget my birthday party is next Friday," Al reminded me, with a grin. "Helen Anne will have my head if you don't stop out. We're having a barn dance."

I promised him I would be there.

I drove home in the early afternoon, Peaches prowling around the passenger seat, and listened to Bill the super apologize for ten minutes before being allowed into my apartment. I'd already left a message with Clark that I wouldn't be able to make supper tonight, afraid I would be unable to behave as though nothing was wrong. Further, I knew it would be impossible to rest right now, even though I'd promised Al I would try, so I took a long walk in the foothills beyond Stone Creek where I lost myself for a few hours, letting the sun soak into my hair and the air into my lungs. I tried very hard not to think about Case and me in another life, both the one in the past and the one I imagined in the present—the one I was terrified to acknowledge.

I returned home to find two missed calls from Robbie; shit, that meant he was either in town or getting close. He was an adult. He could find his way to Ron's cabin without any help from me, and I was in no mood to see him. Instead of doing the polite thing and returning his messages, I took a scalding shower. I shaved my legs and scented my skin with my favorite vanilla body butter. I blew out my hair to its fullest, curliest insanity, applied eye make-up that might best be worn on a call girl in Las Vegas, dressed in my laciest black lingerie, shortest jean skirt, and my red-and-black, cleavage-queen tank top.

What are you doing? What the fuck are you doing?

But I couldn't answer that so I didn't try. Instead, I drove to The Spoke around nine; I parked, heart galloping like the running horse on the tail-gate of Case's truck, which was parked near the back entrance. I faltered, almost restarting the car and fleeing.

Dammit, you're not a coward!

I tucked my keys and a couple of twenties in my pocket and stashed my purse in the trunk before going inside, where it was crowded and noisy. Neon brilliance bathed my skin; a great deal of it was bare in my current outfit.

"Holy *shit*," was the first thing I heard as I entered the familiar bar. Seconds later Travis Woodrow appeared at my side; I was about five inches taller than him in my heeled sandals. He was all eyes. "Lawyer lady, *how-dee-do*."

I couldn't help but giggle, even as additional curious stares flickered my way.

"Who's the lucky guy you're meeting here?" Travis wondered.

"I'm just here to see the show," I explained, my eyes roving for a sight of Case. Probably he was in that back storage room, getting ready. I spied Marshall at a table with some of his friends and he did an almost comical double-take, rising and heading my way, with a low whistle.

"Tish," he acknowledged. "First, glad you're home. And second, *holy fucking shit*. What are you wearing? Never mind, don't answer that. Case is going to break something when he sees you in that outfit."

"Where is he?" I asked. My kneecaps were jittering. I needed a drink and asked Travis, "Hey, would you please get me a gin and tonic?"

"Sure thing," he said, obedient as a school boy.

"Marsh, where is he?" I demanded.

Marshall shot me a long-suffering look. "What the hell is going on? Seriously, what is going on? Case is all nuts tonight, hiding something."

I shook my head, unable to answer. Travis returned with my drink and I downed half of it in one gulp. So classy.

"Come on, sit over here with us." Marsh was aggravated with me but I didn't care right now. He added, "Me and Case are on in just a few."

I recognized everyone at the table and greeted them with as much enthusiasm as I could muster, but sat at the far end, facing the stage, in no mood to be distracted. Pam Heller took a drink order and I asked for another gin, polishing off the first. Marshall was troubled, I could tell, but kept quiet. He excused himself and no more than a minute later he and Case came from the back of the bar. I saw Case looking for me in the growing crowd. Our gazes locked and heat struck me like an arrow he'd fired in my direction. He was wearing his cowboy hat and the t-shirt I had held to my face in his bathroom, his expression stern.

The guys took the stage to cheers and whistles; usually Case appeared at ease on stage but this evening I could sense his strain. He and Marsh bantered, deciding what to play, and a few people called out requests.

I slammed two more gin and tonics, recognizing the stupidity of this kind of drinking, but unable to stop. The room acquired an amber-tinted haze I recalled from college weekends. Time slowed, swimming through honey. I studied Case without letup; even in my drunken stupor I could sense his mounting tension.

The two of them played for over an hour. I waited until they'd almost finished their last encore before stumbling to my feet and making my unsteady way to the ladies' room. The bathrooms were on the opposite side of the front entrance, well away from the action of the bar. I regarded myself in the mirror, hearing the song end to thunderous applause and cheers. I braced on the sink and willed all that gin to stay in place. As I left the bathroom I nearly crashed into Case. My heart responded to this by leaping in his direction.

"You're here!" I might have slurred a little.

"You're loaded," he observed as we stood a few feet apart, regarding me with an unforgiving gaze.

"I am," I agreed. His hair was damp with sweat. His mouth was somber, no hint of a smile. I had just spent the past hour watching those lips as he sang and now I needed them on my body; my nipples were firm against my tank top, aching to be touched. His gaze flickered south before moving back to my eyes. He swallowed, hard.

"Come on," he ordered, firm and resolute. "Let's get you home."

"I'm not ready to go yet." All inhibitions lowered, if not totally eradicated, I stepped forward and put my hands on his ribcage, one on either side, shivering at his warm strength beneath my palms. I leaned against him perhaps more than I actually needed to—but then I understood, like a splash of scalding water to the face, just how very much I needed to lean on him. His eyes held mine and the expression in them was one he was trying very hard to control, I could tell even with my senses all drunk and blurred.

"Come on," he repeated, his voice tight, close enough that his breath touched my cheek. "I'll drive you home."

I let him lead me outside, where I felt dizzier than ever, tiny and insubstantial; a heartbeat from being swept away in a current I could not control. Case walked me to his truck, one arm around my waist, and opened the passenger door.

"Here we go," he said with controlled politeness, as though talking to an acquaintance. One hand beneath my elbow as he assisted me onto the seat. I scooted my legs so he could shut the door and through the partially-open window he said, "I'll be back in just a sec."

A handful of people stood in the parking lot enjoying smokes, chatting over a last beer. The noise and lights from within The Spoke were amplified as Case swung open the door and disappeared inside, coming back a minute later with his backpack slung over one shoulder, carrying his guitar case. I watched the way his shoulders shifted as he crossed the parking lot, his long legs in faded jeans and boots, his cowboy hat shadowing his eyes from view.

It's time, I thought. *It is so time.*

He stashed his gear behind the seat, leaning in from the driver's side, working with quiet efficiency, as though I wasn't even in the truck. He climbed in without a word; when the engine started the radio clicked on and the soft sound of country music came over the speakers. Case shifted into first and then second, taking us out of the parking lot. I studied his profile but he didn't look in my direction, like he usually did. There was no traffic on the road as he drove through town and then turned toward Stone Creek. The silence between us pulsed with tension; I couldn't speak, realizing a couple of things with increasing clarity.

Tish, you fucking idiot.

What did you expect? That he'd thank his lucky stars that you're drunk and take advantage of you?

He's not that type.

Oh God, I want him. I want him, I want him…

Far too soon the truck rolled into the small resident lot at Stone Creek and my eyes flickered to my second-floor apartment, where the light above the sink lent the otherwise dark building a fleeting sense of welcome. I imagined Peaches sprawled in the window sill waiting for me, her tail twitching, and the last thing I wanted was to go up there and lie alone in my bed, longing with every atom of my being for Case to be there with me, all of my petty, stupid fucking seduction efforts having gone to waste.

"We'll go get your car tomorrow," he said, climbing out of the truck, heading around the hood. He took my forearm to help me down and I put my hands on his shoulders, indulging in this excuse to touch him; he left the truck running, communicating his intent to be here no longer than necessary, and tears pulsed in the corners of my eyes. I thanked God that it was dark so he wouldn't notice.

"Do you have your purse?" he asked, stopping short. "Shit, I didn't even think about looking for it."

"It's in my trunk." I let my hands fall to my sides and muttered, "My keys are in my pocket."

"Well, let's get you inside."

Anger blazed a hot path through my chest. I said acidly, "I *got it*, you can go."

"You can hardly walk."

"Go." I stepped around him, teetering in my heels, the ones I'd worn to get his attention in the first place; I felt too unsteady to walk and sank to the curb, kicking off my sandals. Case made a sound of alarm and crouched near my right hip.

"Holy shit, I thought you were falling."

"Falling," I repeated.

Case was only a foot away. I flung the sandals behind me and caught his wrists in both hands. I'd been aiming for his shirt, intending to yank him close, but I miscalculated. He made a low sound, rocking backward as though to free himself from my grip. Barefoot, I rolled to my knees and slid my arms around his neck; still in a crouch, he grasped my hips. I pressed closer, the grass damp beneath my bare knees, and my forehead bumped his hat brim, knocking it to the ground. He stood, taking me with him, preventing my forward motion with an iron grip around my waist. My heart splattered against my ribcage, my breath rough and uneven. When I reached for him again, he clamped my wrists in an unforgiving hold.

"Tish," he warned, breathing hard. Low and with effort, he ordered, "*Stop.*"

"No," I insisted, intent on having my way. I struggled against his hold.

"You are *drunk*."

"So what?" I gasped, even though I knew he was right.

"So what?" Anger crackled in his voice. "So *what*? Are you kidding me? What kind of man do you think I am? What do you want, huh? You want me to take you upstairs and fuck you, is that what you want?"

He might as well have punched me, though I knew he would never consider doing such a thing. That he was basically correct in his assumption only doubled my guilt; wasn't that exactly what I'd been hoping? And for what? So I wouldn't be lonely for one night? So I could prove something to myself?

"I want..." My throat closed. I stopped struggling and tears streaked my face and dripped from my chin, much to my horror. I could not sink much lower; I was a shallow fucking cock-tease and worse than that, I was a user.

His hands moved swiftly up my arms and he kissed me.

I clutched his shoulders to keep from falling to the earth, tilting my head into his hungry kiss, struggling to get closer. He tasted of cola, the interior of his mouth sweet and sleek against my tongue, the heat of him pounding into me so that stars burst behind my eyelids. He took my lower lip into his mouth to run his tongue over it, nipping my chin and then kissing my neck, my jaw, until I was trembling as though with a fever. With a deep, throaty groan, he reclaimed my mouth and I moaned against his lips, holding nothing back as I kissed him in return. He clutched my hips in his strong hands and drew me firmly against him. I felt, with a burning sort of clarity, that I would die if he stopped.

And then, just like that, he did. His eyes flamed with an unholy fire that clashed against the one in my own.

"But I won't." His deep voice shook on those words.

I couldn't catch my breath; I was so wet and aroused that I felt violent. Violent enough that, were I capable of carrying someone much larger and stronger than myself, I would forcibly haul him upstairs. He released his hold on my hips but I clung to him, desire pumping through my blood so that all I heard was a roaring.

"Case, oh God, *please*..."

He broke free and turned away, cupping his forehead with both hands. He made a low sound of defeat and I gripped his shirt. He bent to retrieve his hat, displacing my touch. Settling it low over his eyes, he took my elbow and ordered in a tone not to be challenged, "Come."

I went, so overcome by what had just happened between us and the thick buzz of the gin that I couldn't see straight. He marched me up the carpeted steps and down the hall, stopping in front of 206.

"Where's your key?"

I fumbled it from my pocket, trying and failing to fit it in the keyhole, so Case took it from my hands and performed the task for me, his movements abrupt and angry. Peaches leaped into view as the door swung open, swirling around my ankles.

"You shouldn't drink this much." His voice was tense with what I interpreted as barely-controlled anger.

"My shoes," I whispered, grasping at things to keep him here because I sensed he was going to leave. Heat flared in my cheeks and nipples, burning the length of my spine. In the dim lights of the hall he appeared stone-jawed and stern, his eyes blazing. My hair was in snarls, a strap falling over my shoulder. My eyes detoured to his lips, his beautifully-sculpted lips, before seeking his eyes.

"I'll get them," he said. "You need to sleep it off."

"Sleep it off?" I cried, stung, wounded almost beyond repair. I was so angry I wanted to strike him, stunned by this surging violence. I hissed, "Don't bother!" and slammed the door.

Immediately I leaned backward against it, burying my face in both hands. I could not tell if he continued to stand there or walked away; the carpet muffled all sound. I waited, unmoving, until I heard his truck being put into gear. I jolted forward, tripped over Peaches, and went to my knees. I managed to make it to the kitchen window in time to see his taillights as they signaled to turn out of the parking lot.

And then I went to my knees of my own accord, crying as I had never cried before.

Chapter Sixteen

LATE THE NEXT MORNING I FOUND MY SHOES JUST TO THE right of the door. Case had placed them neatly in the hallway, taking time to straighten the straps and align them just right. I scraped a hand through my hair and regarded them through the headache hazing my vision. Last night I had cried until I thought my brain might explode, just managing to make it to the toilet before puking up what seemed like a bottle's worth of gin.

I woke hours later on the bathroom floor, near the base of the sink, Peaches sitting on her haunches and studying me with her unreadable green eyes. I pretended she was worried about me, that at least someone was, before peeling off my bar clothes and crawling into the shower. I emerged feeling slightly more human and brewed a pot of strong coffee; Al had let me take the coffee maker from the office, insisting he could get us a new one there. I sat at my kitchen table, staring numbly out the window at the restless, stormy sky that suited my brutal mood.

I thought of things I had learned about Case since living here in Montana, about him being left behind to care for his younger brother, their father a drunken wreck who'd thrown them around when his moods were especially black; I sank lower into my pit of self-loathing.

How could you treat him that way last night, as though you only want sex from him? How could you act like that, knowing everything he's been through, knowing how he feels about you? You are a selfish bitch.

I closed my eyes and held the mug of coffee beneath my nose, letting the steam bathe my face. My stomach lurched but I wasn't in danger of vomiting; I had vomited up everything I'd eaten since last weekend already.

Case. How can I tell you that I'm sorry?

How can I make this right?

I let the coffee mug sink to the table and lowered my head; what I wanted right now was all tangled up with what I wanted my future to hold. My future goals, namely living in Chicago as a successful lawyer. What I had been working toward for the last seven and a half fucking years.

Case will never leave Jalesville.

He lives in a trailer.

He has a past.

I lifted my face and cupped my temples in both hands, studying the wood grain on the table. I thought of watching him sing last night, all of the nights I had listened to his gorgeous voice, had studied his hands as he played his fiddle, making it sing joyously or mournfully, depending on the mood of the song. I imagined Case singing a song for me at our wedding, the way Mathias sang for my sister. I let myself imagine having his babies, setting aside my career so that I could be a mother and a wife.

I'm so scared. I'm so confused.

I can't think about these things. I have good, solid job prospects in Chicago, a start at a stellar career. I have to go back to that. To consider anything else is unthinkable.

But the alternative stared me in the eye and I could not look away. To leave meant I would be without Case for the rest of my life. Tears burst and I sobbed again, even as sharp pain made my head seem capable of splitting along the hairline. My phone buzzed, signaling an incoming call, and disappointment compressed my lungs as I saw that it was Robbie. I pressed the decline icon, letting it go straight to voicemail. Almost immediately there was a knock on the door and my heart lurched. Peaches meowed, rubbing against my calves as I stared at the door. What were the odds that Case would be there when I opened it?

But the open door exposed Robbie, clad in khaki shorts and a short-sleeved polo shirt; he lifted both palms and asked, "What in the hell?"

I stared blankly at him, annoyed and crushingly let down. Of course it wasn't Case. What had I been thinking?

"I got to town last night," he explained. "Thanks for fucking caring. I ended up hanging out with Al. Nice guy. I can see why you like him." He narrowed his eyes and asked lightly, "Rough night, Patricia?" Then he snorted, attempting to see past me into the apartment. "Shit, is there a guy here?"

I restrained the urge to shut the door on his knowing leer. I mumbled, "Welcome to Jalesville." Realizing I needed to retrieve the Honda, I asked, "Will you drive me to where I left my car last night?"

"Of course. You're adorable when you're hungover and pitiful, you know that?"

"Come in," I said, ignoring his teasing. Robbie helped himself to a cup of coffee and took a seat at my table as I disappeared into the bathroom. There, I grimaced at the purple smudges beneath my red-rimmed eyes. *Rough night, indeed.* I brushed my hair with more force than required, smoothed some gloss on my lips, and called it good enough. I'd just clicked out the bathroom light when someone knocked on my door for the second time in ten minutes.

It's him.

This time I knew with absolute certainty and my heart smashed against my ribs as though having jumped from the top of a building; before I could move Robbie got up to do the honors for me. There was a moment of crackling-tense silence and I rounded the corner just in time to hear Case say, "I don't fucking believe this."

"Excuse me?" Robbie asked, sounding truly mystified, but I raced around him, barefoot, in pursuit of Case, who was already storming down the steps and shoving through the front doors. My hair streamed behind me as I chased him outside, where the low gray sky had begun spitting rain.

"Case!" I screamed, running across the gravel without thinking. A sharp edge dug into my foot but I was not about to let him go thinking what he did: that Robbie had spent the night here with me. Case's truck was parked in almost the same spot as last night, though he'd killed the engine this time. Rain struck the ground with increasing ferocity, spattering over my threadbare t-shirt and releasing the scent of dust into the humid air. Thunder growled with the threat of something far more dangerous to follow.

"Wait," I implored, out of breath as I caught up to him. He turned, unwillingly, the angry heat from his eyes beating into mine. He was hatless, his red-gold hair bright even in the dimness of the gloomy day, shoulders taut with tension.

Before I could say a word he asked venomously, "Did you wait until I was out of the parking lot last night before you called him? Who the fuck is that, anyway?"

"It's not like that," I said desperately. I thought of how he'd kissed me last night and could hardly breathe with wanting more of him. More, and then only more of this man.

"Then how is it?" he yelled, jerking both hands through his hair. "I guess it's good to know the truth. Fuck, I was coming here to *apologize*."

"He just got here from Chicago!" Angry tears glittered in my eyes, along with the rain, obscuring my vision. I hurried to explain, "He's here to housesit for Ron. I went to school with him."

"Then why is he *here*?"

"I told you, he just got to town! He's taking me to get my car!"

"I told you I would take you to get it!" Case raged, stepping closer, almost as though against his will.

"How was I supposed to know that you'd come back? You left without one word! Without even saying good-bye!" My hands were fisted so tightly my fingernails scraped my palms.

"You slammed the door in my face!" He had me there.

I wanted to scream, *You rejected me!*

But I was too proud.

He lowered his voice to say cruelly, "So you needed to get laid so bad you didn't care who it was, is that right?"

I slapped his cheek hard enough that it hurt my palm and he caught my wrist in a death grip, clearly reading in my eyes that I intended to strike again. He brought me right up against his chest; he looked as tortured as I felt.

"Let me go," I choked out, even though it was the last thing I wanted, as rain spattered our heads. My left hand was trapped between us and my gaze jolted between his eyes and his lips.

"Damn you." He spoke through nearly-clenched teeth, releasing me as abruptly as he'd caught me close.

I shoved his powerful chest with both hands, furious and unfulfilled, needing something from him that I couldn't explain. He held his ground and his shoulders rose and fell with his breathing.

"Fuck you," I gasped, voice shaking, and turned away to see Robbie standing on the sidewalk observing everything with an expression of stun. Behind me I heard Case slam into his truck; I spun around as he drove out of the parking lot in a spray of gravel and screamed after him, "*See if I care!*"

Robbie jogged to my side through the downpour. "What in the hell? Are we in a reality show or something? It's raining buckets, come inside!"

I pressed both hands to my belly, watching Case's truck as it barreled down the road, hearing the roar of his engine as though it was insulting me, too. "He thinks you spent the night here."

Robbie chuckled. "I wish that was true. Jesus Christ, Tish, your dad would *kill* me."

I angled a fraction of my fury at him and he lifted both hands in immediate surrender.

"Let's get out of this rain! You need to get back to Chicago, baby girl. This shitty little po-dunk town is messing with your mind."

"I like it here," I said, and Robbie snorted with pure derision.

"Now I know I really need to get you out of here." He caught my elbow and dragged me after him. Back inside, he seated me at the table, flipped on the kitchen light, and poured a fresh cup of coffee. He then proceeded to sit opposite, folded his hands, and asked in his best attorney-at-law tone, "Now, please inform counsel why in the fuck you just struck a resident of this town."

"Is 'fuck' a legal term?" I curled my cold hands around the warmth of the mug.

"In this case, possibly so," he mused, smiling now. "Ms. Gordon, I assure you that we will examine all possible angles and...*positions* here."

"I'm in no mood for this," I warned.

"Have you been seeing him? Fraternizing with the locals? Patricia," he scolded, lightly slapping the back of my hand. Only half-kidding, I knew, he muttered, "I don't even know if they're housebroken."

"Don't say that!" My anger mildly shocked him.

He sat back and shook his head. "Oh, *Christ*. Don't go falling for some local guy. You have way more sense than that. I hope."

"*Get out*," I growled, and pointed at the door in case there was even a kernel of doubt in his mind. "I am *not in the mood* for you right now."

Robbie gave me a long-suffering look and insisted with zero sympathy, "Chicago. You've had too big a dose of reality here in...where in the hell are we, anyway?"

I was about to chuck my coffee at him and he retreated. At the door he asked, "What about your car? And how am I supposed to entertain myself this week? Shit, don't forget about Al's birthday party next weekend. He invited me, but fuck if I'm going alone."

"I'll go get my car later. And I haven't forgotten the party." I rubbed my aching forehead. "God, just get out."

Robbie was laughing as he shut the door behind him.

My foot hurt as I stood to dump out the rest of my coffee. I bent down, hooking my ankle against the opposite knee to examine the damage. A piece of gravel was wedged in the flesh just above my heel; angry adrenaline must have kept me from feeling it until just now. I hobbled to the bathroom and sat on the closed toilet seat to dig out the tiny rock.

How dare Case act that way!

How dare he imply that Robbie and I are sleeping together?

But what else would he think, showing up to find Robbie already here?

To punish myself I scrubbed soap on the wound, which stung like hell, and then centered a bandage over the cut. I decided that a nap would be in order before I walked the miles back to town to retrieve my car. When I thought about it, I didn't even know exactly where my keys were. Peaches seemed to agree about the nap, curling into a warm ball of comfort against my stomach as I stretched on my unmade bed and closed my eyes against the brooding sky.

Hours had passed when I woke and the storm was gone, leaving a clean, freshly-laundered feel to the air. Mellow sunlight streaked the carpet, indicating late afternoon, and I sat with a sigh, knowing I needed to eat something and get my ass moving. I fought the urge to simply lie back down and sleep until morning. In the kitchen I had the immediate sense that something was different, and cast my eyes around the space twice before I realized there was a set of keys just inside the door, as though someone had slipped them beneath. They were my apartment and car keys on their metal key ring, I realized, stooping to collect them.

Case, I thought at once, flinging open the door. Of course the hallway was empty but I flew outside and sure enough, there was my car waiting for me in the spot marked 'Gordon.' Case must have had my keys from last night; probably he was upset enough this morning that he'd forgotten to give them back. And here was additional evidence of his protective concern, more proof that he watched out for me, no matter how little I probably deserved it, or how little he received in return.

I rubbed my hands over my upper arms, hugging myself, squeezing hard. My stomach churned as I relived slapping his face this morning. There was no excuse for that, no matter how angry I had been. All that fury seemed misplaced now, having drained away, leaving behind only the urgent need to find him and apologize. Beg his forgiveness, before begging him for other things.

It's Saturday, I thought, clamping down on my desperate fantasies. *Where would he be right now? Does he play tonight? Is he home?*

Did I dare drive out to Ridge Road? I closed my eyes and envisioned showing up at the trailer, knocking on the door, apologizing, and then proceeding to explain that I was searching for a hoop earring I'd lost while kneeling illicitly on his bed. Touching his things, taking liberties, all without his knowledge. I roughed up my hair, ran my hands over my face and attempted to center my focus, inhaling deeply of the evening air.

I really do love it here. I studied the darkening sky above Stone Creek, stretching to the horizon where the mountains waited, patient and protective, as they had always been. *I've been here in this place, looked up at these mountains before now, somehow, sometime. I know it.* The truth of this stabbed at my soul. As my eyes roamed the magenta-edged clouds gathering above the peaks, evidence of more rain before morning, I considered suddenly that I had a clue, even a small one, a place to begin researching; despite everything, excitement took root.

I fed Peaches, ate a couple of handfuls of dry cereal while leaning against the counter and staring into space, swept my hair into a ponytail, and then carried my laptop, notebook, and a pencil out to the porch. There, I smoked two cigarettes, justifying this because it calmed my nerves, and opened my laptop. Into the search bar I typed the words *Thomas Yancy*. Nothing promising at first; there was a list of White Page information, advertisements for applications to find anyone, anywhere. I scrolled through all the junk, alert for a hint of something I could focus my energy upon, a puzzle piece, even a scrap of an answer. And then I saw a Civil War ancestry page which had turned up that name.

Thunder growled in the distance and I shivered, eyeing the horizon, where an anvil cloud was massing. I clicked on the Civil War link. The information was sparse. Thomas Yancy had served in the federal army until 1865, and was mustered out in June of that year. No picture available. I drummed my fingers against my lips, considering what Derrick had said at the Coyote's Den, about Thomas Yancy getting shot in the back. Though he'd been extremely drunk he seemed adamant, as though he knew exactly what he was talking about.

Coward, Derrick had said. *Fucker has it coming now.*

Who do you mean? I wondered. *Why does it matter now who shot Thomas Yancy well over a hundred years ago?*

The air chilled with an increasing breeze, the pines surrounding the parking lot rustling with restless whispers, trying to tell me something. On impulse, I typed *Spicer* into the Civil War page search bar. The third hit on the resultant list read 'Returns from U.S. Military Posts, 1865' and showed the name Henry Spicer. Heart clubbing, I backed out of the page and retyped this new name in the general search engine. Less than a minute later I'd broken out in a cold sweat, my breath shallow, staring at the grainy image of a sepia-toned family picture. In flowing cursive, the caption along the bottom edge of the photograph read *H. Spicer Family, 1872.*

Whoa. This is Case's family.

I was certain of this as I marveled at the old tintype, devouring every detail. Henry and his wife were seated at the center, surrounded by their children. Not one smiling face in the bunch, though I understood this was due to the length of time required for exposure; slow-operating cameras of the day. My eyes tracked over the faces of their numerous children, zeroing in on one in particular, a boy of perhaps eighteen, standing tall in the back row. I was touching the screen, caressing his face, before I knew my fingers had moved. Illogical as it was, I realized he looked familiar. *I knew him.* I read the names listed in the caption, each person neatly labeled, until I found the one that belonged to him—*Cole.* Cole Spicer, 1872. Eyes staring directly into mine from the old photograph, handsome and perhaps a little defiant, shoulders thrown back.

Jesus Christ.

I looked at the gathering storm on the western horizon, trying to focus. Attempting to regain reason.

Tish, you're a lawyer. There is no logic to this. You don't know this man named Cole, you have never known this man. There is no way that this is Case in another life—

I minimized the window and opened a second, typing Cole Spicer's name this time. The same image I had just been studying appeared, but as I clicked desperately on suggestion after suggestion, I found nothing more. Nothing useful, no birth or death dates, no further evidence of his existence. I had to call Case. *I had to see him.* I needed this so much that I stood and carried the laptop with me into the apartment. I found my phone and began to dial his number before stopping, holding the phone to my sweating forehead.

You can't call him.

I understood this, though it did nothing to lessen the desire. I did not, however, possess enough willpower to stop searching the Internet. I tried every combination I could concoct. I learned the names of all Henry

Spicer's children, five in total. I surmised that this was the ancestor who had carried the violin to war and then subsequently westward, the beautiful violin that Case still played to this very day.

I tried searching *Thomas Yancy* in conjunction with *Henry Spicer* but came up empty-handed. I discovered that Thomas Yancy had two sons, the younger of the two with the bizarre name of Dredd. At first there was nothing to suggest that Thomas Yancy, former soldier, had been cheated out of land or murdered, or that he was somehow connected to Derrick. Finally I searched Yancy Corps, clicking on the History link on their homepage. It was brief and tidy, citing the founding of the company in Chicago in 1893; the original founder was listed as Fallon Yancy, the eldest of Thomas Yancy's sons. No further mention of the father or the younger brother.

So there is a connection.

I covered my face, defeated and drained. Instead of finding any real answers, I'd only unearthed a thousand new questions. Thunder exploded, startling me; the sky was pewter-gray even though there should have been an hour of daylight left. Lightning sizzled and I smelled the rain seconds before it pelted the earth. Stubbornly, I remained where I was and pulled up the photograph of the Henry Spicer family one more time.

Hours later, I lay sleeping on the couch when a shuffling noise crept into my dream. The thunder had passed but a soaking rain continued to fall outside, numbing my ears to any other sounds. But I knew I had heard something and flung the afghan aside, heart clubbing in sudden agitation.

Someone was in here, just now.

Someone was in your apartment.

The certainty of this paralyzed me with fear—fear that would continue to immobilize me if I let it.

Get up, don't be helpless.

I stood and rushed to the door, flinging it open, unable to contain a shriek as Peaches, who'd been in the hallway, darted past my ankles and leaped atop the kitchen table. I had the horrible sense that if I'd moved only a little more quickly, I would have spied a person in the hallway with her.

"You *scared* me!" I hissed at my cat. The green digital display on the stove read 4:41, close to dawn, though the lingering storm continued to create a sense of deepest night. Mustering my courage, I took the steps to the foyer at a jog, scanning the parking lot, uncertain just what I expected to find. Case, sleeping in his truck, guarding me in the night hours? A part of me had prayed to find exactly that. Instead I saw only the wet parking lot, dim in the gray light of a rainy July morning.

Keeping occupied during the day wasn't a problem, at least not at the law office, where more people than ever were stopping by during business hours to inquire about their legal rights regarding their land dealings with Capital Overland. In addition, Al was busy with his usual caseload, working between the courthouse and the office while I held down the fort. We'd convinced almost a dozen families to reconsider the sale of their property, and though I had not seen him since that night at the Coyote's Den, I felt as though I could sense Derrick Yancy's wrath directed my way like a weapon pointed at my head.

Clark made a point of stopping at the law office on Thursday to remind me to come to dinner tomorrow night, an early one as we all planned to attend Al's birthday party afterward. As much as I hated to lie to Clark I dredged up an excuse, telling him I simply had too much work to do. Clark didn't exactly buy this, I could tell, but to his credit he let it slide.

"Will you at least be at Al's birthday? The boys and I can pick you up, if you'd like."

"I will," I promised. "But I already told Robbie Benson that I would go with him."

Clark's brow furrowed and I rushed to explain, "He's my old friend from school, remember, who's housesitting for Ron?" Not that I'd seen much of Robbie this week—he'd been too busy lounging in Ron's palatial cabin with a booze supply and the satellite dish, the worthless little shit. I was not feeling particularly charitable toward him.

"That's right," Clark said. He studied me with kind eyes. "Tish, are you all right?"

I nodded vigorously, then stood on tiptoe to kiss his cheek. Clark left just as Al returned from the courthouse, the noonday sun bright as a signal beacon on the street outside. Al greeted Clark and then focused his attention upon me. He announced, "I heard word just now that Derrick Yancy is considering pulling up stakes around here!"

"Not just a vicious rumor?" I countered, too wary to get caught up, though Al seemed genuinely enthusiastic.

"Only time will tell. But this is good news! Only thing better would be you telling me that you've agreed to stay in Jalesville."

"I don't even know if I passed the goddamn bar exam," I hedged.

"You passed or I'll eat my hat!" Al was not about to let me rain on his parade, hanging the hat in question on the coat rack. "You know, after I took the exam I spent two weeks on a fishing trip. Shit, and here you are working yourself half to death for me. You can take tomorrow off, if you want."

"Too much to do," I countered.

"At least take off early today." I could sense he wanted to ask me about something.

"What?" I demanded.

"It's not my business..." Al deliberately trailed to silence, a rookie lawyer tactic, the tense pause designed to snag a reluctant answer. I narrowed my eyes and he laughed, knowing he could not trap me in this fashion. "Fine. Is it my imagination, or is there a little something between you and young Mr. Spicer?"

A dense ball of consternation formed in my lungs.

Al said gently, "I thought so."

I bowed to Al's insistence that I leave early; he made me promise that I would take a walk, get some fresh air. He didn't mention Case again, but I drove the wrong direction on Main just so I could put my eyes on Spicer Music. The OPEN sign invited me but I was much too chicken. I rolled by as slowly as I dared, studying his modest little music shop, desperate to spy him through the window, but saw only the red sun refracting from its glass.

So, what is between you and Case? What exactly?

Something more than I could even explain, that was all I knew for certain; something from over a century ago and ten times stronger now, an echo of a time before, the memory of what had once existed between us screaming to be acknowledged. I closed my eyes and pictured Cole Spicer's face, Cole Spicer who was long dead; nothing could change that. Could it truly be plausible that his soul existed within Case?

Was I certifiable for even considering the possibility?

I was so lost in thought that at first it didn't register that someone had parked in my reserved spot at Stone Creek. A flash of annoyance morphed to sickly apprehension as I recognized Derrick Yancy's black GMC.

What the hell?

Again with the power play, taking my rightful place and forcing me to park to the side of his much-bigger vehicle. He was clearly waiting for me; how long had he been here? Did he follow me from the law office? I hadn't gone straight home, instead lingering near Case's music shop, which would have given Derrick time to get to Stone Creek first, if he had indeed observed me leave work. He didn't climb out of his 4x4, watching me approach with his eyes hidden behind mirrored sunglasses.

You spineless little bastard, I thought as I strode to his open window. Adrenaline lent me bravado. *Bring it on, buddy. I've been waiting for this.* For only a second did I waver, wanting Case at my side. But I was far from spineless; I could hold my own against Derrick.

"What are you doing here?"

He sat just above me in his big SUV and I had the distinct impression he liked how this required me to look up, as though he was some sort of royalty, always slightly higher than those around him. The hot sun beat on my head. I could see my angry reflection in his sunglasses; air conditioning blasted from the cab of his vehicle.

"I'd like to talk to you," he said in a perfectly-modulated voice.

"Then start talking."

"Not here," he insisted, and I peered behind him, into the recesses of the SUV; it was empty of anyone but him.

"If you think I'm about to go anywhere with you, you've severely underestimated my intelligence."

"I don't underestimate you at all, rest assured of that." Derrick lifted his sunglasses. His eyes made my stomach cramp—there was so much anger in them, a vicious loathing I knew he couldn't justify even if he tried. I understood, because I hated him perhaps unreasonably, too. He growled, "You are *fucking up* my business here. I won't have that, do you understand? You've done your little duty for Turnbull and now it's time to go home."

"I'll go home when I'm ready." I glared at him, attempting to pick answers from his brain. "There's still plenty of work here." I leaned closer, despite all instincts screaming at me to stay back. "And I won't be scared away, do you hear me? No matter what you do."

His eyes narrowed. "I'm sure I don't know what you mean."

I fixed my steadiest gaze on him, praying he would crack under the pressure of stony silence. Of course he knew what I meant. I was gratified to observe him fidget, messing with his sunglasses. But then, to my horror, his nervous movements stilled. A small smile bowed his mouth and he spoke softly. "Accidents happen, Counselor Gordon. Whether we like it or not. Sometimes, they happen to people we care about."

My knees turned to gelatin; it took all the willpower I possessed to maintain composure. Derrick's smile widened; he'd been successful in his attempt to catch me off guard. He slipped his sunglasses back into place. Speaking my name the same way he would deliver an insult he ordered, "Go back east, Patricia, where you belong. Do you understand me?"

His SUV had long since disappeared before I found the strength to walk inside.

Chapter Seventeen

I SPOKE NOT A WORD TO ANYONE OF THIS ENCOUNTER WITH Derrick Yancy. *He's bluffing,* I told myself. *He's trying to scare you, just like he sent someone to mess up your apartment while you were gone. He's all talk.* But the thought that he might be serious, that something could happen to someone I cared about, tortured my every waking thought. I kept my head low at work on Friday; Al was worried. He reminded me at least three times that it was his birthday party this evening.

"I'll be there, don't worry," I promised. I sincerely adored Al, even though my primary motivation for attending his birthday party was because I was certain Case would be there, as Al had invited nearly everyone in town. I was dying to see Case, furious at him for staying away from me this week.

But my heart ached at the thought of seeing him and being unable to touch him.

Touching him may have been at the forefront of my thoughts later that evening as I proceeded to get ready; that, and the raw, painful hope of him touching me in return. A week apart from Case had left me devastated and approaching desperation. Not to mention I still owed him an apology. I had stopped myself from driving to his place over a dozen times this past week, many more from calling him. I needed to tell him I was sorry in person; if he wasn't at Al's tonight, it would be a sign that I should drive out to Ridge Road after all.

I blew out my hair, letting it fall in curls down my back, and then lined and shadowed my eyes with extra care. Make-up accomplished,

I stood before my tiny closet, agonizing. At last I settled on sweet and simple—pale-pink bra, a tank top made of pretty white eyelet. It had a scalloped neckline and fitted perfectly over my breasts. With this I wore black linen shorts; my black strappy sandals would be perfect as a finishing touch. I fastened my diamond studs in my ears and pressed both hands against the panicked fluttering in my gut.

What if he's not there?

Case, please be there...

Robbie had promised to pick me up and he was late; it was quarter after seven, but what did I expect? Peaches twined around my ankles, swishing her fluffy white tail, and I stooped to pet her; as I did, I heard my phone chirp with a text. It was from Robbie: *Almost there.* And sure enough, I went to the kitchen window to see his sleek BMW inching along the gravel of the parking lot. I could exactly picture the wincing pain on his face at being forced to drive off blacktop with his prized possession.

"See you later," I murmured to Peaches, and then locked the door behind me.

"Damn, baby girl," Robbie drawled, leaning out his window as I approached the BMW. The evening sun was incredible, gilding everything with a rosy luminosity. He let his eyes rove openly over me, making a show of it. "I don't care what your dad does to me, I'm making a play for you tonight. Your tits are incredible, you know this. They're worth losing all job prospects."

"Would you quit?" I muttered, opening the passenger door and settling onto the butter-soft leather. He lowered the music volume with a touch of a button on the steering wheel.

"I'm dead serious," he said, creeping gingerly toward the street. He whined, "God, I hate this gravel. I hate being outside civilization."

"You are *such* a baby."

"Thank God it's just a few weeks. Ron's place is magnificent, at least. Just exactly what we can hope for when we're pulling down six-plus figures in Chicago in the next decade, God willing," he muttered, and I looked out the passenger-side window, watching the rolling foothills in the warm, sinking sunlight. They glowed as though dipped in golden gilt, the scent of sagebrush keen in the air. I inhaled deeply and tried not to let the thought of Chicago and its inevitable pull cause tears to flood my eyes.

Your mascara, I thought stupidly, trying to make a joke of it.

But it was no use.

Robbie was already blathering on about something else but I was far away, my mind flowing through all the things Case and I had shared since reentering each other's lives, all of the expressions on his face, the things he had said to me, the feel of his hands and mouth on my body...

I can't bear this...

"Tish, for real," Robbie complained. "You're in la-la land. Did you hear what I just said?"

"Sorry," I muttered. I looked his way and he lowered his sunglasses to regard me with his perfect blue eyes.

"I *said* I'm hoping to get laid tonight. I'm going crazy. Do you know of any easy girls in this area? Like, who might not have pieces of hay sticking to them?"

"Benson, if you need my help to get laid then you're way out of practice. Be nice. Make conversation. People around here aren't the rednecks you think they are."

Robbie replaced his sunglasses and muttered, *"Right."*

Al's birthday party was being held in his barn; I directed Robbie there and he could hardly contain his disgust, though he masked it behind a façade of lukewarm professional detachment. He understood the game, inside and out, and I knew that's why Dad liked him so well.

"Dammit, will you take my keys?" Robbie asked. "I don't have a deep enough pocket. And of course there's no coat check."

"*Jesus*," I muttered. He was like a little boy. "Yes, give me your stupid keys."

Lanterns were lit and strung between the wooden beams inside the barn, bales of hay intermixed with chairs. The crowd was already lively and bustling, adults clustered around the makeshift bar in the corner; opposite the bar was the raised, pie-shaped stage, where two teenagers were running amp cords even now; the musicians were two older men I didn't know. I saw the Rawleys and welcomed this excuse to separate from Robbie, who looked as ridiculous as one might expect, dressed in black, pencil-leg trousers, suit jacket and formal tie, as though we were dining at a five-star restaurant.

"I'll be over there," I told Robbie, indicating Clark.

"I'll be over *there*," he said, indicating the bar.

Seconds later I was wrapped in Clark's warm, kind embrace. He drew back and studied me with his mustache twitching.

"I'm glad to see you. You've been a stranger this week."

"I know," I whispered, hurting. "I'm sorry. Have you guys been here long?"

"Just arrived," Clark said. I spotted Garth and Becky headed our way; my composure took another nosedive as I scanned the crowd for Case, but he remained nowhere to be seen.

Clark said, "May I tell you how lovely you look this evening?"

"You're so sweet," I mumbled, hugging him again, and then said, "Hi, guys," as Garth and Becky drew near enough to greet. Their baby offered me a sweet, gummy smile. "Hey there, little guy."

"You want to hold him for a little bit?" Becky asked eagerly. "That way maybe I can sneak over to the bar for just a minute..."

I giggled at the anticipation in her voice, unable to refuse. She passed him to my open arms and I settled him on my hip; he was about eight months, completely bald, and studied me with unblinking brown eyes, his cheeks so chubby that they nearly obscured his vision.

"Thanks, Tish," Garth said, taking his wife's arm as they disappeared in the direction of the bar. Probably I would not see them again for the rest of the evening.

I told Clark, "I think I just got snowballed."

Clark smoothed a hand over his grandson's head. "I'll take him when you want to dance, doll."

I didn't want to dance with anyone but Case; and at last, as though conjured by my longing, Clark looked past my shoulder and said, "I was wondering when you'd get here."

Flames leaped from my stomach, igniting my heart in passing. I didn't dare turn around even as I sensed Case come right up behind my left shoulder, pausing perhaps no more than a foot away. I swore I could feel the heat from his body. I wanted to spin around and hug him, press close and tell him I was so sorry that I'd slapped him. That he made me so angry on top of being so aroused that I'd entertained thoughts of forcing him to make love to me that night. As though I was capable of such a thing. I almost laughed at my own absurdity.

"Better late than never," he said; his voice seemed to vibrate in my belly.

"Dad, c'mere!" Wy called from a few yards away.

Clark tipped the brim of his hat, saying, "Excuse me," and went to see what was going on with his youngest. Left alone with Case and the baby, I tried to compose my face enough to meet his eyes before turning around.

I've missed you so fucking much.

There were so many things I needed to say I didn't know where to start; instead, I stared speechlessly. He was wearing his hat, his eyes in partial shadow, lips somber. He was dressed in a gray t-shirt, one I didn't recognize, and his faded jeans, a leather belt with a silver buckle. We stared dumbly at one another for the space of two breaths before he asked quietly, "Did you get your keys on Saturday?"

My words rushing along as fast as my heart, I whispered, "Thank you for that. And I'm so sorry."

He knew exactly what I meant. "I'm sorry, too."

I nodded in the direction of Robbie, who held a plastic keg cup, talking to a couple of girls from town. "That's Rob Benson. He's hoping to work in the same law firm as I am this fall. He's spoiled and arrogant, and I really can't stand him. Please, don't for one minute think…"

Case held my gaze. "I don't think that. I didn't really think that last weekend, truly. I was just angry."

The baby chose that moment to clench a fistful of my hair, tugging delightedly.

"Ouch," I muttered, disentangling his chubby fingers, nuzzling my nose against his impossibly soft cheek, making him giggle as I scolded, "Listen, tiny man, that's no way to get attention."

"But it works," Case said, teasing with both words and tone, and I looked up to see a hint of his smile.

"You've tried it, I presume?" I was immeasurably glad just to be near him I thought of the horrible things Derrick had said in the parking lot at Stone Creek and knew I had to tell Case. Maybe not at this second, but soon.

"A time or two," he allowed.

Touch me, just one touch, even for a second.

He sensed what I longed for and gathered my hair in one hand, lifting it over the opposite shoulder and safely away from the baby's grasping fingers. He let his thumb linger on my collarbone as he whispered, "You are so beautiful it almost hurts to look at you."

My nerves responded by simultaneously supercharging; before I could speak Garth and Becky returned to collect their son, merry and laughing. They'd brought me a beer from the keg.

"Thank you, Tish," Becky gushed. "You're a lifesaver."

"I woulda brought you something," Garth told Case, bumping the side of his bicep with a closed fist, a gesture common to the two of them. "I didn't see you were here yet."

The music started as a man skipped a bow across fiddle strings in a call for attention. The crowd surged with a sound of appreciation, a ripple of applause. The two musicians had taken the stage and one spoke into the microphone. "How're you all doing on this fine, fine evening?"

The last of the sunlight streaked the wooden floorboards and I shivered a little, in pure anticipation; we'd been inundated by the Rawley clan and Case and I were jostled slightly apart. I tried to ease closer to him.

"Gentlemen, invite your ladies and show us what you know!" the man at the mic ordered, lifting both bow and fiddle high in the air before settling the latter beneath his chin and making it sing.

"Tish, dance with me, please, *pretty please*." Wy tugged on my arm.

I couldn't refuse this heartfelt invitation; I held out my right hand

and Wy kissed my knuckles before leading me to the dance floor. The Rawleys were such gentlemen; Wy was only fifteen and yet conducted himself with more politeness and poise than most grown men.

"Two-step?" I asked, concerned as I observed couples dancing as though they'd received professional ballroom training since childhood.

"That works," Wy said agreeably.

"You're a good dancer. I can't believe you don't have a girlfriend." I grinned as Wy flushed. "That Hannah Jasper is one dumb cookie."

Wy led us with the ease of an expert; as we swirled among the other couples, I spied Case, watching us dance. We spun away and I lost sight of him in the crowd. As the song ended, Wy asked, "How about one more?"

But I saw Case headed our way and my breath caught on an inhalation of pure hope. He reached us and said, "Sorry, kid, next one's mine," and Wy grinned and backed off.

Before Case could keep us in a more traditional stance, the way I'd been dancing with Wy, I slid my arms around his neck and pressed as close as I dared. His hands gathered my waist and I saw the expression in his eyes that mirrored the one in mine—what we could no longer hide. My breasts rested flush against his chest and I curled my fingers in the soft hair on his nape, beneath his hat brim. My thighs began trembling and then the trembling moved upward. We danced to the next two songs, wordless, studying each other as though this was the last night we would ever be together. Past images and long-lost memories swirled together. I knew that I had danced with him before tonight.

You, I thought. *It's you.*

He saw in my eyes what I needed and after the third song led me wordlessly outside, into the dark, humid night, luminous with stars, the sounds of the dance receding to the background. Around the far edge of the barn, where I heard only my thrusting heart, he turned to me, buried his hands in my hair and brought my mouth to his, kissing me so deeply and sweetly that I moaned. His hat brim bumped my forehead and I swept it from his head, letting it sail to the ground, clutching him.

And it was so intense, so quickly. Overwhelming need to take deeper his kisses, to feel his skin against mine. He held my face, kissing my chin, my throat, my collarbones, tenderly and with so much heat. I kissed his firm, stubborn chin, his jaws, his neck, running my hands beneath his shirt, over his hard, warm chest. He groaned and our lips were flush again, open and stroking. He slid both hands under my blouse, swiftly up to my breasts, cradling me at last as I made soft pleading sounds, unable to help it as he stroked my nipples. I breathed his name, caressing the front of his jeans; he was hard as a brass rod beneath the warm denim.

"Tish," he whispered hoarsely; he sounded in pain. And then, to my stun, he turned away as he had before, gripping his forehead.

"Wait!" I cried, but he collected his hat with a brisk movement, striding away before I could make contact.

I tore after him; his truck wasn't far. Horrified, I realized he intended to drive away. He climbed inside but I cranked open the passenger door and followed, grabbing his right arm.

"Tish." He froze in place, his voice husky and aching, inciting a riot in my blood.

"Don't go," I begged, my hands all over him, pulsing with energy and desire.

He moved fluidly, hauling me toward him. I straddled his lap, bruising my tailbone on the steering wheel but I didn't care—nothing mattered except tasting his mouth, his hands clutching my hips. I gripped his jaws, begging with wordless sounds. He clenched a handful of my hair and forcefully bent my head, kissing my neck, biting my skin. I clung, afraid he would stop at any second. His eyes blazed like hellfire and heat throbbed between my legs.

"Don't stop," I pleaded, grinding my hips against him. He cupped my breasts with a throaty groan, plundering my mouth with his tongue. I tore my lips from his to beg, "Please, Case, *please*…"

He took me beneath him on the bench seat, bracing above. Pressed flush, I could feel his heart, matching mine thrust for frantic thrust. He was rock-hard, cradled against my pelvis. I curved my thighs around his hips and he cupped my ass, lifting me against him, closing his teeth over my right nipple. I reached for the hem of my blouse, ready to tear it off. Not without difficulty, as I was clinging, he suddenly rolled away, burying his face in both hands, breathing so hard his chest heaved. I was almost too weak with desire to move, dumbfounded by his actions.

"*Case*," I panted, scrambling to my knees, desperate to understand what was happening.

He broke away and managed to growl, "No…"

"*No*," I disagreed sharply; I was lightheaded.

"I have to go." He was barely able to speak the words, I could tell, and yet he was choosing to do this.

"No you *do not*."

His eyes blazed and he repeated, "I have to go."

Fury burned tracks through my blood, so hot that my vision wavered.

"Then go!" I raged, slamming out of his truck. "Just fucking *go!*"

He drove away without fishtailing gravel this time, but the second his taillights began to disappear down the road, I grabbed Robbie's car keys from the pocket of my shorts. I disregarded what would surely be Robbie's wrath, racing to his car and starting it with a vengeance. I followed Case's truck straight out to his place, the sleek little car purring beneath me, determined to finish this once and for all. I was shaking with rage and need, blinded by these emotions. He had barely parked when I pulled beside his truck; I burst out of the BMW and accosted him.

"How dare you drive away from me like that?!"

"I can't bear this!" he yelled, truly furious, as visibly angry as I felt. Mutt and Tiny were jumping around our legs, barking at this unexpected sound of Case in a rage.

"Why? Answer me! Goddammit, *look at me!*"

Case pinned me with his eyes and said in a low, deadly voice, "All I *fucking do* is look at you. I'm tortured every second of every fucking day."

He stormed past me and almost wrenched the screen from its hinges, smacking the kitchen light into existence, me on his heels. In the narrow space between his sink and table, I grabbed hold of his shirt.

"Stop it!" he raged, spinning to face me so quickly that I made an inadvertent sound of fear. But I would never fear him; I only feared the untamed expression on his face. "You can't be here! I can't bear it! It's tearing me up inside! Don't you know *how long I've loved you?* Jesus *fucking* Christ! I've fucking loved you since I saw your picture seven years ago!"

"You didn't even know me then!" I cried, his words pummeling me with both abounding joy and helpless agony. I didn't confess how I wanted him to know me better than anyone else in his life. That I wanted the same from him, in return.

"You think I don't know that?! It's insane, it's more fucked up than *anything I've ever known!*" Anger clashed between us in red-orange waves. "I didn't ask to fall in love with you. Jesus Christ, it's like I'm tormented, fucking *haunted!* When you're not around, I can't get you out of my mind. When you're in front of me it's even worse. I can hardly breathe because I want you so much." His deep voice broke on the last few words even as he continued glaring at me.

I gulped, wanting him so much that my nerves crackled. But there was something far more sobering beating in the vicinity of my heart, something I was terrified to acknowledge.

"Don't worry," he said, acid in his tone now. "I won't mention it again."

"Goddammit," I said, flailing. I recognized I would not be able to turn back from this road, should I choose to head down its length.

But as I stared up at him, the choice was out of my hands.

My heart was furious in my chest, demanding acknowledgment. He went on, in a controlled rage, "I tell myself *every time* that it's the last time. The last time I'll try to see you, to be near you. Do you know what it's been like for me with you here? I feel like I'm on the fucking rack. Just *let me go.*"

I don't want to let you go. Oh Case, I don't want to let you go and I won't tell you so because it would only hurt you. I can't stay here. I don't belong here…

"Just let me go," he repeated, his tone an inch from total defeat. His eyes were dark with anger and need and desire; his gaze dropped to my lips, my breasts, and then he buried his face in both hands, clearly in agony.

The same agony clawed at me. Unable to stop, I closed the distance between us and put my hands on his ribs. He jerked as though I'd plunged a knife in his side but I refused to let go.

"Don't," he ordered, dead-serious.

I tightened my grip.

"I fucking mean it. I should never have kissed you…oh God…" He broke free and stepped back, shoulders squaring. The fury chiseled on his face slashed at my heart. He was beautiful, even in this passionate rage.

"Go," he whispered.

Don't turn me away again. I'll die.

"Go," he whispered, eyes flashing fire.

I spun away and shoved out the door, incinerated by his words. I heard the screen crash open behind me, and so I ran, racing into the humid night. He caught me from behind and we stumbled, almost going down.

"Let me go!"

"Wait," he demanded, just as out of breath.

I struggled, intending to shove him away, but instead I clutched his face. He made a harsh sound in his throat and I opened my lips to take his tongue into my mouth. We went to our knees, Case gripping my jaws in both hands, tilting me into his hungry kisses, our heads slanting one way and the other. I yanked him down over me, tumbling to the ground, latching my legs around his waist as we kissed as though the world would explode before morning's light and this moment was all we would ever be allowed.

"Case, please don't stop," I begged as he broke our kiss, breath pelting my cheek, staring into my eyes with all of the wonder and insanity of what was happening here in his darkened yard. My breath came in gasps, my heart tripping over itself, roaring in my head. His heart matched this pace and then some, pressed to my breasts.

"Tell me…you want me," he rasped, winding his fingers in my loose hair, clutching me almost painfully hard. But it was exactly what I needed, down to my bones.

"I couldn't want you more," I moaned, feeling the rigid hardness beneath his jeans. He caught my wrists as I went for his zipper and pinned them forcefully to the ground on either side of my head. I lifted against him, feverish, and he suckled my bottom lip, running his tongue over it, the heat of this ricocheting between my legs. I couldn't handle another moment of him not touching me.

"*Good*," he whispered cruelly, rolling away, lying flat on his spine and covering his face, knees bent at right angles. Cold and desolate without his touch, I went right after him.

"Look at me!" I shoved at his hands so he would, so aroused that the violent red haze had descended again. "Why are you *doing this to me?*"

"*Doing this to you?*" He clamped hold of my wrists for a second time. "You don't have any idea."

"That hurts," I choked, struggling to free myself from his iron grasp, tear-streaked and miserable, and in love with him. God help me, so in love with him that I couldn't imagine another day without him in it.

"Then you finally understand," he said, low and harsh, hauling me back across his chest. I fell over him, greedy for his touch, my hair getting tangled between us as he rolled us to the side and claimed my mouth, sliding his hand down the front of my shorts. The sounds coming from my throat were purely mindless with need. He kissed me deeply, stroking between my legs until I could no longer sense time and place, my hands fisted around his shirt; I thought he might try to escape if I dared to loosen my hold.

"I need you, I need you so much," I moaned as he freed my mouth to kiss my neck, and at my words he went rigid, ceasing all motion. He lifted his head and withdrew his hands; frantic that he would push me away, I clung even more tightly.

His eyes were flames, burning me alive. "You don't mean that how I want you to mean it, and I can't bear it."

I was not strong enough to stop him from extracting himself from my grip. I scrambled after him, as though we were competitors in a wrestling match, catching his waist as he rolled to his knees, knocking us both off balance. Furious, pulsating with heated energy, I yelled, "Would you *listen to me? I'm not fucking with you!*"

We grappled, falling again to the ground, me over his chest this time. I pinned him as well as I could, bracing on his shoulders. He stared up at me, cast in demonic-red light, his chest rising and falling with harsh breaths; I could see the pulse beating at the base of his throat. He moved fast, rolling us sideways, penetrating my mouth with his tongue, his hands beneath my shirt. I yanked open his jeans, gripping his rigid cock none too gently, devouring his kisses. I latched a thigh around his hip, vibrating with desire, dying with love for him—I tore my mouth away, intending to speak the words aloud…

But before I could, he said, "Right now I don't care how I'll feel tomorrow." The hoarse tone in his voice killed me. "I don't care anymore. When you leave, I want to have at least one memory to get me through the rest of my life."

I took these words like blows from someone with a hammer in hand.

When you leave…

You can't stay here, Tish. You're not good enough for him. You know it's true…

My thoughts raged, swift and horrible.

If you tell him you love him it will only force you to make a choice you can't make.

I can't bear it, I can't bear it either…

Tears gushed from my eyes and I rolled away this time, utterly defeated, hollowed out. I felt as though I should use a whip to peel the flesh from my own back. And even that would not hurt as much as what I had done to him, what I would have to do to myself to prevent this from going any further. I'd pushed it when he told me to go, *to let him go…*

He wrapped around me from behind, catching me to his chest and he was so strong, cradling me this time, as I pressed both fists to my mouth to hold back sobs.

"Oh God, don't cry." His mouth was against my hair.

I hated myself more in that moment than I had ever hated anything or anyone. I wrenched free and stumbled to my feet, blinded by tears, choking on sobs.

"*Patricia.*" His voice was that of someone drowning, unable to surface for the next breath. "Oh God, don't go…please, don't go."

I didn't dare look back as I jogged to Robbie's car, leaving him sitting on the ground.

This time he didn't follow.

Chapter Eighteen

LATER, I DIDN'T REMEMBER DRIVING HOME AFTER LEAVING Case's. Sometime late the next morning Robbie was knocking, calling through the door like a worried little brother. When I didn't respond he texted me, *Can I at least have my keys?*

Go away, I texted in response. *Go the fuck away.*

I wanted to die. I couldn't even cry I was so dead inside. When Robbie refused to leave, I shoved his keys beneath the door and then fell straight back into my bed.

Is this what you want? Is this what's right?

Turnbull and Hinckley is going to call with a job offer any moment.

It's what you want.

You can't stay here. You don't belong here…

I didn't move until some point in the early evening, unable to look at my face in the mirror, because if I did I would have to acknowledge that I was leaving behind the man I was in love with.

Oh God, I love him.

But I can't stay here…

I can't…

Clark called but I didn't answer. I thought about calling my sisters but couldn't bear to talk to Camille or Ruthie right now. I couldn't bear to do anything but drive back to Case's house and tell him the truth. But that would only destroy both of us.

Would he come back to Chicago with me?

He would hate it there.

Could I ask that of him?
Oh God, I want to die. I want simply to die.

I dreamed of Case that night and the next, terrible dreams in which I was a prisoner, my wrists and ankles bound with ropes, sobbing brokenly for him. Somehow I knew he was in mortal danger. I fought the rope bindings until I was slick with my own blood. And then into this dream-scape Derrick Yancy suddenly appeared. Although he didn't look exactly like the man I knew in this life, I recognized him. He crouched beside me and offered a smirking smile. He caught my chin, squeezing as he whispered, *Tell me, Patricia, what does a man do with an unfaithful wife?* When I refused to answer he struck me so hard that sparks exploded across my vision, blood pouring wetly over my mouth and chin.

But that pain could not compare to what he did next, grasping my hair, leaning close. I saw the glitter in his vindictive eyes as he whispered, *You were the one to kill him. Not me. You, Patricia.* And I would wake to morning's light with a shuddering cry, scarcely making it to the toilet before vomiting, realizing on some primal level, beyond all understanding, that I'd been responsible for hurting Case before now—harm had come to him because of me long before this life, and I hated myself all the more wretchedly.

I was silent at work on Monday. I told Al, "I don't want to talk about it," and wisely he didn't press. Thank God Mary was off sick. I worked like a demon, shutting out everything but legal matters. Al had let me take on a couple of minor disputes in the past month, both in the realm of family law, and I spent most of the afternoon at the courthouse, refusing to think about a thing other than the petitions in my hands. Hank Ryan was there, and greeted me with warmth; it was all I could do to return his smile.

When I was through with work it was early afternoon and I considered heading to the records office in the courthouse basement in order to dig up more information about the Yancys and the Spicers—but the thought of seeing Case's surname on old documents, of perhaps running across a mention of Cole Spicer, was too painful to consider. *You made your bed. Now you just have to get through these next few weeks and then go home. Put all of this behind you, forever.* I had driven to the courthouse, even though it would have been easier to walk, too terrified of running into Case. As I drove along the familiar streets of Jalesville, I understood I had to leave for Chicago sooner than planned. I had to go back to the city, now. This week. Maybe even tomorrow.

You coward. I gripped the steering wheel with white-knuckled fists. *You can't back out now. Al is counting on you for at least a few more weeks.*

I can't bear it, I wept, echoing Case's words; my heart was hollowed out, drained of everything. I had done no good here this summer; I had discovered no solid answers. I loved Case and could not admit this to him; I was worse than a failure.

How can this be right?

Tish, answer me. How can this be right?

Immediately after work I drove home and drew the blinds. Jerry Woodrow, the sheriff, had stopped at the law office to tell me there were no leads on the break-in. I didn't mention I knew exactly who had arranged the invasion of my apartment; I didn't care about anything but getting through the next moment. My phone, forlorn on the kitchen table, was lit up like a radio tower with messages, many of which were from Camille. It was well after ten that night when someone knocked on my door. I sprang awake and fell off the couch, heart exploding, thinking it might be Case. Someone knocked again, more insistently, and then I heard Clark say, "Tish, honey, it's just me. You wouldn't answer your phone and I was getting worried."

I went to the door and rested my forehead against the woodgrain. I had to clear my throat two times before I managed to say, "Clark, I'm so sorry." He had warned me and I hadn't listened; I couldn't face my own culpability.

"Can I come in? Will you talk to me?"

"I can't. I just can't right now."

"None of us want you to go," he said, and I pictured him standing in the hallway with his hat in his hands, dear, sweet Clark. "Al called me today, said he's worried sick about you. Thinks you're going to leave early for Chicago. He doesn't want that, either."

I wasn't strong enough to open the door; I couldn't bear to see how disappointed Clark was in me. Aching, bled out, I whispered, "Is Case all right?"

There was a silence that burned right through the door. At last Clark said, "I'm not going to lie and tell you that he is. I can't do that." I sank to my knees, my head still against the door. Tears clawed my eyes and throat, but it was nothing less than I deserved. Clark said, "This next Friday is Garth and Becky's anniversary, hon. We're having a party at The Spoke. We'd all be much obliged if you'd come."

There was no way in hell I could show my face. But I whispered, "Thanks, Clark. Thank you for everything."

I sensed his reluctance to go. He finally said, "I think you should stay, Tish. Please know that." And a minute later I heard the sound of his diesel truck grumbling away.

I went to work every day that week. I couldn't eat, and drank only enough to stay alive. By Friday Al and Mary were ready to conduct an intervention.

"Patty, you've done a world of good here," Mary said, stroking my hair as I sat at my desk, face buried in my arms. By noon I gave up all pretense of trying to work, as I had all week, and just let my head drop. "So many families have refused to sell to Overland because of your efforts. Yours and Albert's. You two should be proud of yourselves."

"Thanks, Mary," I muttered.

Al came near. "Tish, if you're hurting this badly..."

I lied, "I'm just fine. Just fine."

Al made me go home at four, where I crumpled on the floor beside the couch. I was in no way trying to be dramatic; it was just where my knees gave out. Maybe three hours passed and I was half-asleep when the phone rang near my ear, where I'd dropped it. Somehow I knew I needed to take this phone call, even in my semi-conscious state. I fumbled it into my field of view, pulse revving to see a Chicago area code.

Peaches curled near my belly, as usual, watching me.

I cleared my throat but still sounded like a pack-a-day smoker when I answered on the fourth ring. "Patricia Gordon."

"Miss Gordon?" inquired a cultured female voice. "This is Ginny Tinsdale, calling from Turnbull, Hinckley, and Associates. How are you this evening?"

"Wonderful." My mouth was dry as sandpaper.

"Glad to hear it," she said cheerfully, ignoring the way my tone contradicted the word. "I apologize for contacting you so late on a Friday, but you were unavailable yesterday and then earlier today. I am calling on behalf of the partners here. They would like to invite you to return to Chicago to personally accept a position here at our firm. Pending your passage of the bar exam, of course."

A position here at our firm...

'Moment of clarity' were the words that flashed through my mind right then. I sat there on the floor of my apartment, shaking and with a cold chill in my gut, stunned at what I had almost let happen, what I had almost done. Here with my dream job offer literally at my fingertips. Oh God, what had I almost done? How could I have come so close to the brink this way?

"Miss Gordon?" asked the voice in Chicago, when I didn't immediately respond.

"Please tell Mr. Turnbull that I respectfully decline," I said, and for the first time in nearly a week I was able to draw a full breath; I had finally made the right choice, for once in my life. "Please tell him that I've accepted another offer, to work for Mr. Howe here in Jalesville."

A startled silence pushed against my ear before she said, in a completely different tone, "Will do, Miss Gordon. You...have a nice evening."

I will, oh God, I will now.

I rolled to all fours and then to my feet, stumbling as I ran for my bedroom, stripping free of my crumpled work clothes and grabbing jean shorts and a t-shirt, the first clothing I saw. I hit the bathroom only to brush my teeth as fast as I could, freeing my hair from its clip. My eyes were red-rimmed, with awful, bruised-looking smudges beneath, but I couldn't worry about that right now, not when I needed to get to Case as fast as I could.

Call him!

I did, grabbing my keys along the way, slipping into my green flip-flops. Case's phone rang and rang, my heart slicing through my ribs in the silence between each ring. He didn't answer; it went to an automated message and then I was running, my heart alive again. Seconds later dust flew in a powdery cloud behind my car as I flew over the gravel roads; only the thought of the animals slowed me down in his yard. I parked, heart thrusting so hard I put a hand over it, jumping from the car. Mutt and Tiny came running and I hugged them close, calling, "Case! Are you here?"

I ran to the screen door, tugging to find it locked. To the barn next, stepping out of my shoes so that I could move more quickly, frantic as I continued to call for him. Cider and Buck snorted and nickered but I could not waste a moment; several things dawned upon me.

Tish, his truck isn't here.

Calm down. Get a grip on yourself.

It's Garth and Becky's anniversary tonight at The Spoke, remember?

That's where he'll be.

Right. Calm down, drive back to town.

Main Street was already beneath the Honda's tires when I realized I hadn't grabbed my shoes; they were still outside the barn.

Who cares? Just get there.

The amount of cars and trucks at The Spoke caused a spike in my blood pressure. The ground was prickly beneath my bare feet as I ran for the entrance. Need had overtaken me; I needed to tell him the truth, that I was in love with him and planned never to leave his side again. I burst through the front door of the little bar and grill; it was merry and chaotic inside, people dancing to the music, something wild and raucous, lots of fiddle. There was a bunch of helium balloons on the bar and I saw the Rawleys at our usual table. Greetings were called my way; someone asked why I wasn't wearing shoes but I had no time for anything but finding Case. He was not in sight.

Where, where, where?
The back entrance!

I darted outside, where dusk was gathering, racing around the side of the building and smack into the sight of Case and Garth. My heart seized up to observe Case sitting on a chair he'd dragged outside, shoulders hunched, his fiddle bow held lengthwise against his face. His hat was on the ground near his boots. Garth bent down, guitar in hand, speaking quietly, one hand upon Case's shoulder.

I had done this to him.

"Case," I rasped, my throat rough, and he jerked at the sound of my voice, as though I had stabbed him; he had been crying, quietly and devastatingly. I flew to him, but he had already stood up and turned away.

"Wait," I begged, but he yanked roughly from my grip. I hadn't seen him in almost a week but I was determined that I would see him every day and night for the rest of my life, come hell or high water. Starting immediately.

Garth caught my elbow, preventing forward motion, while Case disappeared into The Spoke without a backward glance, door closing behind him.

"Hey." Garth was angry. "Leave him alone. You can't do this to him. Just *go*. He's a fucking wreck."

I knew Garth loved Case and was only protecting him. Further, this was Garth's anniversary party and I should probably offer congratulations, but I jerked from his light grip and decided to explain everything later. I ducked around him and tugged on the door, but it was locked.

"Garth," I begged.

He shook his head; unwilling to waste time, I ran back to the front entrance. There was a huge cluster of people jamming the way.

"Excuse me," I said, using my elbows.

"Tish, you aren't wearing shoes," someone said.

There was laughter but I didn't care, struggling through the crush of bodies. It was like being in a nightmare. Barefoot, wild-eyed, I made it inside just as Case and Garth emerged from backstage. *Dammit.* I knew Garth could have let me in the back door. Case wore his hat pulled low but I could tell his eyes zeroed in on me. I was prepared to storm the stage but it was so crowded. People kept trying to talk to me. Someone else asked why I wasn't wearing shoes.

And then another hand caught my elbow.

"What a sight you make," said Derrick, and I spun to face him, ready to deck him for touching me. I thought of how he'd looked at the Coyote's Den calling me a whore, later threatening me in the parking lot at Stone Creek and then again in my nightmares, telling me I was responsible for killing Case. Whether I liked it or not, Derrick was also embedded in my past. He saw the unchecked rage in my eyes; he showed his teeth in a smile but his eyes returned the fury.

"How can you show your face here?!"

"I told you I wanted to talk to you before you leave. Come outside with me."

"You snake," I hissed, all of the loathing I felt, fair or not, surging to the surface. "You broke into my apartment, didn't you? You were on Case's land! What were you trying to find? I know you're trying to scare me, but *you haven't!*"

"Jesus, let's not make a scene." He leaned closer. "Come outside with me." Then he said something that made no sense—"Please, Tish."

"*No*," I insisted through clenched teeth, tugging at his grip.

"I have to talk to you, you don't understand." His fingers dug into my flesh and there was something in his eyes, deeper than his loathing of me, that I couldn't interpret. I froze as he leaned closer and spoke fast. "There are things here beyond my control. Things you aren't supposed to know. You are in danger if you stay in this town, do you hear me? *In danger.*"

It was too much; on top of everything else, I could not handle being manipulated in this way, by this man.

"Let me *fucking go!*" I raged, and even with the loud music and chatter all around us, more than one head spun our way. And then my world narrowed to a single focal point—I saw him coming, setting people roughly to the side. Case reached us, wrapped a hand around Derrick's forearm, and forcibly removed his grip.

"You *son of a bitch*, touch her again and I will kill you where you stand."

Frustration dug into Derrick's face. "Are you threatening me, Spicer? Fuck you."

"No, *fuck you*," Case said, low and deadly, and with those words strode away, shoving through the door to the parking lot. I raced after him.

"Case!" I begged. My feet hurt like hell on the rough ground but I ran in frantic pursuit, spying his truck no more than fifty feet away. My keys were in the Honda but it was more than twice that distance in the other direction. He would get to his truck and drive away from me. I would not allow that to happen again.

"Stop!" I implored. He reached his truck and I darted between him and the driver's side door, breathing hard, blocking his way. "Don't leave."

"I'm done." His voice was flat with despair. "*Done.* I can't. I'm fucking destroyed. Are you happy?"

I reached for him but he sidestepped, growling, "Don't touch me. What are you fucking doing? What the hell can you possibly want from me?"

"You, I want *you*. Do you hear me? I turned down the job in Chicago…"

He put his hands to his forehead, pressing hard. I had already done so much damage to his heart that my own felt broken, in response. I moved swiftly, getting my arms around his waist, determined to make him listen even if this required wrestling him to the ground. I felt his heart thrusting, his passionate heart that he'd long ago given to me, and told him the truth at last. "I love you, oh God, Case, I *love you*."

"Tell me you mean that." He was rigid with tension in my arms. "Tell me you mean it."

"You *know* I mean it." I clutched his face and he closed his eyes, as if unable to believe my words. "I don't want the job in Chicago. I already told them I'm not taking it. I don't want to leave because I never want to be away from you, ever again."

He swallowed hard and there were tears in his eyes as he opened them. "I told myself I could live without you, that I've faced worse things, but nothing is worse than the thought of that. Not one thing."

Emotion jammed my throat. "Case, *oh sweetheart*, I love you. I love how you sing, and how you love your horses, and how you touch your instruments. I love the man you are. I can't imagine being without you for another second. Please tell me you can forgive me."

He used both thumbs to brush aside my tears. "Will you come with me, right now?"

I nodded and he bent to lift me in his arms, using one hand to open the truck door and setting me on the seat.

"Come this way," I begged. "I can't bear to let go of you."

He climbed in, keeping me close to his side as he started the engine and drove us out of the parking lot.

"Is this really happening?" he whispered.

I took the hat from his head, setting it aside so I could get my arms around his neck.

"I'm so sorry I hurt you." I kissed his temple, his cheek, his ear, inhaling his scent like a forbidden drug. "I should have told you that night in your yard. I missed you so much this week I felt ill. I've been dying without you. You have to know that. Dying."

He took the truck straight over the dark roads to his place. The moment it was parked he hauled me across his lap. "I didn't think I could go on another moment," he whispered.

Cider and Buck loped from the barn; Mutt and Tiny were barking. I laughed through my tears as the dogs jumped up on the truck and the horses stomped and snorted.

"They're welcoming me home, I think."

"That's exactly what they're doing," he agreed, stroking my arm. "Did Yancy hurt you?"

"No," I assured him.

"When I looked up and saw you outside The Spoke, I thought maybe I was hallucinating. I couldn't believe it was really you."

"I can't be without you, not anymore," I whispered, stroking his soft hair.

"It's the same for me," he said, pressing tender kisses to my bare skin—my shoulders, my neck, my eyelids, the corner of my mouth, my ears.

"There's something…" I faltered, almost shy to make the request. "There's something I want us to do. Can we ride Cider? Together, I mean? I've been imagining that."

"You have?" He studied me in the dim glow of the dashboard lights.

"I would love to ride her with you. I would love that with all my heart."

He lifted me from the truck and carried me to the corral; secure in his arms, I wrapped mine around Cider's warm neck, kissing her nose.

"Hey there, girl," I said, scratching beneath her long mane. "I've missed you." And then to Buck, "You too, buddy."

Case asked his horse, "You want to take a ride with Tish and me, sweet girl?"

"I don't have on the right kind of clothes," I worried, then giggled. "I don't even have my shoes!"

"You're perfect," he whispered. "Let me help you up."

He boosted me and I settled atop Cider's warm back with no saddle; she was comfortingly solid beneath me, her hide warm and bristly. Cupping my lower leg, Case leaned to plant a soft kiss on my knee; I shivered and he grinned.

He patted Cider's flank, murmuring, "Down, girl, there's a good girl," and the mare obediently bent her legs so he could mount with no stirrup. Cider accepted this extra weight and straightened, tossing her mane. Case shifted his hips, easing right behind me, and I melted against his chest.

He wrapped his arms around my waist, sweeping my hair to one side so he could press his lips to my temple, hot, soft kisses that sent shockwaves through me. He shifted his hips, curling a hand into Cider's coarse mane; she moved forward in an eager walk.

"There's a good girl," he said to her, and I felt his left knee tighten; he led her toward the edge of the gravel road, keeping one arm around my waist, stroking my belly with his thumb. I tipped my head to give him better access to nuzzle my neck. Against his powerful chest I felt so safe...*so whole.*

"This is so perfect. I wanted this so much the first night we rode the horses together."

"You can't know how perfect this is." His voice was a husky murmur. "I want to touch you."

Slowly, deliberately, he slipped his free hand beneath my t-shirt.

"Your heart is beating so fast," he whispered, pressing his palm there, just at the top curve of my left breast.

"*Case…*" I breathed his name, gripping his thighs.

He cradled my breast, nudging aside my bra cup, his thumb circling my taut nipple with slow, repetitive strokes. Combined with the steady, vibrating beat of Cider's hooves—and no saddle—I was about five seconds from orgasm. But Case took his sweet time; I could sense his joy in prolonging the beauty of this moment. I closed my eyes, letting my head fall back against his shoulder.

"Later, I want to taste this same spot," he murmured, lips at my ear as he caressed my breasts.

I shivered and would have fallen from Cider if not for his arms.

"And this one," he whispered, unbuttoning and unzipping my shorts, moving his incredible touch downward over my pubic hair. I was already so slippery-wet that his questing fingertips almost took me over the edge. I dug my fingernails into his jeans and felt him grin anew against the side of my neck. "Do you know how goddamn long I've wanted to touch you?"

"Case," I moaned, trembling hard now, pelted by sensation. I could hardly remember a thing but his name. He bit my earlobe as he stroked; my breath came in panting gasps as he deepened his touch.

"You feel *so damn good*." He spoke low and sweet, biting the side of my neck. I caught his forearm in both hands, shuddering almost violently as he pressed the base of his broad palm against my pelvis. Cider's hooves crunched the gravel beneath us as she continued walking, unconcerned.

"Thank you," I breathed, steeped in pleasure, and he laughed, low and satisfied, against my hair. I turned so I could press my face to his chest, still trembling, inhaling against his collarbones. I wanted to be held like this for the rest of my life.

I felt the rumble of his voice against my cheek. "You're so very welcome. I'm hoping you let me do a lot more, later."

I looked up at him, his face cast in shadow, the half-moon illuminating the sweeping foothill plains. I traced my fingers along his strong jaws, my thumb skimming his eyebrows, his beautiful chiseled lips. I thought of the shadows beneath his eyes and gently touched him there, aching at the pain I'd caused. I knew his face, had known it in another incarnation in the past, and though I hadn't yet explained this to him, I knew he understood. I knew he felt it, too.

"You don't know how good that feels." He turned his face toward my hand.

Cider issued a low whinny, sidestepping, as though sensing my urgency.

"Can we go back to your place?" I begged in a whisper.

His eyes glinted with teasing, I could tell even in the darkness. "Why's that?"

"I want it to be 'later' right now."

Without another word, he halted Cider and turned her about, then heeled her flanks.

"Oh God, my place is a wreck," he muttered as we stumbled through the screen door. In the dim interior I wasted no time pulling him close.

"It doesn't...matter," I gasped between kisses. We fell against the counter and he groaned as I yanked the shirt from his back; my own made a ripping sound as he freed me from it. With a fluid movement he set me on the counter and stripped off my bra, pressing his face between my breasts. I moaned as he took me in his mouth, one nipple after the other, drawing on me with his hot, stroking tongue.

I repeated his name in disjointed gasps, as though being struck, my legs around his waist as he carried me to his bedroom. He took us to the mattress where I had once knelt alone and then clicked on the bedside lamp, both of us breathing as though we'd just sprinted from Jalesville to get here. He studied my eyes, all of the wonder and love and longing I felt echoed in his expression as he whispered, "I can't quite believe you're here. I've imagined this so many times. You can't know what this means."

"You said a long time ago that you knew I was the one for you," I said, tears brimming, my hands resting on his broad chest. "You were right, Case. It just took me this long to see it. And now I see it with all my heart. I'm so sorry I hurt you. I'm so sorry I fought it."

In his eyes, I saw the pain of the last seven years disappear.

"You are such an incredible man." I touched him without ceasing, caressing his hard, warm skin. "I love that you don't back down. I love that you're so passionate, that you care so deeply about the people in your life. And the animals. I want to be at your side, always." Tears fell over my cheeks, splashing on his hands.

"I told myself I'd just stop at Al's that day, just say hello, and then I would go. But then…" He drew a deep breath. "Then I saw you and knew I was just as much a goner as I'd ever been. A thousand times more. I took one look at you, the woman of my dreams, the only woman on Earth for me, right in front of me at last. I got back in the truck and I was shaking like a teenager."

I pressed closer, touching his face. "I have spent every day since then wanting to be near you. I started falling in love with you that very moment."

"I had almost given up all hope. I don't want to blink for fear that I'm dreaming all this."

"That first day you brought me here I held your shirt to my face," I confessed. "Just so I could smell you on it. I knew I loved you then, I just couldn't admit it to myself."

He kissed my lips with utmost gentleness. "Patricia. I can't tell you how much I love you. There were times I thought my heart might break with it."

"Your heart." I bent to kiss his chest in that exact spot. "I'll cherish it, always. And you have mine. You've had it since that night at Camille's wedding. I was just too stupid to know it then."

"You weren't stupid. I was out of line. But I meant everything I said that night. I knew we were meant to be together. I know it still."

I rolled to my knees to get my arms around his neck. My breasts were at his chin with him sitting and me kneeling, and he pressed a soft kiss between them. Against my skin he whispered, "You are so beautiful. Oh God, so beautiful. Inside and out. Your sweet, passionate soul is what I love the most, I want you to know that."

"This summer is what I've been moving toward my entire life. Toward *you*. We've been together before now, you know that, don't you?"

"I do know it." He looked hard into my eyes. "I do, Tish. I knew it the moment I first saw your face in the photograph, over seven years ago. It's the strongest thing I've ever felt."

"I have so much to tell you," I gushed. "Oh, Case…I came so close to not coming out here at all. I never would have known, I never would have understood…"

"But you did," he whispered. "You're here now, sweetheart, and that's all that matters."

Though I wanted to tell him everything I'd discovered there were a few other pressing matters I wanted to tend to first. Threading my fingers in his hair, I made another confession. "I think about you all the time."

"What do you think about?" he murmured, drawing me closer.

"This," I whispered, trembling. "You holding me…and kissing me…"

I realized both of us were only half-undressed and grasped his shoulders, biting his earlobe and demanding, "I want to see all of you. I've been dreaming about it for so long now…"

He grinned. "And people wonder if there's a heaven."

I giggled, so utterly happy, squirreling to push him onto the mattress. My hair fell all around us as he let me maneuver him to his back, where I ordered, "You lie still. I want to touch you." So saying, I caught his wrists and pinned them to the sides of his head, which he allowed, letting my nipples skim his chest. He shivered and the grin fell from his lips as he warned, "I can only take so much lying still, just so you know…"

"You hush." I released his wrists, whispering against his lips, "Hold still," and he did, though the tension of our desire was about a minute from exploding us to bits. I stood to slip free of my shorts and he groaned with longing; I straddled him, letting my hair glide across his belly, pressing hot little kisses southward down his center, marveling at the freckles patterning his torso, tasting each one I saw as his breath grew increasingly short.

At last I could take no more of my own teasing and unzipped his jeans, rubbing my cheek against his hot, swollen flesh. I opened my lips over his cock and his fingers dug into my hair. I didn't stop him this time, too preoccupied, lifting my head only long enough to order, "I want you to come in my mouth." A small part of me, the part that retained a shred of rational thought, was rather proud of the sounds I was causing him to make. He changed shape against my tongue, swelling even more as he came, and I took it all down my throat; I had never done such a thing and almost choked.

"*Oh…my…God…*" he gasped.

Giggling convulsively, my cheek on his stomach, I implored, "I need…a napkin…"

We were both laughing then, though he was still shaking. He leaned and grabbed the edge of the blanket, hauling me upward and burying his face against my neck as I wiped my mouth and could not stop giggling.

"*Holy shit.* I have never come so hard in my life."

"I should hope not," I teased. "Until the very next time I make you come, that is."

He grinned and slowly shook his head, rolling us to the side. "You're pretty damn bossy, you know that?"

My giggles turned to a gasp as he smoothed one hand over my belly and slipped two fingers inside, taking up a slow, stroking rhythm that had my fingernails digging into his back.

"You're so wet," he murmured, eyes intense upon mine.

I got my arms around his neck; I couldn't bear to not see him, even for a second. "Of course I am. You're touching me…"

"I will never stop touching you," he vowed, as I climbed on top. He was already hard as a stone pillar.

He clutched my hips as I bent forward to bite his neck. I whispered in his ear, "I want to ride you…like Buck…"

"Holy God, *woman…*" And then he could no longer speak, as I did just that. Time swirled into a hot, wet blur. My thighs ached and I gasped for breath. The sheets became a pinwheel of material beneath us, our furious motion taking us to the edge of the bed.

"*Not yet,*" and I slowed the pace, watching his face, overcome by the passionate intensity there; his hands curved around my ass, pulling me into each thrust, his beautifully-shaped hands that cradled a guitar so lovingly, that held a bow poised so perfectly over the fiddle strings as he called forth a wealth of music. And then he suddenly shifted us, his powerful body above mine now as he became the aggressor, spreading my thighs, plunging deeply.

He ordered hoarsely, "I want you to come, oh God, *come all over me.*"

"Let me *see you…*" I begged and he knew what I meant, taking my face in one hand, holding my gaze prisoner.

Tish, he said without words. *My Patricia...*

Case. And then, in the intensity of the moment, I was overtaken by how I had known him before this, how inextricably intertwined our souls; steeped in love and clenched by a powerful, shuddering passion, his long-gone name seared through me. As though outside my own body, calling to him through time, I cried, *Axton...*

～⁓⁓～

Later, we held each other close in the soft lamplight, sweating, tangled together, heavy-limbed with satisfaction.

"I could die right now and I would die happier than I've ever been. My life would have been worth it for these past few hours with you." His deep voice was hoarse with emotion.

"Don't say that," I scolded, and latched my ankles low on his spine. "Don't you dare talk about dying and leaving me. I would die right after that, just so you know."

"Come here," he whispered, parting my lips with his tongue.

My heart surged against his chest. "I need you, Case, I need you inside me again..."

Hours of lovemaking had left my tender skin sensitized, able to accept this gentler passage as a gift. My breath came in panting rushes as Case kept a slow, steady rhythm, holding himself back, allowing my pleasure to swell to a towering height from which I fell at last, headlong and gasping, opened to him in a way I'd never been to anyone. He cried out, thrusting one last time before collapsing over me.

"That was so...*that was so*..." I was beside myself, quivering in his arms; I had never experienced such powerful release.

Case smoothed hair from my sweating forehead, studying me at close range with a satisfied smile gracing his lips. I couldn't catch my breath.

"*You*," he whispered.

I held his face in my hands, imbibing him, heart and senses, body and soul. And nothing had ever felt more right.

Chapter Nineteen

MORNING FOUND US CURLED TOGETHER BENEATH THE sheet. Case's orange cat, Carrot, sprawled at our ankles, stretched out like a kitty-sized throw rug, while Mutt and Tiny poked their noses over the top of the mattress, brown eyes curious, tails wagging. I woke first and giggled, while Case knuckled his eyes and asked with a sleepy husk in his voice, "Everyone is watching us, aren't they?"

I pressed warm kisses to his chest. He growled, teasing me, nuzzling my bare skin. The dogs barked and Carrot prowled the foot of the bed, jumping at my toes under the blanket. I shrieked as Case blew a huge breath of air against my collarbones. He laughed, pinning me and doing the same on the side of my neck. At this noise Carrot flew from the bed as though launched from a cannon.

"Stay right there," he ordered, bracing above me and grinning. My heart thumped like crazy at the sight of him, all warm and tumbled from sleeping. He rubbed his stubbled chin lightly over my breasts as I shivered and giggled. At my ear he murmured, "I have to go feed everyone. But I'll be right back."

"Hurry," I ordered, cupping his face, and he kissed me flush on the lips before climbing from the bed and stretching, twisting at the waist. I lifted to one elbow, admiring his lean, nude body, craving him even as tender as I was from all our lovemaking last night.

He donned his shirt and jeans with brisk, masculine movements and then turned to look at me, lying in his bed on my side, the sheet drawn demurely over my breasts. My curls were a tangled nest. He swallowed hard, with the expression I knew well, that this was almost too much for him to bear, that he couldn't quite believe we were together, at last. I reached for him and he took me back to the mattress with one fluid movement.

"This is the most beautiful morning of my life," he whispered. "Yesterday morning I didn't know how I was going to go on another day."

"You are mine, Charles Shea Spicer." I gripped his ears for extra emphasis, and he grinned at my use of his full name. "We sound like an old-fashioned couple. Charles and Patricia."

"We sound like everything I've ever dared to hope for, that's what." He kissed my nose. "My sweet Patricia. I have something to give you." He leaned to root in his nightstand drawer and sat up with my silver hoop earring. "I found this in my bed, you know."

"I *knew* it." I admitted, "I kissed your pillow that night."

"That just blows me away. Here I was looking for any excuse to be near you, *dying* to touch you and trying so damn hard not to let it show…and you were in my bed without me even knowing?! You know how hard I rode home that night? And then you were gone when I got back here."

"I didn't *want* to leave. I was just too chicken to stay." I traced my thumbs over his chin, confessing, "I knelt right here and touched your sheets and kissed your pillow. It was so hard to drive away."

"If I'd have known you were feeling those things that night, I would have ridden straight to your place and thrown you over Buck on the saddle. I would have brought you right back here." He grinned anew. "Although I had some idea that maybe you liked me more than you let on, when I pulled back my sheet and saw one of the earrings you'd been wearing all day. I felt like I'd found a treasure chest in my bed." His grin grew increasingly wicked. "You kissed my pillow, huh?"

"I wanted to be kissing a whole lot more of you than that, you realize!"

"I do *now*," he said, bending to lightly close his teeth around my right nipple. "You stay here, woman, I'll be right back."

"Hurry," I demanded again.

I curled around his pillow as sunlight fell across the foot of the bed.

I was nearly asleep again, drowsy with warmth and contentment, when Case returned from the barn; we had only relented to sleep a few hours earlier. He shucked his clothes and I murmured happily as he drew me against his chest, kissing my shoulder. He spoke softly. "I thought of something while I was outside. I'm a little ashamed to admit it didn't occur to me last night."

"What's that?" I whispered and he spread one big hand over my belly.

"What if we're parents, around about next May?" He patted me gently, two times.

I'd thought of that, very early this morning. I covered his hand with both of mine and calmly whispered, "Then I hope she has your beautiful hair."

He laughed around the lump in his throat. "I would make you my wife this second, if I was able. Baby or not, I hope you know." He kissed my temple. "Everything will be all right, sweetheart, my sweet, sweet heart. We're together now, from here on out."

"No, your fingers aren't quite there," he said, and I chewed my bottom lip in concentration, almost too distracted by his naked body to think of anything else. I was also naked; Case had instituted a house-wide ban on clothing. It was late afternoon, warm yellow sun pooling in the foothills. We'd managed to venture to the living room couch, after spending the entire day in bed. I was situated on his lap, sitting cross-legged, his guitar braced over my thighs. His chest engulfed my back as he curved forward and cupped his hands around mine. I forgot all about the guitar; his chin rested at the juncture of my neck and left shoulder. He murmured, "Now this is the G chord," and guided my fingers to the proper placement on the taut strings.

Determined to try, I strummed the note; it sounded on-key and I smiled, strumming again. "It's harder to hold the strings down than I would have thought." So saying, I lifted his left hand, inspecting his fingertips for markings; the strings had left rivets in mine.

"It's just that your hands are so delicate." He rubbed his thumb over the grooves left behind in my skin.

"And yours are so tough." I shivered with pure delight, craving those tough, knowing hands all over my body. I begged, "Play something while I sit on your lap. I want to feel like I'm part of the music with you. I wish I knew an instrument."

Case repositioned us, tucking me closer. He swept the hair from my neck, settling its length over my right shoulder. "I'll teach you. And until then, you can inspire the music."

"When I watch you play, this is all I really think about. Being close to you, like this. Being in your arms. You look so…enraptured when you play. I love it so much."

"I knew where you were, every second, when you were at a show with me. I tried to pretend I didn't notice you, especially that first night at The Spoke, but every song I played was for you. What's your favorite, baby? What do you want me to play for you?"

Before I could respond he began strumming out a melody I recognized, sweet and slow, the one I usually requested. I felt the vibrations from the guitar all the way to my toes. When the song was done he held the final chord and then rested his jaw against my temple.

"I love that one so much. Is it an old song?" It sounded like something from an earlier century, I'd always thought.

"It's nearly seven years old," he murmured. "I wrote it for you, August of '06."

"That's *my* song? You mean to tell me I've been hearing it all summer and never knew?"

His eyes were alight with joy. "I prayed that someday you'd know it was for you. I end almost every show with it."

I started crying, tears streaming over my cheeks.

Case set aside the guitar and stretched us full length on the couch. He tucked hair behind my ears and thumbed away my tears. My voice was rough with emotion as I whispered, "Thank you, sweetheart. I love it so much."

"You're so very welcome."

"Can you play it again?" I begged, even as my thighs spread around his hips.

"I promise I will, baby. But first…"

I rocked against him and he exhaled in a rush.

"First I want you to thank me for something else," he said, and drew me firmly closer.

"I have to feed the animals," he mumbled, much later.

The quality of light in the trailer had deepened to indigo. It was late; we hadn't budged from the couch. I didn't know if my knees would support my weight when I tried to stand and smiled at the thought, snuggled against his powerful torso.

"I'll help you," I mumbled, replete with satisfaction. "We should eat, too, speaking of food."

Case folded me even more securely to his chest, hands buried in my hair. "I don't need food. Or water. Just you."

"You've got me," I whispered. "And if you ever get tired of me, too bad. I'm here to stay."

His deep voice vibrated against my cheek as he spoke. "Tish, the entire rest of my life isn't near enough time to be with you. I can hardly bear the thought of you leaving to go back to your apartment."

Overcome with a violence of tenderness and love I clutched his face, kissing the skin beneath his eyes that had borne shadows for too long. "*Case*. You were hurting and I did that to you. I'm so sorry, love. I am so sorry."

The windows were open; the air had grown chill with nightfall. He reached and caught the flannel blanket from the back of the couch, swirling it over us, and I burrowed into his warmth. Despite everything— the decade-old longing for a life and career in Chicago, the challenges and triumphs that had come before in my busy, fast-paced life, I felt as though I had never been anywhere but this evening, this place, with Case. It was as if everything I'd lived through had led to us holding each other in this twilit moment. He smoothed a hand over the back of my head and pressed his lips to my forehead.

"Tell me once more," he whispered. "Please tell me once more."

I could feel his heart beating beneath my cheek; I knew what he needed to hear and whispered, "*I love you.* I love you with my whole heart and you won't doubt it, ever again. Understood?"

We finally managed to separate so Case could feed the animals and I could call Camille, knowing I needed to tell my older sister what had happened last night; I'd purposely maintained radio silence with her this summer, unable to bear explaining what I was going through. But she and Mathias would want to know everything in the world was right again; at least, in our little part of it.

My sister answered on the second ring. "It's about time you called me!"

"Case and I are in love," I said without preamble. Tears blurred my vision and I swiped at my nose with the knuckles of my free hand.

"Oh, thank God, *finally,*" my sister said in response, her voice inundated with relief. "I was getting worried."

"Milla, I'm so in love with him." I was all choked up, trembling. "I turned down the job in Chicago."

"Good, that's so good," Camille breathed. "Oh, Tish, I'm so happy for you two. Let me talk to Case!"

"He's outside. I've barely let him out of my arms since yesterday."

"Everything feels right now," Camille murmured. I could hear Mathias's sleepy mumble in the background. I looked at the clock on the stove and realized it was going on ten, which meant it was close to eleven in Minnesota; I hadn't known it was so late. Away from the phone, Camille said to her husband, "Everything's all right. Tish finally realized that she's in love with Case."

Sounding more awake, Mathias asked, "Can I talk to him? Oh wait, he's calling…"

Case came back inside from the barn, holding his phone between his right ear and shoulder. He came directly to me; I was wrapped in the flannel blanket from the couch and rested my forehead on his collarbones.

Back in Minnesota, I heard Mathias answer. Case said into his phone, his voice all husky, "Hey, Carter. Everything's all right now. Everything's as it should be. I just wanted you to know. Love you, buddy." He disconnected the call and his eyes were so full of love that my phone clattered to the kitchen floor and my arms went around his neck as he swept me into his embrace, carrying me straight to the bed, where we made love for the countless time since last night, wordless and joyous and intense.

Monday morning I decided I didn't feel like driving to town for work. Maybe this wasn't the most responsible attitude, but considering that I had called Al and signed on to work for him for the foreseeable future, I knew he wouldn't mind me taking a day off; he'd been only a *little* smug about my decision to stay in Jalesville. Hanging up in the predawn light of Case's kitchen, I leaned against the counter and set the phone aside. I clasped both hands beneath my chin, smiling as I studied the violet light brightening the sky; the sun seemed to be rising just for us today. I fairly skipped back to the bedroom and scuttled under the covers, naked and chilly and craving him, straight into his warm, sleepy embrace.

"Stay here," he murmured, eyes still closed. "Stay in my arms."

I kissed his neck. "At least I know I'll be warm enough this winter."

He laughed a little, nosing my tangled hair. "You can count on that."

"I told Al I wouldn't be in today," I whispered, winding my legs around his. "He was so happy that I'm staying he told me I could take off the entire week if I wanted."

"I'll make us breakfast in a little while," Case murmured; we had made love nearly the entire night through and he was barely awake.

"You rest, sweetheart," I whispered, kissing his mouth. "We'll get up later…"

It was nearly noon before Case fried us eggs and bacon in a cast-iron pan on the stove, clad in nothing but his boxers while I wore a faded shirt from his high school days, with the word SPICER stenciled across the back in red letters. I sat on the counter near Case while he cooked and we kept kissing, enough that the first batch of eggs burned.

"I love your freckles." I meant this sincerely, though he thought I was teasing. He mixed up a second batch of eggs, which would probably also end up scorched, as I was preoccupied with skimming my fingertips over each and every one on his chest and shoulders. Case's old shirt rode a little higher on my thighs and I wasn't wearing panties.

"Who loves freckles?" he demanded, so damn handsome here in the kitchen, half naked and unshaven, with the contented glow of hours of lovemaking. I caressed his bare torso, smoothing my palms along his ribcage.

"Me," I insisted, smiling as I eased the elastic band of his boxers down over a certain very large swelling, spreading my legs to better accommodate his hips. "I love all of yours. And your beautiful hair. You don't know how long I've wanted to touch it."

"You touch anything you want, baby, anything at all. Put your hands all over me," he said with magnanimous charm. The spatula clattered to the floor and he secured my ass with a two-handed grip, closing what little distance remained between us. He grinned at my gasping cry, burying his fingers in my hair, tilting my head to deepen our kiss. He murmured, "Your curls remind me of a mane."

I knew he meant this as a compliment and tightened my calves around his waist, biting his bottom lip. "Well, you certainly gripped it like a mane last night, cowboy."

"Giddy-*up*," he murmured, rife with satisfaction, and our laughter threatened to uncouple our bodies.

We finally ate breakfast in the late afternoon, the third round with the eggs and bacon. We sat at the table and giggled at the cats as they played on the back of the couch; we'd driven to Jalesville last night, both to collect my car from The Spoke and rescue Peaches before she starved to death. And we talked and talked.

"Tell me about Lynnette," I requested at one point.

Case was forthright. "She never stood a chance. I couldn't truly love her and she sensed that. I tried, though, I really did. I thought she was going to be the mother of my child and I tried with everything I had. I hid away your picture. I'd given up any hope of us ever meeting again and

I was determined to forget about you and love her. We were reasonably happy for a little while."

"I know it's stupid and petty, but I'm jealous of her. *Insanely* jealous. I know it's ridiculous…"

"It's not ridiculous. If you had married someone before now I would have secretly plotted his death. I figured that's what would happen. A part of me always dreaded when Mathias or Camille would call, because I thought they might be calling to tell me that you had gotten engaged."

"Deep inside, I always knew I was coming to you." I studied his eyes.

"We've been together before now, I'm sure of it, Tish. I can sense that, sometimes really clearly, like a memory. A memory of something I don't remember from this life."

I'd told him about my frightening dreams, and the photograph of the Spicer family—and how I thought he might have been Cole. At the very least, related to Cole. I recognized, "And it's getting stronger."

"All of us, you and me, Mathias and Camille, the Rawleys…somehow we've all been together before now."

"And Derrick Yancy." I hated to acknowledge it; if my nightmare was any indicator, I'd been married to a past incarnation of the man. "He's known us before, too…"

Case nodded agreement. I hadn't yet told him about Derrick calling me a whore at the Coyote's Den and making veiled threats in the parking lot at Stone Creek; I was terrified Case would make good on his threat about killing him. I wasn't concerned for Derrick's wellbeing, I simply refused to see Case get hurt or carted to jail, or any of the other possibilities that could arise from me telling him just now. It was the lawyer in me, rationalizing. And though I dreaded the thought, I knew I had to confront Derrick about what he'd meant the other night at The Spoke; he wanted to tell me something. Even suspecting him of massive manipulation, logic suggested that I seek him out. If I was lucky, he'd still be in the mood to divulge information.

"When did Lynnette leave?" I finally asked.

"She found your picture. I told her I had gotten rid of it, and I should have, I should have given it to Marsh, because he loved how Ruthann was in it, too. But in the end I couldn't part with it and Lynnette found it tucked in my things. She ripped it to shreds in front of me. I wanted to hit her. I'm so ashamed of feeling that way, because it reminds me of something my dad would have done…"

I was on his lap and he pressed his face against my hair.

"She left me for good after that. I drank pretty heavily for a few months. And then a year passed, and then one day last spring Clark told me Camille said you were coming to Jalesville for the summer. And that was the day I realized maybe I still knew how to hope. That maybe things truly do happen for a reason."

"They do," I whispered. "I believe that they do."

Clark called to invite us to dinner about an hour later.

"So, I heard you talked to Mathias," I heard Clark say after Case answered; he and I lay dozing in the warm afternoon light, entwined on the unmade bed.

I could tell Case was smiling even though my eyes were closed. He said, "Everything's all right now. I feel it."

"I'm so happy for you two, son," Clark said.

"Thanks, Dad. The past few days have been the most beautiful of my life. I can't even describe it," Case whispered, and I snuggled closer at his sweet words; it struck me that he'd called Clark 'Dad'.

"Aw, son. I love the both of you. You and Tish want to join us for supper pretty quick here? We miss you."

Case put his lips to my ear. "What do you think?"

I said to Clark, through the phone, "We'll be there! We miss you, too."

We decided to take the horses. In the barn beside Buck's stall Case and I held each other close, unable to stop kissing. In the quiet peace of the well-cared-for barn, time seemed to halt. It was only Buck releasing a deep, whooshing whicker that forced us apart.

"Easy, boy," Case said to him, and then to me, "Sweetheart, I'll teach you how to saddle them next time, how's that?"

I nodded agreement, wanting to learn everything about how to care for them. As Case moved to collect Buck's saddle, I asked, "Can we ride double?"

"Of course." Case resettled the saddle on its holder. "It's easier without one, if we ride together. I'll just get his bridle."

He boosted me first before climbing behind, using the corral fence as a ladder since Buck wasn't as polite as Cider. Case gathered the reins in his capable grip, leading Buck to the road with a brief tightening of his knee on the horse's flank. Once we were headed toward the Rawleys' place, he said, "You take the reins, get used to Buck. It's better with me behind you, since he's not near as well behaved as Cider."

I gripped the leather straps and Case held my waist as I concentrated on handling Buck, who was an altogether different animal than his sweet-tempered sister. The big buckskin tossed his head and snorted, then balked, sidestepping instead of moving forward, his every movement conveying impatience—a teenager challenging his boundaries with this new rider.

"*Whoa*," I said, sawing on the reins.

Case tugged his horse back into line with adept movements, putting his hands over mine.

"Quit that," he scolded the buckskin, deep voice stern. "You know Tish. You better get used to her riding you."

I giggled. "Don't make him feel bad."

"He doesn't feel bad, sweetheart, trust me. He's the luckiest horse in the world, with you on his back this way...in fact..." He nipped my earlobe. "I was hoping to get you in the very same position above me, a little later tonight."

I squeaked and elbowed his ribs. "You should *be* so lucky."

"Don't I know," he said, with wholehearted sincerity. "Believe me, I'm counting every last blessing today."

It was a short ride to Clark's and I appreciated every second of it, the feeling of Case behind me on Buck, the summer evening that spread out all around us. The warm air was completely static, perfumed by sagebrush and sweetgrass, as though the foothills were exhaling the scent. The sun beamed low over the landscape, casting it in otherworldly light; it was so intoxicating that tears wet my eyes for the countless time. It seemed I'd never experienced a single emotion before living here in Jalesville. When the Rawleys' double barns came into view, silhouetted against the golden sky, I sighed with disappointment that we'd arrived so quickly.

The front door flew open as Case was lifting me down from Buck and Wy barreled outside, hugging both of us the moment he reached our sides. Buck snorted and tossed his head as Wy all but hollered, "It's about time!"

I giggled, hugging the boy right back, and in short order we were surrounded by Clark and Marshall, Gus and Sean and Quinn, everyone echoing Wy's sentiment.

"You two, I just wanted to crack your heads together," Sean said, roughing up my hair.

"I'm so happy for you guys," Gus said, squeezing Case's upper arm, his eyes wet with tears as he regarded his big brother. "I couldn't be happier."

"So, when's the wedding? There's always lots of hot girls at a wedding," Marshall teased.

We ate dinner outside. I kept smiling, unable to help it, thinking that this place was my home, and would be my home from now forth. Jalesville, Montana, the little town I was trying to save. My Charles Spicer, my musician cowboy I could not live without, sitting just to my left and angling me a soft smile, surely knowing what I was thinking. Beneath the table, I slipped my hand over his right thigh and patted twice.

Later, we all lingered outside to stargaze. I sat on Case's lap, my head against his shoulder.

"It's about time, that's all I can say," Marshall told us for the third time, sitting just to our right, long legs stretched in front of him as he sipped a beer. "I was getting worried. You scared me for a little while, Tish. I thought I might have to take drastic measures to get you two together."

"It's all okay," I murmured, thinking of Case's words. "Everything's as it should be, now."

"Not quite yet," Marsh muttered, almost inaudibly, the tone of his voice sounding very un-Marshall-like. Case and I both looked his way but he only took a long drink from his beer, studying the western horizon with somber gray eyes, and wouldn't elaborate.

Chapter Twenty

A BLISSFUL TWO WEEKS PASSED. I MOVED FROM STONE Creek to the trailer and it was crowded as hell with all of our belongings, but neither of us cared. Peaches was welcomed with varying degrees of warmth by the dogs and Carrot, and tended to retreat to Case's lap when Mutt and Tiny were too much in her space, of which he was rather smug.

"It's the first place I want to be, too," I said. "So I can understand her rationale."

I talked to my mother, who was delighted, and my sisters, my Aunt Jilly, Clinty and Grandma and Aunt Ellen, all of them thrilled at this turn of events. I left Dad a voicemail, wondering why he didn't call me back all the next day before recalling that he and Lanny were vacationing in the Bahamas this last part of summer, as always. Robbie, who showed up at the law office the moment he heard I'd declined the job at Turnbull and Hinckley, was shocked at my choice.

"Gordon, you'll regret this." He studied me with wide eyes.

"Not ever," I contradicted. "Oh God, not ever."

Robbie left, muttering about insanity.

Case and I spent the first Sunday going through the trailer and determining what could be relegated to the barn. It took much longer than we planned because we kept getting interrupted by the need to make love, sometimes sweet and unhurried, with lots of kissing, other times fast and urgent, Case gripping my hips from behind as I bent over the nearest convenient surface. By late afternoon the sun was melting in a hazy, melon-tinted sky, thunder grumbling in the distance; Case and I were sprawled together in the haymow. I turned my head and sneezed for the second time, giggling as bits of chaff fluffed through the air like a dandelion gone to seed.

"Bless you," he mumbled, his face against my breasts. We lay on an old patchwork quilt we'd pulled from a trunk, one that Case said his grandma Dalton had made.

"Are you sure your grandma won't mind us using her quilt this way?" I whispered, stroking his hair, which was damp with sweat. The haymow was as humid as any cedar-sided sauna.

Case rose to one elbow and regarded me as I lay flat on my back, nearly naked and with bits of hay decorating my hair. He murmured, "She'd be honored, sweetheart." I'd slipped my sundress down over my shoulders and bunched its long skirt over my hips, as though wearing a tube top around my belly. Case was also shirtless, his jeans tugged back into place but still unbuttoned and unzipped. Hay clung to his shoulders.

I giggled at his words, removing a piece of chaff from his cheekbone.

"Your beautiful eyes," he whispered. "They're the truest blue I've ever seen. I swear you see right into my soul."

"Yes, I like to think I have superpowers like that."

"I mean it," he insisted, pressing a soft kiss to each of my eyes in turn, as he was sweetly inclined to do. "If you'd have gone back to Chicago, your eyes would have haunted me the rest of my life."

"You wouldn't have let me go," I understood.

"I was ready to chase you there and throw you over my shoulder, if that's what it came down to. But I was so afraid the city was what you wanted and I had to force myself not to stand in the way of that."

I whispered, "Not without you."

He slid both warm, strong hands down my ribs and brought his mouth to within a breath of mine; already my hips lifted in adamant invitation, despite the fact that he'd only left my body a few minutes earlier. Maybe someday, decades from now, we would no longer crave one another in this urgent fashion, but I couldn't imagine that at present. Case licked my bottom lip. "Can I make you come again, sweetheart?"

He cupped one hand between my legs and began stroking gently, in the best possible spot. I trembled, already nearly there, teasing, "I don't know…can you?"

"We'll see," he teased right back, husky and confident, deepening his touch and sliding his tongue into my mouth. I moaned against his lips. Thunder rumbled and rain began pelting the roof, but neither of us noticed.

Much later, flushed and sweating atop the quilt, I whispered, "I can't be without you."

I lay in the crook of his arm, my limbs weak from clutching him as we made love. Rain continued to fall but in a soft patter now, its dusty scent rising up to the haymow.

Case rested his lips to my damp forehead. "We'll never be without each other again, sweetheart."

By that night we'd made a good dent in the closet space in the bedroom, even though I lost focus again after finding a bundle of letters in one of the trunks, the same bunch that Case's mother had once found tucked in with the old Spicer family fiddle. Cole's father—Henry Spicer's fiddle, I was certain. I placed the letters carefully onto the dresser, between a pile of guitar picks and another of my earrings, smoothing my fingertips over the soft old paper, excited to read them. And then I joined Case, who was singing his heart out in the shower.

Case made us breakfast in the mornings before I drove to work since he didn't start his work day as early as I did mine, and I nearly skipped to the music shop to have lunch with him every noon hour. In the evenings I flew home to find him making supper, as he usually beat me to the trailer (and was a much better cook), and we'd make love on the table or couch or kitchen counter, occasionally the bed if we managed to stumble that far, sometimes remembering to eat what he'd made. In the late evenings we rode Cider and Buck out to the wizard rock.

"Do you think we'll ever know what happened here?" I asked one night as we studied the towering structure. It was not lost on me that I hadn't yet sought out Derrick Yancy for potential answers to my numerous questions, too wrapped up in my own happiness; neither had he attempted to make contact with me. But I'd watched his 4x4 roll past the law office these last two weeks, a dark reminder of the world outside my blissful, insulated bubble. Denying the issue would not make it go away.

"I don't know, sweetheart, but we'll sure as hell keep trying."

A few evenings later, Case was making supper when I got home, as usual. I could smell it the moment I jumped out of the car, hurrying inside to his waiting arms. He growled against my neck and I set aside the file folder I'd brought home so I could get my arms around him. "It smells amazing in here."

He kissed my ear. "Now it does. C'mon, baby, I made steak with fried mushrooms."

He was wearing his gray SPICER t-shirt and much-used jeans, a towel slung over his left shoulder. His hair had gotten longer this summer and I stroked it with both hands. I could not accurately describe how much I loved him, so much it almost hurt; I had learned that love worth having is one part pain, even in its moments of purest joy.

"I'm going to change quick," I said. The sun lit the interior of our place with a dusty golden hue; the quiet sounds of the evening, of Buck and Cider in the corral, drifted through the open windows. I happily stripped from my work clothes, letting them fall to the floor, and slipped a pair of his boxers over my panties and a soft, threadbare tank top over my head, bending at the waist to shake out my hair before hurrying back to the kitchen.

Case looked my way just as he moved the pan from the burner, torching the side of his hand on the stove. "Ouch! *Damn.*"

"Are you all right?" I inspected his hand, making a show of kissing the injured spot.

"Holy shit, woman, you don't have any idea how you look, do you?" he asked, with a half-teasing, half-dead serious voice. He wrapped his other arm around my waist.

I cupped his burned hand over my breast. "I thought this might make it feel better."

"Much, much better," he agreed, his deep voice throaty and soft. He stroked my nipple and I kissed his bottom lip. He laughed a little, clasping a firmer hold on my ass. "Baby, you coming into the kitchen like that, so fucking beautiful, all half-naked and wearing my underwear..."

"You like that, huh?" I hooked my right thigh around his hip, forgetting that my period had started this afternoon.

"Are you kidding? Insanely *love*. If my fifteen-year-old self could see you...shit, my almost thirty-year-old self can hardly believe it."

"You have a pretty impressive hard-on for someone so old," I teased, caressing him through his jeans, and he growled again, this time lifting me onto the counter. He was so incredibly sexy and imposing in his desire, his hands on my thighs and sliding higher. It took everything I had to refocus. "Honey, I started my period today..."

Case continued kissing my neck. "We'll shower after..."

"It means we won't be parents in May," I said.

"Sweetheart." He spoke softly, caressing my hipbones. He kissed my forehead and the end of my nose. "Our baby will come when it's time. It's just not time quite yet. I was thinking a lot about that, imagining what it would be like next spring. She'll come when she's ready."

"Does this mean you want us to try? Not to use any sort of birth control?" I asked nervously.

"First let me marry you properly. And then I'll start building our cabin so our baby has a bedroom, what do you say? We'll haul this shitty old trailer out of here —"

I shook my head, effectively interrupting him, protesting, "But this is where we made love for the first time. I love this old trailer."

"I love it because you're in it with me, and that's the only good thing about this piece of shit trailer. I'll build us a beautiful home. We'll spend the winter planning it and we'll start building once spring thaw hits, what do you say?" Holding me to him, he whispered in my ear, "I'll always hold you close, so that you'll know that I've never loved anyone more in a thousand lifetimes."

I cried then, at the intense sincerity of his words. I cried and he held me, and it wasn't until later that we ate dinner, as the sky grew dark. Case lit three mismatched candles, which he positioned on the table. He finished eating before me and grabbed one of my notebooks and a pencil, sketching out our ideas for the cabin. I flipped halfheartedly through the file I'd brought home from work, mildly guilty because I'd been a little bit of a slacker this last week. Al and I were running through ideas about how Highland Power might be able to reopen its doors; the file contained petitions Al had drafted last year. The little red bull caught my eye again, from the Redd Co. logo, and something chimed in my memory.

"Case."

He looked up from his sketching, eyebrows raised.

"A bull." I wasn't making sense. My mind clicked along like a bicycle down a steep hill, gaining momentum. "It's Turnbull."

"Tell me," he said. "I'm not following yet."

I slapped the file folder on the table. "Oh my God. I just remembered where I saw that logo before. Way back, after my first year of school, working at Turnbull and Hinckley in the summer. It was on a letterhead I saw there. It was something I was never supposed to see, something that was supposed to be shredded, but the girl doing the shredding left that afternoon." I put both hands to my forehead. "I shouldn't have stuck my nose in her work but I did. Redd Co. is a Turnbull company! That's who bought out the power plant last December. Fucked over everyone here. Ron *knew* about it. He had to, since his little sub-company arranged the deal. Oh, dear God."

Fairly despicable indeed.

"So Turnbull buys the power plant, knowing it will put enough people out of work around here so that his buddy Yancy can sweep in and purchase all the land. Destroying our homes for a profit," Case understood.

"Ron had me fooled." I was breathless with fury. "He *used* me. He knew I would come out here and…God, he must think far less of me than I ever imagined. Ron probably figured Derrick would seduce me over to his side, all without realizing that he was responsible in the first place. And that bastard *tried*. Oh my God, Case…"

"Hey," he said, curling his hand around mine. "You're way too smart to fall for that. Look at what you've done here this summer. You've done the opposite of what Turnbull wanted, proven him wrong."

I was livid. "I'm calling my dad. And Robbie. I want this to be the equivalent of front-page news." But reality took me out at the knees. "It won't matter to Turnbull. That fucker is untouchable."

Even so, I found my phone and called Robbie. I told him everything I'd learned, emphasizing the fact that there was an angle, likely multiple angles, we were missing; I assured Robbie that I intended to discover the truth if it killed me; Robbie knew me well enough not to contradict a thing I said. I tried Dad next, whose phone went straight to voicemail; he and Lanny were probably still on vacation. I intended to speak to Al tomorrow at work; at last, when it was apparent I could do nothing more this evening Case suggested I let it rest for now, take a bath and relax.

An hour later I lay soaking in the tub, determined to forget about Turnbull and his deep-seated plotting, at least for the evening. I kept the water just shy of scalding, draining and replenishing as needed. Case was out in the kitchen, singing quietly as he washed about a week's worth of dishes. I reached to brush a strand of hair from my eyes, bubbles drifting down my forearm. I loved how he sang so often—while showering, while shaving, doing little chores around the house. He was writing me a new song he called "My Blue-Eyed Patricia," of which he would only sing bits, telling me I could hear the whole thing in its entirety once it was finished.

This is happiness, I marveled.

You finally know.

After he finished the dishes, Case brought me a beer.

"Thank you," I murmured, sloshing soapy water as I reached to accept the icy bottle; I was as red as a boiled lobster.

Case sat on the edge of the tub. "The sight of you in here almost does me in. My woman, all sweet and naked in the bath."

"I'm so happy, honey. I'm so happy to be planning a home with you."

"Me, too. I could die happy right now," he whispered, tucking damp curls behind my ear.

"Don't say that," I reprimanded, catching and holding his hand, entwining our fingers. I hated when he talked about dying.

"How about I climb in there with you."

I smiled at the image of both of us in this cramped little tub; Case had just leaned forward to kiss me when Mutt and Tiny began barking, followed by a sharp rapping on the edge of the screen door.

My heart lurched as Case sat straight, our eyes locking with sudden concern; we never had visitors after dark.

Something's wrong...

"I'll go see who's here," he said, closing the bathroom door behind him. I hurried from the tub, dripping hot water and grabbing a towel, abruptly frightened as I heard Case ask someone, "Can I help you?"

His tone indicated he didn't know the person at the door. And then, to my greatest of stun, I heard my father, Jackson Gordon of Rockford, Gordon and Bunnickle, Attorneys-at-Law, say crisply, "I'm looking for my daughter, Patricia."

Oh sweet Jesus.

This can't be happening.

There was a moment of horrible, tense silence before Case obviously gathered himself together and invited, "Please, come in. She's here."

I don't even have clothes in here!

I hovered in a stupor of disbelief, imagining Case and my father taking stock of each other in our cramped kitchen. Leaving my hair in a messy bun, I slipped into Case's dark blue terrycloth bathrobe; there was no chance in hell of trying to pretend otherwise, that I hadn't just made love with this man in his trailer, in too many ways to count. *Our* trailer, but I decided against sharing that particular news.

I squared my shoulders as I came around the corner into the kitchen, tightening the belt on the robe and meeting my father's eyes without shame. Dad stood just inside the screen door wearing jeans and an ivory dress shirt; I had never seen him look quite so thoroughly shocked. I went straight to Case's side; he tucked a protective arm around my shoulders, as though Dad meant to drag me away by the ear. Though, given my father's stunned expression, uncombed hair, and unshaven face, dragging me away seemed his exact intent.

"Tish..." Dad said weakly.

"Hi, Dad." I kept my voice level. I was astonished to the roots of my hair to see him here in Montana, literally on Case's doorstep, but kept my expression composed. "Case, this is my father, Jackson Gordon."

"Sir." Case spoke with respect, reaching to shake Dad's hand.

The gesture was too deeply ingrained; they shook, and Dad looked pale and sickly.

"Charles Spicer," Case added, and wasted no time with small talk. "I love your daughter, I think you should know that right now. I apologize for meeting you under circumstances like these, but here we are. I love Tish with all my heart. We plan to be married before fall."

I took one of Case's hands between both of mine, threading our fingers, my heart glowing at his somber declarations. "Case and I are in love, Dad. I'm happy here. I never plan to leave this place again."

It was too much for my father; his face lost its incoherent look. "I've heard more than enough. Get your things together this moment. You are leaving with me and I will never hear another word of this, *do you understand?*"

Dad had never spoken to me this way, even when I was a child; he'd always indulged me and let Mom do all the disciplining. To hear him use such an autocratic tone incited within me both bewilderment and anger. "Excuse me?"

Dad heaved a deep breath before letting loose. "You have got to be joking. When we got home and I heard your message, I thought I must have misunderstood. But then I called Ron and he confirmed that you'd declined his offer. I told him that you'd *never* do such a thing, not without consulting me first."

I controlled my voice, reminding myself I was hardly in a position to take a tone with my father, naked and damp beneath my lover's bathrobe. "I'm sorry I didn't call you first. But it was my decision, as I'm sure you understand. I declined that offer because I would die going back to Chicago. I would wither up and die." The thought of what I'd learned earlier loomed in my mind. "Dad, you'll never believe what I found out tonight—"

"I will not hear *another word* of this insanity." A vein bulged in Dad's temple. His eyes moved between Case and me, with incredulous fluster, and he fired his next words at Case. "If you love her, as you claim, then surely you can see how her staying here will destroy her career. Everything she's worked for since she was a teenager. My daughter doesn't *belong* here."

Case's jaw tightened; he held Dad's gaze without flinching. "Tish belongs here more than anywhere else in the world. If you think I'm going to roll over and agree with you, then you have another thing coming."

Dad's eyebrows lowered and I had a sudden vision of him from a decade ago, summer in Landon, the tense and heated July night that everyone found out about Mom and Blythe's relationship. Dad had punched Blythe in the face that night, and gotten his ass kicked for the trouble. Dad wore a similarly ominous expression now and I moved toward him at once, positioning myself between him and Case.

"Dad," I implored, not unkindly. "I know this is a shock for you, I do, and I'm sorry for that. But there is no way I'm coming back to Chicago. I'm not a little girl. I am a grown woman and I make my own decisions."

"I caught a plane the moment I heard," Dad said, as though I hadn't spoken. "I couldn't find you anywhere, until I bullied Al into telling me. And sure enough, here's my daughter behaving like…" Dad choked back what was surely an uncharitable comment and said tightly, "I would never have believed this of you, Patricia. Not *you*. Jesus."

Case set me gently to the side. "You will not speak to Tish that way, especially not in my house. I won't ask again."

"She's my daughter," Dad said, though some of the fight had leaked from his tone. "My daughter, who is going to make a life for herself in Chicago. I funded her entire education with that in mind. I will not let her throw her career away here, in some Sticksville sort of place like this."

I interrupted his tirade. "Dad, I love it here. I have done everything I could this summer to save this town from the Yancys and Ron Turnbull, both. I want to make a career *here*. It's not 'less than' because it's not Chicago. My God, I *matter* here. I belong here, and I will never leave this man's side, not ever again." I tucked myself literally against Case's side. "This is where I belong. And I'm still your daughter, Dad. Jesus."

Dad plunged a hand through his hair. "Does Joelle know about this?"
I nodded cautiously.

"Of *course* she does," he said bitterly, turning without another word and storming down the steps.

I hurried to the screen. "Dad! Wait! I need to tell you about something else!"

Dad didn't look back, throwing his right hand in the air. "I can't hear any more tonight. I'll be at Al's."

He slammed the car door and Case and I watched the taillights disappear down the road, a thin cloud of dust lifting from the tires. Mutt and Tiny chased after the retreating vehicle, barking.

"Oh, boy." I tipped my forehead against the screen, imagining my skin imprinted by a hundred tiny squares from the mesh.

Case said, "I feel like a jerk. If you were our daughter and I saw you for the first time in weeks in some man's house, a man who was a stranger to me, and you were obviously intimate with him…" I couldn't help but giggle at his wording, feeling slightly guilty for doing so; he concluded, "Even so, I won't let him talk to you disrespectfully."

"He'll recover." I was certain of this; I knew my dad. "He's just in shock. But I didn't get to tell him about Ron. I'll call him later."

Case collected me against his chest. I lined his forearms with my own, holding tightly; he rested his chin on the top of my head and murmured, "I liked hearing you say those things. About belonging here. About never leaving my side. My sweet Patricia, you matter so much here that I could never explain in words. Oh God, you are everything to me."

I snuggled closer to him. "I loved hearing you say that we'll be married by fall."

He rocked us side to side. "I would make you my wife right this minute, if I could."

"Will you play me my song?" I whispered.

"Of course," he said, and then his grin deepened as he seemed to notice for the first time that I was wearing his robe. He slipped both hands inside it, grasping my waist. "Aw, baby, I thought your dad was going to faint for a second there. This might have been too much of a shock. I deserve an ass-kicking."

I threaded my arms around his neck; his robe had become a puddle of material at my ankles. "Play my song for me."

"Yes, ma'am," he said, and carried me straight to the bedroom.

After the final note vibrated across the strings, he set aside his fiddle and I dove into his arms, taking him flat to the mattress with the force of my happiness. He settled me over his broad chest, his long legs bent, my hips cradled between his thighs. Grinning, he tucked long strands of hair behind my ears, letting his fingertips linger on my jaw as I rubbed my breasts against his chest. His eyelids lowered in pleasure.

"That feels so good," he murmured, hands all over me as I sprawled atop him.

"I love you," I whispered, punctuating the words with soft, plucking kisses. "I love hearing you play my song."

"I love you too, baby. And I especially love that you're so naked right now." His grin deepened.

"Are there varying degrees of nakedness?" I teased, my thighs spreading over the fly of his faded jeans.

He trailed both hands down my spine, with deliberate intent. Anticipation flowed along my every nerve ending and ignited between my legs.

"Hell, yes," he said softly, grasping my hips, straightening his legs to settle me in the best possible spot. He explained, "You're just so deliciously *naked* when you're naked. No woman could be more naked than you…"

I giggled. "That doesn't even make sense…" My hands were busy unzipping and yanking down his jeans; we shifted apart for just a second, so Case could tug the t-shirt over his head and fling it to the edge of the room.

"It makes perfect sense," he said in defense, reclaiming my mouth with his sweet, lush kisses.

He groaned against my lips, in deep satisfaction, as I shifted to straddle him, taking him fully inside with one smooth motion.

"So naked..." he murmured, eyes blazing with heat as I took up a steady rhythm.

Much later, after Case had long since fallen asleep, I lay in his arms, cool night air entering through the open window, listening to the chirping of crickets, taking a moment to absorb and appreciate my happiness; never mind just now that I had to set aside a large amount of pressing concerns to do so. I would never take my happiness for granted; I knew better. There were so many questions I had to answer—regarding Turnbull, Yancy, the power plant, and Jalesville itself. But I had found Case; there was no question about where I belonged, because the answer was with him.

Tomorrow, I thought, drowsy with warmth and contentment. *Everything else can wait until tomorrow.*

The Shore Leave Cafe series continues in
Until Tomorrow, The Way Back, and Return to Yesterday
coming in 2018.